APARTMENT 16

Adam L. G. Nevill was born in Birmingham, England, in 1969 and grew up in England and New Zealand. He is also the author of *Banquet for the Damned*, an original novel of supernatural horror inspired by M. R. James and the great tradition of the British weird tale.

In his working life he has endured a variety of occupations, including from 2000 to 2004 both nightwatchman and day porter in the exclusive apartment buildings of west London.

He still lives in the capital and can be contacted through www.adamlgnevill.com

ADAM NEVILL

APARTMENT 16

PAN BOOKS

First published 2010 by Pan Books
an imprint of Pan Macmillan, a division of Macmillan Publishers Limited
Pan Macmillan, 20 New Wharf Road, London N1 9RR
Basingstoke and Oxford
Associated companies throughout the world
www.panmacmillan.com

ISBN 978-0-330-51496-5

1 3 5 7 9 8 6 4 2

A CIP catalogue record for this book is available from
the British Library.

Typeset by Ellipsis Books Limited, Glasgow
Printed in the UK by CPI Mackays, Chatham ME5 8TD

Visit **www.panmacmillan.com** to read more about all our books
and to buy them. You will also find features, author interviews and
news of any author events, and you can sign up for e-newsletters
so that you're always first to hear about our new releases.

For Ramsey Campbell,
Peter Crowther and John Jarrold

ACKNOWLEDGEMENTS

The following books provided much inspiration for the interior design of *Apartment 16* and the life of Felix Hessen: *Wyndham Lewis*, by Richard Humphries; *The Bone Beneath the Pulp: Drawings by Wyndham Lewis*, edited by Jacky Klein; *Francis Bacon and the Loss of Self*, by Ernst van Alphen; *Francis Bacon: Taking Reality by Surprise*, by Christophe Domino; *Interviews with Francis Bacon*, by David Sylvester; *Grosz*, by Ivo Kranzfelder; *Diana Mosley*, by Anne de Courcy; *The Occult Roots of Nazism*, by Nicholas Goodrick-Clarke.

Special thanks to Julie Crisp for the faith, careful readings and notes, and to my agent John Jarrold for getting me a shot at the next level. Much gratitude and affection also goes out to Ramsey Campbell, and to Peter Crowther at PS Publishing, who first brought me into print.

For my readers, Anne Parry, James Marriott and Clive Nevill, I have again incurred a debt by exploiting your precious time and critical skills. I thank you.

Finally, a very special thanks to the grand old apartment buildings of Knightsbridge, Mayfair and Marylebone that funded my 'old school' writing residency from 2000 to 2004. I thought I'd never ever escape.

APARTMENT 16

I would like my pictures to look as if a human being had passed between them, like a snail, leaving a trail of the human presence and memory of the past events as the snail leaves its slime.

Francis Bacon, 1909–1992

PROLOGUE

When he heard the noise Seth stopped and stared, as if trying to see through the front door of apartment sixteen, the teak veneer aglow with a golden sheen. Right after descending the stairs from the ninth floor and crossing the landing the sounds began. Same as the last three nights, on his 2 a.m. patrol of the building.

Snapping out of his torpor, he flinched and took a quick step away from the door. Looming up the opposite wall, the shadow of his lanky body stretched out its arms as if grasping at a support. The sight of it made him start. 'Fuck.'

He'd never liked this part of Barrington House, but couldn't say why with any certainty. Maybe it was just too dark. Perhaps the lights were not set right. The head porter said there was nothing wrong with them, but they often cast shapes down the stairs Seth was walking up. It was as if a person descending was being preceded by their shadow; the impression of spiky limbs flickering ahead of them before they appeared around a bend in the staircase, sometimes even convinced Seth he'd also heard the swish of cloth and the *pumpf, pumpf, pumpf* of determined feet approaching. Only no one ever appeared, and there was never anyone up there when he turned a corner.

But the noise in apartment sixteen was far more alarming than any shadow.

Because during the early hours of the morning in this exclusive niche of London there is little to compete with the silence of night. Outside Barrington House the warren of streets behind the Knightsbridge Road are inclined to remain peaceful. Occasionally, out front, a car will drive around Lowndes Square. Or inside, the nightwatchman becomes aware of the electric lights in the communal areas, humming like insects with their black faces pressed against the recalcitrance of glass. But from the hours of one until five the residents sleep. Indoors, there is nothing but ambient sound.

And number sixteen was unoccupied. The head porter once told him it had been empty for over fifty years. But for the fourth consecutive night Seth's attention had been drawn to it. Because of the bumping behind the door, against the door. Something he'd previously dismissed as a random noise in an old building. One that had stood for a hundred years. Something loose in a draught maybe. Something like that. But tonight it was insistant. It was louder than ever before. It was . . . determined. Had been stepped up a notch. Seemed directed at him and timed to coincide with his usually oblivious passage to the next set of stairs, during the hour when your body temperature drops and when most people die. An hour when he, the nightwatchman, was paid to patrol nine storeys of stairwell and the ancient landings on each floor. And it had never before escalated into a sudden eruption of noise like this.

A clattering of furniture across a marble floor, as if a chair or small table in the reception hall of the flat had been knocked aside. Perhaps toppling over, and even breaking. Not something that should be heard at any hour in a place as respectable as Barrington House.

Nervous, he continued to watch the door, as if anticipating its opening. His stare fixed on the brass number 16, polished so brightly it looked like white gold. He dared not even blink, in case it swung away from his eyes and revealed the source of the commotion. A sight he might not be able to bear. He wondered if his legs possessed the strength to carry him down eight flights of stairs in a hurry. Perhaps with something in pursuit.

He killed the thought. A little shame warmed the aftermath of his sudden fright. He was a thirty-one-year-old man, not a child. Six feet tall, and a paid deterrent. Not that he anticipated doing anything beyond being a reassuring presence when he took the job. But this had to be investigated.

Struggling to hear over the thump of his heart in his ears, Seth leaned towards the front door and placed his left ear an inch from the letter flap to listen. Silence.

His fingers made a move for the letter box. If he knelt down and pushed the brass flap inward, enough light should fall from the landing to illumine some of the hallway on the other side of the front door.

But what if somebody looked back at him?

His hand paused, then withdrew.

No one was permitted to go inside sixteen, a rule pressed upon him by the head porter when he first began the night job six months earlier. Such a strict observance was not unusual for portered apartment buildings in Knightsbridge. Even after a reasonable lottery win an ordinary member of the public would struggle to afford a flat in Barrington House. The three-bedroom apartments never sold for less

3

than one million pounds, and the service charge cost an additional eleven thousand per annum. Many residents filled their apartments with antiques; others guarded their privacy like war criminals and shredded their paperwork for the porters to collect in bin bags. The same instruction forbidding access existed for another five empty flats in the building. But during his patrols Seth had not once heard noises inside any of them.

Maybe someone had been given permission to stay in the apartment and one of the day porters had forgotten to record the information in the desk ledger. Unlikely, as both day porters, Piotr and Jorge, had frowned with incredulity when he first mentioned the disturbances during the morning changeover. Which left one other plausible explanation at such an hour: an intruder had broken in from the outside.

But then an intruder would need to scale the exterior of the building with a ladder. Seth had patrolled the front of the building in the last ten minutes and there had been no ladder. He could always go and wake Stephen, the head porter, and ask him to open the door. But he baulked at the thought of disturbing him at this hour; the head porter's wife was an invalid. She occupied most of his time between duties, leaving him exhausted at the end of each day.

Lowering himself to one knee, Seth pushed open the letter flap and peered into the darkness. A shock of cold air rushed past his face and with it came a smell that was familiar: a woody-camphor scent reminiscent of his grandmother's gigantic wardrobe that had been like a secret cabin to him as a boy, and an aroma not dissimilar to reading rooms in university libraries or museums built by the Victorians. A trace of former residents and antiquity, suggesting vacancy rather than use.

The vague light that fell past his head and shoulders brightened a small section of the reception hall inside the flat. He could make out the murky outline of a telephone table against one wall, an indistinct doorway on the right-hand side, and a few square metres of floor tiled in black and white marble. The rest of the space was in shadow or complete darkness.

He screwed his eyes up against the uncomfortable draught that swelled against the front of his face and tried to see more. And failed. But his scalp prickled on account of what he heard.

Squinting into the umbra, he could hear the suggestion of something heavy being dragged at the far end of the hallway; as if a significant weight wrapped up in sheets, or supported on a large rug, was being moved in short bursts of exertion away from the tiny slot of light he had made in the front door. As the sounds receded further into the far confines of the apartment, they lessened, then ceased.

Seth wondered if he should call out and offer the darkness a challenge, but could not summon the strength to open his mouth. Acutely, he now felt he was being watched from down there. And this sudden sense of scrutiny and vulnerability made him want to close the mail flap, stand up and step away.

He dithered. It was hard to think clearly. He was tired. Weary to the marrow, clumsy and confused, paranoid even. He was thirty-one, but working these shifts made him feel eighty-one. Clear signs of sleep deprivation common to the night worker. But he had never hallucinated in his life. There was someone inside flat sixteen.

'Jesus.'

A door opened. Inside. Down in the dark part he couldn't see. Must have been about halfway down the hallway. It clicked open and swung wide on its trajectory, emitting a slow creak until it banged against a wall.

He did not move or blink. Just stared and anticipated the arrival of something from out of the darkness.

But there was only expectation, and silence.

Though not a total absence of sound for long. Seth began to hear something. It was faint, but closing, as if travelling towards his face.

It grew out of the hushed unlit interior of the flat. A kind of rushing sound not dissimilar to what he'd heard inside large seashells. A suggestion of faraway winds. He had a curious sense of a great distance existing at the other end of the hallway. Down there. Where he couldn't see a damn thing.

The breeze thickened where he crouched and peered. Carrying something with it. Inside it. A suggestion of a voice, far off, but still keen to be heard. A voice that sounded like it was moving in a circle miles away. No, there was more than one, there were voices. But the cries were so distant no words could be understood.

He moved his face further away from the door, his mind clutching for an explanation. Was a window open in there somewhere? Could a radio be muttering, or was it a television with the volume turned low? Impossible, the place was empty.

The wind swept closer and the voices grew louder. They were gaining a precedence in the movement of the air. And though they failed to define themselves, their tone was clear, filling him with a greater unease, and then with horror.

These were the cries of the terrified. Someone was screaming. A woman? No, it couldn't be. Now it was closer it sounded like an animal, and he thought of a baboon he had once seen in a zoo, roaring with scarlet lips peeling back from black gums and long yellow teeth.

It was swept away, the scream replaced by a chorus of moans, hapless in their despair but competing with each other in the cold wind. A hysterical voice, relentless in its panic, swooped closer, dominating the other voices that suddenly retreated as if pulled back by a swift tide, until he could almost hear what the new voice was saying.

He let the letter flap slam shut and there was an immediate and profound silence.

Standing up and stepping away he tried to gather his wits. Disoriented by the hammering of his pulse, he wiped the moisture from his brow with the sleeve of his pullover and noticed the dryness of his mouth, as if he had been inhaling dust.

He desperately wanted to leave the building. To go home and lie down. To end this strange sensitivity and the rush of impressions that accompanied lack of sleep. That's all it was, surely.

Taking the carpeted stairs two at a time, he fled down through the west wing to the ground-floor reception. He quickly walked past his desk and left the building through the front doors. Outside, he stood on the pavement and looked up, counting the white stone balconies until his eyes reached the eighth floor.

All of the windows were closed, not open, not even ajar, but shut tight and flush within the white frames, and the interior of apartment sixteen was further sealed by thick curtains; drawn day and night against London, and against the world.

But his scalp stiffened beneath his hair, because he could

still hear, above him, or even inside his head, ever so faintly, the far-off wind and the clamour of unrecognizable voices, as if he had brought them down here, with him.

ONE

Apryl went straight to her inheritance from the airport. And it was easy to find, direct from Heathrow on the navy blue Piccadilly Line to the station called Knightsbridge.

Swept up the concrete stairs by the bustle and rush of people about her, she emerged with her backpack onto the sidewalk. She'd been on the subway for so long the steely light smarted against the back of her eyes. But if the map was right this was the Knightsbridge Road. She moved into the push of the crowd.

Buffeted from behind, and then knocked to the side by a sharp elbow, she immediately failed to move in step with the strange city. She felt irrelevant and very small. It made her apologetic but angry at the same time.

She shuffled across the narrow sidewalk and took shelter in a shop doorway. Knee joints stiff and her body damp beneath her leather jacket and gingham shirt, she took a few seconds and watched the shunt, race and break of the human traffic before her, with Hyde Park as a backdrop, a landscape painting dissolving into a far-off mist.

It was hard to concentrate on any particular building, determined face, or boutique window around her, because London was constantly moving before and about every static feature. Thousands of people marched up and down the street and darted across it whenever the red buses, white vans, delivery trucks, and cars slowed for a second. She wanted to look at everything at the same time, and to know it, and to understand her place in it all, but the sheer energy sweeping up and down the street started to numb the workings behind her forehead, making her squint, like her mind was already giving up and thinking about sleep instead.

Looking at the map in the guidebook, she peered at the short and simple route to Barrington House that she must have looked at a hundred times since leaving New York eight hours earlier. All she needed to do was walk down Sloane Street, then turn left into Lowndes Square. A cab couldn't have dropped her much closer than the subway. Her great-aunt's building was somewhere on the square. Then it was just a case of following the numbers to the correct door. A good sign and one that infused her with relief; the frustration of trying to read road signs and figure out which direction she was heading on streets like this would have been paralysing.

But she would need to rest soon. The prospect of visiting London, and of seeing whatever it was that Great-aunt Lillian had bequeathed her and her mother had disrupted her sleep for over a week and she'd not managed so much as a micro-nap on the plane. But when could a mind ever rest in this place?

The short walk from the station to Lowndes Square confirmed her suspicions that Great-aunt Lillian had not been poor. On the map, the very fact this neighbourhood was so close to Buckingham Palace, and Belgravia with all those embassies, and Harrods, the store she had heard of back home, made her realize her great-aunt had not spent the last sixty years of her life in a slum. But that knowledge was still no preparation for her first sight of Knightsbridge: the tall white buildings with their long windows and black railings; the plethora of luxury cars gleaming at the kerbs; the thin blonde English girls with clipped accents, teetering about in high heels and clutching designer handbags that made her backpack feel like a sack of shit. With her biker jacket, turn-ups and Converse boots, and with her black hair styled like Bettie Page, she felt the tension of discomfort bend her head forward with the shame and diffidence of the miscast.

At least there weren't many people out in Lowndes Square to see her in this state: a couple of Arab women alighting from a silver Merc, and a tall blonde Russian girl talking angrily into a phone clamped to her ear. And after the melee of the Knightsbridge Road, the elegance of the square was soothing. The apartment buildings and hotels formed an unbroken and graceful rectangle around the long oval park in its centre, where short trees and empty flower beds could be seen through railings. The unlaboured harmony of the mansion blocks stilled the air and deflected the noise else-where.

'No way.' She and her mom now owned an apartment here? At least until they sold it for a stack of cash. A thought that immediately rankled. She wanted to live here. It kept her great-aunt here for over sixty years and Apryl could see why. The place was classic, flawless, and effortlessly exuded the sense of a long history. She imagined the polite but indifferent faces of butlers behind every front door. Aristocrats must live here. And diplomats. And billionaires. People unlike her and her mother. 'Shit, Mama, you're just not gonna believe this,' she said out loud.

She'd only ever seen one photo of Great-aunt Lillian, when Lillian was a little girl. Dressed in a curious white gown matching that of her elder sister, Apryl's grandmother, Marilyn. In the picture Lillian held her big sister's hand. They stood next to each other with sulky smiles in the yard of their home in New Jersey. But Lillian and Marilyn were closer at that time than they ever were after. Lillian moved to London during the war to work for the US military as a secretary. Where she met an English guy, a pilot, and married him. She never came home.

Lillian and her granny Marilyn must have exchanged letters or cards because Lillian knew when Apryl had been born. She used to get birthday cards from Lillian when she was little. With beautiful English money inside. Pounds. Really colourful paper with pictures of kings and dukes and battles and god knows what else on them. And watermarks when you held them up against a light that she thought were magical. She wanted to keep them, not cash them for dollars, which looked like toy money in comparison. It always made her want to visit England. And here she was for the first time.

But Lillian went quiet on them a long time ago. They even stopped getting Christmas cards before Apryl was ten. Her mother was too busy raising her alone to find out why. And when Granny Marilyn died, her mother wrote to Lillian at the address in Barrington House, but there was no response. So they just assumed she'd died too, over in England, where she'd lived a life they knew nothing of, the weak connection with that generation of the family finally severed, for ever.

Until two months back, when a probate lawyer sent a letter to inform the last surviving relatives of their inheritance following the 'sad passing of Lillian Archer'. She and her mother were still in a daze. A death, occurring eight weeks previously, and leading to the bequest to them of an apartment in London. Knightsbridge, London, no less. Right here where she was standing, outside Barrington House: the great white building seated solemnly at the foot of the square. Rising up, so many floors dignified in strong white stone, the classicism tempered with slender art-deco flourishes around the window frames. A place so well-proportioned and proud, she could only feel daunted before the grand entrance, with its big, brass-framed glass doors, its flower baskets and ornamental columns either side of the marble stairs. 'No way.'

Beyond her reflection in the pristine glass of the front doors she could see a long, carpeted corridor with a big reception desk at the far end. And behind it she received an impression of two men with neat haircuts, each wearing a silver waistcoat. 'Oh shit.'

She laughed to herself. Feeling ridiculous, as if ordinary life had suddenly transformed into cinematic fantasy, she checked the address on the papers they had received from the lawyer: a letter, with a contract and deeds that would get her the keys. To this.

No doubt about it. This was the place. Their place.

TWO

The figure was there again, watching Seth from across the street. This time it stood at the kerb between two parked cars and was not slouched inside a shop doorway, or peering from the mouth of a side street as it had done on three previous sightings.

Closer now, open to his attention, the small form was more sure of itself. Unperturbed by the slanting rain, it just stared. At him.

It.

Seth thought it was a boy but couldn't be certain. Even though the head was no longer dipped, inside the hood of the dirty parka he could see no face. Just a child then, hanging around instead of being at school, where any youngster with parents who cared should be at this time. And directly across the road from the Green Man pub, where Seth lived in an upstairs room.

So perhaps the child was merely waiting for a father or mother inside the bar. But the figure's attention was directed at him, as if it had been waiting for him. And it had been on the same stretch of the Essex Road for the past three afternoons he'd been off work.

It was such an unusual child: wrapped from the legs to the head in the faded khaki parka. Or was it grey? It was hard to make out the colour of the fabric against the dark background, or the wet silvery air beneath the smudgy red sign of the fried chicken takeaway. But it was one of those old snorkel coats. He'd not seen one in years. Didn't even know they were still being made.

Dark trousers too. Not baggy jeans or tracksuit bottoms like most kids wore these days, but trousers. Schoolish trousers. Badly fitted and too long in the leg, as if handed down from an elder sibling in a poor family. And completed by black shoes with a chunky heel. He'd not seen anything like those either, not since he'd been at junior school, and that was during the early seventies.

Usually as he marched through London he did his best to ignore the people on the streets, and took extra care to avoid the eyes of any youths on this stretch of road. Many of them had been drinking, and Seth knew what a stare could lead to. There were plenty of them running wild in this area. They had acquired the privileges of adulthood too early, and played at their version of maturity for long enough to eradicate genuine youthfulness. But this one was different. Set apart by its vulnerability, its isolation. He was reminded of his own youth and he was drawn to the figure out of pity. Every memory of childhood was painful, marked by a terror of bullies he could still taste like ozone, and by a quick stab of heartbreak that lingered twenty years after his parents' divorce.

But what surprised Seth most was the curious and sudden feeling preceding his sighting of the strange watching child. The mere presence of this figure projected such a force that he reacted with a slight shock and temporary bewilderment, as if a voice had suddenly been directed at him, or as if there had been an unexpected hand around his elbow within a crowd. Not exactly intimidating, but enough to give him a start. To wake him up. But before this sense of significance could fully form in his mind, the feeling would pass. And so would the child. It never stayed long. Just long enough to let him know he was being watched.

But not this afternoon. The hooded figure lingered at the kerb.

Screwing up his eyes and facing the figure, Seth expected his attention to force the cowled head to turn away, uncomfortable under his glare. It didn't. Not a twitch. The figure in the coat remained at ease and just continued to stare from out of the dark oval of dirty fur-trimmed nylon. It appeared to have been in the same position for so long it could have been a permanent fixture on the street, a sculpture indifferent to the people walking by. And no one else seemed to take any notice of the child.

The situation soon began to feel intimate. Speech seemed inevitable. As Seth tried to think of something he could call across the road to the kid, the door of the pub opened behind him.

He heard a series of disquieting sounds from inside the bar. Someone yelled 'Cunt', a chair was scraped violently across a wooden floor, pool balls snapped against each other, there was a raucous eruption of laughter, and a muffled love song rose from the jukebox as if trying to calm the other sounds. Seth turned to face the bright orange doorway. But no one entered or left, and the noise only lasted for as long as it took the door to swing closed by itself; everything growing fainter until the hot and noisy innards of the pub were completely shut off from the street again.

When he turned back to face the road the figure had gone.

Walking into the road, he looked up and down the wet street. There was no sign of the child in the coat.

The Green Man was the last surviving Victorian building on the corner of a scruffy street. Now, the character of its brickwork and buttresses was spoiled by the rubbish at street level. Survivors of the Blitz and looking as if they hadn't been cleaned for decades, little could be seen through the pub's murky windows from outside but a variety of posters tacked to the inside of the glass. There was an advert for Guinness he remembered from his teens. Now, the Guinness in the pint glass had faded a lime green in colour, like sucked liquorice. Other adverts for coming attractions, like *Quiz Night* and *Sky Football: Big Screen TV*, were only bright and colourful where the windows had been blotched by rain.

He'd lived there long enough to learn something of the customers and culture of the Green Man. Some of the punters were market traders, retired from the stalls but still doing business in the bar with East End accents so broad he was tempted to suspect them inauthentic. There were casualties from labour patterns as sketchy as his own, who drank their benefits from opening until closing, or played the fruit machine. A miscellany of other characters would be positioned about them in the gloom, like unrelieved sentries. This final subculture had no peers in Seth's experience with whom to be compared; they represented new strains of dysfunction caused by personal tragedy, mental illness, and drink. How long now before he completely gave up on himself too? Some days, he wasn't sure he hadn't already.

Weary from waking late in the morning after only a few hours' sleep, he shrugged off the residual effect of the staring child and approached the door of the pub. His rent was due: seventy quid across the bar once a week. Stepping over some dog shit, he entered the bar.

His vision began to jitter, as if he was being bounced along on someone's shoulders. He only ever seemed to get fleeting impressions of the place: a panorama of yellow eyes, the foamy sides of pint glasses, Lambert and Butler cigarette packets, an evil fox's face behind glass, a tier of champagne bottles under genuine cobwebs, a nicotine ceiling, a pool table, a small dog with bristly fur before an opened bag of scratchings, one Arsenal shirt, and a once pretty woman with eyes still attractive but mostly sly. Several heads turned to take him in, then turned away.

Seth nodded to Quin, who was working the bar today. Quin's skull looked as if it had once been cleft by an axe. The wound ran from his hairless white cranium to his pink forehead and still shined with scar tissue. Quin nodded without smiling. He leant on the bar to accept Seth's money.

'There's a kid,' Seth said.

Quin squinted and his glasses moved up his nose. 'Huh?'

The music was loud and someone with cheeks like corned beef was shouting on the other side of the square-shaped bar.

'There's this kid outside. Watching the place. Have you seen him?'

'Eh?'

'A kid. Just stands over the road. And stares at the pub. Wondered if you'd seen him.'

Quin looked at Seth as if his words confirmed something he'd long suspected: *He's gone a bit funny in the head, this one. Up there on his own all the time. No girlfriend. No visitors.* Shrugging, Quin turned to stuff Seth's rent in the till.

Feeling ridiculous, Seth moved to make his way back to the door, but someone stood in his path. 'All right, son.' It was Archie. Archie from Dundee, though he hadn't been back to the wife and five kids for over twenty years. He was the live-in cleaner and handyman responsible for the rooms above the pub. Though the irony of the position never escaped Seth, as Archie was the prime contributor to the mess and disrepair inside.

Small and old-man-bony, Archie seemed to hover more than walk. But he was still in possession of an incredible thatch of grey hair, cut into the shape of a Saxon helmet. Cragged and sprinkled with whiskers, his face appeared grandfatherly, as if capable of compassion. Archie always called Seth 'son', too, though it was only because he couldn't remember his name.

'Have ye got a fag on yer?' Archie asked.

Seth nodded. 'Sure.' Seth gave him a crumpled packet of Old Holborn with a last tuft of tobacco in the bottom.

Archie grinned. 'Ar, yer a pal, son.' He had one tooth, an incisor, bottom right, that Seth could never stop staring at. Nor the masking tape that held the thick lenses inside the plastic frames of his glasses. 'Run out. Dinne get paid till Tuesdee,' Archie said, grinning at his booty.

'Listen, Archie. Have you seen that kid who hangs around outside the bar? Wears a hooded coat.'

Now he had the tobacco, Archie lost interest in conversation. He was also drunk and had to concentrate on rolling the cigarette. Seth moved out of the bar and back into the porch. He jabbed his key into the lock and climbed the dark staircase that led to the rooms above the bar.

*

On the first set of stairs, the skirting boards were painted the red of fresh blood. Over the walls a white paper decorated with the impression of grapes had turned sallow and peeled away from the seam. In places, vast swathes had been torn down to the plaster beneath.

On the dark landing of the first floor, Seth guided himself by the light falling from the doorway of the communal kitchen. He could smell the damp beer towels in the washing machine. Bacon had been fried recently on the old gas stove and the fat had cooled. Its smell now mingled with the scent of ripe rubbish, which meant that Archie had not taken down the bin bags. There were mice in there, but no rats, yet.

Across from the kitchen was the bathroom. Frosted glass had been fitted into the top half of the door, but was not quite opaque enough for privacy. Seth switched the light on and peered inside to see if the shower unit above the bath had been fixed. It had not. 'Cunt,' he said, and then wondered when he would give up checking on the progress of the repair. Aged thirty-one, with two arts degrees to his name, and he had been reduced to washing his entire body in a sink.

He climbed the second grim flight of stairs to his room. The banisters were painted the same colour of murder as the skirting boards in the rest of the building, but the pattern and colour of the carpet had changed three times by the time he reached the second floor. He shared this storey with two other men he'd never spoken to. Up here, the lack of both natural and electric light plunged Seth into oblivion.

'Shit!' He banged a knee against something sharp. Flailing, Seth slapped a hand up and down a wall until it happened across a light switch in a splintered plastic surround, where a fist had once applied too much force. All of the lights were on timers. Pushing the large circular button activated the unshaded bulb hanging from the ceiling.

The passage between the three rooms, each fronted with a red door, appeared all the more gloomy and cramped because of the furniture stacked against the walls. It was a fire hazard he navigated daily. Hurrying forward to get to his room before the lights went out, he trampled amongst the broken bones of a discarded sofa bed. By the time he reached the door to his room the passage was dark again. Seth hit the closest switch for another five seconds of sight while he fumbled with his keys. Crossing the threshold of his room, the darkness returned and swallowed everything behind him.

On Seth's first day at the Green Man, twelve months earlier, it was Archie who had shown him the room. And Archie didn't hang around for long, as it had been his job to prepare the place for the new tenant. Of the two window frames neither had net curtains and only the window on the left side had fabric ones, the same colour as dress-patterns in the copies of *Woman's Weekly* that survive decades in doctors' waiting rooms. The sash window on the right side had become skewed at a tilt in the frame.

'Aha,' Seth had said, in horror and disbelief.

But Archie had merely blinked at him.

On the side of the room opposite the windows, the mattress of the double bed distinguished itself with Auschwitz stripes and gang-rape stains. Of the furniture, there were two badly assembled wardrobes and a little cabinet beside the bed. Still coated in mug rings and make-up, it added a faintly reassuring feminine touch.

Beside the bedside table was a single radiator, painted yellow and speckled with dark droplets. Dried blood. He'd never been able to get rid of the stains and once asked Archie who lived in the room before him. To which Archie had raised his eyebrows and said, 'Lassy. Lovely girl. Had boyfriend troubles. They was at each other all night.' Archie had then relished his role as storyteller. 'Before her was a real strange fella. Quiet as you like. But when the police come, they caught him in here with his step-daughter. And her friend.'

The whole room smelled like old carpet that had been stored in a garage for years. But at least it was dry.

He'd never done much with the place after that, just moved his stuff in and picked some broken glass out of the carpet. The sheer dilapidation of the room made any attempt at improvement seem futile. And now his piles of discarded magazines and Sunday papers made the room look cluttered but somehow vacant at the same time. Desperation led him there; despair kept him there.

During his first night he remembered being filled with a combination of self-pity, feelings of abandonment, and a subtle terror that would have been choking had he let it grow. But he couldn't afford anything else after moving to London with twenty unwanted paintings to his name. And with the big south-facing windows, he told himself the room would make him a good studio. Old school.

Seth closed his bedroom door and locked it. The other tenants often got drunk and fell about in the dark passageways; he could never relax until the door was secure. He dropped his bag on the bed and switched the kettle on. Then he turned it off again and opened the fridge, remembering he had a can of beer left over from the four-pack he bought the day before.

He sat on the edge of the bed and glanced at the cardboard boxes still stacked in the corner of his room. All of his art materials were back inside the boxes, gathering dust in a corner. The paintings were in plastic bags, stacked inside the wardrobe. He'd not done so much as a sketch in over six months and wondered whether he'd finally given up on all that, or if he might go back to it someday.

Not bothering with a glass, Seth drank from the can. He thought about a sandwich, but now he'd sat down he was too tired to move again. Still wearing his coat, he lay on the bed covers and sipped the cold drink. Time to get out. Tomorrow he'd make a start. Decide on his next move.

He looked at his watch: four o'clock. He'd have to leave for work at five thirty. Deciding a quick nap would make him feel better, he put the can on the floor, turned on his side, closed his burning eyes. And dreamed of a place he'd not been shut inside since the age of eleven.

The gate to the chamber was made from iron bars, thickly covered with black paint. Instead of windows there were two arches, one on either side of the gate. These were also blocked with vertical bars. There were no other entrances into the chamber.

The back wall, the two sides and the ceiling that completed the rectangular building were bare white stone. Smooth marble tiles made the floor hard and cold under Seth's bare feet. In here, he was always stepping from one foot to the other; the soles of his feet felt as if they had turned blue and stayed blue.

No bigger than fifteen feet square, the chamber had no

decorations. It was also devoid of furnishings. There was nothing to sit on. The cold made his back ache, but the floor was too chilly to sit upon with naked buttocks.

From the ceiling a light was suspended on a brass chain. The light bulb was housed inside a square glass shade, like an antique lamp on the outside of a horse-drawn carriage. It gave off a bright yellow light, all night and all day. He could not prevent himself from trying to warm his hands against the glass shade. But every time he reached up and touched the glass it was cold.

Looking through the locked gate he could see a deciduous wood: damp, thick and wild. The foliage was dark green and the sky above the tallest trees was low and grey. Three wide steps descended from the chamber into the long grass that grew in a wide arc around the face of the structure before the tree line. A cold wind blew through the iron bars.

His world had been reduced to a few colours.

He was inside this place because he had allowed himself to be led there and locked inside. That was all he knew. Beside that, he had vague memories that his family had visited long ago. His mum and dad had come together; his dad had seemed disappointed in him, his mother worried but tried not to show it. Another time, his sister and her husband had come. They had stood at the bottom of the steps and his brother-in-law had cracked jokes to make him feel better. Seth had kept a grin on his face until it began to ache. His sister had said little and seemed frightened of him, as if she didn't recognize her brother any more.

He'd told them all he was all right, but was unable to tell anyone what he really felt about his imprisonment in the strange stone chamber; he was unable to explain it to himself. After they passed from sight, a lump had filled his throat.

Confused, his memory failing, he had no idea how long he had been inside the stone chamber, or for what specific reason he had been locked inside in the first place, but he did know he would be there for ever; always frozen, always hungry, never able to sit down, just stepping from one foot to the other, fretting.

THREE

She might have just boarded a luxury passenger liner, a *Titanic* or a *Lusitania*. Inside, Barrington House was like a movie lot designed for a film set on the high seas between the wars, photographed in copper and sepia.

In a daze, she followed the tall head porter, Stephen, through reception and into the east wing. Along corridors lined with silk wallpaper, illumined golden brown by the lights inside patterned glass shades, and through the peculiar smell of tradition. Not quite churchish, but not far off: wood and metal polish, fresh flowers and the fragrance of precious, preserved things insufficiently ventilated, like an old and private museum never open to the public.

Stephen talked as he walked ahead of her. 'We've forty apartments spread through the two blocks with the private garden in the middle which draws the light into the rear of the flats. It's a bit confusing at first. But if you imagine a giant L shape, with the roads along the outside, you soon get your bearings. And there are twenty parking spaces under the building, but I'm afraid your aunt's flat doesn't have parking.'

'That's OK, I don't have a car. And the novelty of using the subway hasn't worn off.'

The head porter smiled. 'It may do, ma'am. It may do.'

'Apryl. Call me Apryl. Otherwise I sound about a hundred and ninety.'

'And you may live to be that old. Your aunt was eighty-four when she died.'

'Great-aunt. She was my grandmother's sister.'

'Still, a good age.' He paused and looked over his shoulder. 'Though I am truly sorry for your loss ... Apryl.'

'Thanks. But I never met her. It's still sad though. She was the last of that generation in my family. We had no idea she was still alive. Or that this place was like ... Well, like this. I mean, it's spectacular. We're not rich. We couldn't even afford the service charge – it's about how much I make a year back home. So I won't be here long.'

At a guess, when they eventually sold the place, neither she nor her mother would need to work for a long time, if ever again. They'd be rich. Just the word seemed incongruous, even silly, when applied to them. But there was no one else with a claim on the inheritance. Lillian died childless, and Apryl's mother, like Apryl, was an only child. End of the line. And at twenty-eight, if she didn't get a move on herself, the Beckford family would vanish with her. The last spinster.

'It's all a bit of a fairy tale. My mom is just gonna die when I tell her about this place. I mean you porters and everything. I could get used to this.'

Stephen nodded, his smile polite but stiff. He seemed weary, but also preoccupied by something, though not by the tattoos peeking from under the sleeves of her shirt. Reflected in the mirror of the elevator they looked like the open pages of comic books.

'So you never knew your aunt Lillian?' he asked warily,

as if weighing up something awkward he would have to tell her.

'No. My mom kind of remembers her, but not well. And Lillian wasn't that close to Granny Marilyn either. They just kind of went their own ways during the war. Which I never got, being an only child. I'd have loved a sister. We just guessed Lillian died years ago. I mean, my grandmother's been dead for fifteen years. And my mom was too busy raising me to find out about Lillian. I was quite a handful.' She was rambling, she knew it, but was too excited to care.

Stephen bit his bottom lip, then sighed. 'Your aunt wasn't well, Apryl, I'm afraid. She was a lovely woman. Very kind. And I'm not just saying that. We were all very fond of her here. But she was old and her mental health hadn't been good for a long time. Not for the ten years I've worked here, and my predecessor said as much. A few years ago we arranged to have meals delivered. And a carer visited her every week. The management used to cash her cheques and pay the bills on her behalf.'

'I never knew. Must make us sound terrible.'

'I didn't mean to suggest anything. It happens all the time in this part of town. People become estranged from their families. Cut off. Money can do that. But Lillian's state of mind was getting worse. A lot worse in the last few years before she passed away. She shouldn't have been here really. But this was her home and we all pitched in – the porters and the cleaners – to make it possible for her to stay.'

'That was very kind.'

'Oh, it was nothing really. Just milk and bread and fetching things she needed from the shops. We do try and be helpful. But we were always concerned she might have fallen or' – he paused to clear his throat – 'become lost.'

'Didn't she have any friends?'

'Not that I noticed. Not a single visitor since I've been here. You see . . .' He paused and rubbed at his mouth. 'She was quite eccentric. That's the politest way I can put it, and I mean no disrespect.' He looked uncomfortable as he said it. Even his voice dropped. *Crazy* he meant.

But she wanted to know everything about the great-aunt who had left her and her mother a whole bunch of real estate in London. Once it was sold, she'd make sure those who'd made the old lady comfortable toward the end were rewarded in some way. Her mom wouldn't object. She'd feel guilty too. Just like Apryl did right now. Though neither of them should. It was never wilful neglect on their behalf: Lillian had been a distant relative who lived on the other side of the earth.

'Do you remember her husband? Reginald?' asked Apryl. 'I think he was a pilot in the war.'

Stephen looked away, his pale blue eyes flitting, glancing above and around her head as if he were inspecting the lights in the elevator, which were dim and cast a grubby shadow over the mahogany panels and brass trimmings. 'Mmm, no. Passed away before my time here. But I would hazard a guess his death affected her greatly.'

'Why do you say that?'

But then the elevator stopped with a wheeze followed by a clunk. The doors slid open and Stephen seemed eager to step through them.

She followed him onto the landing. It was carpeted in dark green, and the walls were decorated in the same restrained tone as the communal corridors downstairs. There was a radiator opposite the elevator, inside an ornamental covering that looked like a Victorian tomb. A broad, gilt-framed mirror glimmered above it and a staircase rose and fell on either side of the elevator shaft. On the walls of the staircase she could see prints in elegant frames. At each end of the landing was a wooden front door, numbered in brass.

'Well, here we are. Number thirty-nine. Right at the top. Unfortunately, the heating isn't so good up here, so I put portable radiators in Lillian's bedroom and in the kitchen, the only two rooms I can ever remember her using. At some point I'll need them back.'

'Sure.' Apryl watched the back of Stephen's neat silver head as he rattled the fob to free the right key. Under the shiny grey waistcoat, she could see how strong his shoulders were. He exuded ex-military; the kind of authority she imagined was popular with the residents. Her great-aunt must have felt safe with Stephen around.

'I'm afraid it's quite a mess inside. She didn't want a maid and wouldn't let anyone move a thing. I doubt she threw anything away in sixty years. Anyway, here are the keys. We have another set in the safe downstairs – standard practice in case of emergency. I'll have to dash off now. Contractors are coming to look at the satellite dishes on the roof. But call reception if there is anything you need. Piotr is on the desk until six thirty, and then Seth, the night man, will take over. I'll be on site pretty much all day, every day. You can call the front desk from the phone in the kitchen. Just lift the handset and it'll connect you.'

Stephen looked into her eyes. He could probably guess she didn't want to be left alone in the apartment. 'I'm afraid you've got your work cut out, Apryl. I doubt it's been cleaned in years. And it's the only apartment with the original bath-room still intact. If you are going to sell, it'll need a lot of work. Maybe a complete renovation to get the right price.' Stephen left her outside the open door and trotted down the stairs.

The drapes must have been drawn inside the apartment, for even though Stephen had reached inside the door and turned the hall light on, little was revealed beside a dowdy and cluttered hallway from a different age.

The very thought of entering made her feel vulnerable and guilty, like she was a trespasser. And the dross of age was reluctant to remain within the confines of its walls. Even outside on the landing the place smelled old. Real old. Like her grandmother's bedroom in Jersey, which hadn't altered one bit since the forties either. But this smell was a thousand times stronger. Like the windows had never been opened and everything inside was ancient and faded and dusty. The past contained and reluctant to leave. Like the rest of the place, if she were honest, now the excitement of her first impression had passed. Gloomy stairwells and dim hallways. It was like going back in time. Maybe the residents liked it that way. Traditional ambience or something.

She poked her head inside the door and felt a foolish urge to call out her aunt's name. Because, curiously, the place didn't feel empty.

The head porter wasn't kidding: Lillian had been a shut-in. The hallway was choked with bundles of old newspapers, magazines and plastic bags, their shiny sides bulging taut. Apryl peered inside the bag nearest the coat stand. It was full of junk mail, colourful intrusions from the modern world

31

standing no chance in here, but kept for some reason, imprisoned.

Under the soles of her boots the carpet was crispy. With the dim hall lights on, a host of dead moths visible through their glass shades, she could see how the carpet was worn down to the weave. What had once been a complicated pattern of red and green was now mostly the colour of compressed straw along the middle. Worn down by her great-aunt's feet.

The furniture in the long hallway was definitely antique. Dark and shiny wooden legs appeared between bales of yellowing newspaper. Embroidered cushions on the chairs were partially hidden by blanched telephone directories. Elsewhere, carved wood, mother-of-pearl inlays, and frosted glass with intricate decorations peeked out from among the garbage sacks, as if humiliated by their surroundings. Apryl was no historian, but even she knew they'd stopped making cabinets, clocks and chairs like this in the forties. And if it wasn't for the piles of trash and stained walls the apartment might have looked elegant. Or maybe not.

The wallpaper had once been a cream silk, with silver stripes running vertically through it, but was now mostly yellow and discoloured by brown clouds where moisture had dried near the dirty wainscoting and above the skirting boards. Beneath her fingertips, the walls felt fuzzy like the worn fur on a stuffed animal.

In the kitchen there was cracked yellow lino and a perimeter of ancient enamel appliances. Dark wooden cabinets were fixed to walls once painted buttercup but now blemished like ivory. The gas rings on the stove were dry and dusty, the deep sink bone dry. Only the surface of the kitchen table showed signs of use. There were lines made by a knife on the chopping board and crumbs in the bread bin. A solitary chair, with a tartan pattern on its cushion, was tucked beneath the kitchen table.

The scant evidence of her great-aunt's domesticity suddenly made her sad, right down to her toes. But it was the sight of the silver teapot on the tray decorated with birds of the British Isles, next to the stub of a packet of lemon cookies on the table, that thickened her throat with emotion. She thought she might cry.

There was a single china cup beside the teapot, a strainer, a sugar bowl and a tea caddy. The gold rim of the cup was chipped, probably the last of a set. Maybe a wedding gift when she and Reginald were married. Apryl touched the handle, but couldn't bring herself to raise the fragile vessel. This was Lillian's cup; she drank tea out of it. Up here on her own in the kitchen, at this little table by the plastic bin with the swing lid, surrounded by the relics of nearly a century on this planet. Apryl sniffed a tear back. She could see why rich people sealed themselves off inside retirement villages in Florida and rode around in golf carts wearing polo shirts. What was the point of being different if you ended up like this?

She wiped at her eyes. 'You could have come and lived with us.'

Inside the cupboards on the walls she found a motley assortment of crockery – three china dinner sets, incomplete and now combined in an incongruous medley of patterns. There were some old pots and pans in the cupboards. She doubted the pots had been used in years, except for the one with a rind of dry milk inside. And besides the three tins of soup and some packets of sweet cookies, there was nothing to eat. Inside the fridge she saw a plastic bottle of lumpy milk. Her great-aunt lived on tea, cookies and soup and made it to eighty-four.

Stephen said nothing had been touched since Lillian died. And how did she die? Was it in here?

Apryl dropped her backpack from her shoulder and leant it against the kitchen table. She couldn't shake the sense of being an intruder in a stranger's home. Already she was dreading the thought of spending a night here. Would there be clean sheets? Had her aunt died in bed? She suddenly wanted to call Stephen and get him up here and not let him leave until she knew everything.

With an effort of will she calmed herself. She was tired, excited, her nerves were strung out; she couldn't possibly have anticipated any of this. She just had to remember this was a great opportunity. Something totally radical and beyond her experience.

But when she opened the living-room door, her resolve vanished again. She didn't manage more than two steps inside. Why hadn't Stephen told her about the flowers? All of the dead flowers. The sloping pile of brown stalks and shrivelled petals that rose from the carpet to the sill of the big window overlooking Lowndes Square. They reminded her of flowers on old graves, left to wither and collapse and to bleach of colour. Seeing so many emaciated stems and dead leaves in the thin, brownish light made a shiver pinprick up her spine and then fizzle at the base of her skull. This must have been going on for years. This pile built one bunch at a time. And all roses, by the look of the few petals on the top that remained as dark as wine. Behind them, the grey drapes with the plaited golden trim were drawn closed.

She turned the main light on to better investigate the flowers and see the pictures on the walls, but the room was still so shadowy and dim she realized she'd be better off with the drapes open. But when she leant over the flowers and tried to pull them apart she discovered they had been stitched shut. She stepped back quickly from the window and stared at the neat bindings of red thread that joined the drapes in the middle, permanently.

'What the fuck?'

Alone and crazy, Great-aunt Lillian had sewn her drapes shut with thread, and then mounted before them floral tributes that covered half the room. She turned around to look about her. The room was empty of furniture, the floor still thick with dust, but the corners where the walls met the ceiling were free of cobwebs, so you still could see the photographs. On all of the walls, black-and-white photographs in antique frames reached from the height of her waist to the ceiling. And the pictures all featured the same couple. Every single one of them.

Handsome with a pencil moustache, like Douglas Fairbanks Junior, his hair slick either side of a parting, she saw her great-uncle Reginald for the first time in her life.

His eyes were dark and intelligent. And smiling. Just looking at him made her grin. Reginald always dressed in a suit and tie or wore silver slacks with a white shirt open at the neck. In one photo a little terrier lay at his feet as he sat in a cane chair. A pipe often featured in his strong left hand. Lillian's husband: a man she always stood proudly beside, close, either holding his elbow or standing behind him with a hand placed upon his shoulder. Like she couldn't let him go. Like she loved the man so much being without him would drive her crazy.

And Lillian had been a beautiful woman. Like a movie star from the forties with big brown eyes and the sharp bone structure you rarely saw these days. Always dressed elegantly in tea frocks, or cocktail dresses to the knee, or ball gowns sweeping around the white toes of her glossy shoes. But it was the way they looked at each other that affected her most. You couldn't fake that. This sad, brown and mildewed space which Lillian roamed and dreamed in and haunted for sixty years suddenly made more sense. Two people once lived here who should never have parted. And the place was in mourning because the widow was heartbroken. Maybe mad with a grief that never eased. Did hearts still get broken like that?

Apryl knew Reginald died in the late forties. After serving in the RAF in the war and surviving dangers she couldn't even begin to comprehend, this happy, handsome man with a beautiful young bride had died suddenly. She didn't know the details, but her gran had told her mom that he died after the war. That's all they had to go on. A sketchy oral history passed down from one solitary old woman to another, and so on to her. But glimpses into Lillian's life hung all around her on the walls, and were packed into those boxes in the hallway, and into whatever else Apryl might find in the three bedrooms and dining room. And hadn't Stephen said something about a storage cage under the building?

She'd budgeted to arrange a quick sale of the flat and a hasty disposal of Lillian's possessions in two weeks. But she didn't want that any more. She wanted to stay here and learn about her great-aunt and uncle. She wanted to examine and consider and collect and preserve. This wasn't junk. It meant something to Lillian. All of it.

There had to be letters. Maybe a diary. She'd have to sift and discard in here like an archaeologist, in between dealing with real-estate agents and all of the legal stuff. Work fast and maybe see a bit of London too. But Lillian had to come first. If it meant cashing the rest of her savings and quitting her job back home, so be it. She would know every single thing there was to know about her great-aunt.

FOUR

Changed into his uniform, with a cup of tea in his hand, when Seth came up from the staffroom he was hoping Piotr had already made his way down to the basement garage where his rusted shitbox car was parked. Instead, Piotr had merely pulled his red anorak over his sweat-clouded polyester shirt and was waiting for him. Grinning, he held up the duty log. 'Ah, Seth being seeing the ghosts again! We all laugh so much when we read the log. Maybe he drink the whisky in the night and he see things, eh?' He rolled his eyes and raised a hand as if to simulate drinking from a glass.

'I didn't say I saw anything. I reported a disturbance. A noise. Someone's been in sixteen. I heard them.'

But Piotr wasn't listening. 'You should polish the brass at night. I tell Stephen but he no listen. Then you being doing work and not have the time to see the ghosts.' The door closed on the swishing anorak and beaming face.

He wouldn't make another report, no matter what he heard. Fuck it. He'd done his job; if something was stolen, he'd warned them.

He collapsed into the chair and thought again about the dream he'd had that afternoon. It left him nostalgic but uneasy. As a kid, he used to visit that chamber in nightmares. Trying to scream, while strangely mute, as he was pushed inside the chamber against his will. It started around the time his dad left. Over and over again, he used to find that weird stone chamber in his dreams. It was an actual mausoleum he'd once seen with his nan, as they walked through an unkempt corner of the cemetery where his grandfather was buried. All the flowers were dead and the names of people were worn off the stone tablets and markers. It terrified him. He could not accept that his mum and dad would die and leave him one day, and then end up inside one of those stone enclosures or the mausoleum. And that he would die too. His nan said, with a smile, 'Not for a long time, Seth.' But the cold marble mausoleum with the little light inside, and the locked gate and barred windows, haunted him. He imagined being put in there. Being dead in there. Where he would stand on the wrong side of the little gate crying for his mum and dad who couldn't see him. Would watch them walk away through the headstones. He used to see them clearly, starting the white Allegro before driving off and leaving him behind the gate, sobbing, hysterical.

He shook himself. Even now he didn't like remembering it. As a kid, the fear of the chamber used to tighten his chest so much he couldn't breathe.

He should call his mum. His dad. His sister. The dream made him want to. He couldn't remember the last time he had spoken to any of them. He'd let everything go.

Seth sighed and glanced over the duty clipboard to force himself to think of something else. Only twenty of the forty apartments were in use. Same situation as during his four shifts the previous week.

Most of the penthouse suites were either holiday homes for the absurdly rich or corporate flats for employees working in the city. Although some of the flats were occupied by troublesome permanent tenants, he was rarely bothered during the night. Though he noted one addition in flat thirty-nine in the east wing. Someone had moved in. The old girl, Lillian, had died. In a taxi or something a couple of months back. Stephen had told him the day after, but he'd never seen the woman during his shifts. She never came out at night. The new tenant was listed as Apryl Beckford. He wondered what she looked like.

When he finished the last dregs of his tea, he walked into the ornamental garden built at the intersection of the two wings. He rolled and then smoked a thin cigarette while listening to the fountain. The memory of the dream dimmed and he began to feel something like relief to be back at work. There were few chores, only the occasional patrol to make and guest to sign in. It was less demoralizing than life at the Green Man, and more comfortable too. Once, before he started work at Barrington House, the building had even been featured in *Hello!* magazine, on account of some footballer who used to live there. An ideal old-school job for an artist, he'd once hoped, but he'd stopped sketching as soon as he took his place in the leather chair in reception. Now he suspected he had put himself there to forget and be forgotten; to ease himself out of mainstream life in the most comfortable way possible. And that notion no longer troubled him.

After his spent cigarette landed in the fountain he returned to the chair and began to yawn. Another restless night. Arab teenagers in performance cars circled Lowndes Square. He checked his watch. Still another ten hours before he could leave in the morning and fall into a deep sleep. Preferably a dreamless coma.

Leafing through the television listings in the *Evening Standard*, he was suddenly startled by the buzzing of the house phone. On the brass panel he could see a red light next to the label for apartment forty.

'What the fuck do you want?' he whispered to himself. It was Mr Glock, the middle-aged Swiss playboy, and the rudest man Seth had ever met. He picked up the handset to stop the deafening trill from the panel's speaker. 'Seth speaking.'

'I need a taxi for Heathrow. Do it now.' Mr Glock hung up.

No other tenant so reinforced his long-held suspicion that the rich were an unpleasant crowd. When he first began working in the building, the tenants and their absurd wealth intimidated him, as if their very presence shone lights about his stained tie, the scuffs on his shoes and the gaping holes in his curriculum vitae. It had made him ridiculously diffident in their presence. But after half a year of taking their stinking rubbish out and witnessing countless demonstrations of self-importance before his desk, compounded with their affected accents and vulgar furnishings, his awe had gradually reduced to a simmer of resentment. He'd little respect left for any of them. Especially Glock. Working here assured Seth that money favoured the worst kind of people.

He took the lift up to the fourth floor, where Glock's bags would be waiting. On the way up he mopped his face with a paper towel. The texture of the paper hurt the hot, delicate skin of his forehead and cheeks. Remembering an Asian man who sneezed on him in the cinema, he wondered if he'd picked up a tropical illness from a foreigner. He rubbed at his neck, feeling the beginning of a tickle in his throat. Then recalled that nasty cold air he had sucked in while looking through the letter box of apartment sixteen, and winced. He thought he could still taste the dust.

Once Glock and his bags were taken care of, Seth rolled a cigarette and watched the cab pull away from the kerb and drive out of the square. He told himself it was absolutely the last time he was getting out of the chair for the duration of the shift. He felt like shit. The tickle at the back of his throat had turned into something raw. Under his blazer, his shirt clung to his back.

But his respite slumped behind the desk was short-lived. The next person to demand his attention was Mrs Shafer, the elderly wife of an invalided American stockbroker. They lived in apartment twelve.

Standing outside the building's front doors, she began ringing the bell. The incessant buzzing tone that sounded behind his desk carried the full force of her annoyance. She appeared even more grotesque than usual, with her hair piled into a messy arrangement of scarves from which strands drooped around her doughy face. Fucking Halloween in a bandanna. He shivered with disgust. How could a woman let herself go like that? Especially one with so much money?

Seth buzzed her inside via the switch behind his desk. As she trundled into reception on her thick legs, a severe frown eroded her forehead. 'What is the point . . .' There was a long pause. 'We have trouble with it!' She pointed at the door. Seth winced. Although accustomed to her hysteria and un-predictable temper, she never failed to frighten him. She was mad. Only the head porter, with his graceful manner and soft voice, seemed able to manage her moods.

She began to take short, shuddering steps towards his desk. 'Don't bother yourself!' she shrieked at him. One of her arms flapped in the air until she resembled a dinosaur, the bulky body set forward at an angle, with short, fetal arms clawing out front. Mrs Shafer expected the porters to rush to the doors and manually hold them open as if she were royalty. Then it was customary to escort her from the lift to the front door of her apartment. This was a precedent set by Piotr and his relentless hustle for tips, but Seth refused to take part in the charade. It made him think bitterly of his wasted education – four years at art school, a master's degree to follow – only to be reduced to placating a demented, rich bully who terrorized her tiny, disabled husband before the eyes of the door staff.

Mr Shafer rarely left the apartment. On the rare occasions he was seen, he was always accompanied by his shrill wife. He looked like a puppet with dried-out wooden limbs barely suspended above the ground, as if most of the strings had been severed. His wife would tug the old man about her massive skirts and constantly berate him, while he used all of his concentration and energy to balance as he took one slow step after another. Both the Shafers stank of stale sweat.

Seth stood up in front of his chair and said, 'Good evening,' so quietly he barely heard himself.

She flapped her arms again in exasperation and her face turned bright red. 'Get Stephen! Phone Stephen now!'

She only stopped shouting when the lift doors opened behind her. For a moment the sound flustered her, then she shambled inside. A final mumble from her became a shrill cry that Seth could make no sense of. He had no intention of bothering Stephen; by the time she reached her apartment, she would have forgotten the altercation.

But he was to get no peace that night. Every arsehole in

the building seemed involved in a conspiracy to make him work. By nine o'clock, Mrs Pzalis had phoned down three times from flat twenty-two to complain about the television reception. As did Mrs Benedetti from flat five. He wrote it in the log, but could see that the satellite company had been up on the roof twice since his last shift. At ten thirty, Mrs Singh in nineteen complained about a smell of smoke in the west wing, and before he could go and investigate, Mrs Roth in eighteen called down to tell him the same thing. There wasn't a peep out of the fire and smoke alarms, but he had to check it out.

If Singh and Roth could smell it inside their apartments, then the smell was up by sixteen. A part of the building he'd planned to avoid on each of the three patrols he was obliged to undertake during the shift.

'Cunt.' He took the lift to the ninth floor.

The moment he left the lift and stood on the landing, he could smell it too: burned meat, singed clothing and something like sulphur. But there was no smoke, the doors were cold, and the rubbish stores were empty. It was a dead scent, but a deeply unpleasant miasma like the residue that lingered in a place where there had been an accident with fire. It was strongest near the door of number nineteen. Old Mrs Roth's place.

He looked about him and was reminded why he'd never liked the building upstairs. Any of it, if he were honest. Even during the lighter evenings of the summer, when the fading sun reinforced the electric light in the communal areas, he found it gloomy. The old brown wood, the dull brasses and the thick green carpet seemed to absorb any illumination, particularly on the stairwells. They reminded him of those parts of old houses that remained forever in shadow. But despite the absence of human traffic in the stairwells and corridors, the place had an active energy. A kind of swarming, bustling sensation in the air, as if the presence of former activity was locked in place and unable to escape.

He descended to the eighth floor in a feverish, breathless daze. He decided to proceed swiftly across the landing and not stop, regardless of what he smelled or heard bumping and scraping about inside apartment sixteen. But it was not to be.

As he took the stairs two at a time and swung onto the landing he almost collided with a figure. A figure dressed in white and hunched over. It was standing a few feet before the door of apartment sixteen.

'Jesus Christ,' he whimpered in a breathless voice and felt every hair stand up on his scalp.

The figure turned to stare at him. For a second he failed to identify the crumpled face and the curved bonnet of thin silvery hair. But then recognition struck. His shock passed and an immediate sense of relief washed through him. It was Mrs Roth. But in her nightgown, alone, and clearly distressed.

'He's come back,' she said, on the verge of tears. Her needle-thin arms and arthritic hands trembled. Through the thin, silky material of her gown he could see the sharp bones of her shoulders and pelvis sticking out. Absurdly scrawny legs, knotted with veins, jutted from beneath the hem. Her clawed feet were bare.

'He's come back for me.'

She was ninety-two. He could do nothing but wonder how she had managed to walk down a flight of stairs on those legs. Mrs Roth was largely confined to her bed, being taken out for lunch just twice a week, with the help of two walking sticks and her Filipino maid, Imee.

Seth stood still and stared at her. He tried to swallow but it was too painful.

She pointed a disfigured hand at the door of flat sixteen. 'Open the door. I want to see for myself.'

He shook his head. 'I can't, Mrs Roth. Let's get you back into bed.'

Angrily, she swatted the contortion of bone and thin skin that serviced as a hand. 'I don't want to be in bed!'

She wasn't sleepwalking. And, despite her age, Mrs Roth had never seemed prone to even the vaguest confusion. In fact, she remained unfailingly rude and unpleasant at all times. Though she rarely bothered Seth at night, her mal-treatment of the day staff was legendary. Even the head porter was terrified of her.

'Please, ma'am. You shouldn't be down here.'

He realized his mistake as he was speaking. Her face pur-pled with rage. She turned on him; pointed a finger, bent like a hook, at his face, so only the knuckle of the second joint was directed at his eyes. 'How dare you!' The normally per-fect halo of transparent wisps on her head, fashioned into a bouffant, became disturbed. A few strands hung about her ears. Through what remained in place, he could see her pale scalp and the liver spots discolouring it. Her neck was thin and the flesh hung from her collarbones like loose leather. She reminded him of a bird. A beaky, fierce-eyed bird with a few feathers remaining on its plucked skin.

'He's back, I tell you! I heard him. I heard him laughing.'

Ordinarily, a man in his position would be prone to an embarrassed laugh or a nervous smile when confronted by a raving ninety-two-year-old woman in her nightgown, but there was something about her determined face and wild rheumy eyes that made Seth uneasy. Particularly considering what he too had heard on the other side of that door.

Seth made a bold move. He stood close to Mrs Roth, nodding in sympathy. 'I know. I've heard noises in there for a while now. But what is it?'

'What? Speak up. Don't be ridiculous. What are you saying?'

He nodded his head towards the door. 'In there. At night. I made reports. About the noises. The bumping. In the hallway. Furniture being knocked over. Things. Like that.'

Mrs Roth's pointed face blanched a sickly shade of pale. The tremble in her frail, monkey limbs became a shake. He thought she might fall over, and moved forward to take her elbow. She clutched at him for support and dropped her head.

'No,' she whispered. And then, 'No,' again, but to herself. She looked up at him like a child after a fright. 'Take me home. I want Imee. Get Imee. Where's Imee? I want Imee.'

Tense and uncomfortable in the face of her indignity, he walked her slowly towards the lift door and then summoned it from the ground floor by punching the button in the polished brass plate. As he waited he realized his shirt was drenched with sweat again.

The groaning cables seemed to take an age to haul the heavy but elegant carriage up from the ground. And all the while, in his discomfort, Seth tried to reassure Mrs Roth with comments about Imee and bed, until she told him to, 'Shut up, just shut up,' and waved a hand at his face.

When he opened the outer doors and guided her inside the lift carriage, she screwed her eyes closed and seemed more decrepit and bent-over than ever, as if being forced to remember something especially painful. Something that broke her. Broke what little spirit remained in that old frail body.

Up on the ninth floor, the door to her apartment was still open, and Seth rang the bell to raise Imee, who came swiftly from her little room at the end of the long hall. Clutching her blue dressing gown across her front, as if to protect her modesty from the eyes of the porter, she snatched Mrs Roth off him, and cast him a sullen, angry look, before closing the front door on his whispered explanations. Mrs Roth had begun sniffing and crying the moment she saw Imee.

'Bitch,' Seth muttered at the closed door, and took the lift down to the staffroom in the basement. Where he pondered, with some discomfort, who Mrs Roth had been referring to outside the front door of apartment sixteen.

FIVE

'Mama, she never threw anything out. Nothing. I'm not kidding. You should see the clothes in her room. There's like a hundred dresses and suits and coats and stuff. Going back to, like, the forties. It's all still here. Like a fashion museum or something. We inherited a goddamn museum. The Lillian collection. And some of the dresses are so beautiful.' Apryl walked back and forth in her great-aunt's bedroom, her cell phone pressed to her ear.

But she knew her mother could never comprehend what she'd uncovered in her great-aunt's rooms. Not unless she saw it herself. Which she never would, due to her pathological terror of flying. And Apryl felt unable to describe her discoveries adequately, or to impress upon her mother the atmosphere of the apartment: the faded grandeur, the ever-present sense of loss, the chaotic defence an old woman had built against the world outside, the disturbed inner life still evident in unoccupied rooms with shrines and rituals and habits long maintained but now just plain mystifying.

Two of the rooms, the smaller bedrooms at the end of the cluttered hallway on the right side, were choked with debris. In each room she'd found a single bed with an ancient eiderdown coated in a fur of dust. About the beds, cardboard boxes and old suitcases filled with bric-a-brac were stacked.

What she was to do with any of it remained a mystery. An inventory would take weeks, even months to complete.

At least Lillian's bedroom remained uncluttered around the two giant wardrobes and clothes drawers. There was also a huge bed and a beautiful bureau with three locked drawers, the keys for which she couldn't find, but she guessed Lillian's personal papers must be stored inside. And she'd never seen so many perfume bottles arranged in a herd on top of the chest of drawers. Cosmetic companies never made glass like that any more, nor the porcelain jars for cream and make-up, most of their contents hard and cracked like the baked soil of distant planets.

'Mama, I'd like to bring the clothes back. I think they all fit me. Isn't that crazy? I tried on two fur coats and three hats and it was like they were made for me.'

'*Honey, where are you gonna put it? In your tiny place? I've no room here, you know that. And think of the cost, sweetheart. We just don't have the money for that kind of thing and now you're talking of giving up your job too. I'm worried.*'

'Don't be. Mama, we're not going to be short of green soon.'

'*We will be if you carry on like this. You have to be realistic, honey. The apartment could take a long time to sell.*'

'I can cover the shipping from my savings. But Lillian's stuff I want to keep will have to come to you first and go in the basement.'

'*Honey, it'll cost a fortune. You can't bring it back here – you'll have to sell it in England.*'

'No. I'll be careful. I can stay here until the apartment is sold and just work my way through all this stuff. The furniture will have to go. I don't know anything about antiques, so we'll have to get an expert to value them. But the really personal stuff I want us to keep. Mama, it's so beautiful. It's just the clothes and the photos and a few other things.'

'Oh honey, I don't know about this. You were only going there for two weeks to empty the place and sell it, and now you're talking like a crazy thing.'

'Mama, Mama, this is our history. We can't just throw it out. I mean, the photos of Lillian and Reginald, they're just heartbreaking. They were so glamorous. Like movie stars. You just won't believe it when you see them. That's someone in our family up there on those walls. A woman with so much taste and class and style. She's like my icon already. You know how much I love that look.'

But her mother sounded tired; she should never have agitated her like this. Added to the strain of her only daughter being overseas, the intrusion of anything new or foreign into her immaculate New Jersey bungalow would be the cause of severe anxiety. She should have broken all this to her mother slowly, but Apryl couldn't contain her excitement.

The forties and fifties had long been the inspiration for her own retro stylings back home in New York, where she sold alternative and vintage clothing in St Mark's Place. And had done for starvation wages for the last five years, which had slipped by and left her without much of a CV, or apartment, or standard of living. But this cache could raise thousands on eBay. Not that she was intending to sell it all; she intended to wear the majority of these outfits to the retro clubs downtown and in the Village when she got home. This was her inheritance; her aunt wore these clothes *back in the day.*

The dresses were so exquisitely made; she'd found six immaculate silk and taffeta ball gowns, two dozen suits in cashmere and wool, and twice as many figure-hugging black and cream dresses, folded into cases, that her great-aunt must have worn into the sixties with, perhaps, a single strand of pearls. And the sight of the costume jewellery had made her shriek out loud: three boxes stuffed full of colourful brooches, necklaces and earrings all tangled together.

The vintage underwear they stopped making in the early seventies, and some of her great-aunt's girdles and corsets were made at least as far back as the forties. She'd long fantasized of such finds in used clothing stores and garage sales, and had never stopped scouring factory closures and charity stores for vintage accessories for her own wardrobe, or to sell in the store. There were enough clothes in her great-aunt's room to start a business from scratch or fill an auction room. There were at least thirty packets of real nylons unopened in the top drawer of the dresser, with names like *Mink* and *Cocktail Kitty*. Some of the older stockings were still sealed inside tissue-paper sheets within flat cardboard boxes, the manufacturer's details embossed regally on the lids.

Lillian could not have discarded any of her clothes. As decades and styles changed, she seemed to have preserved and stored everything until she stopped buying new clothes some time in the early sixties. She had no contemporary clothes at all. So she must have worn old classic styles right up until she died. If she had done, the family resemblance was uncanny; Apryl rarely wore anything that didn't look as if it had been made in the fifties.

Only the shoe collection disappointed. Apart from a pair of velvet pumps with Cuban heels and two pairs of silver sandals, Lillian had worn out all of her shoes. Heels were sheared down to wood and leather uppers were split or scarred with deep creases, all unsalvageable. It was as if her great-aunt had done a lot of walking, but very little in the way of replacing her footwear.

'Mama, look, don't worry, it'll be OK. Everything will be fine. I'm just real tired. I've been up since five thirty. All this is so exciting and sad and I don't know what. I still can't get my head around the fact that Great-aunt Lillian lived here. Knightsbridge is like Park Avenue. With the money she had in the bank and the sale of this flat, we're going to be rich, Mama. You hear me? Rich.'

'Well we don't know that, honey. You said it needed renovating.'

'Mama, this is prime real estate. These places get snapped up right away. Even in this condition. It's a penthouse, Mama.' She heard the front-door bell trill like a little hammer going crazy inside an iron bell. 'Mama, someone at the door. I gotta fly, and anyway my cell is nearly out of juice.'

'Your cell? What are you calling me on your cell for? It'll cost the earth.'

'Love you, Mama. Gotta fly. Call you soon when I know more.' Apryl air-kissed the phone then ran from the kitchen to the front door to let the head porter in.

'I guess I really want to know what she was like. Especially at the end. I mean, she's left all of this. In here . . .' To unravel, she wanted to say. Lillian had not made it possible for her to just throw things out and sell up. It was as if the dead woman was enforcing an involvement in her crazy existence.

Apryl sighed as she sat in the kitchen with the head porter.

'I promise not to keep you long – I'm just beat myself. I'm so wrecked I'm starting to hallucinate. So maybe this isn't the best time for me to start asking questions, but ... some of this is kind of freaking me out.' She couldn't keep the emotion out of her voice. She coughed and took a slurp of her black tea; she usually drank coffee, but Lillian was all out.

Stephen was no longer on duty and had taken his tie off, but even though it was after ten, he still wore the white cotton shirt and grey trousers of his uniform, which suggested he didn't have much life besides his service to the building. While Apryl sat at the table in the kitchen – the only room serviceable enough to entertain a guest – he leant against the counter and held the mug of tea she'd made for him.

He nodded. 'It must be a lot to take in. I was thinking it might have been easier for you to deal with as you never knew Lillian. But of course, having not known her is probably just as taxing in a different way. You want to know her before you let this place go.'

'That's about the size of it. And already I'm seeing things here that remind me of me. If that makes any sense.'

Stephen smiled, as if in prelude to a confession. 'It does. I noted a resemblance right away. In your eyes. But it's ironic. Often the residents are closer to us porters at the end than they are to their own families.'

'And I guess no one ever thinks of you guys.'

'Oh, we don't mind. We're paid to do a job. But when you work in people's homes for a long time, you can't help becoming a part of their lives. Like family.'

'You liked Lillian, didn't you?'

'Yes. The day porters did too. But I don't think the night staff ever saw her. Not once.'

'Why was that?'

He shrugged. 'She always made sure she was home and indoors in plenty of time before it got dark.' He could see Apryl was confused, and tried to elaborate. 'It's what happens when you spend a twelve-hour shift here. We never pry, but you just can't help noticing things. And we're paid to be observant.' He was preparing her for something. She could see he was a man with impeccable manners and very professional, who didn't want to speak out of turn, or be garrulous. Maybe it was against staff policy. But she was tired now and just wanted him to be straight with her. If Lillian never had visitors or friends, the staff at Barrington House were the people to talk to. It looked like the porters were all Lillian had at the end. And the very thought of a life recollected only by them made her morose again.

She gave Stephen a tired smile. 'Please, Stephen. You can be candid. I just need something to go on before I hit the hay. My curiosity is killing me.'

He nodded. Looked at his feet. Ran his tongue over his gums. 'Like I said before, she was very eccentric.'

'But in what way, specifically? I mean, did she talk to herself out loud and—'

'Yes. Yes she did. Half the time she lived in her own world. In her head. And she never seemed particularly happy when she was there.'

Apryl felt her mouth sag.

'But there were often moments too when she was completely lucid. She was unfailingly gracious. She had beautiful manners, your aunt. Real quality. Though we never really passed more than the time of day with her, on her way out. Once every day. At eleven, like clockwork. But . . .'

'Go on.'

Stephen's smile was awkward. 'It's not often you see a woman wearing a hat these days. With a veil. But Lillian never went out without one. Or without her gloves. And only ever dressed in black. Like she was in mourning. She was quite the local celebrity. Everyone around here knew her. And took care of her. Local residents and shopkeepers and the cabbies would all bring her back when they found her wandering about confused.'

'What do you mean, confused?'

Stephen shrugged. 'She'd go out as right as rain, your aunt. But then get all upset and have to be brought home. Most of the time she'd perk up when she came within sight of the building. And eventually, if I could spare them, I had one of the porters follow her whenever she left the building. Or I'd go myself. She never went far, but never seemed to take the same route twice. She'd always turn up in a different place.'

'It sounds terrible.'

Stephen shrugged, his expression helpless. 'But what could we do? We're not nurses.'

'I wonder what was going on in her head.'

'Before she set off she'd always say, "Well, it's cheerio, Stephen. If I don't see you again, take care my dear." And she took the same bag with her. A small case and her black umbrella, as if she were going on a trip. But every day, she'd be back within a couple of hours. More than anything else we worried about her getting lost. Some of the cabbies would stop when they saw her and say, "Hop in, Lil, I'll drop you home." And if she was ready, she'd climb in and say, "I shan't get any farther today. Not today. But I'll try again tomorrow." Same thing every time, without fail. They all said so. And they'd bring her back. In a way, I always thought it refreshing to know there's still a sense of community, at least among the local workforce. They all knew your aunt Lillian.'

'What about the flowers? There must be a thousand in that room.'

Stephen shrugged. 'She never told me what they were for, or why she collected them. But she came home with them, for as long as I can remember. Roses every time. She was caught twice taking them from the front gardens of Chesterfield House in Mayfair. Fortunately, I know the head porter, so there wasn't any trouble. But it could be awkward. She'd even get them out of bins, and walk out of florists and forget to pay.'

'And how did she die? It says heart failure on the death certificate.'

Stephen wiped at his mouth. He was having difficulty meeting her eye. He tried twice and failed.

'Please, Stephen. Tell me.'

'She died in the back of a cab, Apryl. She'd had quite a fright out there. On one of her walks. A cabby saw her first. Really distressed. She had made it as far as Marble Arch too. The furthest I'd ever known her go, and that's quite a distance for a woman of her age. But that day, she was different. You see, usually, when someone found her, she'd be talking to herself and striking at the air with her umbrella or cane. Nothing odd about that. We'd all seen her do it. Very involved in an argument with someone who wasn't there. And usually this would happen, this agitation, just before she turned and headed for home. Or, as I said before, when she was picked up and escorted back here. But the morning she died, the driver said she looked ill. Really worn out. She was leaning against the railings of the park. Very pale and almost ready to keel over. She'd used up all her strength getting so upset about something. So he stopped and helped her into the cab. But she never broke out of the trance like she usually did. She seemed . . . to be in shock. Just wasn't aware any longer of where she was, or where she was going. The driver put his foot down and phoned the main desk to tell us to call an ambulance. But she died on the way here. It looked to me like a massive stroke. That's what I thought. And the oddest thing . . . well, she came out of her trance just before she died. As the cab entered the square. The driver saw her in the mirror. Upset. Really upset at the end. Well, afraid, you could say. Of something. Almost as if someone was sitting beside her.'

Apryl looked into the dregs of her tea. After a long, uncomfortable silence she spoke. 'Wouldn't a care home have been a better place for her?'

'Yes, probably. But she did have a carer, and when she was here Lillian was fine. Eccentric, but capable and lucid and able to look after herself. She was quite a strong woman for her age. It was only when she went out – only when she left the building – that she . . . well, had a funny turn.'

Lillian could have been suffering from anything: Alzheimer's, dementia. If only she and her mother had known. 'Poor Aunty Lillian,' she said.

But Stephen didn't seem to be paying attention. He was preoccupied with his own thoughts. 'But the strangest thing that day,' he suddenly said, 'was her bag.' The head porter frowned at his shoes in puzzlement. 'She had a plane ticket in there. To New York. Along with a passport that had been out of date for fifty years. It seemed she really was planning on leaving us for good that last time.'

After Stephen left, Apryl ate some pasta parcels with pesto she'd bought from the little store on Motcomb Street and then ran a bath. There was no shower, or even a shower attachment to fix to the cloudy steel faucet. So she sat on the little cushioned stool beside the tub and watched the thick cascade of water splash with a hollow sound against the worn enamel. It set off a whole series of clanging and gassy whooshing sounds behind the discoloured and patchy walls of the bathroom. Waiting for the tub to fill, she went and unpacked the few clothes she'd brought with her and put her vanity case on the dresser in Lillian's bedroom.

She found herself looking for things to do. Trying to distract her mind from dwelling both on the prospect of sleeping alone in the apartment, and on what her great-aunt spent her time doing at night. The two end bedrooms had long been out of action and were just used as storage, so it was doubtful Lillian ever went in there other than to make deposits. The living room was never used for anything beside the delivery of fresh flowers to cover the dead flowers of the window shrine. That room was sacred to her aunt. And the furniture in the dining room was covered in dust sheets. There was no television or even a working radio in the apartment either. Earlier, she'd found an old broken radio set with a Bakelite casing, wrapped in newspaper and plunged deep inside a box of pewter tankards. But apart from that and a few books in the bedroom, none of them recent titles or publications, she couldn't even begin to guess how her great-aunt occupied herself during so many nights indoors and alone. No wonder she talked to herself; Apryl had been there for a day and she was ready to do the same thing.

After her bath, in which her eyelids closed themselves three times and abandoned her to a doze – lasting until the water cooled – she made her way to the bedroom and shut the door. The bed linen under the ancient quilted eiderdown looked clean, but she couldn't bring herself to climb beneath the sheets. On top of a wardrobe she found some blankets and made a temporary nest with them on top of the covers.

When she turned off the side light, the profound darkness of the room shocked her a little; made her pause before lying down. But she forced herself to quell her silliness; she was just too tired for it. In fresh underwear and a Social Distortion T-shirt, she curled into a fetal position facing the door, like she always did when sleeping in a strange place.

As she settled down, she listened to the purr of the occasional car passing below the window of the room, down in Lowndes Square. She cast her slowing thoughts out there, into London, rather than let them turn and begin exploring the apartment, reaching to the strange and cluttered rooms upon which a darkness and heavy silence had fallen.

Pulling her knees further up and into her stomach, she clasped her hands together and sandwiched them between her warm thighs, like she'd always done since childhood. And was immediately aware of herself slipping into a thick slumber, one that would last for hours, all night. Down she went, and away. At last her mind was still. Though the room beyond her closed eyelids was not.

She dismissed the rustle and the subtle padding of feet on the floor, moving swiftly from the door to the foot of the bed. It was only her roommate, Tony. Tiptoeing the way he did, in a kind of hasty walk to fetch something he had left in her room earlier. Too tired to open her eyes, in a very distant and shrinking part of her consciousness she knew he would be gone soon. Gone.

What did he want now, then, standing at the foot of the bed and leaning over her? She felt the long presence extending across her feet, the indentation of a knee at the foot of the mattress.

She snapped awake in a panic, sweat cooling on her forehead. Utterly disoriented, she stared into total darkness. Sat up. Said, 'What do you want?' Which went unanswered and left her unable for a few seconds to understand where she was or how she came to be there.

Until her memory supplied a few vital details. There was no Tony here, no roommate. She was in London. In the new apartment. Lillian's. Then who . . .

With one hand she smashed about the bedside table looking for the lamp. Found it. Groped around for the switch. Whimpered. Clambered onto her knees, her body feeling painfully vulnerable while exposed to the standing figure so close by in the darkness. Her fingers found the old ceramic fixture with the clunky switch and clicked it. The heavy base of the lamp rocked on the table. Then suddenly the brownish room flooded with pale light.

No one there. She was alone in the room.

Her every fibre and sinew relaxed with relief. She gulped at the air like she had just sprinted up a flight of stairs. It was the drapes wafting in a draught, or the old floorboards correcting themselves. Like they do in old buildings you are unaccustomed to.

She put her face in her hands. Shock drained from her, to be replaced with a blush of foolishness.

But the experience of such acute alienation, and the terror of intrusion, shook her sufficiently to make her try and sleep more lightly, by sitting up, with the bedside lamp on. And she left it shining all night. Something she hadn't done since the first and only time she had watched *The Exorcist*.

SIX

Some time after midnight, the residents stopped bothering Seth, and the smell of sulphur and old smoke on the upper floors of the west block dispersed during his third investigation, as he hunted for its source in the rubbish stores. But the inertia that prevented him from concentrating on the *Evening Standard* increased once he was back behind his desk. His head was soon dropping across his chest every few minutes. Which was odd; he never usually dozed until around 2 a.m. at the earliest. Must have been the virus his body was busily cultivating into something more than just a temperature and scratch at the back of his throat.

He decided to nap for a few minutes. Then he'd wake up refreshed and able to keep his eyes open, at least for another few hours.

He fell into a deep sleep.

It lasted for what felt like a few seconds, before a swish of movement nearby and the darkening of a shadow across his closed eyelids woke him.

Seth sat up, alert.

The reception area was empty.

He shivered, and then relaxed back into his chair.

And dozed off again.

But awoke a moment later. Because this time he was

certain a face was pressed against the glass of the front doors opposite his desk. But when his eyes snapped open and he lurched forward in his chair, noisily clearing his throat, all he could see in the dark glass was his own reflection peering back: a solemn, thin face with dark eyes.

Unsettled, he went downstairs and smoked two cigarettes and drank a cup of coffee. But despite his best attempts to stay awake, within moments of returning to his chair behind the reception desk his chin began to drop. And he slipped off a ledge and eased into a welcoming depth of sleep.

Until once again he heard the brush of clothing right next to his ear. And a voice. Someone said, 'Seth.' And then again, 'Seth.'

Sitting bolt upright in the chair, his heart thumping, he peered about. Stood up, already mumbling an apology as if expecting to find a resident in a dressing gown leaning over the desk. But there was no one around. He'd imagined it. But how? The mouth had been right against his ear; he was sure he'd even felt the speaker's cool breath.

The glare of the white electric lights in reception bruised the back of his eyes.

Still uneasy, he returned to his chair and turned the television on. Clawed at his face with two hands and shook himself. But it was as if he had no choice and there was no controlling his mind's insistence on slumber. Or on the dream that came with it.

From the corner of the wood, a small figure emerged. Wearing a grey coat with the hood pulled over its face, it just watched Seth as he stood in the stone chamber with his hands clutching the cold bars of the gate that kept him locked inside.

Stepping from one foot to the other, Seth swallowed and secretly wished the figure would not disappear or pass by.

Trying to smile, he found he had no control over his facial muscles; it must have looked as if he were about to cry. He stopped trying to smile, and waved. Embarrassed when the hooded figure never so much as moved, he let his hand drop to his side and wondered whether he should crouch in a corner and never bother anyone again. That's why he was here.

The figure moved forward away from the trees. Slowly, it wandered through the long grass, avoiding big clumps of dark wet nettles, until it reached the edge of the stone steps. The urns upon them held dry brown stalks. The figure looked up at him. Inside the hood, Seth could see no face.

'What's ya name?' the boy asked.

'Seth.'

'Why you in there?'

Seth looked at his feet. He paused to swallow, then looked up and shrugged. 'Dunno.'

'I know why. You got scared and crazy. Same as me. You'll be in there for ages. And then some place much worse.'

Inside the stone prison, Seth began to feel something cold skitter about his stomach. His skin goosed and his vision flicked about. It was hard to breathe.

'Makes you shit-scared, don't it?' the boy asked.

Tears burned Seth's face and he gripped the bars of the gate so tightly that all the feeling disappeared from his hands. He kept squeezing even though he knew it would leave bruises. 'It's too late,' he said, in a thin voice that broke around the edges.

'It ain't,' the hooded boy said with defiance. 'I can get you out.'

'But we'll get in trouble,' Seth replied, and hated himself for saying that.

'Who gives a shit? And anyway, no one thinks of you. Not no more. You're forgotten.'

Seth tried to say *no* but knew the hooded boy was telling the truth.

'Do yous want to come out?' the boy asked, rummaging in a deep pocket.

Snuffling back his tears, Seth nodded.

From his coat pocket the boy withdrew a large iron key. But Seth never really looked at the key; he couldn't take his eyes from the boy's hand. It was purple and yellow and just the sight of it made him feel sick. The skin had melted and then gone hard again. Some of the fingers were stuck together.

Crooked fingers folded around the key's large butterfly-shaped handle and turned it in the lock of the gate. The mechanism made a groaning sound before the barred portal swung open.

Too frightened to move his bare feet from the marble floor of the chamber, Seth remained inside for a while, shivering. The boy retreated to the bottom of the stairs and looked up at Seth. He put his hands back inside the pockets of his snorkel coat and assumed his usual posture: relaxed but expectant.

The sky over the wood turned dark. Either night was coming or the clouds brooded closer to the treetops.

The hooded boy began to look over his shoulder and watch the woods. Seth instinctively knew he had to hurry and make up his mind. Did he stay or leave? It was as if another much bigger gate had been opened in the world outside the chamber and if he wasn't quick enough it might close again and leave him stranded. And together for too long in the same place, they could attract attention. He had a sense they might be spotted at any minute by someone in the trees.

Seth ventured out through the gate and into the grass on weak legs unused to exercise. He thought of his limbs as spindly sticks of vegetable left to go soft in the bottom of a fridge.

He stood in the grass and marvelled at how the stalks felt on the soles of feet so used to stone, at the pluck of the breeze against his naked skin, and at his excitement at the sight of a path that led into the thick, deciduous foliage of the wood.

The hooded boy moved toward the trees. Anxiously, Seth followed.

From the edge of the wood, he took a last look over his shoulder at the chamber and its little yellow light. Further up the path, the boy encouraged Seth to follow by doing nothing more than waiting and staring at him until they stood by each other on the path inside the damp wood.

'Where are we going?' he asked the hooded boy.

'Away from this place.'

Seth swallowed and tasted panic.

'If yous go back we won't be able to get you out again. Yous'll stay in there. It always happens. There are lots of people trapped. I see 'em all the time. They don't know how to escape.'

'How do you mean?'

'Only a bit of yous is still alive, Seth. The rest of yous is here, always. And when you die you'll come back to this place again. For a long time.' The hooded head nodded in the direction of the marble cage. 'That's what happens. Then yous get the darkness, when you can't see nuffin'. Or remember much. Then it's like you're in the sea at night. Cold and drowning and no one comes to help yous.'

Nervously, Seth began to take short steps back and forth.

'I'm your mate, Seth,' the boy said, in a more decisive, grown-up way. 'You're lucky we came. Yous can trust us.'

'I know. I know. Thanks. Really, thanks.' Seth felt better and grateful, but awkward too. He wanted to ask so many questions but didn't want to annoy his new friend who'd let him out of the chamber. 'Who . . . what I mean is, you said *we* and *they*?'

As if he had not heard, the hooded boy continued to move along the path away from the chamber. Overhanging branches and wet bushes whipped against the nylon of his coat. Seth continued to follow until they were moving faster and had gone so far from the chamber he wondered if he'd ever find it again. Dew soaked him and nettles stung his shins.

'Don't be scared, Seth. It's just strange at first. Everything will look strange to start with. But after a while it's OK. I was only ten when I got stuck. I was stuck in a concrete pipe near a playground.'

'Really, a pipe?'

'Then I was done in with fireworks, by me mates.' The hooded boy slowed down. He took his hands out of his pockets and Seth saw a flash of deformed joint and purple flesh before the long sleeves fell down to cover his fingertips. 'Now you're out of that place you're gonna see things as they really are, Seth. When people like you and me are on the out-side of the places we get put, we see it all. Then we do what we were supposed to do.'

'Really?'

'Yeah. And you're going to paint what you see. They's

gonna show you how. You's gonna be brilliant, mate. The best. They told me. And then you'll do stuff for us too, like.'

'Yes!' Seth said, suddenly excited, although it was not clear to him what he was going to do.

'It'll be really scary at the start. But you'll never want to go back. I never did once I was let out of that pipe.'

Seth nodded, enjoying the new sense of liberation he felt outside the chamber. Yes, there was a real difference now; a real freedom he could not properly define. It was unformed but its new presence made him shiver with pleasure. It was something he'd waited most of his life for and then forgotten about. He couldn't remember the last time he'd felt enthusiastic about anything.

Soon, the wood started to thin around them. The air became colder and the sky lightened to a watery grey. 'This is my bit,' the hooded boy said. 'I wanted to show yous where I got stuck. Most people go back to a place when they die, like I's told you. And can't get out. Till those places go all dark. And you don't want to be in the darkness, mate. Nah-ah. I seen it. That's the end of everyfing. But we's going to show you how to move around all the others down there, mate. They's fucked. Don't mean you have to be, like.'

They emerged from the wood and onto a wide plain of waste ground. Sparse, struggling grass grew from mud that pulled at his bare feet and made him slip about. In the distance, to their left, Seth could see a cluster of sheds with plastic sheets on the roofs and polythene windows that were ripped. Between the sheds were allotments grown over with weeds. Straight ahead of them, he could see a playground.

They walked towards it. Every few feet they would pass a coil of dried dog shit and shards of glass from smashed bottles. The hooded boy started to skip and hum to himself. He seemed pleased with the way things were going.

In the playground there was a slide and four chain-link swings with plastic seats hanging from an iron frame, and a roundabout made from rusty sheet metal with wooden bars across the top. It had been solidly anchored into a concrete square. The bright paint on all of the apparatus had chipped down to brownish metal and then been varnished with the grease from many little hands. There was a giant sandpit full of broken glass and slugs. Part of a smashed plastic doll languished in a rain puddle. Its head was cracked. Seth could see a dark hole through its curly blonde hair. The wound looked real. An eye was missing too. The violence of the thing made him shudder. Beside the doll were a few pages from a porn magazine. Glancing at it, Seth saw a woman with her legs open and one finger between her big purple lips.

'Shit hole, ain't it,' the boy said.

Seth nodded and followed the boy out of the playground until they came to two enormous tower blocks rising so far into the clouds the height of them made him squint. There were no lights on and they looked derelict. Graffiti covered the walls up to the height of a child and there was rubbish blowing about the pathways between the buildings.

Seth looked at the things around his feet – crisp packets, cans and tins with faded labels, a tyre, something from a car engine, a smashed television and a pair of tights that had been soaked by the rain and dried out so many times it took him a while to work out what the crispy thing with long tentacles was. The remnants of a child's scribblings, drawn with coloured chalk – pink, yellow and blue – had stained some of the paving slabs. The rain hadn't managed to wash it away. And it must have just rained. All the concrete was wet and there were still some puddles on the pavement. Seth assumed the place was always damp. He shivered. Wrapped his arms around his ribs. Even in summer it would be horrible. The closer they got to the buildings the stronger the smell of urine and bleach became.

As they walked between the giant tower blocks, a gust of wind whipped between the walls and made Seth cringe from the cold. When he looked up, the buildings seemed to be tilting and ready to fall down on him. He put a hand against a pebbled wall for support.

Next they came to a small, brackish stream that dissected the endless, flat, dull landscape and its struggling grass full of excrement and glass.

The mud of the banks and bed of the stream were bright orange and smelled of the spaces beneath kitchen sinks where plastic bottles are kept. Under Seth's feet, a lethargic trickle of water moved between a rusty paint tin and a broken pram that had been made for a child to wheel its dolls around with. Purple canvas hung in rags from the white plastic frame. Further down the stream, Seth could see a large grey sewer pipe. Inside the mouth the concrete was stained orange. He looked down at the hooded boy, who nodded without speaking. What a place to die.

They crossed the stream. As far as he could see the view never changed: disused allotments, empty playgrounds, litter, and tower blocks dotted about the stagnant plain. It went on for ever.

'There's toilets too,' the hooded boy said, without turning

his head to look at Seth. 'I never showed you them. And in some of the flats I found people.'

'They trapped too?'

The boy nodded.

Seth shuddered. 'Can't you get them out?'

The boy shrugged. Then he said, 'Nah. They're done for. I found a mongol kid with a plastic bag on his head that he couldn't get off. He couldn't understand anything I said to him. And there was an old lady who breathed in fumes from a boiler. She was just lying on the lino in some sick. And I found a man too that I didn't like. He was sitting in a chair by a gas fire and asked me to look at his pee pee.'

'Can we go? I'm cold,' Seth said.

'Yeah. Just wanted to show you my old place.'

'Thanks.'

'Most people can only see these places in the dreams they forget in the morning. And when they die it's too late. They come back and wait for the darkness.'

They walked back the way they had come, towards the wood. 'Who got you out of here?' was Seth's final question as they left the waste ground.

'A man,' the hooded boy replied. 'He's an artist. Like you. And some people you know done bad things to him.'

'Who?'

'He's gonna help yous. He's your mate. Yous'll meet him, Seth. Soon. But you's got plenty to do for us first.'

Sitting up with a start, it took Seth a moment to realize where he was. Looking around him, he saw familiar things: the semicircular desk that he sat at with the house phone and the metal panel for the intruder and fire alarms connected to every apartment, a portable radio, the yellow walls of the spacious reception area, fake plants, an orderly pile of *Tatler*s and *London Magazine*s on a cane coffee table, and the security monitors on the desk before him, glowing yellow-green. Anxious, he expected someone to shout at him, or at least be standing before his desk shaking their head because he had fallen asleep on duty.

There was no one there. Both lift shafts were quiet behind their sliding metal doors. The fire exits at the foot of each staircase were closed. The front doors were locked. No one had been into reception and seen him sleeping.

Glancing at the clock, he could see it was nearly four o'clock. He'd been asleep for over three hours. The ache in his lower back attested to time spent in the same cramped, seated position. He breathed out and straightened his tie. Rotating his head slowly, he heard a crunch inside his neck before his muscles warmed and became flexible again. Then he stretched his legs. Both knees had gone stiff from hanging over the front edge of the chair while it was reclined.

He had never slept so soundly at work before. Not to wake up for hours was new, unthinkable. And that dream again. He recalled bits of it; remembered enough of it to know he'd dreamt of that place again. The stone chamber, the mausoleum, set on the edge of the wood. But there were differences. The boy with the hood and the burnt hand hadn't been in the first dream.

It was that kid who'd been watching the pub; his subconscious had inserted the figure. With remarkable clarity, Seth remembered what it was like to be a child again. It had all come back in the dream. And he had been crying with frustration as he slept. Against his cheeks the salt tracks cracked when he yawned. He almost wanted to sleep again to recapture the exhilaration of escape, the comfort of a new companion, the anticipation of adventure.

But he began to shiver and could barely swallow. His throat felt peeled. His face burned with fever. He wanted to lie on the floor and die. A lingering sense of duty made him scan the monitors. Glancing over the bank of screens, he could see no one in the black-and-white street outside, or in the mews that ran behind the ornamental garden, or in the basement garage.

And then he paused, and looked to his left. Sniffed. Stood up. Hastily smelled the arm of his jacket, and then both of his hands. They stank – of sulphur, maybe gunpowder, and the thick greasy smoke that belches from open cooking fires. He reeked of it, and so did his desk and the reception area, all the way down to the lift doors.

SEVEN

There were no mirrors in the bedroom, as far as Apryl could tell in the thin morning light struggling through the parted drapes, so she went to the bathroom and checked the sills of the window behind the blinds and the little cupboard that contained floor rags and a bottle of disinfectant – but still no mirrors. So she rifled about in the two end bedrooms for another five minutes. But there still wasn't a single mirror to be found.

She returned to the master bedroom and sifted through the boxes of cosmetics for a hand mirror. Nothing. But she noted a vacant space at the back of the dresser, between two wooden uprights, in which she was sure an oval mirror must have once been fixed.

Curious, she returned to the bathroom and found four small holes in the wall above the sink. Drilled holes with brown rawlplugs still pressed inside. Holes for screws that once held a bathroom cabinet in place. A cabinet that most likely featured mirrored doors.

On the wall behind the bath, she noticed two more holes. These were wider, for longer screws that went deeper, to support a larger mirror. It too had been removed. And yet the room had not been decorated or newly painted, so the mirror and cabinet had not been removed in order to modernize or brighten the place with a lick of paint or some gleaming tiles. The watery yellow walls, blotched with clouds of dried damp, had remained unchanged for a long time.

Back out in the hallway, she took a closer look at the long walls reaching down to the bedrooms. Their surfaces warranted nothing more than a cursory inspection the day before because they made her feel uneasy. It was the stains and the worn paper peeling off in places that affected her. Had Lillian been so unwell, so incapable for so long? It was hard for Apryl to accept, considering how precise and neurotically tidy her granny Marilyn had been, and how elegant and beautifully groomed Lillian appeared in the photographs.

But the mystery of the missing mirrors insinuated itself uncomfortably through her mind when she noticed a total absence of any other decorative feature on the walls in the apartment. Not a single picture frame or ornament in the hallway. Or in the kitchen or the three bedrooms. She hadn't noticed that the day before. And now, the closer she looked at the ageing paper in the cluttered hall and at the disorderly bedrooms, she noticed further evidence of screws and steel fittings that had once held paintings, mirrors and ornaments that her great-aunt had taken down at some point and removed from the apartment. And she was certain that when she searched the boxes and cases in the two storage bedrooms she had seen no watercolours, no seascapes, no hunting trophies, no oil paintings, or whatever it was with which Lillian and Reginald had once furnished the walls of their home.

They had been removed, not merely taken down from the walls, but eradicated from the apartment itself. Stephen said Lillian had been a hoarder, that she had thrown nothing away during his time as head porter. Which left the storage cage under the building as the only possible repository for the pictures and mirrors. Frowning, Apryl fingered the small black iron key attached to the same ring as her front-door keys.

'And the Mrs Lillian throw the nothing away,' said Piotr. He sweated so much. His suit looked unbearably tight and his face was pink and moist. She thought of a hot-dog sausage, with its reddish meat bursting through the membrane of skin. And he never stopped talking with a forced jollity devoid of humour or wit. Her polite smile began to hurt her face as he irritated her with so many questions, usually about money, with no pause for an answer. 'And maybe the Mrs Lillian keeps the gold here, no? Maybe one of the boxes is full of the money, eh? Then you don't need the lottery tickets, no?'

And down to the basement they went. To what the staff called the 'cages'. Beneath the millionaires' world of dark carpets and teak doors, of heavy drapes and marble floors, they entered a netherworld, coexisting below the luxury and silence of the world that it served above.

Down here the walls were of painted cement and the floor was rough and stained with oil and scuffing; wires and rubber-coated cables swung in loops from the ceiling. African cleaners moved slowly with buckets and detergent bottles, their skin coal-black but sheening purple under the lights. Steel doors warned of high-voltage dangers; a vast boiler wheezed and smouldered and sent a ripple through the concrete under the thin soles of her Converse sneakers. And then there were the cages. A labyrinth of black mesh cubicles filled with bicycles, boxes, and looming objects concealed by dust sheets. One cage for each flat. She hoped Piotr would leave her alone once the cage was open.

'Ah, here is your one.'

More boxes, and long sheets draped over packing cases. There was just enough room to stand inside the cage with the metal door open. 'Thank you, Piotr. I'll be fine now.'

'But you might need the help to take the boxes, no?'

'I'll be fine. Really. I'll swing by the desk if I need a hand. But thanks.' She had to repeat this three times as he hovered, too close, sweating and smiling and flitting his small eyes past her to the contents of the cage. When he finally waddled away, wiping the sweat from his forehead, she wondered where the thrill of discovery had gone. Just looking at all the stuff made her weary. It was like moving house, only a hundred times worse. Because although these things legally belonged to her, she didn't feel like they were really hers, and there was so much, and she didn't know what to do with any of it, or if any of it was valuable. A reckless part of her suggested she just junk the lot and then go out sightseeing.

Starting from the edge, she began to lift the sheets and was soon amongst piles of aged drapes and musty bed linen, old-fashioned skis and tennis racquets in cases, fishing tackle, tartan blankets, a wicker picnic hamper, two old tea sets, tarnished silver trophies and six pairs of wellington boots. Beneath and behind all of this she found the missing mirrors. Eight of them of various sizes and shapes, packed in brown paper, neatly tied with string, and carefully stowed away.

And within flat wooden cases with the hinges so old and corroded they were mostly dust, she found the paintings that once adorned Lillian and Reginald's walls. Seascapes and line drawings of Grecian figures, lithographs and RAF squadron plaques. Then there was the largest picture. The one at the very back she reached last of all, in the early afternoon, when her stomach burned with hunger and a litre bottle of Evian rolled empty at her feet. Her discomfort was immediately forgotten the moment she unveiled the painting and was confronted by an image of Great-aunt Lillian and Great-uncle Reginald, depicted in their glamorous prime by a skilled hand. This was the first time she had seen them together in colour. For a few seconds Apryl stared without blinking.

It was a full-length portrait. Lillian's beautiful, imperious face stared out, as if unimpressed with the sordid location now inflicted upon her eternal image. Ice-blonde hair was pulled back beneath a sparkling tiara, and her forehead was porcelain-smooth. A perfect nose, the thin arches of her clipped brows, and full red lips completed a composition of arresting beauty. White satin gloves shone to her elbows, a necklace glittered around a princess's neck, and a long white dress hugged her wonderful lines and curves. But it was the arctic eyes that astonished Apryl. It hurt to look into them; it was impossible not to. Eyes filled with curiosity and intelligence. Passion, too. But above all else, they were vulnerable. Deeply.

She attributed an impending tragedy to the figures, knowing these qualities in Lillian would flounder into a slow madness after her beloved husband's death. It was as if the painter had been commissioned just in time to capture the last of her extraordinary intelligence and beauty before it became something else entirely, until she would eventually suffer a confused and frightened death in the back of a hackney cab.

And Apryl struggled to believe there had ever been a more handsome and distinguished man in uniform, standing beside such a society beauty. A hint of prettiness in his eyes and long, dark lashes were offset by the masculine angles of jaw and pronounced cheekbones. The slight bump of a nose that had been broken and healed crooked was an imperfection not detracting from his beauty but adding the same character as a duelling scar. While flecks of silver speckled his temples, most of his hair was as black as fresh oil.

Their hands were together. Fingers entwined. A sudden glare of intimacy that Apryl's eyes were pulled toward. Somehow incongruous in such a formal pose, but not inappropriate. A sign of devotion they were unable to contain even at this moment of their immortalizing.

A lump came to her throat. She whispered 'Sorry' to their faces. Sorry for rummaging through their private possessions. For planning on selling these things they had collected together and once cherished. She felt like an intruder, a trespasser, a vulgar little urchin with dusty hands and smeared cheeks where she had wiped at her hair falling from beneath the red headscarf.

Their home and its furnishings, most of its valuables and bric-a-brac, all from a different time and world, would have to be sold to the highest bidder. But not this painting, and the elegant dress-mirror, nor her great-aunt's clothes that she would model before it. They were going back to the States, so the poor branch of this family could marvel at these once proud and beautiful people who shared their blood.

Outside, night had fallen early, at about four o'clock, in a dense ocean of black, and now the rain pattered against the windows of the apartment. Inside, the radiators and pipes glowed too hot to touch and banished the chill into the corners and near the windows of Lillian's bedroom. Apryl had warmed her bones with another hot bath and a spicy Lebanese takeout, but at the prospect of dressing in Lillian's clothes she'd been edgy with excitement, like a young girl given permission to play with her mother's make-up. This was her time. Tired after a day in the basement rescuing another weight of memorabilia to assess and discard, she would fill her evening with the styles of the past. And in this solemn place she was a bright little ghost, come back to prepare herself for evenings and days long gone.

By the time the clock chimed ten she had tried on the dark suits, sleeveless dresses, and sparkly gowns, overlaid by fur coats and complemented with hats and their smoky veils that instantly made her eyes mysterious in a way no eye shadow could. It was uncanny how they fitted. Tight, but not uncomfortably so, over her trim hips and small athletic bust.

She covered the bed with tailored tweed, wool, cashmere, silk, satin and clattering wooden hangers. Put her hair up in the easiest forties' victory roll she could manage with the hairpins from one of Lillian's porcelain pots. Then creamed, brushed and powdered her pretty face and upturned nose with her own cosmetics, and found herself unable to resist a dab of Lillian's scent from a crystal stopper on her neck and upon each pale wrist.

In Cuban-heeled shoes or glittering silver sandals, depending on the outfit – a fitted suit with box jacket, a floor-length ball gown with diaphanous shawl – she strode, pranced, pirouetted and sat with affected poise before the oval mirror she'd rescued from the cage, while the drab backdrop of an old woman's bedroom formed a brown murk around her reflected silhouette.

Against the muscular curve of her calf muscles her aunt's

nylons gleamed in the thin light. Sheer as cobwebs but slick as glass, making her legs look more aerodynamic than the imitations she bought back home ever could. With nails red as clots of blood, cheekbones rouged and eyes dollish in the false lashes she found in a drawer that also contained long opera gloves, she twirled and danced a three-step jive. She was transformed, and her great-aunt was suddenly alive all around her, and inside her.

Transported by her finery, she took no account of the time and gave no further thought to the heaving of boxes, the calling of antique dealers, and the complications of dispensing with real estate that would come in the days ahead. She emptied her mind of all but the atmosphere and imagery of the past so suddenly filling her imagination and lightening her soul. In the painting that Stephen had hung above the cluttered dresser, her great-aunt and uncle looked down in silence.

All this excitement . . . until she was forced to stop in her tracks. To pause and do a double take like a flapper in a silent film. In the mirror she saw her face suddenly seize with shock at the movement behind her reflection.

Quick in motion, a rushing forward from the gloom. Intangible apart from its thinness and the suggestion of something reddish where one would have expected a face to be.

The brief sight of this form in the polished mirror made her turn and cringe like a cat expecting a blow.

And when she took a second look into the mirror she saw nothing in the dour light but the wardrobes on either side of a rumpled bed. And herself, petrified and alone.

Breath rushed back into her body and her balance returned. She stood up straight and felt ice crystals shiver and then melt all over her warm skin. She swallowed the tightness in her throat.

It had been nothing. The faint glow of the stained lampshades had fooled her into seeing something in the mirror where there was nothing. But still she teetered across the room and hastily departed, running down the hall to the front door, where she paused, breathing hard.

In this long-silent place of shadow and clutter, had someone been hiding all along, crouched down on thin limbs, with something red fastened tight about a face that only a nightmare would cherish?

EIGHT

Three other passengers on the bus were aware of him talking to himself. They pretended to be unmoved by his muttering presence. Embarrassed by the realization that his inner voice had become audible, Seth stopped whispering and looked out of the bus window instead, peering down to the street to keep his mind distracted from its inward meanderings.

What was happening to him? It was hard to say. Hard to remember what he was like before this. The normal business of humanity had begun to appear strange to him. Alien. He wondered if he was more enlightened now, or just losing his mind.

The entire front of his face burned and the skin was tender. In his joints, any movement created a painful grinding of the ball in the socket. Every muscle felt like it was being assaulted by a yellow acid that responded angrily to exertion. A pulsing headache forced his eyes into a squint or closed them entirely near strong light. And the further he travelled from his room the worse he felt.

Below in the street the beggars sat, their legs under dirty white blankets on the cold pavement; but at least they seemed capable of salvation, of a second chance, when he had finally been consigned to an incurable demise, a disintegration both physical and mental. That's what it felt like. A long and tangled series of disappointments, habits, unfortunate choices and periods of introspection had brought him to this.

He couldn't stop his thoughts now; they raged and changed direction and reappeared unexpectedly like a bush fire. And it was as if the last vestige of his former self only survived to impotently monitor the transformation.

Furious with himself, he tried to fathom why he had left the Green Man. Fever had prevented him from getting more than a few hours of fitful rest between his shifts at Barrington House. And every time he woke during the day, he'd found his sick, sweating body had turned the bed into a cold swamp, while the sunlight filtering through the thin curtains of his room seared his eyes and made him groan and then cry out with a pillow held over his face. If he kicked the blankets off for relief from the heat, he would quickly freeze and be forced to pull the damp bed linen back over his cramped body. Eventually, he'd risen at three in the afternoon to gulp water and swallow painkillers. Perhaps then, some deluded sense of duty, some sad parody of a Protestant work ethic, had obliged him to dress and leave his room for work.

But it was something more than that. He felt almost compelled to go back. As if some important business connected to his bizarre dreams and Mrs Roth was to be concluded. Or maybe his judgement was now so impaired that he couldn't account for his actions at all. It was possible.

After alighting from the bus, he trudged from Hyde Park Corner to Lowndes Square. Sweat covered his forehead and re-soaked the back of his shirt and jumper. There was so much cloudy liquid leaking out of his pores even the lining of his overcoat was sodden by the time he pulled himself up the back stairs of the building. Each footstep hurt his head and jarred his lower back; his breathing was ragged and painful in his hot lungs, yet still he smoked himself nauseous.

'Ahh,' he said, and put his hands over his hot ears when Piotr appeared.

'Today, you would not believe what happened. There will be the big trouble. The Jorge was out driving when he should have been here. I cannot be responsible for the building with him gone so long . . .'

Seth ducked into the stairwell and fled down to the staffroom, clutching his head and the fragile swollen cargo inside. Meningitis. Maybe the tissues of his mind were inflamed and pressing against the inner walls of his skull. Piotr's voice chased him down the stairs: 'And he get paid for this driving. When it say in our contract that we cannot maker the money outsider the building. It is not fair. Why is he allowed . . .'

He could die in that chair behind the semicircular desk tonight. Maybe the dreams were the prelude to a coma. Yes, he'd driven his mind to the point of extinction; slowly unravelled himself until he realized there was no point to his existence, so nature was kicking in to relieve the species of a burden. He giggled and then sniffed.

In the staffroom Seth stripped down to his pants and socks and washed his body with cold water from the sink. Using paper towels he then dried himself under his arms, around his neck and in the small of his back. By the time he'd dressed in his uniform – grey polyester trousers, a synthetic white shirt, a pullover, tie, and navy blue blazer – his body was slick with sweat again.

He turned the lights off and lay on the small couch beside

the water cooler. Sipping a hot lemon drink full of paracetamol, he waited for his shift to begin.

Over the next few hours his illness allowed him to do
nothing but exist inside it. He rocked back and forth in his
chair with a hot face clasped in both hands. The bright lights
of reception burned his eyes and the gurgling radiators threatened to desiccate his body. Covered in his overcoat, he passed
in and out of consciousness.

But just after midnight, Seth became aware of a presence
in the communal areas of the building. As if locked in with
him for the night, someone seemed to be out there, flitting
between floors, pointlessly running up and down the stairwells and taking short, inconclusive rides in the lifts. Like a
bored, restless child might do after gaining access to a private building.

Half an hour later, he struggled from his chair to investigate the most recent noise close to his desk: a swish of
clothing and the bumping of quick tiny feet. Most of what
he had heard when half asleep seemed too distant to be of
pressing concern, occurring far off and upstairs. But the most
recent sounds raced across reception and past his desk until
a creak and whump of the fire doors leading to the west
block staircase brought the commotion to an end.

Pursuing the noise into the stairwell, he heard the faint
sound of running feet retreat up one floor, and then stop. He
went up to investigate.

The flats on both the first and second floors of the west
wing were empty. One apartment was for sale, and the tenants
of the others were overseas, so there should have been no
one up there for any reason he could think of. It now
appeared that somebody was.

Allowances had to be made for the presence: wind moving through the air risers; a maid or a nurse from the upper floors – there were two he knew of – wandering about to smoke a cigarette or to make a call from a mobile phone; or maybe it was a resident coming downstairs only to find they had forgotten a wallet and returning to their apartment.

Above him, at the foot of the next staircase, a light in the ceiling flickered. But everything else was the same as it always had been at this time of night. Or was it? There was a smell. Again. Faint, but undeniably present, and growing stronger the further he investigated. Walking around the corridor and sniffing, he noticed a trace of sulphur in the hall. It was as if someone had not long struck a match. A hint of smoke, too, in the way it clung to the clothes of one recently in the presence of a bonfire. And something else: a cooking odour. Yes, a kind of chargrilled, meaty smell like roasting animal fat. The same thing he'd smelled up by flat sixteen last night. 'What the fuck?'

In front of each door he passed on his ascent Seth sniffed at the letter flaps to determine whether anyone was inside the apartments cooking meat. But the odours were stronger in the middle of each of the landings and virtually non-existent near the apartment doors. It was as if someone passing through the building was leaving a scent.

The stairwell above had fallen silent, and lacking the strength to go any higher he walked back down to the ground floor and sat behind his desk. Unable to keep his eyes open because of the painful pressure behind his face, he closed them. And fell into a deep sleep.

A glance at the clock told him that it was shortly after half past one when the disturbance began again. This time it was more insistent. From behind his desk he heard the west block lift click, groan and whirr into life. Up it ascended, through the dark shaft to the higher floors.

Someone had summoned it from above. Seth glanced at the metal panel beneath the lip of the desk. A red light moved behind the digits until it showed that the lift had stopped at the eighth floor of the west wing. Flat seventeen had been empty for four months, since Mr and Mrs Howard-Broderick had moved to their apartment in New York. Flat sixteen, he knew well enough, had been empty for half a century.

From his chair he watched the illuminated panel. Observed the lift descend. Floor by floor, from the eighth down towards the ground floor. His floor. Right where he was waiting.

With a hydraulic wheeze the lift slowed, then settled with a clunk on the ground floor. The door remained shut.

Gingerly, Seth moved out from behind his desk and walked across reception. He peered through the little window in the outer door of the lift. And saw nothing but the mirrored rear wall. Anxious the inner doors might suddenly slide apart as he peered through the little glass square, he stepped back and pressed the button to open the door.

The carriage was empty. He saw nothing more than his own pale face peering back from the mirrored interior. He sniffed and winced. Once again he could smell smoke and burnt fat, pungent inside the lift, even worse than it had been in the stairwell.

He closed the outer door and shut his eyes. The brief exertion had worn him out. He was too ill to care about a bad smell and a faulty lift. The virus had returned with vigour and these scant movements felt like they had nearly killed him. He was barely able to stand, and clung to the railing as he staggered down to the staffroom to gulp chilled water from the cooler.

But relief was still some way off. After he returned to the desk and slumped into the leather chair it was as if the nocturnal disturbances were only just beginning.

At two in the morning, for the second time that night, the lift in the west wing clanged to a halt on the ground floor. But this time it wasn't empty.

Dizzy and blinking, Seth stood up and leant on the desk with his elbows. Squinting through a migraine that travelled through his head in waves, he saw something crawl out of the lift carriage on a number of legs he couldn't count. Only as it scuttled near to his desk did he recognize the shrunken face of the thing to be that of Mrs Shafer.

Covered in a vast silken kimono, the bulk of her body traversed the carpet with a surprising swiftness. The sack-like head rested on the tabletop of her back, dwarfing her shoulders. Clumsily pinned under a tapestry of scarves, her hair was wet. Tendrils of it glistened on her forehead and temples where a few pins had dislodged. 'How many times do we have to ask before the job is done properly?' Her voice was on the verge of a scream. 'They've been on the roof time and time again, and still we can't get a picture. Are these men not trained?'

She'd made this complaint before. Behind her on the carpet a slug trail of moisture leaked from her abdomen. It reeked of meat gone bad in a rubber bag.

'My husband,' she said to Seth, who held a hand across his mouth to withstand the stench, 'is a very important man. He must see the financial news. He doesn't just sit around on his fanny all night.' A small front leg waved in the air to add emphasis. There was a tiny human hand on the end of the thin limb. 'I want Stephen, *now*!' Seth backed away from the edge of his desk.

Swinging the bag of her head around on an oily neck, she then shrieked, 'And who might you be?' She was addressing the hooded boy who stood and watched Seth from the main doors of the reception area.

'I told you, didn't I? That you were gonna see fings the way they really are,' he said to Seth, ignoring Mrs Shafer, who raced back across the floor of reception shrieking for the head porter, until her bulbous body finally stuffed itself back inside the lift. When Seth glanced over to the front doors the hooded boy had vanished. The entire foyer was empty and silent again save for the humming of the wall lights. And the smell of burnt meat.

Seth stepped out from behind his desk. He checked the carpet for Mrs Shafer's stains. There were none. He thought he was going to cry. When he sat back down, the desk and security monitors seemed somehow larger, looming over him and coming closer until they held him in a corner. Then the front doors of the building retreated into the far distance, as if he were looking at them through the wrong end of a telescope.

Seth shut his eyes and pulled his coat over his head until his breath turned wet against his face. After taking his shoes off he sat on the floor behind the desk and curled his body under the coat.

'We need help,' an elderly voice said. 'Please come with me.' It was Mr Shafer who woke Seth. But he was not as Seth had ever seen him before.

Naked, Mr Shafer tottered beside the desk on his long, bony feet. All of his toenails were yellow and cracked. His limbs were wizened and his ribs pushed against the thin bluish skin of his torso. Hook-nosed and unshaven, his grey head appeared too big for the spindly neck to support. Below the hollow pelvis, Seth looked at the stub of genitals and the shrunken sack and then looked away. Such was the state of his emaciation it seemed impossible that he could still be alive.

'Can you come up please?' Mr Shafer said, politely, a tone that usually served as an antidote to his wife's shrieking.

Obeying instinct, Seth stood up and walked around his desk until he towered over the shrunken old man. Like a child, Mr Shafer held Seth's elbow with his long fingers. There was no strength in his touch.

So slowly, it was as if Mr Shafer were walking on a tightrope, Seth led him to the lift. And stared at the enormous hump deforming the elderly resident's back and shoulders. Under the taut skin, a vast network of gristle and black vein had grown to a hillock. It disgusted Seth, but he felt an urge to touch it and see if it was hard.

'What's wrong?' he said, and felt immediately foolish for asking such a question, when Mr Shafer had come down to reception naked and his wife was a grotesque arachnid. But Mr Shafer said little more apart from mumbling about it being 'the right time'.

As soon as they entered the Shafers' apartment on the sixth floor, Seth covered his mouth and nose with the sleeve of his blazer. But that did little to keep out the stench. Scores of bin bags were piled up against the walls of the long corridor that ran the length of the rectangular apartment. Each sack had been labelled with a yellow sticker that read 'Medical Waste'.

All of the doors to all of the rooms branching off the hallway were open. A brownish gloom filled every room, as if the smell was visible. Each was filled with more of the plastic bags, and with piles of newspapers and magazines, plates encrusted with dried food, and crumpled clothes; it was as if nothing had ever been discarded from their long and miserable occupation of the suite. Under his feet the carpet was moist and covered in whitish stains.

There was no sign of the nurse. 'Where is your wife?' Seth said in a tense whisper.

Mr Shafer lifted the chicken bone of his forearm and pointed forward, to the living room at the end of the corridor.

'Your nurse?' he repeated, desperate to keep control of his voice. 'You have a nurse.'

'She was no good,' Mr Shafer said and blinked his milky eyes. 'Your help will be sufficient.'

'What can I do? Is it the television again?'

Mr Shafer cut him off with a shake of his grizzled head. 'It will be fine.' His voice changed to something Seth found unpleasant; there was a wheedling aspect to his tone and something sly about his smile. Of more concern, as they neared the shadowy living room, old Shafer began to make a sighing sound that seemed sexual, and his limping sped up so his head began to dramatically bob up and down next to Seth's shoulder. Around his elbow the bony fingers tightened their grip.

At the mouth of the living room Seth thought he might be sick. In the far corner of the room he could see Mrs Shafer. She was on her knees, head down, with her great back towards them. Still covered in the dirty gown, she turned her face to them as they entered and then raised her broad buttocks. The slight movement seemed to push a fresh gust of putrefaction across the room and right down Seth's throat.

Mr Shafer released Seth's arm and began to excitedly stumble about the floor of the living room. Ungainly, he looked like the skeleton of a dead child taking its first unholy steps around a crypt; a child with one leg shorter than the other.

Mrs Shafer watched Seth closely; her tiny red eyes were fierce in their disapproval, but also expectant. 'Are you capable of helping this dear man with his medication?'

Mr Shafer pranced on his bird legs to a cardboard box with Chinese writing on the side and a large inky stamp to show it had been through Customs. From out of the box his needle fingers pulled a length of rubber hose and an old glass syringe with large metal hoops for the injector's fingers. He dropped them on the dirty floor and then rummaged in a second box. Polystyrene packaging spilled over the lid and fell about his gnarly feet. He pulled a jar out but the weight of the object seemed ready to pull him over and onto his face.

'Why, help him!' Mrs Shafer roared.

Seth broke from his appalled trance and moved to Mr Shafer's aid. He took the glass jar from the old man. It was dusty and filled with a yellowy fluid. Preserved in the serum and crammed against the side of the glass, Seth could see a soft shape the colour of a kidney. When it moved and opened a little black eye he dropped the jar.

'Be careful!' Mrs Shafer screamed. Her husband fell to his knees and began scrabbling near Seth's shoes, clawing at the glass container. A rubber tourniquet was already tied around one wasted thigh.

'The treatment is more expensive than you could imagine, and we don't have much left! Are you an idiot? Can't you do anything right?' Mrs Shafer demanded, her voice trembling with hysteria. 'We pay your wages. This is not much to ask.'

Mr Shafer sat on the floor with the jar between his legs. Hastily, he stabbed at the metal lid with the end of the syringe. His head began to wobble from some kind of palsy, and either his face was screwed into a smile or the man was on the verge of tears.

Inside the jar, the small creature began to move in a series of contractions that appeared defensive. But the activity behind the smoky glass only served to excite Mr Shafer even more and he stabbed at the lid with a greater vigour. A strand of saliva hung from his chin and swung like a pendulum from the energy of his efforts. When his clumsy attack on the metal lid eventually created a puncture, something hissed from inside the jar. It could have been air escaping, but Seth thought it sounded like a tiny scream.

'You're hopeless,' Mrs Shafer said to Seth with exasperation in her voice.

When Mr Shafer finally pushed the needle of his syringe deep inside the jar, Seth stood back and put his hand over his mouth. Yellow fluid sprouted from the metal lid and ran down the side of the glass. Seth wanted to believe what he then heard was a sudden wheeze of excitement from the old man, but he knew it had actually been a rasp of pain from the thing inside the jar.

Whatever fluid was then withdrawn into the syringe Mr Shafer wasted no time injecting into his groin. Seth looked away.

'Is that good, darling?' Mrs Shafer called out to her husband.

'Is it working?' And then added to Seth, 'We ordered boys. They usually cheat us with girls. But these are definitely boys.'

'I think it's better,' Mr Shafer mumbled, but seemed at once unsure and confused.

It was not the response Mrs Shafer wanted. Her face coloured and her great body began to shake under the kimono. 'I said to you we should never have swapped brands.' Then she turned her outraged face to Seth as if for his support in an argument. 'He will not listen to me. Spending a fortune on this rubbish. It has to come all the way from China. Romania was closer, and from their stock at least we got results!'

Mr Shafer looked dejected and more tired than ever. 'I didn't like the last company. I told you. They were crooks.'

'Everyone is a crook!' she screamed. 'And now what is to become of me? You've known for months this is my time.'

Mr Shafer lifted his skull and grinned at Seth. 'He can do it.'

This seemed to placate his wife. 'Well, don't just stand there,' she said to Seth.

'What?' he said.

Mr Shafer shook his head. 'Another idiot. Not a bright man, are you?'

'You could get a monkey to sit behind that desk downstairs,' his wife added. They both laughed together, enjoying their first moment of agreement in what seemed like a long time.

Mr Shafer stood up and pressed a coin into Seth's hand. 'Here. This might help.' Seth opened his hand. There was a ten-pence piece in his palm.

'Now you see,' Mrs Shafer said. 'That's what it takes. How

did I guess? This is a service we have already paid for. You have no right to expect a tip.'

Seth tried to pull away from Mr Shafer. 'What are you doing?' The old man's fingers had suddenly become busy as knitting needles about Seth's belt buckle.

'Please. No. I don't want to.'

'It's not like it's much to ask. Do you think Stephen would be pleased to hear about this?' Mrs Shafer said from the corner.

Seth swatted Mr Shafer's insistent fingers away from his crotch. His attentions seized by what Mrs Shafer did next, he took a step away. 'Oh God, no.' In the corner, she'd pushed her abdomen higher in the air and drew the kimono slowly from her rear in a parody of seductiveness. Revealed for the moment Seth could bear to look at it was a wet slit with grey lips and pinkish insides, opened in the middle of her hirsute backside.

'Well?' she then shrieked at him.

'Be careful, Seth!' a voice called from behind.

The hooded boy stood in the doorway of the living room.

'Who is he?' Mrs Shafer screamed, pulling her great skirt down and mercifully concealing the fleshy eye.

'What is the meaning of this?' Mr Shafer asked Seth. His eyes had become squinty and his mouth stretched into a mean suture.

'But what can I do?' Seth asked the hooded boy. His words quivered and his jaw started to tremble.

'You got to do 'em. They deserve it.'

'Call Stephen!' Mrs Shafer screeched at her husband.

'I intend to,' her husband replied, and staggered across to a phone on top of a stack of medical catalogues.

'How?' Seth asked the hooded boy. Never had he felt so weak and useless. 'I can't.'

'You have to. They had it comin' a long time. They knows it.'

Seth gritted his teeth and felt the comforting glow of anger replace his panic and fear. Soon, a great molten power coursed through his every limb. Mrs Shafer could sense it. 'Hurry, dear,' she said to her husband. 'I think he's unstable.'

The old man groaned under the weight of the handset. He squinted at the keypad and one of his fingers hovered above the buttons. Seth walked across to him and seized the phone. The old man held on. 'How dare you?' he said. And then, 'Let go or you'll be very sorry.' Seth pushed him away.

Immediately, the old man collapsed on the dirty carpet and began to moan. The phone fell after him, down and into the petrified deformity of bone and parchment skin to crack against his skull.

'Now you've done it!' Mrs Shafer shouted, before she began to scream. The noise was hideous and deafening.

Seth looked at the hooded boy. Who nodded.

Seizing the brass stem of a lamp stand from behind the wreckage of a dozen cardboard boxes, Seth pulled the whole thing free of the floor and wall. The electric cord snapped from the base and left the plug in the socket. He strode towards the corner of the living room where the bulk that was Mrs Shafer trembled. She stopped her screaming to ask him, 'Have you lost your mind?'

'I hope so.' He brought the heavy base of the lamp down against her upturned face.

'Oh,' she said, in a daze after the thunk of antique walnut and metal against her tiny features. Then she sat up and tried to regain her dignity. She wiped a strand of bloodied hair from off her forehead and pouted her lips as if to apply lipstick.

Seth brought the lamp down even harder. Like wielding a pickaxe, every muscle and tendon in his back and arms went into the second blow.

'That's it,' the hooded boy said from behind, his words partly obscuring the crunch of skull.

Seth laughed to prevent himself from falling to his knees and weeping. Mrs Shafer stopped talking but her lips still moved. He brought the lamp stand down again and again and again against her face, hoping the great body would stop trembling under the kimono. It didn't seem ready to stop so he slammed the base of the lamp into her abdomen. After the second strike against her distended belly he heard something tear under the kimono and her entire body appeared to soften and finally relax.

'My wife. My wife. My wife,' Mr Shafer cried out in a weak voice from the floor, where he lay tangled in his own disability.

'Don't feel sorry for him,' the hooded boy advised Seth. 'They'll all feel sorry for themselves at the end, but they had this comin'.'

Seth nodded in agreement and walked across the carpet to finish Mr Shafer off. Under his feet something squelched. It was fluid seeping from under Mrs Shafer's kimono.

'It's not that hard once you start,' Seth said in amazement to the hooded boy. 'You just lose your temper and go all hot.'

'That's right.'

'But what amazes me most is that they're nothing. In the end, they mean nothing.'

The hooded boy nodded excitedly.

Seth brought the lamp stand down into the middle of Mr Shafer's body. It was as if a giant metal foot had trodden upon dry twigs on a forest floor.

'There's another fing you need to see tonight, Seth. I's been told to show you,' the hooded boy said.

'No, please. Not in here.' Seth stood outside apartment sixteen. The teak veneer shone like gold, and from beneath the heavy door a reddish glow dispersed across the green carpet of the landing. From within the flat he sensed a resolution to a journey that filled his body with panic. And with it came the far-off sound of something he'd heard before but could not place. Voices. Swirling about. Rotating, but going backwards like a record. Faint, like the sound of crying children inside a distant house, heard on a winter's afternoon, just as the sun is dying into dark clouds. Forlorn. And fast becoming a much bigger chorus. Inside the apartment but elsewhere. Above him.

His body rigid with fear, he tried to step away, but the door just moved closer.

'You have to,' the hooded boy said. 'He wants to show you all them other ones, them down there that can't get out. They's all waiting. He's got it open just for you, mate.'

Twisting and pushing his limbs against the heavy thickness of air that swelled against his back and threatened to topple him forward, Seth tried to resist. He knew instinctively that if he were to cross the threshold of this place something terrible would happen. He would be forced to confront something that could stop his heart with a bang.

And then they were standing in a red hallway on the other

side of the door he never saw open. Side by side. Him and the boy that smelled of burnt flesh, of exhausted gunpowder and singed cardboard. A smell that filled his nostrils and seared the back of his throat. Made it difficult to breathe, while the circling sound of the chattering crowd moved closer like a playground full of terror. It was coming from further down the reddish hallway, as if a room behind one of these heavy doors contained a whirlpooling violence of air in which so many people were caught up and dragged backwards, around and around, until they were too dizzy to do anything but scream.

Already he could sense himself falling a long way down if he opened the wrong door. So far down into that sound and at such great speed.

The boy stood behind him. 'Go on, Seth.'

The hooded presence pushed Seth forward. His legs were numb, his feet beset by pins and needles. His jaw seized up and he struggled to breathe. But down the hallway and across the black and white squares of marble he went. Beneath the old glass lamps that threw out the dirty light that never reached the ceiling which he couldn't see, and that was too dim to illumine much of the reddish walls. Ox-blood red around the big pictures in the gilt frames. Heavy gold frames, acting like the frames of windows beyond which existence had stopped while the void moved.

The void. Absorbing his stare. Pulling it from his body, leaving the rest of his face behind. Tugging it towards the flat darkness of the pictures. Paintings of an absence that made him feel both cold and afraid of heights at the same time, as if he could fall through into it.

But if he stared long enough at the darkness inside any

of the frames, things could be seen. Ever so faintly, emerging like pale fish from still, lightless and forgotten waters.

Here and there he began to think he could see things moving quickly. A flash of grey bone. A smudge of face looking back over a shoulder. Teeth yellow and chattery. Then gone. Or was it just a trick of the faint light that distorted any real sense of shape among the swirls of paint?

But as he passed the largest rectangular frame he was sure he saw the wet brick walls of a shaft descending away from the picture frame. And within the tunnel the pallid silhouette of something turned and scurried away, but backwards.

Gradually, as he passed more of the large, dark backgrounds in the picture frames, new shapes emerged and took more definite form. And the paintings began to resemble distant unlit rooms. Inside them he caught sight of things huddled and twisted. The faces were covered or turned away from the light. Other frames issued impressions of fleshy presences, whose mottled skin was like discarded clothing, empty of the rigidity supplied by muscle and bone but still moving. Moving against thin pins that nailed the flayed opacity to walls stained with rust or rot.

And then he too was moving forward. Pushed onward against his will, flitting past the occupants of so many dark rooms within the frames he passed. Wanting to look straight ahead, or at his feet, at anything but the terrible walls and what hung upon them, he wrestled with his neck to stop his head whipping from side to side. But he still caught glimpses of things at the edge of his vision, or up ahead in other picture frames, as his eyes stubbornly refused to obey his will. He clenched his jaw to stop himself screaming at the tangled things, gnawed to the bone. The torn things. Fragments of fleshiness ripped like cloth. Sometimes a smudged whitish face, caught in the act of a scream, hung in space. Until, on either side of the walls, a terrible momentum gathered. As if a call had gone out and summoned the subjects of the portraits to gather for an audience.

Dim faces, transformed by animal features, soon pressed outward from the darkness. Limbs dangled with an increasing frequency. All obscured by the poor light as if a full revelation would be too much of a shock, even in a dream. But the women still tried to show him their dirty teeth. And the men, tied in knots, revealed a rapture of pain so great it made their shrieking faces turn blue and disintegrate around the edges.

And then he was inside another room off the middle of the corridor where the swirling sound was at its loudest. He had to cover his eyes and crouch down, to make himself small, where he shivered against the cold air that swooped about his body. Air that carried a hundred voices all telling a frantic story.

Against the wall. Against the wall. Smash it against the wall.

I can't. I won't. He said he'd come back. Wait here. I know it's cold, but wait here, love.

Stamp on it. Break it.

Seth peeked through his fingers, terrified but compelled to see who was speaking and shouting and screaming all about him.

Bleached faces groaned but kept their eyes closed. They rose and faded on the dark walls.

I coughed it up. Coughed up my heart.

Was that an ape? The thing with the hair around the mouth?

I fink he's coming. Fink he's coming down. There'll be hell to pay now.

Could an old woman have such teeth?

Excuse me. Please. Excuse me. I think I fell down.

He saw three baby-things with big heads and doll bodies hanging against some wet bricks in a sewer.

Are you all asleep? I'm sorry, but are you all asleep? I need the doctor. But the door is locked. I'm sorry to wake you, but they turned all the lights off.

The walls were paint. The ceilings were paint. It was still wet. Reddish but dark, like blood or moist rust.

He turned to look at a black beak that said, *Blood. It's in the blood*, but it vanished and he watched hind legs kick away into the liquid shadows.

Oh Jesus Christ.

There were no angles where the walls ended and the ceiling began. What had been a room was now just a space.

To his left, at head height, four women turned about on their hands and knees. All of their joints were in the wrong places. Teeth and hair grew in clumps from out of the grey and pink flesh of their bodies.

Hello? Is somebody there? Who are you? Please help me.

In between a procession of bluish bony things that dragged themselves through the darkness in a circle, round and round at the edge of the room, up near where the ceiling should have been, following each other's paralysed legs and useless hooves, and beyond the chitter-chattery teeth, clacking like the muzzles of wooden horses, was an intense blackness. It moved. Seethed.

Seth screamed and a terribly thin figure rushed at him on all fours, its wisps of hair wild in the freezing wind, but then suddenly fell away, or was yanked backwards, so that something else, inside a sackcloth bag, could struggle forward on its elbows, its eyeholes stitched shut, hissing and desperate to reach him but blind and unable to locate him.

Am I awake? Please. Can you tell me, am I awake?

Everything in here was suspended in a freezing ether. An eternity of living oil in which so many things drowned and resurfaced before being sucked back down again. The room had transformed into a terrible broth of liquid and gas in which these things were all stuck and barely aware of each other. Some crawled blindly and bumped into others they then challenged or screamed at, insane with fear. Others hung silent, or were pinned fast against the darkness momentarily, before fading back into the void once again. The roar of the wind was the roar of tens of thousands of voices. Vertigo tried to turn Seth's stomach inside out when he realized he was but a pinprick in a seething that stretched forever.

He covered his eyes. Stood up and started to stagger about. To feel for the door he'd slipped through. There was no door. He had to peek between his fingers again, but it was so dark now he couldn't even see his feet. And things were brushing against him in the moving air. Something like a tongue lapped between his fingers. A dry, bristly face pushed into his stomach. Was it speaking or gnawing? Thin fingers touched then pressed against his face. The tips were cold but urgent in their examination as if suddenly surprised to find him here in the darkness. A hand grabbed his thigh and squeezed. A woman screamed. A hide of scabs brushed the back of one hand. An awful sexual panting erupted behind him and he sensed the feverish motion of something wet and raw directed at him in the darkness.

Seth staggered towards where the walls had once been. He'd taken no more than a few steps when the temperature plummeted. His body froze. Shivering with a violence that made it hard to breathe, and even with his eyes closed, he sensed that he stood near the edge of a precipice. The floor of the room had become nothing but a small platform in a bottomless night. A darkness overcrowded with suffering and confusion and madness. And it was all crawling onto the platform with him as though the room were a solitary life raft in a freezing black sea.

He fell to the ground and clung to the floor, while the deformed and fragmented subjects of what he had mistaken for paintings in the hallway clambered over him.

It was the phone ringing that pulled him out of sleep with a cry. It was a strangled sound that suddenly disintegrated into an anguished sobbing, a noise he had never heard himself make before. And as the bright yellow light of the reception area burned into his wide eyes, and the solidity of the leather chair pressed against his back, his sobbing turned into panting.

Tears dried on his face. He coughed to clear his throat of mucus. His hands gripped the arms of the chair until they became bloodless, as if they were still obeying some command designed to prevent him from falling from a great height.

Seth looked about him, the sudden shock of consciousness sobering him from terror. The familiar world of security monitors, clipboards and ringing house phones reassembled around him and chased the vestiges of suffocating darkness out of his mind. The nightmare drained away, as, mercifully, did his waking notion that all he had just witnessed had been real.

He was ill. Really ill. He must be.

Someone wanted him. On the phone. Jesus, how long had it been ringing? What time was it? He swung about in his chair and yanked the receiver from the switchboard.

He cleared his throat and quickly and instinctively spoke into the phone. 'Seth speaking.'

Bad line. But someone was speaking inside the crackles and static. 'In here,' he thought they said. Or was it 'Down here'? It was a man's voice, but not one he recognized. He looked at the switchboard. The red light was flashing for flat number sixteen.

Recalling bits of the dream, Seth dropped the phone.

NINE

The mirror was turned so it faced the wall. All night long it had reflected nothing but the noble image of her great-aunt and uncle in dusty oil paint, instead of her lying frightened and tense in bed.

She had turned the mirror round because it frightened her. But it was just a long mirror in a dark room, in an old apartment, in a strange city, in which a tired and excitable girl had become overwhelmed by all the things she had seen, thought and imagined. Just an overwrought mind imagining a presence in a mirror. Nothing more.

Dim morning light hovered around the window frames, emitting a thin greyish haze through the net curtains. She hadn't closed the drapes the night before in order not to feel trapped, as if the windows above Lowndes Square offered the possibility of a quick escape. All the lamps were still on too, along with the ceiling lights.

Confounded by how her mind had invented terrors to torment her, she clambered out of bed and looked out at the sky, already dark, and rippled with stripes of tangerine. It was as if night was ready to reclaim the earth again at nine in the morning.

Tired and tense, as if she hadn't slept at all, she pulled the net curtains back to allow more light inside. As she rearranged the gauzy fuss, something hit the floor at her feet and bounced. A blue and white saucer lay upside down on the carpet and near it was an iron key with butterfly-wing handles. About the right size for the drawers of the bureau. She moved quickly to the heavy and dark piece of furniture opposite the foot of the bed.

The key turned in the first lock with a tiny thump that she felt in her fingers rather than heard.

There were so many tickets in there. For train and plane travel – even tickets for journeys by sea. They were arranged into stacks by year and then secured with red rubber bands in the uppermost drawer. But not a single ticket had been clipped, stamped or torn along the perforated strip. These were tickets for journeys planned but never taken. And most of them listed the United States as the destination. From as far back as 1949, Lillian had been planning to go home.

Apryl thought about what Stephen had said about Lillian's final farewells as she left the building for her morning wanderings. There had been a little case with her too, with an expired passport and a plane ticket inside, clearly packed for an overseas journey, on the day she died. But why had Lillian broken contact with her sister and family, when the United States was such an important a place for her to reach? It didn't add up.

She'd heard of ritual obsessives and their precise but irrational routines, and this was further evidence of her great-aunt's deteriorating mind. A demise beginning four decades earlier. Wearing an antique hat and veil and launching out of the building with America in mind as her destination, only to return confused and disoriented an hour later, before she reset herself and began the process all over again the following day. If it hadn't been her own aunt and benefactor she might have smiled at the idea; but instead she wondered how in this day and age so wealthy a woman had been allowed to go on like that for so long.

In the drawer below there were copies of birth certificates for Lillian and Reginald, some old unfranked stamps, Reginald's service medals, his wedding ring, and hair clippings in a plastic sachet. Beneath all this lay a densely stacked assortment of private papers that looked like investment statements, insurance documents and household bills, neatly ordered inside linen envelopes. Her aunt had been meticulous as well as batshit crazy. Apryl figured she'd have to make sense of it all later.

The opening of the bottom drawer, unless there was a safe or bank vault somewhere, represented the last undiscovered remains of Great-aunt Lillian's estate. The scent issuing from it pierced her sinuses with the strong but not unpleasant fragrance of pencil shavings, dust, and dry ink. It clouded over her face and then quickly sank back into the dark wooden space that she could see was full of books. All with plain covers and from a time when book binding and production was seen as a craft. Each volume had a woven fabric or leather cover. Dusty and neglected but of some quality – which just about summed up the end of her great-aunt's life.

Opening the red book on the top of the stack revealed lined pages filled with handwriting, but with no dates given. She flicked through the stiff pages and soon realized that a separate sheet had been used for each entry, written by an unsteady hand.

The writing was difficult to decipher. Was that a *b*? And

what at first looked like an *s* was actually an *f*. It also slanted so far to the right that the longer strokes were in danger of lying flat and crushing the vowels against the blue lines on the paper. She flicked through to the last entry. It said something about 'trying again in the morning'. And 'taking the Bayswater Road, which I've not seen in years'.

Going back to the first page, she pressed her finger under each word and moved her lips like a child learning to read, slowly moving through parts of the scrawl, and abandoning whole sentences and paragraphs when the jumble of letters and scratchings defeated her. But on occasion an individual word would stand out, or even a clause, such as: 'further than before here. Years ago.' And: 'There are cracks to get through where he won't follow. Or be waiting.' At least that's what seemed to have been written, but she couldn't be sure and the tiny muscles behind her eyes were beginning to strain. The light in the bedroom was too dim for the task.

She put the first journal aside and raised five more out of the drawer. The writing in these was similar to the first, but at least one volume had months written above the entries, though there were often question marks following them – 'June?' – as if Lillian were unaware of the date as she wrote.

There were twenty of these journals in total and Apryl placed them all on the top of the bureau in the exact order in which they had been removed from the drawer, assuming that Lillian's arrangement followed a chronological pattern, with the oldest diaries at the bottom.

She was right. The writing was much clearer in the last journal to leave the drawer. It was nearly all legible and very attractive to look at. And there were no errors, as if what had been written had been carefully composed.

Delaying the phone calls she had to make, Apryl went back over to the bed and sank into the musty goose-feather pillows. And from the first journal she began to read pages at random:

Highgate and the Heath are entirely lost to me now. I have accepted this. I went there to remember so many of the walks we took together. But they will have to live on in memory alone. And I haven't seen St Paul's in at least six months. I cannot get near the city. It is too difficult. After my episode on the underground, I have sworn off travelling below ground. The breathlessness and anxiety may be acute outdoors in the street, but they are doubly so below ground in those tight tunnels. Even my afternoons at the Library and British Museum in Bloomsbury are in jeopardy.

Not those too? I keep asking myself in despair. When will this tormenting end and what will I finally be left with? The tightness in my chest and the flickering of my vision has occurred twice in the reading room like the slow onset of some appalling migraine. I had water brought to me. The second time a man with terrible breath tried to take advantage of me.

Doctor Hardy still insists I am healthy. But how can I be? Doctor Shelley claims I am an agoraphobic and will insist on meddling with my childhood memories. Soon I will have exhausted the wisdom of Harley Street. I dare not tell them about the mirrors. The rest shall have to go downstairs too.

Most of the other entries in the journal were along similar lines. Catalogues of fatigue and curious bodily sensations in different locations around London that Apryl couldn't picture or even place on a map. But it seemed that her aunt had suffered acute anxiety attacks whenever she strayed too far from Barrington House.

Increasingly, the entries became lists of directions she assumed her aunt had tried to follow in order to leave, or even escape, London. Train stations abounded: Euston, King's Cross, Liverpool Street, Paddington, Charing Cross, Victoria. Lillian had tried to reach them all but succumbed to an attack of nerves combined with unpleasant and paralysing physical symptoms at each attempt. Something she began to refer to as *the sickness*.

Or maybe she was attempting to test some kind of boundary she felt had been imposed upon her freedom. Sometimes it seemed these obsessive journeys were taken as a form of reconnaissance.

Some entries involved other people who were never described in any real detail, because her dead husband, to whom these journals were addressed, was already familiar with them:

East, I can reach no further than Holborn. To the West his boundary encroaches deeper. Today I was forced to call Marjory from the street to cancel luncheon. I can go no further in that direction than the Duke of York's Headquarters. Bridge is an impossibility because Holland Park may as well be in China considering how far I can reach out these days.

With every cancellation the girls wonder about me. I can hear it in their voices and they are nervous with me, though they are good enough to try and conceal it if they ever come to dinner in Mayfair. If I cancel many more appointments or refuse invitations I fear I shall have no friends left at all. And I'm satisfied that crossing the river is not an option. I have been thwarted on the Westminster Bridge twice after setting off with my head held high, only to be overcome by the profound dizziness and weariness that made me faint before I was helped to a bench like an unfortunate blind woman.

It is so hard to countenance now as I sit here writing to you, as clear-minded and upright as I have taken for my right in life. But along the Embankment to Grosvenor Road I can do little but crawl like a cat miserable with some internal injury and gaze across at Wandsworth as if it were paradise. A place I never wished to visit when you were alive, darling. But would gladly go barefoot and penniless amongst the cranes and concrete if it meant I could be free of him, and this sickness he has brought me. And the others have it too. They cannot fool me. Beatrice has not been further than Claridges for a year now. And when I told her I had been sick on my shoes in Pimlico she stopped returning my calls as if I were the contagion. She is a cowardly thing, and a terrible bully. We can't keep the staff. She takes this imprisonment out on those who are not to blame. She will not allow the idea that he is behind this appalling situation to even enter her mind. And the Shafers are sweet enough to me, but have begun to complain of bad hips as if they are already old and infirm. Their silly heads are firmly buried in the sand, my darling. As long as a few old friends still visit them they tell themselves they do not need to leave the building. And they still will not tell me what happened the day they tried to flee London from King's Cross.

TEN

Weakened, his stomach hollow and burning, Seth woke in his room. Pissing into a large saucepan and drinking warm tap water from an old bottle, he had kept himself alive and maintained a basic toilet until the worst of the fever passed.

Through the thin curtains he could see the glow of electric lights spreading in the apartment building at the back of the Green Man. It was dusky and darkening already. The travel alarm clock told him it was four o'clock. Avoiding all daylight now seemed inevitable in this life he led. When he finally saw it, he wondered whether the sun would replenish or kill him.

Upstairs at the Green Man, all was quiet; the other tenants must still be at work, or out wandering, or down inside the bar. Soon they would return and begin frying bacon and eggs in the kitchen. It was all the others ate, fried breakfast. The thought made his stomach deflate.

Wrapped in the duvet, Seth edged off the bed and took the one step required to reach the fridge. He turned the kettle on and opened the fridge door to retrieve the plastic bottle of milk. The vanilla light from the fridge hurt his eyes. There was only a dribble of milk left and he sniffed it. It must have begun to turn some time during the morning when he was out cold. Without milk he couldn't eat cereal, and there was no bread. He looked across the shelves and saw a nub of hard cheese, some spice bottles with coloured lids, three stock cubes, soy and Worcester sauce, a dried garlic clove and a half-empty carton of withered mushrooms. Nothing to constitute a meal, in combination or if taken separately. On the fold-out table in the centre of the room two small apples had gone soft and become dusty. It would be like biting into the stuffing of a cushion.

It couldn't be avoided: he would have to go out.

Feeling faint, he sat back down on the end of the bed and rolled a cigarette. Three drags made him dizzy.

Should he wash in the sink downstairs before he ventured out to the supermarket? He decided against the idea. This place was unclean; it was for the unclean.

The kettle was boiling. He poured the water on to a tea bag and heaped four spoons of sugar inside the mug: that would get him up the road to Sainsbury's. Looking at the floor, he sipped the tea. Cherishing the warmth of the mug in his cupped hands, he thought of the hallucinations of the last few days and nights but was surprised by his lack of concern. The horrific nature of the dreams, their macabre themes and terrifying situations sustained night after night, the reappearance of the hooded boy: all this, surely, gave cause to question his mental state. But to him there seemed to be something both natural and necessary about it all: even the execution of the Shafers in that long and tortuous dream. What followed that nocturnal sojourn in their wretched apartment, he refused to dwell upon. The vaguest recollection of the indistinct apparitions in apartment sixteen still jangled his nerves.

But for the first time in over a year he was intrigued by

himself. Never had nightmares seemed so real, though he could not account for this. Perhaps he was just too miserable and lethargic to be bothered by any further signs of slipping away from the path that others walked. Inertia killed motivation. Isolation made him paranoid. Poverty left him wretched. He knew all this. Put yourself through it and you never know how you will react. Hardship was supposed to be good for art. But what kind of art and at what cost?

One month previously, an uninterested doctor had tried to give him Prozac again. 'Stop working nights. It obviously doesn't suit you,' he had said, bored, his pen poised over a prescription pad. But it wasn't as simple as that, Seth had wanted to tell the man. People make me manic. They exhaust me. They drain me. Isolation is my only defence. I have to be awake when they sleep and asleep when they are awake.

'Fuck it.' He stood up and stubbed the cigarette out in the saucer he used as an ashtray. There were over twenty butts in there already, stiff and gnarled like the fingers of old puppets. A cloud of fine grey ash erupted from the dish when he put it on the dining table. What did his lungs look like? That would be worth painting. An exhibition of one man's decay; his mind and emotions and morals represented in the colours and shapes of his dissected body. Maybe he should try a sketch later.

Seth sat down and rolled another cigarette.

Although they were creased, damp, and a little short in the arms and legs, Seth wore the same clothes he'd worn two days earlier. The cold came through them.

Out on the street it was hard to see anything clearly. It was like looking at this tiny rumple of the world through the watery windscreen of a car with ineffective wipers. Darkness swallowed the yellow street lights. Drizzle smudged definition. But he did notice one thing when standing on the pavement under the creaking sign and dripping gutters of the Green Man: a small boy in a hooded coat on the other side of the road, waiting solemnly between two parked cars.

He flinched at the sight of the urchin who had led him through his own dreams. But once the quick jolt of shock dissipated he attributed a sullen insolence to the small figure, imagining a weasel face inside the dark hood, grinning like a bully at the surprise and alarm on the face of its victim.

Leaning into the rain, Seth dug his hands deep inside the pockets of his overcoat and strode away from the pub and the watching figure.

A swift wind buffeted his unprotected head. Blankets of newspaper, made heavy by water, slapped into his shins. Kicking out at the tangled mess, he lost his balance and tumbled into the plate glass of the bookie's window. It took his weight. He straightened up, swore, and tried to hurry on into the blowing air and pinpricking drizzle. Even the buses and cars on the road seemed to wheeze and struggle against the energy that came down the street like a flash tide. Raising his face in acceptance of the rain and swirling vapours, he called the universe a cunt.

Outside the paper shop a news stand displayed the *Standard*'s headline: *Police give up hope on missing Mandy*.

Anger turned to shame. That kid in the hood was out in the rain and cold and darkness. Impulsively, Seth turned towards him and raised an arm. But in the air his hand dithered, useless and indecisive. Did you wave these days or do the thumbs up? Or was some kind of rap salute the only thing cool enough to guarantee a response from a youth? He slid his hand back inside his pocket and waited for a bus to pass the kerb where he had last seen the hooded boy. When his view of the road was clear the child had gone.

Wiping a rivulet of rain from his nose, Seth turned and pushed on to Sainsbury's. With only nine coppery pennies in the pocket of his jeans he would have to go somewhere where a bank-card transaction was possible. 'That fuckin' kid,' he said to himself, and dodged between two women carrying umbrellas to get to the pedestrian crossing opposite the taxidermist's shop.

But something was wrong with the supermarket.

Despite most of the shelves displaying a wide variety of products, he could see nothing edible.

As usual, scores of people were pushing and nudging against each other as they filled their wire baskets. But Seth wondered how they were finding anything fit to eat. He was tempted to stop someone and ask how they intended to prepare and then consume the things they were taking off the shelves. But the young woman nearest to Seth filled him with disgust. What was wrong with her skin? Mottled pink and grey and white, it resembled the surface of luncheon meat that came in cans with a self-opening lid. And her red feet made him recoil. Even in December she wore flip-flops. Her feet looked like defrosting beef, with yellow crocodile toenails hanging over the ends of the rubber soles. Her clothes smelled of damp.

Seth moved away from the overripe tomatoes she was prodding with a finger. He would not be able to touch anything in that part of the fresh produce section knowing her salty pork face had been near it. She turned towards him and elbowed him aside so that she could inspect the hard, dry onions. Her muddy eyeballs had a blunt glaze. Her mobile phone began to ring. Clawing it from her clutch bag, she cocked her head back, delighted with the opportunity to shriek in public.

Seth walked away. But none of the other produce was fresh either. A bunch of spring onions that he held before his face sagged between his fingers. When he saw it was priced at one pound and seventy-five pence, he crushed it and threw it into the yellowing Chinese leaves.

His hunger was desperate, but what could he find to eat here? Turning his face away, he dropped celery and a round lettuce into his basket. 'Compost. I'm buying compost,' he said with a smile full of teeth.

He turned to look for fruit. The bananas were brown, the pears were fluffy. No oranges left either and everything else was too soft, split, white with thick pesticide, spindly, old, or rotten.

About him, people with grey faces and cheeks encrusted with pimple scars scurried and clawed at the plastic baskets and shelves to gather up rubbery mushrooms, gamey fish portions, fatty mince and expensive imported chillies sealed in jars filled with a murky red embalming fluid.

He tried another aisle, but found himself unable to stop staring at a fat old woman who was collecting bricks of lard in waxy paper. She was going bald and stank of sweat. Through her coat and pink cardigan he sensed the texture of her back: fleshy but slick, possibly fungal.

He shook his head and covered his nose and mouth with the back of his forearm. Burping gassy hunger air from the pit of his stomach, he began to feel faint and leant against a long refrigerated bin full of frozen paper they were selling as chips. Breathing deeply with his hands on his knees, he gathered his wits before moving on.

But in every aisle he became hemmed in, shoved, sneered at. The faces of the children were like Halloween masks, carved pumpkins, spiteful and grinning. They banged into his legs and gobbled freely the sweets that smelled of chemicals. Scruffy old men in dirty trainers shuffled around the tinned beans.

Near the bakery counter he was overwhelmed by the stench of human piss: briny, kidneyish, raw. 'Oh, for Christ's sake!' he said, and appealed for understanding from the couple in dirty denim jackets and flared jeans who selected tiny misshapen loaves made from organic flour. 'Can you smell that? It's piss.' They looked at Seth with their pale fish-belly faces and then exchanged glances with each other. When was the last time they'd slept? Dark circles around their eyes had begun to look like bruises. They said nothing and turned their backs on him as if he were raving.

Dropping his basket against the tiled floor, Seth shook with a rage that made him dizzy. Clenching his fists, he stared at a row of birthday cakes; the coloured icing was smothered with fingerprints. Someone had taken a bite out of a chocolate fudge cake and returned it to the shelf.

The smell of piss was even worse by the naan and pitta bread selection. He watched a woman in a smart business suit who had greasy hair arranged in a ponytail. She picked up the spoiled fudge cake and dropped it into her basket. Her leather shoes were misshapen by her long feet and masculine toe joints. Seth wanted to leave.

Vestiges of the fever were still alive in his body. That's why the world looked this way. Every now and then he would shiver and huddle his arms inside his coat. Bitter white and glaring, the ceiling lights scalded the back of his eyes and made him squint.

A trolley was pushed into his shins. The mother-of-three behind the carriage looked daggers at him and bared her dirty horse teeth. Her breath was a gust of sour yogurt.

'Fuck off!' Seth said, his voice cracked. Grabbing her children against her legs, she stumbled away from him, repeatedly looking back over her shoulder as she took flight. Even at ten feet he could see her moustache.

The tins of tuna that he picked up to buy had something sticky on their dented lids that smelled rancid. Contaminated. He put them back. Inside the sardine tins he knew the silver bellies of the dead mothers were full of tiny brown eggs. Seth burped and wiped a layer of milky sweat off his forehead.

Down an adjacent aisle he found it impossible to believe that a cluster of people in smelly coats were buying bags of rice in which moist rodent droppings were clearly visible through the polythene wrappers.

There was nothing in his basket but soft celery and a brownish lettuce. He added a few bottles of still water. The wire handle dug into his tender fingers. He threw out the lettuce and celery. He would have to find things sealed inside metal that had not been tampered with or touched, sniffed at, breathed upon. But not the fish. He wanted uncorrupted edible matter, so much the better if it were a tasteless paste that had been processed by the metal fingers of robots who stood in long lines in dust-free factories. He wanted nothing that had come into contact with people.

Soup! Of course. Seth smiled and walked quickly into the central aisle and looked above his head for directions on the hanging signs. On his third trip down the length of the main aisle his neck ached and still there was no sign of soup.

Someone touched his elbow. 'Sir.'

Seth wheeled around and saw a black man in a white shirt and blue tie. His eyes were yolky and bloodshot. Above the shirt pocket a plastic name tag revealed his identity: Fabris.

'Oh, soup,' Seth said, hurried, harassed, desperate to communicate. 'Soup. Soup! I can't find the soup.' His gibberish was slow and interspersed with swallows. Inside his skull a thick insulation of white fibres seemed to prevent him from putting the words in the right sequence. His tongue was swollen and clumsy. He hadn't said much in days; it was like he had already forgotten how to push sound from his mouth. Seth cleared his throat so aggressively the security guard took a step back and held his hands out, peroxide palm first.

'No. No,' Seth said. 'Soup. It's the soup. I can't find the bloody soup.' At last! His voice had come back. 'Where the fuck is it?'

'Follow me, sir,' Fabris said.

Seth smiled and nodded. 'It has to be in tins,' he told the man. 'I've got water. But I need soup in tins. Won't touch anything else. People . . . well, you know, you work here. I can't stand stuff that's been touched. They don't wash very often in London. And their clothes. Stink. Someone pissed on the bread, Fabris.'

Seth was led down the aisle and back towards the fruit and veg. Another two black men also wearing blue ties and trousers joined Fabris. Between the four of them they should find the soup.

'Now, what a crazy place to put it. By the bloody news-papers,' Seth said. 'The tinned stuff is usually way over there. How weird.' He waved his free hand in the air.

Fabris gently took the basket from Seth's fingers.

'No. It's OK,' Seth said, touched by the gesture. 'I'll carry it. And you don't have to call me sir.'

Fabris insisted and took the basket.

Fabris and the other two men, who were now smiling and trying not to laugh – it must have been his observation about the ludicrousness of putting the soup by the newspapers – formed a tight semicircle behind his back and led him with firm hands past the papers and the cigarette kiosk. It was only when Seth felt the cold on his face sweeping through the main entrance from the dark street outside that he real-ized what was happening. There would be no soup. Fabris and his colleagues were throwing him out of the shop.

Wheeling around to face the three men in the mouth of the door, he suddenly noticed a large crowd watching him. Three women on the checkouts had paused in their scanning of products across the little red eye to observe his ejection from the building. 'What? Why?' he said.

It was then he saw the mother-of-three with the long yellow teeth and moustache standing beside a manager in a suit and tie, by the frozen orange chickens that smelled of antiseptic. She must have complained about him.

The sense of injustice boiled. 'What? Because of that fat bitch with the fucking beard, you're throwing me out?' Fabris and his allies stared at him, straight-faced. 'She slammed her trolley into me. Outrageous. And the condition of the food in here! You're bloody lucky anyone comes in at all.'

Fabris took a step closer. 'I'm gonna ask you to leave now, sir.'

'Fuck you!' Seth shouted, and his voice carried a note of triumph he hadn't intended. He left the supermarket with a dramatic swish of his overcoat and barged his way through the crowd outside to get away from the burning white lights.

By the time he reached the main road he was laughing in the rain. Uncontrolled belly laughing that hurt and made him think of suffocation. For a few moments he felt totally free and weightless.

Shaking from the confrontation, Seth walked to the nearest cashpoint. He withdrew a ten-pound note. A beggar sitting inside a cardboard tray asked him for change.

The rain was coming down harder and he needed soup. With money he could go to the twenty-four-hour mini-market; it was nearly all tins in there. Expensive, but what choice did he have? And he was close to passing out. From now on he would have to bestow his patronage on local shopkeepers.

In the cold and rain he found it hard to believe the episode in Sainsbury's had taken place. Nothing like that had ever happened to him before. He was well behaved, well brought up. But it was the city. It did terrible things to people: made their hair greasy and their skin blotchy and grey. Everyone around him had that pallor, induced by old air, exhaust, dust particles, bad milky water from Victorian pipes, rotten food at high prices, stress, isolation, pain. Nothing worked here: lights, phones, wires, roads, trains. You couldn't rely on anything. And this darkness, the eternal night of soot and black air. His chest went tight. It was hard to breathe. Where were all the dogs and cats and pink babies in pushchairs?

In the mini-market the shopkeeper never slept. A Bangladeshi man with coal-black skin and half-open eyes operated the cash register without looking at his fingers on the keys. 'Than you, sssur,' he said all day and night by the light of the fluorescent tubes overhead. He sold vodka to teenagers and cigarettes to children. 'Than you, sssur.' It was too dangerous around here to say no to anyone. The empty bottles were smashed outside the Green Man and in the bus stop.

'Do you have soup?' Seth asked.

'Yes, sssur.' He pointed to the back of the shop. Seth squeezed around the old Irish men who tottered and swore by the two-litre bottles of dry cider. They stank. Today everybody stank. Didn't people have time to wash?

As well as six tins of soup, Seth bought hard crackers that must have been compressed to a wooden consistency by a large machine. He added bleach and a bottle of water to his purchases. The bill exhausted all of the ten-pound note.

His face hidden inside the round darkness of his hood, but slightly raised and cocked to one side in anticipation, the boy was waiting for Seth as he jogged across the wet mirrored pavement towards home. This time things were different. Contact was unavoidable. The boy had moved to his side of the road. Seth smiled to himself. Maybe speaking to the real version of this figment of his crazy subconscious mind would dispel the spectre from his sleep.

He stopped running and stood beside the wall of the pub. The boy waited on the pavement near the kerb. Rain had turned the khaki of his coat black.

Seth looked up at the sky, an impenetrable murk of ink

with flashes of silver water falling across the sodium of the street lights. He wiped a hand over his face. His overcoat felt heavy and sodden but underneath his body was warm. His muscles loose, his skin hot, he had gone past the point of tiredness and hunger and fatigue. He looked down at the boy who waited and watched quietly. 'Seen you round here a bit. You in trouble?'

There was a long, mute pause followed by a shake of the head. In the bottom half of the hood Seth thought he caught a hint of something red, but wasn't sure. 'You lost? Homeless or something?'

Another shake of the head.

'So . . . what? Why are you here? I mean you can be here if you want. There's no law against it.'

The boy didn't speak.

'But it's wet.' Again Seth looked at the sky.

'Don't bother me,' the boy said with a shrug. The voice was strong enough to let Seth know he wasn't scared.

Seth smiled, but felt his smile didn't penetrate the hood, which seemed to be a silent and empty space. 'And cold,' he mumbled.

The boy shrugged again. One of those kids who can stay up late, call adults by their first name, never go home, ring doorbells when families are sitting down to eat, and look blankly at anyone who shouts at them. He sensed something hard and insensitive inside that cowl, but not callow, not mean, not delinquent. Just lost and able to bear it without question or feeling self-pity. 'So your parents are inside the pub?' Seth asked, and immediately felt both foolish and wary at the way the question sounded. It was the kind of thing he imagined white-haired men saying inside the warm interiors of cars as they leant across the passenger seat to invite someone else's child into the vehicle. He didn't want this kid to think he was a nonce.

The boy shook his head and then looked down the street. There was something hopeless about the way he confronted the road.

'You should go home where it's warm. Watch television.' What could he say to connect with the boy? 'Why hang around here? It's a dump.'

Still no response. He thought of offering some money for sweets or cigarettes, but realized he had none to give. With a sigh Seth turned to go.

'I seen worse.'

'At least stand under the porch. You'll get soaked.'

'Don't bother me.'

'Your mum won't be pleased if you get pneumonia.'

'Don't got one.'

'No mum? Your dad then.'

'Live with me mate.'

Was this some rehearsed ploy to extract sympathy? 'Well you better take off. It's no night to be out.'

Two girls walked by without raincoats. Their blonde hair was pulled back tight from their foreheads and Seth wondered if the rain was able to penetrate the smooth hair. It always looked wet in that style. They wore training shoes without socks, tight black leggings and baggy sweatshirts with Reebok logos hanging in the loose folds at the front. A cigarette was passed between them. The taller girl held a bottle of Bacardi Breezer in her ring-encrusted fingers. They both looked at Seth and giggled. Both of their freckled faces suggested something dog-like – wet and snouty and ill-disciplined. 'What you doing out then?' the one with too much green eye make-up said, mimicking his voice.

'What?'

'You should take your own advice, mister,' the one with the bottle said.

'I wasn't talking to you.'

The girls stopped. 'Who was you talking to then?'

'Don't, 'Shell,' her friend said, giggling at the same time.

'To this lad here.' He gestured towards the hooded boy.

The girls turned and looked at where he was pointing and then laughed in a hard, humourless way.

'Piss off,' Seth muttered. You couldn't stop on this road for long before someone bothered you. You had to keep moving.

'Piss off yourself,' the taller girl said. Her breath smelled of pineapple. They carried on walking and laughing and chewing gum.

'Don't worry about them,' Seth told the boy.

'Don't bother me. Not no more.'

Seth turned towards the pub, his interest in the children of the night exhausted. 'Anyway, I better get on.'

'Can't do nothing to me.'

'Eh?'

'Them girls. Can't do nothing. Boys neither.'

'Glad to hear it.' Seth walked away.

The boy followed him to the entry of the Green Man. Seth groaned to himself, realizing the terrible mistake he had made in talking to this character. He should have ignored him like everyone else. Now he could be stuck with the kid every time he left the building. The boy came closer until he was standing inside the entry with Seth, the hood bowed so the hidden face could peer down at the dog shit by his chunky heeled shoes.

'Sorry. You can't come in. Get yourself home.'

'Ain't got one.'

'Eh?'

'Go where I like.' The boy removed a hand from inside a pocket. A collection of burnt and deformed fingers were revealed.

Seth was meant to see them. 'Do . . .' He had to clear his throat. 'Do I know you?'

The hooded boy nodded.

'From where?' Seth moved out of the entry and back into the rain. It was better to stand in the cold and wind than with the stench of sulphur and burned meat that lingered in the confined space of the entry.

'Seen you a few times.' There was something cocky about the voice and the angle of the head now. Inside the blackness he guessed the child was grinning. From head to toe Seth prickled with static.

'Told you fings was going to change, didn't I?' the boy said.

Seth shook his head and closed his eyes. Then opened them. The boy was still there looking up at him in the wet street. 'You seen it in the shop before they chucked you out.'

Seth could not speak or swallow. He retreated back up the main road. The boy came after him. 'That's just the start. It'll get bad, Seth.'

'You know my name.' Seth broke from his stupor. 'Is this a joke? This is a fucking joke.' His voice was a whisper.

The boy shook his head. 'It's what you wanted. You takes your chances.'

Seth stepped into the path of an elderly man carrying an umbrella. Somehow he found his voice. 'Excuse me.'

The old man looked startled. His whole flabby face quivered.

'This kid?' Seth pointed at the hooded boy, who turned to face the old gent. 'You can see him, right?'

The old man dipped his head and walked around Seth, only to stop once he'd gone a few feet to look back at him with a mixture of boredom and curiosity.

'Him!' Seth yelled and pointed into the chest of the boy. The man turned and hurried away.

The boy giggled inside his hood.

Seth forced himself to smile politely at a West Indian woman who struggled past with a cluster of shopping bags. 'Excuse me, ma'am.'

'Yes?' she said, her face on the verge of a smile but held back by instinctive suspicion.

'This boy here is lost.'

'Eh?'

'This kid here. He's lost. I want to help him.'

'You is lost?' she said. 'Where you wanna go?'

'No. I'm fine. I live here. But this kid. Here. This one. Do you know . . .'

She looked to where he was pointing and then screwed up her eyes to stare at Seth, puzzled for a moment and then wary. After a moment of silence she said, 'Come out of it. I got to go home. I got nothing.' She waddled away from him.

Seth looked at the boy and swallowed. 'No,' he said, and

then ran back into the doorway of the pub. He dropped his shopping bag to fumble a key into the Yale lock. Scooping up his bag of tins and bleach, he fell inside the building and slammed the door behind him.

ELEVEN

Sometimes I believe I am marked and scrub my skin red raw. How else is he able to follow me? I cannot countenance the idea that he can read my thoughts and guess my intentions in advance. And does he leave the building when I do, after sitting outside my door like some cruel dog, patiently waiting for me? Or has he been inside here with me since the last time we saw him? Now I'm beginning to sound like you, my darling.

Apryl sat in bed with the second journal and skimmed through another series of aborted trips and paranoid fantasies. More crazy stories about how Lillian and her friends in the building were being terrorized. Haunted even, by someone she had yet to name.

When she spoke to her mother an hour after midnight, she didn't mention Lillian's madness, or her own unease in the apartment. And to her mother's delight she even hinted that it might be possible after all for her to return to New York on the date previously planned. She then rang off and cuddled back under the eiderdown with a mug of camomile and honey tea, promising herself she would only read the beginning of the third journal before getting some sleep. The

antique dealer was due at ten the next morning, and an auc-
tioneer at noon, so her alarm was set for eight thirty.

But two hours later, after delving into the third volume,
she realized the last thing she would be able to do was sleep
in this bedroom:

*My darling, these past two weeks I have tried to get
away from here through the parks. But things have
changed there too. If the sickness and the sudden confusion is not enough I believe he has now positioned
sentinels to keep us inside here.*

*On Monday I set off at five, at first light, won-
dering if this would make any difference to my chances
of getting out. But I began to feel nauseous halfway
along Constitution Hill. Determined, and so upset I
had only made it thus far to be suddenly stricken with
the sickness, I set off north instead through Green Park
with Piccadilly in sight. It was then I spied a woman
who should not have been in the park. Not at that
time of day, or at any time if I am to be honest.*

*Seeing her gave me such a shock I didn't leave the
flat again until Sunday morning, and I had the porters
do what shopping I needed.*

*Even after all I have endured I am still ready to be
shaken to the marrow by the strength of his influence.
I still question what I saw, and still leap from denial
to acceptance on an hourly basis, but I must accept
these new sightings are a change in the strategy he
employs to keep us in.*

*In my nervous state of mind I was ready to dismiss
the individual in Green Park as some kind of actress.*

Perhaps they were filming nearby. Or maybe she was one of these strange youths I read of in the papers who are so fond of dressing up. But from her appearance I would have placed her with the Victorians and not the current 'swinging' Londoners, or whatever they are now.

She wore a long black dress that swept the path, and a bonnet on her head which concealed her face from me. And could I have imagined all of those ribbons in a detailed frill around her bonnet, as if she were in mourning? It was the details that convinced me this silent and unmoving figure was real. But she was so tall and so unhealthily thin beneath the dress that stretched up to her throat, she made me suspect I was seeing a person on stilts playing some prank on whoever was about at that time. And she was pushing a black perambulator out in front of her. A big old-fashioned thing with wheels like a cart.

I turned away and pretended to ignore her. But, as I proceeded to go on, she just seemed to come quickly out of the mist that was clearing from the base of the trees, and she approached along the path I needed to cross to reach Piccadilly. No matter how much I slowed down or sped up it seemed impossible that we would not meet at some junction ahead.

I veered to the right but she kept pace with me, so I cut directly upwards and tried to avoid a collision I instinctively felt would be unpleasant for me. By this time I was stumbling. Losing my balance because I felt so wretched. My hair had come loose and fallen across my face and I was in such a state, darling, but I tried. I really tried.

She was there when I reached the path. Waiting, not more than a few feet away. Almost at my side. So silent, but determined to greet me, I felt. I only looked at her quickly, but could not see any evidence of her features inside that bonnet. It was angled down, but still, I thought, where is her face? Though what I did see in that solitary glance were her hands, clenched upon the handle of the pram. And I could not take another step after observing the state of them.

They were all bone. Brownish and mottled, not white as you'd expect bones to be. And in that moment she reached out and spread these hands over the top of the pram. As she unhooked the black veil from the hood and reached inside, her fingers made a clatter as if she were wearing lots of loose wooden rings on her thin fingers. I thought this sound more dreadful than the sight of them. And what she raised from the pram made me scream. I remember hearing my voice as if it came from someone else. It simply didn't sound like me.

I must have fainted, because when I woke, the sun was warm on my face and the woman and her horrid pram were gone. A tramp stooped down and asked after me, but he frightened me too and I staggered all the way home in tears.

A week to that day I tried again. First, to reach the trains to Brighton at Victoria, and then to push across the river by the Albert Bridge where I had been unable to get through some years before. But there were more of them. Waiting for me.

Near Victoria I was greeted by something hunched

over and wearing a flat cap. The face under the peak was all chattering yellow teeth. And on Cheyne Walk, three days later, my heart nearly stopped when I was surprised by the sudden appearance of three little hairless girls with the strangest misshapen heads, all long and thinnish. They were wearing surgical gowns tied at the neck and they did a horrible little dance on their stick legs, right there on the pavement before my eyes. Under the gowns I think their bodies were stitched together. But it was the way they moved . . .

I tried to run around them and get across the Albert Bridge but saw something caught up in a tree. I thought it was a kite, but it was fleshy. A face, in fact. With small pox scars on the skin and no eyes. Just hanging there alone in its own grief and pleading with me.

It was as if I was being held down in a nightmare and unable to wake. I doubt I shall ever try and go south again. Down there, it is worse than anywhere else.

Of course I am losing my mind. I know it. As you did at the end, my darling. But we both know where we saw such things before. He brought them here, into the building and into our homes. We never got rid of them. Not after all that burning.

Apryl closed the book. It had gone two and she couldn't bear to read any more. Lillian was a schizophrenic. But how had it gone undiagnosed for so long when she was seeing so many doctors? Maybe it was Alzheimer's. Didn't that make you see things too? Did they even know what it was in those days?

There were no cars at all in the square outside the building. She missed the swishing sound of their tyres on wet tarmac. They were the only company she had as she lay alone with the lights on. Lights that were so dim they barely lit the room. She was no longer sure how she felt about the big wardrobes either, and wondered if she should go and turn the keys in their doors and make sure they were locked.

She looked at the ceiling. The paint was cracked around the light fitting. Three times she felt herself swoon into sleep, but forced her eyes to open each time. She was desperately tired but wanted to stay awake, because when you are asleep you can't keep watch. But the next time her eyes closed they never reopened to lift her from sleep.

Until, in the faint far-off world outside her sleep, she heard a door open and close. A door inside the apartment. And after that came the sound of feet moving swiftly across the floorboards of the hallway.

Then she was awake and sitting up with her heart in her throat and her body stiff with fright. And as her eyes travelled to the doorway they passed over the mirror still facing the wall and the painting of Lillian and Reginald. But she didn't look at the bedroom door for long because she was compelled to return her gaze to the painting. There were now three figures in the picture where there should have been only two. And the one standing in the middle, between her aunt and uncle, was terribly thin.

TWELVE

At midnight Seth was still pacing his room. Moving from the cold by the windows to the warmth near the radiator and then back again. Cigarette after cigarette moved between his fingers and his lips until he felt sick and tight across the chest. 'Jesus Christ.' He was seeing things. He'd lost it.

He sat down on the edge of the bed and stared at the floor, seeing nothing. His heart was beating too fast. Sweat cooled under his arms and smelled sour. He stood up and began to pace again until he could stand it no more and threw the window open to gulp at the dark, wet air outside. It sobered him enough to feel the need for an immediate escape from the confines of his room, to flee outside, to make fast feet and pumping legs exhaust the angry bees swarming inside his chest and head.

But he didn't venture further than the toilet, one floor down, where it required all of his remaining concentration to stand still long enough to finish urinating. By the time the last droplets of clear pee vanished into the sodden toilet paper clogging up the bowl, anxious thoughts of the world outside the pub, and of what might be waiting for him on the street corner, coaxed him back up the stairs and into his room. A thick mist of smoke clung to the yellow ceiling.

He tried speaking to himself in a fast whisper so the neighbours wouldn't hear, urging himself to calm down; repeating simple sentences in a mantra as if the act of speaking was doing the job of gravity, preventing his body from rising to the ceiling, where he would writhe in the exhaled smoke and tear at the chaos in his own belly with long, dirty fingernails.

He tried to distract himself; he had to do something to channel this electricity under his skin into an outlet before his stomach, and then the rest of his body, combusted. He remembered a photograph of a woman's leg in a pile of ash beside a gas fire. As a child he'd seen it in a book of mysteries. If anyone could incinerate themselves by pure thought or emotion it was him, right now.

He giggled.

There was no use resisting the desire that had been stagnant in him for so long. Because recently it had begun to simmer again. Right now it was boiling. Without a distracting thought of where it would lead, whom it would please, or what it meant, Seth plunged his hands into the cardboard boxes full of paper, paint and pencils and set a rime of dust loose into the air.

With thick charcoal stubs and a large sketch pad, he fell into an immediate frenzy of creation, only pausing to shake some feeling into his cramped and aching fingers and wrist. Standing up at the table, or sitting cross-legged on the floor, he dragged his papers and pencils about looking for better light, or shifting to appease the pains erupting in his soft, untrained body, but always working constantly.

Violent, hurried, unthinking, he spilled images onto paper in a continual outpouring as if some tremendous turbulent inner pressure had found a tiny pore to squeeze itself through. The pinhole became a sluice.

Tearing one sheet after another from his pad and then discarding the fragments of sketches about him on the hard carpet to start new ones, he attempted to give some shape, an impression, to the faces and images and hideous things that had been pressing upon him or finding peculiar narratives in his dreams. When his hand cramped into a claw, he clenched his teeth against the ache and tried to photograph this crowd in his mind, terrified it would vanish before the lines and smudges of his pencil had captured it, even in part.

It seemed immediately and shockingly vital, this congested stream of image and sound and smell that whirled through him. He was sure he'd never imagined anything so significant before, nothing of this clarity or power. It was original. God, he was being original.

Whenever he paused to change position he would catch sight of the discarded sketches left in his wake across the dirty brown carpet, and be immediately startled by the absurdity, the inhumanity of what he had drawn. Only when the little travel clock read 08:00 did he stop. Still weakened by illness and feeling concussed by sleep deprivation, he absently dropped his pencil and fell upon his bed.

With a trickling sound the central heating came on. A radio began to play upstairs. But moments after dousing the bedside lamp, Seth was asleep, fully clothed.

'We shouldn't be in here.'

'I wanted to show you some stuff.'

Seth's whispers were tense and hurried in the humid air. 'But this is someone's room. It's private.' He stood beside the hooded boy in the only available floor space in the shabby attic room.

'We can go anywhere.'

The ceiling curved under the arc of the roof. It was dark, but the one arched window above the bed let in an infusion of gassy yellow and grey light. It filtered through the smudges on the glass, and although it seemed to die a few feet in front of the window pane, where it was further suffocated by a haze of stale air and shadows from slouching walls, it still allowed Seth to see silhouettes of furniture and flotsam on the floor of the room. Black spore fungus erupted behind the painted plaster and the carpet was brittle as stale bread under his feet. When his eyes grew accustomed to the gloom, he could see more. Much more.

Milk bottles in varying states of emptiness were littered among tousled newspapers, scraps of discarded clothing, oddments of cutlery and kitchen utensils, stained plates and steel pots dull with grease and dust, from which a kidneyish aroma wafted. Closing his eyes, Seth covered his mouth and nose with one hand in a vain attempt to suffocate the taste in his mouth.

'Fought you should see it.'

He looked at the slovenly disorder of mismatching linen and rough blankets on the bed. There was no sheet on the mattress. Red and purple stripes like a stick of rock showed through the tangle of soiled bedclothes in which Archie slept. From out of an orange wicker bedspread a gnarled and toothless head protruded. It looked impossibly large, too big for the scrawny remains of the body. Beneath the head Seth could see a suggestion of thin, naked limbs. But it must have been a trick of the light to coat them in so much long white hair.

The hooded boy stepped towards the bed. 'Look.'

'Don't.'

Too late. The boy grasped a handful of bedspread and the sheet that had the texture of a towel and raised it above Archie's sleeping body.

Yellow bones, shaped like hooves, were revealed as the natural conclusion to Archie's wasted ankles. Large knees, with surfaces like bleached nut shells, broke through the carpet of white hair – or fur – that covered the rest of the emaciated legs and malnourished groin. But worst of all was the terrible smell of livestock – wet straw, slimed nostril, stale urine – that belched from under the sheets and hit Seth full and hot in the face. Coughing to clear his throat, he took a step backwards and kicked over a milk bottle, discharging a lumpy soup across the carpet.

Archie stirred. In his sleep his oversized hands, stained yellow at the fingernails, clawed at the air to retrieve the missing blankets. Blue home-made tattoos looked like bruises through the hair on his thin forearms. Archie then rolled onto his other side, his sleeping mind still hoping to regain the lost warmth by facing the other way.

After a glimpse of the spine, covered by violent pink skin and more of the white hair, Seth turned away, unsteady on his feet, and breathed through his fingers. He lived in this place; below old goats who pissed in their straw.

'I want to go. He might wake up.' Seth's voice was faint.

'We're in this old bastard's dream, mate. When he dies, this is where he'll come back to. And stay for a long, long time.'

'I feel sick.'

'But there's more.'

'No more, please.'

'Just a little bit. Look closer. By 'is 'and.'

Between two of Archie's swollen sheep knuckles a thin plume of bluish smoke rose from a hand-rolled cigarette. Around the arm the mattress was dotted with black holes and scorch marks.

'Christ, he'll kill us all,' Seth said.

'And your pictures will be burnt to ash.' As the hooded boy said this, Seth noticed a smell of burning wood and flesh that coincided with a brief deepening of the boy's voice.

'What do you mean?'

In the dark room the boy raised his face. Inside the impenetrable blackness of the hood, Seth sensed a grin. 'You's good at them drawin's, Seth. But this lot don't care. No one does. They mean nuffin' to them. They'd be happy to burn 'em. Like they did to *his* pictures. But you should paint what you see. That's what our mate told me. You'll be the best.'

Seth flushed red. It was the first encouragement he'd had in years.

'Honest. You been spotted. He'll help you.'

'I don't understand. Who?'

'He told me to tell you.' The hooded boy said this slowly like he'd been practising it. 'He's been watching you. And what's inside you, all tight and twisted. He told me to show you stuff. Then you paint it like it is. You know it anyway. You know these things are here.' He pointed at the bed where Archie lay contorted in the sheets. 'You always known it. But you too scared of it to draw it. You been stuck in one place for too long, behind bars. I told you before. You know how things really are now. You're lucky you been shown, mate. You's can be the best. Like our friend was, before them shits wrecked it all. So it's not much to ask for you to do summat for us, like.'

'What? I mean, what do I have to do?'

The hooded boy walked confidently across a yellowing newspaper and vanished through the door. Seth followed. Behind his back, Archie kicked out with a hoof.

Seth stood in the place he recognized as his own room. These walls he'd stared at for hours, only half seeing them as his mind looked at other things. But he noticed the paint was fresher and not such a watery yellow. Thicker and more sickly now, like vanilla ice cream. And there was a shade over the light bulb that contained all the colours inside a tin of fruit cocktail.

Same windows though, and just as grimy. And the same fridge, but the reddish stains down the door were new – soup or blackcurrant. Same curtains too, but stiffer, brighter, and the carpet was soft. Looking at the wardrobes, he saw the doors were not broken any more. It was someone else's room now, or back then.

All the things he had thought and done in here suddenly seemed trivial. His whole anxious occupation was more irrelevant than ever.

The hooded boy spoke. 'Everything is in the same place. Even the old stuff that's stuck in here. None of it goes away. If you stay long enough you get to hear all the old voices and see some of the faces. But in here, I only ever find the same fing.'

Seth looked down at him, at the back of the water-stained hood and threadbare fur trim.

'Look at the bed,' the boy said calmly, self-assured, knowledgeable and content, proving his point.

Seth turned and flinched as if the solitary figure had leapt from where she sat against the vinyl headboard, the plastic cover faded to a dirty cream by hand grease. 'Who is she?'

Lank brownish hair fell to the shoulders of her pink cardigan. Pointy chin on scabbed knees, hands clasping white knee-length socks about the bony ankles, scuffed sandals on the brown and yellow blanket, the girl stared at the door, grim anticipation a rictus on her pale face. She couldn't have been older than ten, but her eyes were blank. Seth took in the thin thighs, mottled with a raspberry-ripple blemish all the way up to her cotton pants, and quickly looked away. There was something indecent about her pose, but not intentionally. It was as if she were immune to the scrutiny of strangers. Tears and snot had dried on her face; the red rims of her eyes were sore from crying. Chocolate wrappers were littered around her grey pleated skirt. There was an old-looking camera, made from metal and painted black, on the bedside table. And a ball of green twine that Seth remembered seeing on roses in his parents' garden during the hottest summers of his childhood. Rough, fibrous rope that tasted bitter, like creosote. Couldn't be snapped no matter how hard you pulled, it just hurt your fingers.

'She used to come here to see a man.'

Seth tried to smile to overcome the dread that filled him up. He swallowed, but couldn't move or speak for a while.

'Police took him.'

Seth remembered Archie's story. One of his eyelids twitched.

'Young ones and the old ones don't go easy. They stuck all over the place. Even if she got older, which she never did, she'd be back here again, one day.'

'Enough.' Seth's voice started to crack. 'Get her out. You

were let out of that pipe, and you got me out of that chamber, so get her out of here.'

'Can't let 'em all out, Seth. Too many of 'em, mate. Can't have 'em hanging round us, like. What can she do for us? She don't understand nuffin'. Best leave her be. All she knows is it's the afternoon and she's waiting for her step-dad to come up from the pub.'

'How long's she been here?'

'Dunno,' the boy said with disinterest. 'Long time. No one wears them sandals no more. If she was waiting a few hours before he come in, then it'll always feel like a few hours. For ages. Till it goes dark.'

'Where is he now?'

'Told ya. Down in the pub.'

'Can she see us?'

'Sometimes. But it don't do no good. Watch.'

The hooded boy went and sat on the bed by her feet, bouncing his body down as if to try the springs in the mattress. 'All right?'

'Right,' she said, without taking her eyes off the door.

'You wanna go?'

'Nah. Me dad's coming soon. He told me to wait.'

The hooded boy turned to Seth. 'She always says the same thing. She's stuck.'

'But . . . but how can she always be there?'

''Cus she is.'

'Not at the same time as me?'

The hood nodded with enthusiasm. 'Always. Now you'll be able to see her too. And all kinds of stuff that's stuck, with more and more coming in all the time.'

*

This was the biggest room in the guest house above the pub. It overlooked the main street outside. But when Seth found himself inside the room, the jumble of pizza boxes, beer cans and unwashed clothes of his landlord's occupancy were absent: during trips to the bathroom in the morning, he often caught glimpses of the room as Quin came out wrapped in a dressing gown.

Free now of dust and clutter, the bed was made with a white sheet turned down over a tartan blanket. The doors to the wardrobe were shut and the articles of furniture had been polished and set at right angles to the bed. There were no clothes or shoes in sight, besides a single black overcoat hanging on the rear of the door, and the only personal effects were arranged on a white sheet of notepaper on the bedside table: a watch, a wedding ring, a silver fountain pen, loose change neatly stacked. The room could have been described as spartan but well-maintained.

All of this detail should have been in the background, at the periphery of his vision, but Seth's eyes were avoiding the slim figure of the old man who hung by his neck from the light fitting.

Still swaying from the infinite momentum of stepping off the chair, after his weight jolted down with a snap, the man's limbs had straightened inside the dark suit, and his manicured hands were relaxed. From his left trouser leg, a liquid dripped onto the polished upper of his black shoe, ran off the toe and fell a few inches onto the carpet.

Seth didn't look him in the face, but knew the man's eyes were open and bright.

THIRTEEN

The difference in their offers was not great, a matter of two hundred pounds. But the antique dealer with the thick, coppery eyebrows couldn't collect the furniture for two weeks. And the auction house who offered the best price wanted the portrait of her great-aunt and uncle, to complete the set of four paintings that had been kept in the storage cage and were originals by a fine artist who had once been exhibited at the Royal Academy.

Neither dealer wanted the bed. Dismantling the ponderous, heavy frame and throwing it in the skip seemed inevitable. Lillian and Reginald's marital bed was now firewood. Another belittlement from a world they had departed.

Still feeling too distressed from her upheaval the night before, Apryl was in no mood to haggle, and accepted the disappointing sum of five thousand pounds offered by the antiques dealer for everything. He didn't break so much as a smile when the offer was accepted.

Having been convinced of the presence of a third figure in the painting the night before, April was strongly tempted to let the portrait go as well. But after having breakfast and a few cups of strong coffee, the sighting felt like a figment of her imagination. What had actually been seen? Something tall and thin and pale, standing bolt upright and grinning through a reddish murk. Like the flitting thing she had glimpsed behind her reflection in the mirror the night she wore Lillian's clothes, the quick suggestion of a movement of brittle limbs across the floor towards her. She must have seen or read something that put these apparitions into her mind, because they weren't anything she could just make up.

The place was getting to her. And Lillian's journals were not helping, yet she couldn't leave them alone. Once her business was concluded with the valuers, and she had booked a contract cleaner over the phone, she found herself at the kitchen table with the fourth journal open. But only after a brief inspection of a *London A–Z* with a plain black cover she had at first mistaken for another of Lillian's diaries. It was in the same drawer as the journals, and the brightly coloured maps inside, featuring central London, were heavily marked with biro in various colours.

In the margins cramped notes detailed street names in Lillian's handwriting, and inked lines snaked in every direction from Knightsbridge, representing her great-aunt's attempts at exodus. Lines extending no more than a mile in any direction from the building.

That's why nearly all of Lillian's shoes were worn out. Her obsessive endeavours over such a long period of time were astonishing; the height of paranoid delusion. Apryl wondered again if Lillian's love for her husband was so great that she wouldn't allow herself to leave the last place they were together. When she mentioned her theory to Stephen when he called to ask if she would require the hire of another skip, he looked uncomfortable and apologized, as if expressing his condolences all over again. Her great-aunt's eccentricity clearly embarrassed him.

At the kitchen table, armed with a pot of fresh coffee, she continued reading the fourth journal. The entries in this diary were shorter and more disjointed than the previous three, but all the more disturbing for the change in style:

I see them everywhere. Their thin silhouettes hanging in all of the windows. Not fully formed or half concealed by the shadows. Sometimes they just push uselessly against walls in the entries of basement flats, or crouch muttering in the quiet, dirty corners of mews streets or in the wasted spaces behind buildings. They populate the dead ends. It is in the places the sun never reaches where they exist. But their faces are the worst of all. I see them whenever I look up in Mayfair. Horribly white and thin, they peer down at the street from the oldest windows. Their mouths move but I cannot hear what they say. If they had lips I would try to read them.

In Shepherd Market, a place that even today refuses gentrification, they crowd and jostle in the empty rooms behind boarded-up doors. These ones I can sometimes hear, whispering through the cracks. They have spoken to me from where they hide. 'Is he coming back?' a woman kept asking me, and through a hole in the wooden boards I could see the bone of her ribs and spine.

'I can't seem to find them,' another old thing whispered to me over and over again. I never knew whether it was a man or woman down there on its hands and knees behind some bins. Their milky eyes don't seem to see me. It's no use talking to them; they're unaware

of anything beside their own suffering, but seem to sense me momentarily.

Oh darling, I am half in this world and half in another. Like you were at the end. Now I understand and I ask your forgiveness for ever doubting you. I never looked too long at the things he had on his walls, as you and the others did. Never heard him speak as you did. And it was you who confronted him. Perhaps because my part was so slight the contagion has been slower to take effect. But maybe he was right after all, as you suspected at the end, and maybe what he told us was true.

But how did they get out from down there with him? How do they get into the things that once hung on our walls and into all of the mirrors? How can they appear before my eyes like this in daylight? Must I live alone in silence between bare walls until the end, and not risk any channel through which they can enter? Is hell so overcrowded they are coming back?

There were pages of it; lists of the strange and hideous visions her poor sick aunt encountered on the streets that must have once been a paradise of social appointments, luncheon engagements, dinner parties, shopping trips and clubs. And who was this individual she continually referred to? '*And all the time* he *was calling them down. All of the voices and shadows and things that were not right in this building, on the stairs and in our rooms came to* him *when* he *called . . .*'

Apryl began to leave bookmarks of notepaper and to write anything down that seemed pertinent to the actual building. She suspected some event had occurred, involving both Lillian and Reginald, upon which her aunt blamed Reginald's death, though there were never any specific details of his demise. If any resident of Barrington House from this period was still alive, she would like to know how her great-uncle had died. Lillian also wrote as if she had been condemned by some terrible act committed by her husband:

When you burned it all, you thought everything had been destroyed with it. But how could this survive fire? Yet they are here again despite what you did for us. For all of us.

The others won't speak to me any more. They think I am to blame because I was your wife. I can see it in Beatrice's eyes. She won't open the door to me now. The manager has written me a warning, and so has her barrister, threatening me with legal action if I do not stop hounding her. Hounding her? I tell them there is strength in numbers. And that we are all in this together. But it does no good.

The Shafers will not see me either. Sometimes Tom calls and whispers into the phone when Myriam is in another room, but he always hangs up when she comes back. She controls him like she always did.

They're all cowards. I tell myself I am better off without them. And they can't throw me out because I can't leave. The irony makes me laugh, but not with any joy. We're to stay here while he plays with us and torments us for what we did, or we are to put an end to ourselves. But I cannot do that, my darling. Because I cannot know for sure whether it is a cruel trick or whether it is you I sometimes hear, behind the walls.

After closing the book in the late afternoon, in an effort to move her thoughts away from her great-aunt's insane narratives Apryl went shopping in Harrods to buy some treats from the Food Hall, and then browsed in the clothes stores with sales on in Sloane Street and the King's Road. But the street names and some of the landmarks only served to remind her of the routes Lillian had walked into her eighties, wearing a hat and a veil and broken-down shoes.

The rain drove her back to Barrington House when the stores closed at eight. It was cold and angled at the back of her neck. But at least the apartment had lost much of its clutter, and the hallway was now clear. And with another monumental effort on Friday, she figured she could rid the two end bedrooms of everything but the furniture and ornaments earmarked for sale.

But the increase in space in the apartment did not lead to an increase in light or comfort. With Stephen's help, even after she had refreshed the lamps and overhead lights with new hundred-watt bulbs, a musty brownish haze still filled the air. And the extra illumination only served to attribute a sickly luminance to the paintwork of the ceiling, wainscoting and skirting boards, giving it the discoloured effect of weathered pottery in museum display cases.

She feared no one would want to buy it. Unless it was stripped, gutted and renovated from floor to ceiling, any future inhabitants would be forever trapped inside an old photograph. It was a demoralizing place, the smell of dust and dried damp and old furniture somehow a fitting reminder of her great-aunt's lonely, despairing and whispering entrapment until death.

The irony didn't escape Apryl: she was in one of the oldest and most exclusive apartment buildings in the swankiest part of London, one of the most expensive cities in the world, but was reduced to using an old bath, to inhabiting a dismal space between stained and peeling walls, surrounded by half a century of dross and the neglected detritus of a crazy dead relative's life.

By nine o'clock she was in bed with another journal open in her lap, and a glass of white wine on the side table. And once again she was quickly immersed among the things that scurried about her hallucinating great-aunt:

It moved like a monkey around me ...

... She said, 'They should be here soon. Shush, I think I hear them now,' and then put the little thing's mouth to her shrivelled teat ...

... On such thin legs it came after me, chattering ...

... Wrapped in a stained white gown, with no hair on the yellowish head, it threw its long arms up in the air at the sight of me. I'm sure it saw me down in the street. The building was very old and in one window a blanket had been nailed to the sash frame ...

... Someone brought me home. I don't remember the journey. Then a doctor was called for. But not my doctor; a man whose hands I didn't like came instead ...

In all this she found a man's name repeated twice:

. . . I've looked for his name in other places. The book shop on Curzon Street, where Nancy used to live, ordered what they could for me on his period. But he was unknown. As you once said, 'no self-respecting or decent gallery would hang his abominations on their walls.' You always said he was insane. And he must have been to have been enthralled by such things. But Hessen has no publications or listings in journals or catalogues. The means that brought him here must have been private. I've asked around the last of our friends who know anything of painting and only two of them had heard of him. But they could tell me no more than what we already knew and nothing in relation to his art. Only that he went to prison with Mosley during the war for being a traitor.

I cannot reach the British Library, or even a local branch now. So maybe Hessen was a false name. Doesn't the Devil assume different guises? And was all of this created solely to horrify us? Maybe he never had another purpose. There is no intelligence I can pursue to equip me to defeat him, or to at least evade his influence and escape. I have tried everything. The clergyman who comes here to see the dying Mrs Foregate in number seven thinks I am mad whenever I accost him.

Yet we are all still here and falling apart. If I was taken by force from here I would go hysterical. I would die in a fit. So why do I cling on to this pitiful existence, darling? Because it is the thought of where I will

go that is more powerful than the bliss of release, that
prevents me following you. How can I be sure that
part of me, with even less free will, won't remain here
for ever? To be powerless like those things outside.
Hunting through the dark for people and places and
things they have already forgotten.

Apryl wrote the name *Hessen* in her diary alongside the
names of the residents mentioned by Lillian. She wanted a
psychiatrist back home to read some of these journals too.
To explain to her what was wrong with her great-aunt's mind
and to reassure her it wasn't hereditary. And she would have
been inclined to dismiss this evidence of a painter tormenting
Lillian as illusory if it weren't for the repeated references in
the text to Reginald's role in some dispute.

You were the first to be firm. To take action. I am still
in awe of you my darling as I was when we were
together and so much closer than we are now. Because
I tell myself every day that you can hear me. It's the
only thing that keeps me going.

You were a hero in the war and you tried to become
the hero for all of us here. You refused to move away
as the others did. To flee the shadows that came up so
many stairs and slid along the walls and entered our
private rooms, and our sleep. You wouldn't be turned
out of our home by a horrible little Hun like Hessen.
And neither would the Jews who had lost all of their
family in the war. But I'd never heard you talk like
that before. It frightened me. Now I understand you
were afraid too. To hear you say 'we should have

finished this business the night he had the accident.'
To think back now on how we helped him and let him
survive, only to have him come back with a greater
darkness. It fills me with despair.

You tried to do the best for all of us. But what was
silenced began to speak again, and show itself. It still
does, darling. It still does. I only hope you can no
longer see it. The thought of you being among them
would finish me.

I wish with all my heart that we had left when we
had the chance. Why must fate be so cruel? You came
back to me after so many missions when so many were
lost, only for me to see you taken away again. Right
from my hands. And before my eyes.

With the lights on as usual, and the mirror and painting now
not merely turned around, but placed in the hallway outside
her bedroom door, Apryl sank down among four fat pillows,
half upright as if she neither wanted nor expected to sleep.

High up on the ninth floor the windows were occasionally whumped by the wind. Outside the apartment the faint
whirr and clank of the elevator could be heard. Sometimes
a front door closed and sent its noise up the dim stairwells
and through her great-aunt's flat. The knowledge that there
were others in the building gave her comfort.

She pushed her drowsing thoughts into tomorrow's activ-
ities – the wrapping of the photographs in cushioned plastic
sheets, the bundling of the dead roses into bin bags, maybe
a phone call to thank the taxi driver who brought Lillian
home that last time. Maybe. Estate agents. Maybe.

Was she asleep? It was as if she was sleeping but somehow

still aware of the room around her. Like she was just under but not completely. Not something that happened to her often, but the feeling was familiar, as she lay alone, the sole inhabitant of the apartment, but aware of what was around her in the bedroom.

So who was that, leaning over the bed?

Other people in the building must have heard her scream. For a while, after she sat bolt upright among the pillows, before scrabbling out of the bed, a foot caught in the sheets and then kicked away like it was a hand pulling her down to somewhere that terrified her, she heard voices. In the distance. Beyond her own heavy breaths and whimpers, she heard voices. Like the sudden burst of sound from a distant school playground carried on the wind.

The wind: it was outside the windows and walls, but elsewhere too. Up on the ceiling. The ceiling that had become dark and endless around something that had looked like a face, drawing away. Something red was tight about it. A face retreating into the darkness where the main light should have revealed cracks and yellowing paint and not that depth of no colour and such bitter coldness. A coldness that went through the skin and into the bones.

But where was the face now, and the voices, and the wind?

As Apryl stood by the bedroom door and looked back at the bed from which she had fled, her whole body shaking, dressed in just her underwear, her great-aunt's room now looked the same as it had done before she fell asleep. The lights were on, the walls were bare, and there was no one else in there with her.

FOURTEEN

Thirsty and thick-headed, Seth sat up in the hot bed and reached for his tobacco and cigarette papers on the bedside table. Disoriented from another long and deadening slumber, he tried to remember the time before he had fallen asleep; it seemed so long ago, yet it was still dark outside.

He lit the cigarette with one hand, while the fingers of his other hand scrabbled on the bedside table to locate the small travel alarm clock. He turned his head to look for it, and then swore, clenching his eyelids shut. The light from the little table lamp, burning the whole time he'd slept, hurt the back of his skull.

Slowly, turning his face away from the scorching bulb, he raised the alarm clock up to his blinking eyes. Six thirty – though he didn't know whether it was the evening or morning. Or precisely what evening or morning of which day. He even struggled to remember the date of the last day he'd been awake.

A litter of sketches were strewn about the floor and furniture. Aching muscles in his right arm and fingers, still stiff from cramp, attested to a recollection of frantic sketching. He'd slept all day then. Maybe two days. He'd slept through the hours of watery daylight and awoken in darkness. He wondered whether he should be back at work tonight, if the new shift pattern had started. No one had called. It must be a day off.

Wind shook the windows in their peeling frames. Rain pattered against the grimy panes.

Coughing, he clambered out of bed. Tasting the rich broth of cigarette tar in his mouth, he surveyed his work by the light of the bedside lamp. From the radiator to the blocked-in fireplace, under his desk and between the legs of the dining table, his drawings, or fragments of sketches, lay scattered.

A cigarette dangling from his bottom lip and his tatty overcoat pulled around his shoulders, he considered his work, that resembled something that a prison warden might find in the cells of the insane.

The images were shocking. Bestial in their savagery. Absurd. Sickening. Grotesque. But not without merit.

Hastily gulping at water from a plastic bottle, he saw with some satisfaction the life in these drawings. Vitality. A curious animation in the twisted limbs of the dark figures. And in the eyes a cruel intelligence, a sly appreciation of another's misery, a gleeful seeking of mischief, an incinerating, glaring envy: the eyes of the world. It was like nothing he'd ever drawn, but seemed to be a glimpse of that incoherent inner force he'd always been too afraid to form with charcoal, paint or clay before. The only worthy parts of his pitiful former efforts were those bits that vaguely resembled what appeared before him now; the incongruous shadows and colours his tutors at art school had noticed and been mystified by. Something he was ashamed of. Something he quashed. A streak of expressionism he was too timid to explore. But not any more. It was the only part of his ability worth a damn. It just needed cultivation.

After switching the main light on, he crouched down and peered at the face of an unborn child pressed against glass, its features smudged by an umbra of pickling fluid, but the eyes were clearly Asian. Beside the sketch of the fetus, he found a depiction of Mrs Shafer's head, messily wrapped in scarves, drawn from three angles, the eyes small as olives and black with fury. Then another of her head on top of an arachnid bulk, the shell smooth and polished like onyx, half covered by a kimono and risen in loathsome provocation to the silhouette of her wizened stick-husband, who teetered on baby steps towards his mate.

There was also a sketch of Mr Shafer's death mask with grey crumpled papier-mâché features, and another of his puppet body, suspended in the gossamer threads recently excreted by his wife's abdomen. A final sketch of the elderly residents featured a cluster of eggs, opaque like pearls with a wet sheen, and kept warm next to a radiator in a box of soil.

Seth smiled. It felt odd around his mouth.

But most of the sketches, desperately scrawled as some aperture of his mind opened for a short time, were studies of a single and familiar figure.

Hooded and withdrawn inside the parka coat, protected from unwelcome scrutiny, Seth had depicted the solitary child with the blacked-out face obsessively.

'Jesus Christ.' He suddenly looked around the room, at the pile of soup tins stacked on the refrigerator, at the broken wardrobes, at the lurid thin curtains billowing in draughts, at the dried-up carpet and its confetti of paper. He marvelled at how far he'd let things go. It was all the result of working nights. Had to be; the madness of sleep deprivation. And of struggling to get by in London. Of loneliness, despair, the difficulties of coping with the details of existence. Or maybe this was predestined. As though he'd always secretly needed to be here. Cornered and forced to unravel himself, to peel away every layer, to doubt and reconsider everything he had been taught until he was dragged to the depths inside himself where the dark things lived. He had been led to the discovery of a place where three decades of experience had amassed, filtered through, and then sunk, only to re-form as some vile underlying truth. His truth. The truth.

So here it was, his artistic vision.

But did he want it?

Face in hands, Seth peered through the cage of his fingers at the ceiling.

This could be an extraordinary gift he was about to spurn. A great gift carrying a heavy price. To engage with the world on this level – it was seductive. If he had integrity then it shouldn't bother him what anyone else thought. If he was compelled to cultivate this vision then there could be no room for vanity or dignity. No restraint. He would have to give himself wholly to this submerged world until it consumed him or reached completion. There could be no thought of success or failure. No deadlines. Only a dedication to what he saw and felt.

Dare he?

He looked down. Another brief appraisal of his drawings filled him with disgust, but also with a peculiar excitement that made him uncomfortable. The vision would destroy him; he knew it at once.

Seth sat on the bed, lowered his head between his knees and rapidly sucked a cigarette down to the filter. He thought of the nightmares, the hallucinatory sightings of that boy. God, he was even talking to figments of his own diseased imagination. And there was his uncontrollable anger, his torpor, his inability to function, to clean himself, to feed himself, to communicate with others.

He had a chance to step back from the mad place now. Maybe the remains of his old self were issuing a final warning in a moment of sobriety. Or maybe it was some infuriating and in-built sense of caution that would always step in to prevent him achieving his potential as an artist. He could not decide what to do, and had no one with whom to discuss the crisis. All he knew for certain was that he was frightened of himself, could no longer trust himself, or predict how he might react in any given situation.

FIFTEEN

Something was taking a toll on Stephen. Dark flesh bruised his eyes, his face was too thin, and the movements of his head and hands were slow, as if everything about him as he stood behind the reception desk was delicate and required careful gestures. Apryl had begun to find this more noticeable, the last few times they'd met. And to pick up on his agitation, as if he was nervous around her. Anxious even. Not a reaction she was aware of ever having caused in others before now.

But then his wife, Janet, was ill. And she'd learned from Piotr in the middle of one of his attempts to chat her up that the couple lost their only child years ago in some awful accident. And on top of that, the poor man rose at six every morning to oversee the exchange of nightwatchmen and day porters, before working until six in the evening himself. A twelve-hour shift playing diplomat and servant to the residents. He had told her as much in his quiet, undemonstrative way. And though she did get the impression he liked to help her and that there was nothing inappropriate or amorous in his interest – it was kind of fatherly – she was beginning to suspect that her arrival at Barrington House was causing him grief. Not an inconvenience so much as a reminder of something difficult, even unpleasant. Maybe it was something in her American character that troubled a reticent Englishman.

'Good morning, Apryl. Making progress?'

'Oh, you know, two steps forward, three back. No, I'm kidding. It's fine. Really.'

'Well, you've certainly put your mind to the task. I saw the skip.'

One more day, I think, and I'm done.'

'The new skip will be here by Friday.'

'Thanks. Thanks for everything. You've been such a help. I don't know how I would have got this far without you.'

He wafted the praise away, and almost smiled. 'It was nothing. Glad to help.'

'But I was wondering if I could ask you something else. About Lillian.'

He frowned, and returned his eyes to the ledger. 'Of course.'

'Well, she kept a diary. Diaries to be exact.'

He squinted and underlined whatever he was reading with a fingertip. 'Oh?'

'They are ... well, pretty strange. Freaking me out if I'm honest.' Her voice started to falter. 'Kinda confirms the impression you gave me. She was like really paranoid. I think she was sick. Like really sick for a long time. In her mind.'

Stephen nodded sagely, but couldn't conceal his discomfort whenever the exchanges became more than just passing the time of day.

'But she often writes about other people in this building. There are no dates in the journals, but I'd guess I've kinda reached the seventies now. Just from picking up little details.

And I was wondering if there are any residents still living here from way back then who knew her.'

Stephen pursed his lips and looked down at the desktop. 'Let me think.'

'Do you remember someone called Beatrice?'

Stephen nodded. 'That's Betty. Betty Roth. She has been here since before the war. A widow. But I'm not sure she knew your aunt. I never saw them speak.'

'No way! That's amazing. Beatrice is still here? She and Lillian were friends. Back when both their husbands were still around. I'd love to talk to her.'

At this Stephen winced. 'It's not often I hear that request.'

'Why so?'

'She's a rather difficult character.'

'And for you to say that, it means she's a total bitch, right?'

'I never said a word.' Smiling, Stephen raised both hands palm outwards. 'You can try, though I don't think she'll see you. And if she does you may come away either in tears or too angry to breathe.'

'That bad?'

'Worse. Her own daughter is the sweetest woman you could ever wish to meet, and she leaves here in tears after every visit. Her relatives are terrified of her. Most of Knightsbridge is and they won't let her shop in Harrods or Harvey Nicks anymore. Not that she goes out much these days. And she's the main reason I lose so many porters.'

'But . . .'

'I know. She's just an old woman. But woe betide anyone who underestimates her. I think I've said enough.'

'Thanks for the heads-up, but I have to try. She might

know how my great-uncle died. And Lillian mentions a couple called Shafer. Pretty much said dynamite wouldn't budge them from here.'

'Well that's true enough. They still live here and I've never known them go further than the shops on Motcomb Street, even before Mr Shafer's hip replacement. They're very old now and he has a nurse. He can hardly walk these days. He's in his nineties, you know.'

But Apryl was still replaying Stephen's remark about them going no further than the shop around the corner. Even so many years after she had written them, her great-aunt's crazy journals suddenly resonated with something that was more than just paranoid fantasy. 'Could you . . .'

'Call them. Sure. Betty will be down at eleven thirty sharp for lunch. I'll ask her then. She never misses her Claridges.'

'Is that far away?'

'No. Just the other side of Hyde Park Corner.'

Apryl nodded, unable to conceal a renewal of her discomfort. 'That would be so cool. And say Lillian's great-niece was asking after her. You know, family history stuff. And that she'd be real grateful for anything. Just a few minutes of her time.'

Stephen made a note on the desk pad. 'I'll call you upstairs. Or let you know if you're passing.'

'Cool.'

'But I can't make any promises. They tend to keep themselves to themselves.'

'I understand. And there was one other person she mentioned. A painter who used to live here. Some guy called Hessen. Must be his surname.'

Stephen's fingers paused as he scribbled his note on to the pad, but he didn't look up at her.

'You've heard of him?' Apryl asked, her stomach tensing with excitement.

Stephen squinted, looked over her shoulder, then shook his head. 'Painter? No. No. Not in my time. And we've no blue plaques on this building,' he said, explaining how these signs commemorated the homes of famous people in London.

'Uh huh. This would have been like ages ago. I think he was small potatoes too. Not famous.'

The desk phone began to ring. Stephen's hand darted to the receiver. 'You'll have to excuse me while I take this call.'

Apryl nodded, trying to keep the disappointment from registering on her face. 'Sure. I better fly. See you later. And thanks.'

She set out through the sodden green landscape of Hyde Park in search of a street called Queensway. It was in Bayswater on the north side of the great open common, beyond the Serpentine and through the maze of paths and trees.

Moving off the path and into the grass until it soaked through the canvas of her Converse, she moved at a diagonal trajectory, passing through an assortment of gardens, past the colossal Albert Memorial, and then walked alongside Kensington Palace where Princess Diana had lived. It felt refreshing to suck in the cold air. To see ordinary people doing normal things – nannies with prams, and children in their padded coats; joggers who staggered by, puffing, on steaming pink legs, or who strode lean and bony-shouldered past her. It wasn't just her imagination – the further she moved away from Barrington House, the lighter she felt. Unburdened of the sense of gloomy enclosure in the cramped, brownish rooms of the apartment.

Taking a quick look at the white hotels and dripping garden squares and passing through a constant stream of tourists, she thought Bayswater would be the best place to relocate to from Barrington House. The idea of spending another night alone in the apartment made her feel sick with nerves.

She was scared of it. Afraid of the stained walls, the rotten carpets, and the silence so tense with expectation when night came. The prolonged incubation of a crazed and lonely woman had altered the place. Crumbling into dementia within the dour prison of her home where too many memories changed shape and flitted like spectres through the uncounted hours, it was as if Lillian had infected the place with a psychic damp that seeped its bottled terrors and paranoia into her own thoughts.

She couldn't explain exactly how it had happened, or how her strange sensitivity to such things arose. But now she felt warm with foolishness at the absurdity of it all. That a place, a simple physical environment, could change her so much. But it could. Last night was proof again.

She wondered how she might explain her move into a hotel room to her mother. More white lies. The mere thought of breaking the news made her feel tired. Later, she could deal with that later. Because Bayswater had a kind of Mediterranean charm that she wanted to enjoy – even the sky broke into blue – and it seemed exclusively equipped for visitors from abroad. It was all luggage shops, chain restaurants and tacky tourist shit, but she liked the tall white buildings and Greek Cypriot groceries. She bought olives and hummus to snack on, from the Athenian grocery on Moscow Road where the old men behind the counter wore blue overalls and wrapped her purchases in white paper.

Once she'd bought an hour of time on a computer, and made herself comfortable with a cappuccino in the Russian Internet cafe on Queensway, she found that only three pages of a Google search contained anything relevant about a painter called Hessen. And there was only one artist by that name: a man active during the thirties in West London. He was known by few, but those still aware of him seemed enthusiastic enough. It was him. Had to be. The first name of her great-aunt's nemesis was Felix. Felix Hessen.

Some guy called Miles Butler had written a book on him a few years before, so most of the links were to reviews of that book. It was published by Tate Britain, so she scribbled the details down: Miles Butler, *Glimpses into the Vortex – Drawings by Felix Hessen*. There was also an organization called the Friends of Felix Hessen. It was based in Camden and had a freakish website. All black and red graphics designed by an amateur. She read the gushing introduction about 'Hessen's rightful place as a great surrealist painter', about his 'contribution to Futurism', and about him being 'a precursor to Francis Bacon', whom she'd heard of.

She clicked on the link to the biography, which ran for several pages, but there was no mention of Barrington House that she could see during an initial skim-read. He was a Swiss Austrian immigrant, but just about as obscure as an artist could be. For a 'great painter' he wasn't exhibited in a single art gallery during or after his lifetime. His surviving sketches were now in America at the New Haven archive.

The biography webpage claimed his father was a successful merchant and sent the young Felix to medical school in Zurich. For some reason his wealthy parents then emigrated to England and Felix Hessen ended up studying fine art at the Slade, where he excelled as a draughtsman. The Introduction argued that his support of something called the British Union of Fascists, and a man called Oswald Mosley, before the Second World War, was responsible for a left-wing conspiracy in the arts banishing him into oblivion. Hessen was even locked away in Brixton prison for 'acts prejudicial to public safety or to defence of the realm' for the entire war. And there was speculation that he'd met the top Nazis in the thirties too – maybe even Hitler – to try and interest them in his art. Which they never liked. So he had to make do with being a communications officer for the British fascists, who didn't like him either.

No wonder Reginald hated him.

After his release from prison he became a recluse at the family home in West London. And only his sketches from the thirties survived, along with one copy of some arts journal he started, called *Vortex*. It lasted four issues and had fewer than sixteen subscriptions when Hessen gave up on 'a philosophical medium to ideas incommunicable in language'.

Apryl knew a loser when she saw one.

Hessen then disappeared in the late forties, but the website didn't give an exact date. He was listed as missing by the family lawyer years before he was finally declared deceased in official records. The estate was sold by a distant branch of the family in Germany. He never married, never had children, and survived his parents, who both died before the war and before their son's brief notoriety.

He was hardly mentioned in records of pre-war art either, although someone called Wyndham Lewis thought he showed 'uncanny promise' before they soon fell out, while Augustus John recommended his work to the Royal Academy, though Hessen had no interest in the institution. And in memoirs of the time there was only the briefest mention of him. One of the Mitford sisters, Nancy, thought him 'unjustly handsome and vile'. He was even expelled from Crowley's occult society, Mysteria Mystica Maxima, very quickly after they 'doubted the path of his enlightenment'. Allegedly, he tried to bribe and then blackmail Crowley to hand over the knowledge required to conduct summoning rituals far beyond his status as a mere adept. Rumours in occult circles at the time suggested that Crowley did indeed impart both the knowledge and the relevant tracts for a significant fee in order to feed his morphine and prostitution habits. It was highly volatile material that the Great Beast Crowley had used himself, with some success, in a lengthy summoning ritual at Boleskin in Scotland, on the shores of Loch Ness, after a considerable period of fasting. A poet called John Gawsworth remembered Hessen being ejected from the reading room of the British Library for conducting rituals between the desks that had made the lights dim throughout the entire building.

But soon after the war he was gone. Vanished. Probably a suicide.

There was no mention of him being a lousy neighbour in Barrington House.

The Friends of Felix Hessen organization dismissed the Miles Butler book as part of the liberal arts campaign against Felix Hessen.

The website also published over thirty essays on his missing oil paintings, the sketches for which were allegedly only preparations for Hessen's 'great vision of the Vortex'. According to the website, the missing paintings were part of another conspiracy. They had been suppressed or hidden to this day by arts councils because of the painter's associations with fascism.

The Friends met fortnightly to listen to guest speakers, and to take part in the 'Hidden Landscape of London Sessions', whatever they were. There was a meeting this coming Friday night in Camden on 'Hessen and the Nazi Occult', with a guest speaker from Austria called Otto Herndl. The phone number for a guy called Harold was given to call for details. Apryl quickly browsed through the other topics on the Friends' forthcoming itinerary: 'Felix Hessen and the Cult of Dissection'; 'Banquet for the Damned – Felix Hessen and Eliot Coldwell's Unseen World'; 'The Puppetry Grotesque in Pre-war Painting'; 'The Feral – An Eye For The Bestial'; 'Surrealism and the Modernism of Ezra Pound – Glimpses of the Vortex'.

It all sounded like a load of Greek salad and she quickly found her eyes glazing at the unfamiliar words and obscure references. But she made a note of Harold's number. He was a doctor after all, of metaphysics. She wasn't sure what that meant, but he seemed like an authority on Hessen because he was the author of most of the essays and of a book soon to be published by the group.

But when she clicked on the link to the gallery of Felix Hessen's surviving sketches, the back of her neck began to prickle. Once they had fully downloaded, picture by picture, she went dizzy and had to refocus her eyes. If she needed a visual depiction of her great-aunt's persecution fantasies, of the hideous things Lillian described crowding and pursuing her back to Barrington House, then Hessen had drawn them in charcoal, gouache and ink. And he had done so in the thirties, before Lillian's journals were even written.

Apryl stayed in Bayswater for the rest of the morning, drinking coffee and eating flaky sugary pastries. For hours she was content to stare through the rain-blurred windows of a Lebanese cafe. All the time trying to make sense of what she had first stumbled across in Lillian's journals and now found on an obscure Internet site. She wished she'd never looked at the journals. But could not stop herself trying to figure out why her great-aunt and uncle had been so obsessed with this man who lacked a single redeeming feature and who drew the most awful pictures of dead animals, human corpses, and those puppet things that seemed to be a combination of the first two subjects. She hadn't liked looking at them online, and now bits of them had taken possession of her memory. The image of something that looked like a dark monkey with horse teeth came again into her thoughts and made her shudder. Just looking at the picture made her think she could hear it scream. But suppressing the image only made a second appear in its place – like that thing, a bit like a woman, a very old woman, and more bone than flesh, looking up from a basement window.

Sitting at the little table in the cafe, she made a decision. She would read the Miles Butler book on Felix Hessen, the man Lillian claimed was responsible for making her life so wretched. She would go to the Friends of Felix Hessen meeting on Friday. And she would speak to anyone left in Barrington

House who knew Lillian when she was younger. She would do it for Lillian. Otherwise, no one else would give a damn. At least she could spend Friday in Camden checking out the market before the lecture in the evening, where she could talk to one of these experts. Just to get a better sense of this artist – the man who drew those terrible things.

By noon there was one other thing she also knew for certain: she would not be spending another night at Barrington House.

In a hotel room in Leinster Square she forked through a takeout from a Vietnamese place on Queensway, sipped her Chardonnay and opened Miles Butler's book at the introduction.

The paperback was only one hundred and twenty pages long and mostly filled with the prints of Hessen's sketches. There had been no more than a dozen copies of the book left at Tate Britain in Pimlico, and all had been reduced. 'Never did that well', the assistant told her in the gallery bookshop. 'Not most people's cup of tea.' They were about to be 'remaindered', whatever that meant.

'My great-aunt knew him,' she'd told the assistant, with a weird sense of pride. But he didn't seem impressed at all.

From the gallery she went back to Barrington House to pack an overnight bag with some clothes and toiletries. On her way out of the building she stopped at the front desk to talk to Stephen, catching him before he finished his shift.

He didn't question her decision to stay in a hotel. She suspected he was surprised she hadn't done so sooner, considering the state of the apartment. Or thought that possibly he was even relieved that she might not be bothering him so much now. But he did tell her that both Mrs Roth and the Shafers had declined to see her.

'But why? They knew her.'

Stephen had shrugged. 'I asked nicely and said the very charming niece of Lillian was over for a while and would like to know more about her aunt, who she never met. But they said no. A bit mean-spirited, I thought. So I tried to talk them round. But that set Betty off.' Then Stephen shook his head and looked more tired than ever.

What was wrong with these people? Didn't the old love to talk about their memories? Apparently not. Her disappointment simmering, she took a cab up to Bayswater and checked into the hotel. After a hot shower – the best she could ever remember taking – she settled on the soft bed with the Miles Butler book. And immediately congratulated herself on her decision not to study it at Barrington House. It felt safer to deal with these things here. In another world, one clean and bright and comfortable and modern; the antithesis of the home Lillian could never escape.

Glimpses of the Vortex was much better written and less hysterical than the text on the Friends' website. But the author didn't include much more biographical detail than she'd already read online. Most of the text was an analysis of the imagery and symbolism in the surviving sketches. She found this difficult to understand and skimmed it because it made her feel stupid. But the illustrations she had seen online were all here on expensive shiny paper and all the more disturbing for it. It took a conscious effort to prevent her eyes wandering from the text to the relentless suggestions of the savage, the bewildered, the terrified and lost figures in the drawings. Those with elements of colour being the worst of all. When she turned a page, she got into the habit of covering the illustrations with a napkin so she could focus on the text. They made her remember whole passages from her great-aunt's journals. And these comparisons were so disturbing she began looking about the bed and the small, well-lit room as if she suddenly expected to see someone standing there, watching her.

She shook the feeling off and skim-read the section about Hessen's early medical training and the fuss a tutor at the Slade had made over Hessen's drawing of cadavers instead of live models, and for having 'no interest in beauty'. The only mention of Barrington House was brief – it was merely cited as the place where he lived reclusively after the war.

His imprisonment during the war, the author suggested, had broken Hessen and foreshortened his career as an artist: 'Hessen was a privileged and acutely sensitive man unused to the stigma of being a traitor or the harsh conditions of prison.' The only way Hessen could be studied was through his art – the actual drawings. And only through a study of them from a psychoanalytical angle.

His life was an inner life, and the only true glimpse of who he really was, and of what he tried to achieve, exists in his art.

It wasn't what she wanted to read. And maybe the author was incorrect anyway. Maybe there was something else. She had a hunch an entire chapter of the painter's life remained unwritten: the Knightsbridge years – a story hinted at in Lillian's journals that could be backed up by the testimony of his surviving neighbours, if only they would speak to her. Maybe the others – this Betty woman and the Shafer couple – had seen his paintings too, or at least been told of them by Lillian and Reginald. A long shot maybe, but something she knew she should tell this Miles guy about. The back of the book listed him as a curator at Tate Britain, so he wouldn't be impossible to track down if he still worked there.

She continued to skim through Miles's interpretations of the art until she happened across anything specifically concerned with Hessen. And what little had been recorded about the painter portrayed him as irascible, unpleasant, spitefully vindictive, and ultimately indifferent to the feelings of others. His short temper was repeatedly attested to, and blamed for alienating what few remnants of friendship he had before the war.

He was already deeply withdrawn before his incarceration in Brixton prison under Regulation 18b, which allowed imprisonment without charge or trial. The author suggested that a bipolar illness could have already consumed him prior to his arrest, describing him as 'exhausted, listless, paranoid, possibly even exhibiting signs of schizophrenia, and hypermania'.

An acquaintance and sculptor called Boston Mayes claimed Hessen didn't appear to sleep and his face was cadaverous. He talked to himself in front of others and often forgot they were there. He was utterly distracted, absorbed and forgetful. 'A mind at the end of its tether.'

There was evidence in some of the memoirs of Hessen's unwise investigations in the twenties into Enochian magic and black magic. But apart from his sporadic esoteric, philosophical and political writings in *Vortex* in the early thirties in support of fascism, which pretty much sullied his reputation for all time, Miles Butler admitted he didn't have much to go on besides the surviving drawings. And so it was these he tried to decode:

> Hessen's work was an idiosyncratic and deeply personal investigation of an inner vision, something he'd spent his entire adult life evolving. He prepared himself with psychic investigations while a student, and with extreme political disciplines afterwards, until he realized the answers he sought didn't exist in any other ideology or set of beliefs. Philosophy and fascist fervour were, in Hessen's opinion, merely vehicles that skirted round the Vortex – they were methods to it, or symptoms of it – preparation. And it was only through his art, with reference to occult ritual, that he even came close to realizing his vision.
>
> The Vortex was a region Hessen believed to be, in effect, an afterlife, the true and final destination of human consciousness: a terrible, lightless and turbulent eternity that gradually reduced the soul to fragmention, in effect a perpetual nightmare in which an inhabitant possessed no control over their inevitable demise. Personality and memory became mere residues, and a final awareness was only able to register terror, pain, bewilderment, entrapment, disorientation and isolation. In effect, hell. Paranormal activity merely represented the last flickers of those lost souls, struggling to return to their lives at the edge of the Vortex, where the walls separating it from this world were at their thinnest and most permeable.

Another chapter detailed Hessen's obsession with death. He believed his only chance of interpreting existence began with a study of its end:

> ... *when a consciousness became aware of its end and the sudden consuming dialogue with extinction.*
>
> *The best evidence of what follows this life is glimpsed in a death mask, a livid facial expression, especially if the eyes are still open. They give us a vague approximation of whatever we call the soul, and what it has slipped into. In these eyes I first glimpsed the Vortex.*
>
> *And what we have become in this life, at the most profound depth of ourselves, determines our position at the next level.*

From what she could grasp of all the psychobabble, it seemed Hessen was convinced of a kind of duality – like Freud and Jung, but in a more mystical and sinister way:

> *From his studies of psychic phenomena in the twenties, and of people who possessed the talent to speak in tongues, he believed two selves, in essence, were always conducting a simultaneous existence within the same body. The one shown to the world and called a personality was, at best, a flawed construct: an approximation of what we created, out of necessity, for survival. But when that was abandoned, at the moment of death or in the midst of madness, or another altered state of mind, or most often during sleep, the other self would be glimpsed.*
>
> *Hessen spent his life trying to find it through any*

*method of displacement at hand – through removal
of the conscious self through occult ritual, or via hypnotism, automatic writing or painting. He had no
interest in anything but the other self. And by com-
municating with it, knowing it and ultimately
controlling it in this life, he believed one could achieve
not only an awareness in the following existence,
inside the Vortex, but the equivalent of sentience – or
life after death – an animation that bridged both the
mortal plane and the afterlife, that terrible region very
close to, but concealed from, the naked eye and the
primary senses.*

*Not easily described by logical or reasonable means
afterwards, his art was to act as a pure and sudden
glimpse of the 'other', of what was only ever seen in
dreams, or in times of euphoria or mental disintegration. Of what actually existed inside the Vortex – what
Hessen called the population of the Vortex. This was
something only understood and interpreted by the
'other' — in his case, his art.*

*Despair, feelings of dislocation, altered states of
consciousness, a psyche unravelled and paralysed by
depression; all of these were aspects of the restless,
infinite Vortex, and represented a closeness to its
relentless surging around our short and inconsequen-
tial lives.*

Sipping her wine and changing position to ease the cramp
in her elbow, Apryl frowned as she went back to reread
the earlier chapters about the surviving sketches; Hessen's
early studies of dead animals and human deformity. Even as

a teenager at the Slade, using ink, pen and pencil he had been faithfully depicting the heads of dead hares, the bleached grins of skinned lambs and the horrors of congenital disease:

No classical nudes survive from this period, when it was compulsory to produce them at the Slade. Only his fastidious depictions of dead animals and human deformity have been found.

Stillborn triplets, the preserved faces of those who had perished through disease, and the bulbous skulls preserved by the Royal College of Surgeons were his favourite subjects. In all the awfulness of nature's distortions visited upon children, he attempted to distil and re-create the full impact of specific images that caused horror and revulsion in an onlooker. The sudden uncomfortable surprise, the inability to prevent the stare, the gaping open perception and astonishment at the malformed: it was this reaction he wished to inspire.

'It is so much more plentiful than beauty,' Hessen had written in his failed journal. In decay and deformation and ugliness he found far more evidence of what existed within the Vortex.

Imbuing his obsessive drawings of cadavers and body parts with a peculiar life, he created an animism. As if, after life, after the end of self, a new animation existed through a sense-memory of the physical remains – a sign of what one would become after death, or rather, of what one would become trapped as, inside the Vortex.

And in the chapter about Hessen's re-creations of animal and human hybrids that followed this phase – 'the grotesque figures stricken by despair and painful contortions that gained Hessen a small posthumous notoriety' – Apryl learned more than she cared to about his slide into primitivism.

Still controlled, his expression is not quite free enough from, or unconscious of, what he learned at the Slade while exposed to the Italian masters. 'Figure Bowed Clutching Face', 'Toothless Woman Drinking Tea from a Saucer', and his other earlier figurative drawings reflect his radical affront to traditional aesthetics and notions of beauty in Western art, and yet they only hint at his own voice, at the signature that would become shockingly apparent just before his work ceased. Here, towards the end of his surviving portfolio, his drawings are full and pulsing with an acknowledgement of the essential ugliness of mankind as he saw it, and the attendant isolation and bewilderment of existence. Subjects are barely recognizable as the people he'd observed in streets, cafes, pubs, and shops. Some of the figures appeared more canine than human. Others had limbs more reminiscent of the goats and jackals he'd drawn at Regent's Park zoo, and the figures possessed the faces of apes. They were drawn with the surety of someone observing life, more than simply showing what had been imagined. Hessen himself claimed that this was actually what he had trained himself to see in those around him.

Apryl read on, uncomfortable with the mind the biographer was unravelling for her. A mind that had inflicted its terrible vision on Lillian and Reginald.

When he began to use gouache, ink, chalk and water-colours, 'the influence of surrealism and abstraction on Hessen became visible.'

Miles Butler went on to describe the backgrounds in these works, with detail that Apryl found deeply unpleasant. She'd only begun to notice the backgrounds of the drawings the second or third time she'd looked at the pictures.

Half-formed misty landscapes drifting into a sense of a moving nothingness, of infinity, at the edge of each picture. Around the thin silhouettes at windows, or the hunched figures in corners or holes, he tried again and again to portray a sense of vastness. Never static but alive, seething, turbulent, cold and vacuous. There is an absence of shape or solidity surrounding and swallowing the claustrophobic studies of these figures trapped in dingy rooms, or performing seemingly repetitive tasks alone. Most are reduced to all fours and resemble apes or puppets, their faces pushing relentlessly against walls in a futile attempt at escape.

So he was a nut. But the last chapter about his painting was more relevant to what she wanted to know. Though no easier to read. Frowning in concentration, and ignoring her glass of wine until it had gone warm and tasted sour, she squinted at the sentences and often read them twice over, struggling to connect these bits of information to his influence on Lillian:

Why would a man who spent so long pursuing such a vision, and perfecting the line in order to capture it, suddenly stop creating? It didn't make sense if he never considered his sketches to be anything but preparatory notes – preliminary studies before the greater work was attempted: a depiction of the Vortex in oil.

Maybe prison put an end to his frightening ambition, or he destroyed his own work. That was all the author really offered to explain the fact that not a single painting by Hessen had ever been found.

His intentions were clear in the surviving issue of Vortex, *as was his frustration at the amount of preparation needed to equip him sufficiently to achieve the vision. But of course he painted at some point. He must have done. Hessen was too determined, too single-minded to be distracted from a work before which all else had become secondary. Was it really feasible that such a monstrous ego, with such an epochal vision, would never progress further than line drawings and gouache? Most probably these ultimate works were destroyed by the artist's own hand.*

He couldn't have destroyed them, because Lillian and Reginald had seen the paintings. The author also questioned what Hessen did alone for the four years after his release from prison before his disappearance. These remained the two mysteries debated endlessly by his admirers and critics alike:

There is little information in existence about this period of his life. Even before the war, he was largely an enigma. And the few visitors and models whom Hessen allowed into his studio in Chelsea in the thirties told conflicting stories. The painter Edgar Rowel, who rented a studio close to Hessen, attested to seeing paintings he found 'profoundly affecting in Hessen's rooms'.

Contrary to this, not one of his acquaintances from his time at the Slade claimed he showed any evidence of ever having painted a single canvas. Nor did he ever admit to such. But contradicting this position again, a model called Julia Swan mentioned locked rooms, dust sheets, the existence of art materials, and the smell of paint and cleaning spirits in his mews studio in Chelsea – all the paraphernalia of a painter at work in his own lodgings.

There is also another mention of Hessen's studio in Chelsea in the memoir of the French painter Henri Huiban, who assumed Hessen was a sculptor due to the loud noises he made at all hours. And there was a rumour of actual oil paintings spread by the alcoholic poet Peter Bryant, who briefly befriended Hessen at the British Library. He wrote of 'giant paintings glimpsed in Felix's darkened rooms'. But in the Fitzroy public house, Bryant was also fond of declaring himself the reincarnation of a Celtic king, so his testimony is, at best, dubious.

Giant covered canvases stacked together, but turned to face the wall, were also reported by Brian Howarth, an acquaintance of Hessen's from the British

*Union of Fascists, who once called on him at his studio
to collect some papers.*

Infuriatingly, the book asked more questions than it answered, but at least the author admitted this:

*And where did the artist go? How could a man of his
wealth and position just vanish without a trace?*

But traces did exist. Traces that were rapidly vanishing as time passed. It was becoming, Apryl realized, a case of no one having looked in the right place.

SIXTEEN

His vision was jerky, unable to fix on anything. Instead, his eyes flicked about and took in fragments of things on the street. Short of breath and clumsy, he repeatedly tripped over paving stones or veered drunkenly as if unused to walking upright. By trying desperately to move away from the other pedestrians, he was somehow drawn off-balance towards them. He became enraged and wanted to shout.

He should not be in London. But he had damned himself to it with some vague romantic foolishness about art. He'd stranded himself here. Shipwrecked himself among the dreadful screeching of the apes.

It could be felt as much as observed; this alteration in the environment, in the very atmosphere. Wherever people congregated in the street, in this drizzly cold, lit only by street lamps and flickers of fluorescence, outside the little supermarkets and off-licences, fast-food restaurants and dreary pubs, he felt a total aversion. Some invisible contamination made his guts seasick with nerves. Some kind of unseen pressure, perhaps electrical, filled his head with a buzzing static noise, indecipherable transmissions or echoes of somewhere else, but now here too, as if he travelled beneath or between what everyone else was experiencing.

But it was hard to describe exactly how the world had

altered. Only a visual vocabulary would suffice. Did he have the clarity? His sketches were probably nothing more than gibberish and graffiti. And wouldn't that be the worst frustration of all: to be at last presented with some insight into the true nature of things – a truth so blurred by the media, by education, by these endless social systems and codes, the benign totalitarianism that distorted existence – and yet to find his new perception incommunicable?

When he finally reached the tube station, Seth leant against a tiled wall to roll a cigarette; he was unable to speak when a beggar asked him for a smoke. He had forgotten how. His lips moved but the triad of vocal cord, tongue and jaw refused to coordinate. He swallowed and then produced a rasp.

He wondered why he was here. What had compelled him to leave his room again. His original purpose was lost to him.

The blue light of the cash machines and the red and white illumination of the Angel underground station stimulated some vague anticipation of travel. He briefly gravitated towards the lights, but was soon warded off by the crowds pouring out of the tunnels.

He moved past the station but was halted by an impassable crossroads of hurtling traffic, slapping winds and jostling elbows. It all vibrated through his bones. A crowd waited for the lights to change. But no amount of perfume could disguise the fishy-vinegar reek of the women. Had he once thought these creatures attractive? There was something physically wrong with all of them. Lipless, protruding eyes, overlapping teeth, misshapen noses. Ears too red, discoloration of the skin under make-up, pink-rimmed eyelids, calcified hair. Seth shuddered. The men fared no better with their apelike swaggering, wet dog nostrils and blunt shark eyes. Intimidating, dangerous animals with a brute strength increasing its potential to explode as every drink was quaffed. Murder beasts reeking of dung-straw and brewer's yeast.

Seth didn't manage to cross the road; a moment's hesitation, and another flash flood of cars, bikes and buses shook past, further blurring the smudgy buildings with their headlights, and leaving him stranded on the pavement.

It was as if he had been abandoned in a foreign city without a map and failed to understand a single word spoken. An overwhelming desire to be free of London made him shake with frustration. Anything, even to be penniless in another town, was better than merely existing, baffled and buffeted, in this unfeeling place.

Head down and defeated, he moved away from the traffic. He couldn't go back along the Essex Road; there were too many people down there. He'd slip back through the adjacent side streets. But as he tried to remember a route home, he spied an empty-looking bar set underneath an ugly concrete office building. Maybe he could shelter in there, in a quiet corner by a radiator, and drink whisky.

Already it was as if he could feel and taste the fiery, revitalizing liquid in his cheeks and throat. He moved towards the door of the bar and lingered outside. There was music inside and one or two loud voices trying to rise above some other noise. The idea of entering made him anxious, as if such a move was no longer an easy thing to accomplish. And even if he could reach the bar, he wondered if he would be able to speak. After whispering his own name down and into the lapel of his coat, Seth pushed the door open.

It was like walking onto a well-lit stage. His instant immersion into bright light and sound made him giddy and afraid. A lump formed in his throat. Gingerly, keeping his eyes down, he concentrated on placing one foot in front of the other in case he crashed down among the tables and chairs. At the bar he looked up, doleful and insecure, and waited to be served.

There were only a handful of people in the scruffy place, and all gathered around a giant video screen to watch a football match. He was glad of the distraction; it saved him from attracting their eyes.

He looked dreadful, he realized the moment he saw his disgraceful reflection in the mirror underneath the optics; pale and creased and stained and downtrodden. He cringed with shame. But it had been a long time, nearly a year, since his appearance mattered. He could see the results of a chronic inattention to grooming, diet and lifestyle. There was a miserable and lined aspect to his mouth. His eyes had shrunk to tiny, hard things, set deep in the bruised skin of the sockets, as thin as tracing paper. There was an unnatural lividity to his complexion too, the only colour provided by the networks of broken blood vessels across his cheekbones. He looked sixty, not thirty-one. This was a death mask. He saw callousness, despair, revulsion, the loss of all hope and all compassion. His face was the one true work of art he'd created in the last year: a detailed and living representation of the city.

At a corner table away from the other customers, his euphoria for escape grew with every shot of whisky downed. Sipping at speed, the glass was never out of his hand or far from his mouth. The alcohol made his thoughts go faster.

And he could no longer think of a single reason to stay in London. It had been a rapid and grim descent from day one. Uneventful months smudged into each other to become a year; a long, dismal and greyish smear of existence. A year in which he had ended up barely civilized, almost inhuman, like the others.

But it had always appeared impossible to get out of the city. And improbable that he could change this life, or slow the momentum of decline, with so many things conspiring against him. He'd never been able to find the time between night shifts to organize himself. It was not possible to think clearly with so many thoughts, so many memories, so many scenes playing out in his imagination. The whirlwind in his skull had always kept him rooted to his chair, or perched at the end of his bed, smoking. And perhaps he'd resisted the only true alternative – a shame-faced return to Mother's spare room – out of a conviction that it would destroy him. But little was left to be destroyed. At least there he could recuperate, stop working nights, catch up on sleep. On so much sleep. He could change this debilitating pattern, rediscover his will, regain some enthusiasm. Yes, he saw it all in the fifth glass of whisky. Going home was not so bad. He wouldn't fool himself a moment longer: getting out was now simply his only chance of survival.

He'd phone his mother the following day, and then hand in his notice at Barrington House in the evening. Then get out. So easy it seemed, on that stool in the bar. The smile on his face felt strange. Stiff. These features had moved so little of late. He suspected the tiny muscles of his face had atrophied.

He stabbed out a cigarette in the ashtray and hastily

dropped his tobacco and lighter into the side pocket of his overcoat.

Outside, he experienced a sudden trepidation at the mere thought of returning to his room. He worried the familiar torpor would overwhelm him once he was back at the Green Man. That the same urgency for escape could be gone tomorrow afternoon when he woke after a long, dead sleep.

He had to act right now, tonight. Start packing. Anything. Already he sensed the aperture through which he must escape was closing. The rain, the blowing litter, the wet stones, the endless thoroughfare – these were all ropes intent on binding him with knots that his cold fumbling fingers could only paw at ineffectually.

Bowing his head, Seth pushed out at the wind. Huddled into himself, he made mental lists of tasks to be completed. At least he had some money in the bank. His wages were pitiful, but he'd stopped spending money on anything but food a long time ago. There was enough in his current account to get him out, back home, and to tide him over for a few months.

Perhaps, he thought later, had he been allowed to get back to his room at the Green Man without delay that night, all would have been well; he would have followed through with these plans and saved himself. And saved the others too.

But as he walked past the overflowing bags of soiled clothes and broken children's toys left outside a charity shop, his future was decided.

All of the motion and light in his mind was instantly obliterated.

For a moment he was not sure of anything – which way was up, which way down, which direction he was facing, where his arms and legs were. His entire body was weightless until his shoulder hit the window of the charity shop.

Inside the shop, unwanted teddy bears, a tiny porcelain teapot and a book about cats all shuddered on their shelves. He had been thrown against the window. When the cold glass slapped his face, the world and its dimensions reassembled around him.

Bent over, looking down, off-balance on unsteady legs, it was then he saw the shoes on the wet pavement. Three pairs of whitish trainers surrounding him.

Suddenly he was upright again, wheeling backwards on both feet, throwing his arms into the air, chin raised. Inside he was all white and jerky, but the left side of his head felt different: it was a gigantic numbness.

The cold was forgotten, the cyclone of mental listings vanished. His darting eyes tried to assess the situation and size up all those involved.

'Cunt,' a gingery mouth said from nearby.

'Come on. Fuckin' come on,' a dark face barked from under the peak of a baseball cap.

Their eyes were full of cruelty, and a strange anticipation too, as if they were impatient for a predictable reply. Both of the assailants were in their late teens. And Seth had seen the gingery youth before, slurping arrogantly from a bottle of Diamond White cider he later smashed outside the betting shop. The third one he couldn't see, but sensed him behind, standing too close.

There was a moment of silence – a suspension of everything – and then the world was a rustling of nylon sleeves as a salvo of punches from small hard fists came in at him.

The first blow hit his cheekbone but didn't hurt. He took the second punch against his forehead and the third impacted against the side of his neck. His head flicked back and forth, but the punches made no sound and there was no pain at first. It felt like he was being pushed by different hands while trying to move in a straight line. For some reason he tried to walk away as if nothing was happening. This made his assailants really angry.

More rustling, more prodding fists and kicking feet made all the strength drain out of Seth's arms and legs. He couldn't feel his hands or feet. He said 'Fuck off' in a weak voice without thinking. Warm air filled his body and he felt buoyant. He seemed to weigh nothing.

But inside his head something slapped around his skull like an animal trapped in a cave. It made him feel sick and so scared he would have done anything to become one of the unwanted teddy bears on the shelves of the charity shop, instead of this – a piece of meat to be kicked, punched and tenderized by the white trainers and red knuckles.

He couldn't speak. His eyes were flicking everywhere but not fixing on anything. Then he was yanked around by small iron fingers, and the knocking from side to side started again. The gingery kid in the white Tommy Hilfiger jacket was flailing his arms at Seth so fast it was as if he was afraid his target would disappear before he got his freckled knuckles into its face.

Twisting and ducking, Seth took most of the punches on his shoulders, the back of the head, against an elbow, and in the ribs. But now they began to hurt.

He jumped at a space between the flailing arms to get away, but a hand seized the collar of his overcoat and kept him upright so his face would remain exposed to the flurry of fists.

He made a sound like a crying baby. He tried to think what he might have done to make them so savage. Nothing could explain the urgency of their fists and feet. There just wasn't enough time for them to properly destroy another human being. Gravity slowed them down and infuriated them.

When a coal-black fist hit Seth's teeth, his head filled with cracking ice. Linen ripped inside his mouth. The same hand came in again, again, again. The smudgy, jerking world disintegrated into bright white motes, all falling downwards.

I'll die. They're not going to stop until I'm dead. Seth went cold. His eyes were full of water. There was something crackling and tingling inside his nose. A big loop of spit and blood came out of his lips, to be smashed flat against his cheek.

He thought of trying to jump away from the fists again, but the thought never became action. It was getting hard to think of anything.

'Cunt! Cunt! Cunt! Cunt!'

Their breathing became grunting. They were trying to punch and kick so fast they were getting tired and slow. In his dark upside-down world, lightning was flashing.

When Seth fell over, they stopped shouting 'Cunt!' But as he lay on the unforgiving pavement, he heard a whinny of excitement from one of them.

Another one hurt his foot with the first kick. The other two began a scuffling, kicking kind of dance, putting their toes into Seth's face, shoulders, back, thighs, stomach. It was the stomach they wanted most.

Seth tried to get to his knees. The panicked child in his mind was screaming now.

Was it never going to end? The kicking just went on and on. Both of his legs were dead from the thigh down and one arm had become useless. The pain in his ribs stopped him from moving. Had splintered bones speared his purple organs inside? He could see it all inside his shrinking mind.

So that's it, a tiny voice said inside the white sphere in the middle of the darkness, where all of him had withdrawn. Soon, it'll just all be black. This is how it ends. And then, close by, beyond the swollen, hot darkness of clenched eyelids and hands over face, he heard a bus shudder and wheeze to a stop. Feet then slapped down to the pavement from the platform.

Saviours were coming to drag these hyenas off, to call the police and an ambulance, to make him comfortable on the ground with a jacket under his head. Warm hope expanded the tiny sphere of consciousness inside his skull. He almost cried out with relief. But then he heard the bus drive off, and the stamping resumed.

All that kicking in soft training shoes was hurting their toes. It was much better to stamp a cushioned sole down onto a body. So they smashed him flat. Bent his arms and legs. Compacted an ear into his head and made it hot and whistley. Ripped hair out from the root with rubbery training shoe traction that made a sticky-tape sound; these soles were designed to grip in all weather conditions.

Someone walked past, stopped, and then sang, 'Easy, easy,

easy,' in a lazy though joyous voice. The stampers stamped. The final kicks hurt the most; the second to last one pushed his belly into his throat and made his eyes pop.

When they were finished, worn out, limping from kicking a body so hard, they swaggered away, tired, euphoric, and fulfilled.

It was too hard for his mind to register all of the parts of his body that were damaged, so it flooded the whole of him with a fluid warmth. And, impossibly, he stood up with no trouble at all from broken bones. He looked down at his body. Not too bad, he thought. Dirty and wet from being kicked around the pavement, but no blood or meat on the bone. There seemed only to be footprints from the stamping, criss-cross brandings from the soles of their footwear. He felt almost disappointed that he had nothing to show for his labours; nothing to show the jury. But when Seth decided to walk, the idea never got past his hips. And all the stabbing hell of bodily pain rushed into the marrow of his bones.

He fell down.

Then dragged his broken-doll body into a shop doorway.

Too scared to move in case the white heat of pain grew any worse, he lost track of time, slumped in the porch of the charity shop. He wanted to puke and weep at the same time. He was waiting for the ambulance, the police. They must have been called. So many people were on that bus. Scores of feet had walked past since he'd been on the ground, since those dirty feet had finished their kicking and stamping.

A little rocking back and forth seemed to ease the pain for a while, until it made things worse. There was no way to sit or lie down without the agony swelling up like a gigantic wave. The skin of his face was hot and tender and tight because of the huge lumps growing out of his head – lumps that were hard like bone. To breathe he sucked in shallow whispers of air because his ribs felt as though they had been smashed like old wooden banisters and the splinters had gone everywhere. His left hand was numb and his right knee had grown as big as a deformed vegetable made out of salty, fibrous flesh. That leg could not be bent, and even the weight of his jeans and the shoe on that foot hurt it terribly; it might never bend again. The right side of his neck was raw and sticky.

People continued to walk past in the rain. They sped up when near him. Twice he called out for help. Two girls looked at him, but walked on, their pace quickening after they had seen his ruined face. Could they see the big black crack in his skull? It was there, he could feel it. All of his soft pink-grey brain was pushing at it, trying to get out and into the air after decades caged inside its watery prison. The stamping feet had tried to free that tortured organ. He wanted to get to a hospital and be injected with morphine.

His breathing sped up at one point and he passed out, then woke up dizzy and was sick down his coat. When the choking terror passed, he rose to his good knee. Using his numb hand and letting the uninjured knee take the weight, he pushed himself up against the glass door. It was about half a mile to the Green Man. It could take all night, and he was sure he could slip into a coma at any time. He would call for help from his room if he could make it that far.

He briefly closed his eyes to recover from the exertion of standing, but was made quickly alert again by the sound of feet coming from the left. A burly shape staggered up to him and thrust out a hand. Seth flinched and jumped back at the same time, crashing against the door of the charity shop.

'Yer man down there is too fine to drink wi' the likes of you and me. But I'll tell you something. And I'll tell you for nothing . . .' The tramp's face was a mess of scar tissue and broken veins. Each eye looked in a different direction. His smell was choking; alcohol, scrotal rot, unfathomable layers of sweat in second-hand wool. A black can was shoved under Seth's nose. He moved his head to one side and breathed out through the side of his mouth.

The tramp was standing too close, leaning in, spitting on his face as he talked about 'yer man'. Who was yer man? Seth was confused. The soiled arm of the tramp went around Seth's neck. There was a sleeve patterned with grey and red diamonds, brown and unravelling at the wrist. The pain of that dreadful wool on his neck made him cry out. 'I've been attacked. I've been fucking attacked. Don't touch me. Don't hold my neck.'

But the tramp wasn't listening; he just wanted to talk about 'yer man' and to spray his rotten breath all over Seth's bleeding face.

Dragging his straight leg behind him, his head bowed in concentration, Seth lurched away from the vagrant and began the hardest and most exhausting journey of his life, where every crack in the paving stones or slight incline in the road registered in every damaged nerve and made his skin repeatedly coat itself in cold sweat. The tramp, who had mistaken Seth for one of his own, followed him home, raving about 'yer man'.

It was as if none of these events had been random. As if

there was nothing coincidental or accidental about his fate that night; as if this was all the deliberate work of something in the city, or of the city itself. Whatever it was, this malign intelligence, it wanted him humiliated and reduced for daring to forsake it. It had been watching him. It knew he had few defences and claimed him for its own.

He began to sob. The tramp swung his arm around Seth's swollen neck again and nearly pulled him down. He came close to passing out from the pain. No amount of punishment would ever be enough. To be kicked and stamped close to death was not enough for one night. He had to be dirtied as well. Assaulted by a madman with sweat that smelled of vomit. The night and its torments must now stretch forever because he had dared to defy the will of the city. Had planned to reject it, to reject the role and the misery it had bequeathed him.

'I'll fucking break every stone in two,' he whispered to the damaged man in the rotten jumper. 'I'll bring the whole thing to its knees, I swear by almighty god. Then I'll turn the fucking heap to rubble.'

The tramp laughed and offered him the black can. Seth had made contact. Broken through. Their eyes were the same. They spoke the same language now and shared the same secrets about the city.

This is what you get when you call 999 and asked for the police. There had been a long wait for someone to pick up the phone. Then a recorded message about all the operators being busy. Seth's chest grew tight with an indigestion of frustration. The message was always clear: Don't let anything go wrong or happen to you because there is no help, only the promise, the illusion of service. But surely this wasn't the case with the police as well?

Seth hung up. Slammed the handset onto the receiver so hard the entire phone crashed down the side of the bookcase and bounced onto the floor.

Dumbfounded, bent over in pain, he rocked back and forth, cradling his ribs and a swollen hand. There were bitter tears until the weeping hurt and had to be stopped. Weeping uses the stomach muscles, the lungs, the throat, the face, even the spine: he never realized this until they were all too damaged to squeeze out the tears. His assailants had even denied him grief. He just had to take it, to be in pain, to not complain, to allow their empowerment.

Loose bleeding teeth filled his slack mouth. Blood bubbled over his lips. Fantasies were entertained. Red, wet ones in which the gingery weasel died slowly beneath Seth's skull face; it was the last thing he would see, had any right to see. And a butchering for the black one, who held the collar of Seth's coat so fists could break his teeth; equal opportunities for all the swaggering dog boys.

First he tried lying on the bed, but the pillows and mattress and bed linen felt like rope burns. Then he curled up against the radiator, but the floor was merciless. A chair offered no relief and standing up was agony. He crunched on handfuls of paracetamol, but they were like tiny firefighters, uselessly directing thin streams of water from the ground up and into roaring walls of flame that turned both solid and liquid into a gas of pain.

He could only comfort himself with visions of the next confrontation, after he had hunted them down. He must refuse to let time and the inevitable healing process soften

his murderous resolve. He could not allow his mind to protect itself by repressing their faces. The dog faces. The animal
yellow eyes.

Seth clawed around the dry carpet for paper and a pencil.
One of his eyes was filling with smoke and jelly. He found
it difficult to see the lines, the definition. The lights were too
dim. And the sketch pad was too pitiful a canvas on which
to placate his desire to capture these faces that kept rearing
up in his mind; the universal faces of ignorance and cruelty.

He could settle for nothing less than a vast depiction of
this parasite corrupting the flesh of mankind: the antithesis
of reason and talent and progress. Such a work would need
long, bold, primitive strokes; an absence of subtlety. Blue fists.
Tommy Hilfiger. Raw meat. Gucci. Black gums. Stone Island.
Yellow eyes. Rockport.

He wanted to roar like a lion on a cement floor. And
bellow like a polar bear with yellow fur worn down to pink
skin against the tiles of an enclosure in a zoo. The disgust
must come. Let it drip down the walls. Scorch the ceiling
black with hatred. Liberate rage. Forgiveness is overrated.
Compassion is dead.

Seth opened the paint tins and went at the walls with wet
hands.

SEVENTEEN

Miles Butler smiled. 'But what I can't figure out is why you'd have any interest in Hessen.' In his intelligent eyes Apryl glimpsed mischief. Since they'd met at seven for dinner in Covent Garden, she hadn't stopped laughing. He was one of those rare men who won you over by being modest to an extreme degree and who seemed never likely to take himself too seriously, while being accomplished at the same time. An underplayer, but a player all the same.

His face was thoroughly lived-in, but still handsome, distinguished. Even the lines around his blue eyes were sexy. And Apryl had fallen in love with his vintage hairstyle, reminiscent of an army officer in the Second World War: grey now, but shiny and neat and graded up the sides. His clothes looked classic too: high-waisted trousers worn with suspenders that she noted when he took his jacket off and draped it across the back of his chair. The only thing she would have added to his wingtip shoes, his white shirt with cufflinks and his retro silk tie was a trilby hat. They complemented each other in a way she couldn't have anticipated: she'd worn one of her great-aunt's exquisite woollen suits, seamed nylons that were called *Cocktail Hour*, and Cuban-heeled shoes with a little bow over the toe strap.

'And anyway, what's so weird about me being interested in art? Do I look like a schmuck?'

Miles laughed and shook his head. 'No. But you're, well, not like any other Hessen enthusiast I've ever met. You're too attractive for one thing, Apryl. And far too stylish to be messing around with the *Puppet Triptych*. Let alone *Studies of the Lame*.'

'Should I be in Harvey Nicks trying on Jimmy Choo shoes instead? Or chasing Mr Big around an office?'

'Absolutely. Why spend so much of your vacation investigating an obscure European artist? And not a very wholesome one at that.' Miles might have been flirting, but he wasn't dismissive of her. She could tell he was genuinely intrigued by her reasons for calling him and enquiring about Hessen. 'You are a mysterious girl. Quite the enigma.'

She laughed, and drank from her wine glass to hide the warmth of the blush suffusing her entire body. Why hadn't she thought of dating older guys before? 'Well there might be a family connection.'

'Yes, you mentioned that on the phone. I'm all ears.' He took a mouthful of his linguine vongole.

'My great-aunt Lillian lived in the same apartment building. Barrington House. And she passed recently.'

'I am sorry.'

'It's OK. I never knew her. But she left the apartment to my mom. And because she's terrified of flying I came over to sort out the estate.'

'In return for half the spoils.'

'I've already earned it. You should see the place.' She thought of making light of the mess, but levity seemed inappropriate;

the apartment just wasn't something she could laugh about. 'She writes about him in her diaries.'

'You're having me on.'

Apryl shook her head, relishing his interest, the pause of fork from plate to mouth. 'And they never got on. But the thing is, Lillian, my great-aunt, wasn't well. You know? She was really disturbed, and she kind of blames Hessen for it, so I just had to find out more about him. And I found this website and read your book. And . . .'

'Now you're smitten.'

'Not exactly. I find his pictures like really creepy, but . . . this whole mystery about him and his connection to my great-aunt, it's quite a kick. I never guessed I'd be into all of this, but I have to know what happened to Lillian and Reginald in that building. What he really did to them. Because he did something. And the more I find out about him and his art and the people that knew him, the more I just know there's something not right. Something terribly wrong, in fact. My great-aunt may have been crazy, but she wasn't making it all up. I'm convinced about that now. But what was he doing to her, and how did he do it?'

She then bit down on mentioning her own experiences with unexplained phenomena inside the apartment. He'd think her mad.

Miles nodded, and began to refill her glass. 'Did you know that everyone who was at all close to him had a personality disorder? They all died young or ended up in institutions. He attracted the disturbed, the damaged and the eccentric. Misfits and outsiders all of them. People who couldn't function in the world they were born into. Individuals who saw things. Other things. And not necessarily what everyone else was able to see. They orbited him. But I think you are suggesting that he made your great-aunt that way. Which is a novel perspective. So maybe it was his effect on others that explains their behaviour. An idea I never considered.'

Apryl's glass was full. He rotated the bottle to avoid a dribble. He was trying to get her drunk. To remove the last vestiges of her nervous formality. She decided she didn't mind at all. It was good to unravel a little. London was a bewildering place, but just when the city had begun to make her feel really low, it suddenly had this romantic side too. It had been ages since she'd made a real effort and dressed up for a date. And tonight, it was the sense of infinite opportunities in the city that seduced her. How could you ever get to the end of such a place? Miles filled his own glass.

Apryl took a sip of her wine, narrowing her eyes over the rim. 'You know so much about him. But can you respect a man who was so fucked up? Why *you* are into him is more interesting to me right now.'

Miles smiled. 'I like the underdogs in the art world. And he was interesting. Fascinating, in fact. He felt compelled to try and complete an artistic vision outside the values and tastes of his own time. I'm impressed by that. It must have taken courage. Great courage to go where he went.'

'To draw corpses? And skinned animals? And those nasty puppets? A fairly bleak world view, isn't it?'

'It is. But then his world changed so much, from the end of the nineteenth century onwards. Imagine what Darwin and Freud did to religious belief. Not to mention the horrors of the First World War. Mechanized slaughter. And industrialization. The rise of Marxism. The beginnings of Fascism. The great war of ideology brewing. The flux was represented in so many ways. Fractious, discordant, chaotic ways. Modernism, if you like. And he took his place there, but his reputation could only be posthumous. I think he knew it all along. But he wasn't interested in acclaim. He never cultivated peers or curried influence. He did it for its own sake. And for himself. Don't you find that incredible? Especially these days? To dedicate your life to one vision with no thought of reward?'

Apryl smiled. 'Sorry, I was only playing devil's advocate. It's a bad habit.'

He winked at her. 'It is. Life could have been very comfortable for Hessen. Privately wealthy ... educated at the Slade ... handsome ... erudite ... cultured ... talented. Come to think of it, he was a bit like me.' He said this with a straight face until she began to laugh.

He offered her the basket of bread. 'He had access to the great minds and talents of his age. Not to mention the queue of eligible connected beauties who would have fawned over him. But he made decisions guaranteed to make life difficult for himself. Incredibly difficult. He looked for and drew death, constantly. The moment of death in hospitals and the moment after death in the morgues and operating theatres. He obsessed over medical curiosities. Deformity. Disfigurement. He spent his best years trying to understand death and the idea of being trapped. By disability, and by social immobility. Wallowed in it. Spent his weekends bribing undertakers in funeral homes, his days sketching skinned sheep and offal in the abattoirs of the East End. Or drawing the deformed limbs and faces of the poor wretches who suffered every conceivable disease and incapacity.'

'Must have been a barrel of laughs.'

'Precisely. And what about his evenings when he was a younger man? No parties for Felix. Instead, he investigated every mystic, seer, and black magic practitioner in town, or attended séances held in front rooms and parlours. There is no evidence of him ever relaxing. Or being in love. He never seemed to do a single thing not directly connected to his vision. I know of no other artist so determined. To spend a decade trying to perfect line and perspective, and then to launch into distortion, which he claimed was the only true vision. A recreation of the Vortex. The absolute epitome of wonder and terror and awe. A place after this world, accessed only by madness, by dream, by the deep subconscious, and by death itself.'

'You really think he was that good?'

'Hard to say. Because what of that did we see? What survived? Those terrible final drawings of the human and the animal, imprisoned in those unformed landscapes. You see, I think Hessen is more interesting from the perspective of what he was trying to achieve. The drawings are only studies. Initial plans for the paintings no one has ever found. And to also go public in support of fascism with his Vortex paper – how could I not be fascinated by the guy?'

Apryl smiled. 'I'm convinced. What was his name again?'

'Don't make me come over there.' He raised one eyebrow and looked at her in such a way that she felt part of herself melt.

'I looked on Amazon and there's only your book.' She didn't mention the dozen bad reviews written by members of the Friends of Felix Hessen.

'In this country, we're very bad at looking after our artistic heritage. America is the place to find anything of value about

British painting or poetry in the twentieth century. Ironic, I know, but there's nothing left of him here. Though I believe there was very little to begin with. Hessen's contribution to modernism is hard to gauge. That's the problem. The myths that surround him are far greater than any actual evidence of his ability or influence. Besides the drawings there's nothing left. Had he painted it would have been different. But sketches and chalks are not enough. Some of them are extraordinary, I know, and perhaps hint at a formidable vision. But I doubt it was ever realized. No one ever saw a single painting apart from a few acquaintances. And one must, surely, cast some doubt over the reliability of their testimony. I mean, they all saw something different.'

Miles took a long draught of his wine and she liked the way his face flushed with excitement as he talked. And that voice. She didn't want to interrupt his flow. He could have been reading from the back of a detergent box for all she cared. She could listen to that voice all night.

'But he was ahead of his time. He potentially created a new visual language, steeped in an anti-aesthetic, and in philosophy and radical politics. Outside vorticism, futurism, cubism, surrealism, he operated alone, and followed his own creative discourse from an early age. You could even call him an occult philosopher. Misunderstood in his own day and virtually ignored ever since. The scourge of middle-English conservatism and safe Bohemia. A painter who saw art as the worship of something supernatural. And as the means of finding it. What's more startling is that no one wrote of him before me.'

That mention of the supernatural made her feel suddenly uncomfortable. It nearly spoiled her mood. 'Do you think . . .'

'What?'

'That he had powers or something?'

'Powers?'

'I know it sounds freaky, but my great-aunt was really scared of him.'

'Well, he was steeped in occult ritual. Was probably tutored by Crowley, the Great Beast 666, in the most advanced summoning rituals. Who knows what Felix could have suggested to the impressionable.'

'But what if it wasn't all suggestion?'

Miles laughed and tore a bread roll apart with his fingers. 'You're pulling my leg again.'

'I guess.' It was a foolish question and one she immediately regretted having asked. All around her people were eating and talking under bright lights in a modern restaurant. Outside, taxis were trundling past and people were lining up to enter an opera house. This was a world of cell phones and credit cards. There were no ghosts. Maybe she was starting to lose the plot by filling her head with so much of Hessen's and Lillian's madness.

'And the mysticism, of course, is not in his favour as far as the critics are concerned,' Miles continued. 'In fact, all the informed responses from art historians and curators who were familiar with Hessen were the same when I was researching the book. They all thought him absurd, and a minnow in comparison to his contemporaries.'

'I guess you can believe anything you put your mind to,' she said quietly.

Miles didn't hear her but was looking intently into his wine glass at the syrupy crimson surface. She took a sip from her own glass. 'Do you really think he painted anything?'

'I don't doubt he painted something. But I suspect he destroyed it when it fell so short of his ambition. Which was considerable. He was hard on himself. Set himself unfeasible expectations. Either that, or prison ruined him.'

'I wonder about it. You know, whether he did produce paintings, and if people really saw them. Like my great-aunt and uncle.'

'You think there is some dusty cache of crates filled with his work? Some have suggested he produced paintings more radical than any other modernist, or than any artist since his time. Now that would be nice. But where are they?'

'You're taking the piss.' She liked the expression, had picked it up since arriving in England.

'No. I'm not. I'm merely echoing my own disappointment at finding nothing. And you know I looked hard. I contacted the estate, distant relatives,. and the children of anyone who ever mentioned him. Not to mention the family of the collector who acquired the sketches prior to Hessen's imprisonment. Hessen gave them away. They had served their purpose. But I didn't find one genuine lead to provide reliable evidence that he produced a painting.'

'But what about after the war? Did you find out anything about him then?'

'Barely ventured beyond the front door of his flat. Became a recluse. He never had more than a small crowd of acquaintances, and they were mostly gone before the forties. And there's no evidence of any correspondence after his release from Brixton prison. So even if he painted something, who would have seen it? I once wondered if he might have given away any paintings he produced before he disappeared, perhaps to a private collector. But unless that individual comes forward, or their descendants, it's gone. It's tragic. I do believe he was on the verge of painting something incredible, but for some reason he either never began it or he destroyed it. I find the latter the more likely course of action. For all of his determination and grit, he was very unstable.'

'I still wonder.'

'I did too.'

'And I'd still like to show you my great-aunt's journals. Just to see what you think. You'd have more idea what to make of them than me.'

Miles smiled. 'Apryl, I'd love to. I'm sorry, I suspect I've been an awful bore.'

'Not at all. I'm kinda reaching saturation point with Hessen though. It was never supposed to be about him, but about my Lillian. I wondered if I could learn anything about her by finding out about him. I'll go to that Friends of Felix Hessen meeting. And there's a couple of people I'd like to talk to in the building, but then I'm done with him. For good. In case I end up like Lillian.'

He frowned at her, then raised an eyebrow. 'Well, I know what you're saying, but . . .'

'What?'

'But I have a little suspicion about you. Despite your physical charms and the doors they must sweep aside, Apryl, I suspect you're an outsider like Hessen, and are secretly drawn to his mystique.'

She blushed. The thought of him making a pass suddenly made her afraid but also thrilled. 'Maybe I am an outsider, but I'm no fan of Felix Hessen. And I'm not a mystical kinda girl. Anyone connected to him is crazy.'

'Me included?'

'Particularly you.'

They both laughed at exactly the same time.

'I wonder what happened to him,' Apryl mused. 'He's supposed to have disappeared, but Lillian's journals give the impression that he never left. It's weird.'

'Well, everyone loves a good mystery. And to vanish without trace is a trite legacy, but a legacy all the same, and one that might amplify a limited reputation and not just keep it alive, but give it the potential to grow into something it never was in the first place. Especially irresistible to those of a mystical bent – vanishing along with his so-called masterpieces.'

'The Friends of Felix Hessen disagree with you.'

'I never expected too much from them. They're enthusiastic enough for amateurs, but not an academic organization. More of an occult outfit. It's the ritualistic side of Hessen they're obsessed with. Though they do make claims of being rigorously scholarly, I seem to remember. In their publications and so forth. Bit of a weird bunch. You'll probably meet a few oddballs if you go to the lecture. I know I did. We used to get petitions from them to view our archive at the Tate. They sent them to all the galleries. They were after the secret cache of his forbidden illustrations. Stuff we've apparently suppressed for being sympathetic to the Nazis or some such nonsense. But despite it all, I do have a soft spot for the gifted amateur.' He laughed. 'And who knows, old Felix may have been pleased to have been the inspiration for a cult convinced of his importance who periodically harass the major art galleries. And maybe, after all is said and done, it's the likes of the Friends of Felix Hessen who have the right idea. Perhaps the occult route and the interpretation of dreams is the only true method available to understand him.'

'You don't believe that?'

'No, you're right, I don't. But I did stop looking. And not only because I drew such an almighty blank.' He sat back in his chair, dropped his napkin on the table and sighed. 'And I don't have much interest in him any more either. Lost my appetite a bit.'

'Why?'

Miles shrugged. 'He got under my skin.'

Apryl laughed.

'No, I mean it. You look at his work for too long and you might feel the same way. It even gave me nightmares. It's very strange. I felt he was getting closer to me, but I was getting nowhere near him. What he was all about, I didn't like it. And I feel much better since I finished the book. To be honest, I shan't be upset when it's out of print. I don't like being reminded of it. The period in which it was written . . . it was a difficult time for me, personally. There were other things on my mind, but his art didn't help. It started to change the way I thought. I became something of a nihilist. Because that's what Hessen was. He couldn't see anything but the end of life. Misery. The essential loneliness of death. And his predictions of what came after were equally grim. I'm not actually a masochist, Apryl.'

Apryl thought about what Miles had said. It made sense. After looking at Hessen's sketches and reading about him for any length of time, she'd also felt a need to reintegrate herself into normal life. To go to a movie, to eat in a restaurant, to walk amongst other people. His vision was so oppressive. So consuming. So crazy. It managed to suck her inside herself and make her morbidly introspective.

'It's a shame you don't live in London,' Miles said, after a final gulp of wine. The bottle was empty. They both had purple mouths.

'Why?' she asked softly, deliberately lowering her eyelids. It had been so long since she'd had an opportunity to be provocative. It felt good.

'Because I'd like to see more of you. We could join the Friends of Felix Hessen together. Go on dates to their meetings. It would be so romantic.'

Apryl giggled. She wouldn't mind staying on in London for longer if hanging out with Miles was on the cards. At last she'd met someone sane and gregarious, and sexy in that British way. And someone who could help her understand the maniac who'd had such an impact on her distant family. She couldn't help feeling seduced by his quiet confidence, his dry humour, that deep voice and the wicked smile in his eyes. All of these things were ganging up on her now. Making her feel wanton. She'd never lacked attention or been accustomed to rejection from men, but some guys made more of an impact. Or did she just have a crush on him?

'What is it?' asked Miles. 'You have a very strange look in your eyes.'

'I'm just wondering whether I have a crush on you.'

Miles swallowed and used his napkin to dab at his forehead. 'Better ask the waiter for some smelling salts.'

'Is there a Mrs Butler?'

'Not any more. I wasn't sure I wanted to be a father. I wasn't sure I wanted to be a lot of things she wanted me to be.'

'Girlfriend?'

'Nothing serious.'

'Lying bastard.'

Miles raised his hands. 'It's early days. That's the truth of the matter. But if she knew we were having this conversation, she'd be furious. And hurt. And I'd feel like a shit. Which I'm not fond of. My head's complicated enough.'

'But I'm sure you could get over it.'

'With you as an incentive, I'd say I could get over most things.' Just for a moment, as he spoke, the smile slipped from his face and Apryl detected a brief look of longing. It stopped her breath. And she felt its impact between her legs.

So he did like her. And maybe more than she suspected. But why did everything have to be so complicated? That's the way it was once you were approaching thirty and still a single girl. Particularly as the older, charismatic men like Miles were invariably married. She'd read about women who had affairs with them. These guys were always married to someone they underestimated and took for granted, but for whom they rediscovered an unbreakable attachment when it was time to make a big decision. Handle with care.

'That's sweet of you to say,' she said, a little too bitterly for her own taste.

'It's the truth. You are lovely, Apryl. Why wouldn't I be interested? You're a beautiful young woman. A bright one too. And a little crazy in a nice way. Irresistible, in fact.' The smiling eyes were back.

Her composure regained, Apryl detected a reticence in him about taking a chance with his emotions. Something else they had in common. If they never saw each other again, they'd think about each other.

'It must be the wine. Or I'm a slut. But I came very close to asking if you wanted to come see my great-aunt's apartment.'

'Not exactly conducive to passion.'

'You're not wrong on that account. Unless it was something really kinky, like S and M.'

'Get your coat. You've pulled.'

Apryl giggled, but couldn't stop feeling churlish with disappointment. 'Your girlfriend wouldn't thank me for keeping you out late.'

'Stop it. Now you're misbehaving.' But even being told off by him was not without its appeal. 'Seriously, though, I'd love to see inside Barrington House. I wonder if it's changed much since Hessen lived there.'

'I don't think so. It's like totally retro. And Lillian's apartment hasn't had a lick of paint since the forties.'

'This diary, too, I'd love to see it.'

'Her journals? Sure, you can borrow them. The ones that are legible. The later ones are just unreadable. But you have to be careful with them – I want to take them back home with me. We're not going to have much else of Lillian left when the place is sold. Just some photos and her journals.'

'How many of them are there?'

'There's a stack of them. Twenty.'

'Really?'

'They're all about your beloved Felix.'

He looked at her with such intensity, his face was almost stern. 'All joking aside, are they really about Hessen?'

She nodded. 'If you'd been listening earlier you'd have realized just how much. But you have to read them yourself. I couldn't even begin to describe what they're like. They're frightening. And they're the main reason I'm staying in a hotel from now on.'

*

'Well, you weren't exaggerating,' Miles said, looking around the hallway. 'This is incredible.'

'Isn't it? But you should have seen it before. I've cleared most of the junk away. Lillian never threw anything out. There were London telephone directories here from the fifties.'

'Some of it could have been valuable.'

'I'm not an idiot, Miles. The dealers bought anything of value.'

'Ouch.'

'And luckily for me, she also kept her clothes. This belonged to her.' She twirled around to show off her suit, which she felt he hadn't paid enough attention to.

'I thought it had the look of authenticity about it,' he said, studying the thin seams on the back of her calves.

'And the smell too, unfortunately. I'll have to mask them with perfume until I get them all dry-cleaned.'

'It really suits you.'

'Thanks.'

'I mean, it *really* suits you.'

She pulled a Betty Boop pose and blew him a kiss. His eyes darkened. With desire, if she wasn't mistaken. She turned and teetered deeper into the apartment, and Miles followed.

'Your great-aunt had problems?' he said, as if to clear the air of the erotic awkwardness that seemed to keep surfacing.

'She wasn't very well. But she was ... haunted. By the past I think. I don't think she ever got over her husband's death. She didn't have any friends. Just rattled around here on her own, planning to escape from the city. She thought Hessen had trapped her inside here.' Apryl wanted to mention

Lillian's suggestions about 'the burning' of something – possibly Hessen's work – and the torments Lillian imagined the artist had inflicted on her and Reginald, but she couldn't bring herself to do so. She wanted Miles to like her and not think her flaky with any talk of evil spirits or ghosts or anything kooky like that. She'd let him read the journals and make up his own mind.

In the living room he looked through the packing crate filled with the photographs she had taken down from the wall. 'Sad, isn't it?' he said quietly, while holding a picture of Lillian and Reginald standing in a sunny garden somewhere. And she knew exactly what he meant. For this to be the end of you; a box full of photographs in the hands of people who never even knew you.

Already the place was destroying her mood. Tonight with Miles was the best she'd felt since she'd arrived. 'Come on, I'll show you the rooms and then you can see me into a cab. I want to get out of here. I've spent way too much time here already. I want to have a bit of fun now before I go back to the States.'

Miles looked around the stained walls. 'It's no place for a wee young thing. So damn gloomy, but affecting in a way, too.'

'You should try spending a night here.'

'Is that an invitation?'

'You're welcome to on your own. I'm not sleeping here again before it's sold. I told you, it gives me the creeps.'

'But your great-aunt lived here. You're wearing her clothes and you seem to think the world of her.'

'I know. And I do. But it's the place itself. The whole building, if I'm honest. It's just not right.'

Miles frowned over a smile. 'Really, what makes you say that? It's just old. I thought you liked old.'

She shook her head. 'No. It's not even the age of the place or that the apartment's never been looked after. It's not that at all. It's the actual place. The building. I know this sounds crazy, but it changed everything for Lillian. And I think it played a part in whatever happened to Reginald. The place is all wrong. It's bad. You spend enough time here and you'd feel it too.'

Miles frowned at her.

'You think I'm being silly. But read a few of the journals and you might see what I'm talking about. This place is all about madness and nightmares. It's a sick building, Miles. Very sick, like Hessen.'

In the bedroom, while she rummaged in the dresser for the journals, Miles said, 'Why is the mirror turned around? And is that a painting? May I see?'

'Oh yes, that's my great-aunt and uncle. I found it in the basement. I brought the mirror up so I could try on her clothes, but . . .'

'What? It's a beauty.'

'It is. But I don't know. It just made me feel a bit freaked out.'

Miles began to laugh but then stopped when he saw her face. 'I'm sorry. I'm not making fun of you. This place *is* kind of creepy. It could do with some new lighting.'

'This is as good as it gets. The walls and floor just seem to swallow it up.' The room wasn't at all cold, but she shivered as she spoke.

He wrapped an arm round her and looked down into her eyes. 'You want to get out of here.' She nodded. 'Thank you for these.' He held up one of the journals she had given him. 'I can't believe I'm about to read something on Hessen from someone who actually knew him after the war. This is quite a find.'

'She was obsessed with him. And I warn you, they are really weird. Don't read them before you go to bed.'

'I promise. And maybe I can help you find out what was going on here.'

She nodded. 'I'd like that.' Impulsively, she raised herself to her tiptoes and kissed him. When she drew away he looked surprised. She was about to apologize, but Miles leant down and drew her into a longer and deeper kiss.

EIGHTEEN

At 3 a.m. Seth let himself into apartment sixteen. And until twenty past the hour, stood still.

The moment he flicked the lights on, shards of a recent nightmare fell out of his memory: the black and white marble tiles, the long reddish walls of the hallway, the ancient doors, the large rectangular paintings arranged in perfect symmetry, and all lit up by the dirty light struggling to escape from the discoloured glass of the shades. Yes, he had been here before. It was like a prolonged sense of déjà vu and it defied all the rules in life he'd taken for granted.

But one significant detail was different. In the dream, the paintings had been uncovered. Now, they were concealed by long sheets of aged cloth. Seth closed the front door behind him. Wincing, he dropped the steel key ring from his damaged hand into the pocket of his trousers.

Something had drawn his attention to this place. Something that moved within as he passed the front door. Something that had called out to him through the house phone and implanted visions in his sleeping mind. Something that had followed him home.

His troubles had intensified right after the first disturbance in this flat. What he had put down to depression and sleep deprivation and isolation could be attributed to this place. He felt it.

Impossible, but confirmed. Right here and right now.

And it was inevitable he would come in here. He had been summoned.

He shuddered. It felt like shock, seeing this. But the circling of his frantic thoughts ceased. For the first time in so long, his mind was clear of everything but a terror that escalated into awe. A feeling so acute he could barely draw breath.

Into the hallway he walked slowly, on unsteady feet, unable to postpone any longer this rendezvous with a place that had been empty for half a century.

All of the interior doors off the hallway were closed, and he recoiled at the thought of opening the middle door on the left-hand side, the door leading into the place where the definition of walls, floor and ceiling had been worn away by a freezing infinity of darkness, where things he had mistaken for paintings suddenly moved. At first around him, and then all over him. The sensation had come out of the dream with him, still clinging.

Pausing by the first painting in the hallway, Seth willed himself to lift the dusty muslin from the picture frame. It was the size of a large window. With trembling fingers he unhooked the fabric from the bottom corner of the heavy frame. He tried to raise it slowly. But as he disturbed the bottom of the sheet, so loosely wrapped about the frame, it dropped with a heavy sweep and landed on the floor with a *whump*.

Like a blow to the gut, the impact of the thing depicted in oil paint hit him immediately. This shock swiftly turned into nausea and disorientation, as if the contorted thing in the suit and tie was transmitting its torment directly into his own body.

Seth staggered backwards, unable to take his eyes from the painting, or to even blink. What was it? This thing torn apart, with a face wiped away by a sweep of whitish pain? And yet he instinctively understood the smouldering angst of its exposed entrails. At once he felt an involvement with the figure's violent demise, its loss of itself, its disintegration.

It was not a depiction of anything human or animal. But it suggested both. There were elements in it he could distinguish – the open howling mouth; teeth covered in a film of blood; an oversized tongue flapping; the suggestion of a throat twisted in a choke; an eye, or something that resembled an eye, only positioned on the wrong part of the blurred head, wide open and so full of its own capacity for terror and torment that Seth could not meet it with his own stare. He wanted it covered again, that blood-filled eye, that scarlet pupil, engorged and ready to burst. It looked so real, despite its distortion in the swirl of a missing face.

Whoever the figure had once been was now destroyed. Remnants of its suit and tie were still in place, in some dreadful parody of formality, but the limbs had gone. Ragged stumps mingled with the ochre aura that seemed to sanctify its mutilation.

These were the throes of death. But suspended in this terrible black space for all eternity. Not life, but an animation of sorts. A motion after death, repeated to infinity. He understood the message immediately.

Seth turned his back on the tortured statement, the wet meat encased in fabric. But he experienced a kind of euphoria, an awe at the hand that had managed to capture the very height of terror and obliteration. He thought of his own sketches, littered about the crusted carpet of his room at the Green Man. Remembered the hooded figure in his dream, wandering through a landscape of dog-shit grass and pissed-on concrete, who whispered mad child logic about getting stuck in things, in places, after death. Trapped for a very long time. Until the darkness came. Was this the darkness?

The next painting, stretching six feet high and at least four wide, impacted against his excited mind in the same way that being drenched by a thrown pail of freezing water shatters comprehension and creates disorientation. It immobilized everything inside him except the electricity of terror. And that was its whole purpose: to be something only the insane would look upon and be able to bear.

And after he gathered his breath, his balance, his shaky sense of place and self, he noticed the background in which the figure was suspended. This performance of violence and fragmentation was nothing without the depths behind it. Baboon-snouted and eyeless, but horribly twisted in the vestment of a floral housecoat, bloodied and still moist, the figure hung upon complete darkness. A total absence that still managed to transmit the cold of deep space and the ungraspable length and breadth of forever. It was the most marvellous use of impasto, he thought, ridiculously, while wanting to laugh hysterically before the dripping blasphemy. A background surface that pushed its subject out as if it were about to drop at his feet, where it would howl and thrash its broken claws in an agony that had continued for so long it made a century seem barely a beginning.

Yes, he knew at once he was catching glimpses of things that had risen to the surface of an endless freezing darkness. An eternity where terrible things were deposited, but would flood upward towards a pinpoint of light whenever an aperture was made. As it had been in here. This place no one could live in. Where no one was supposed to be. But someone had been in here to depict these things.

Seth staggered drunkenly from frame to frame and hauled the coverings down. He let them slide off images that struck him so mute he couldn't manage a scream. Nothing but an occasional babyish mewl in the face of things skipping on their animal bones, or blinded by stitched-up flaps, spitting like dying cats with black gums and needle teeth, kicking like the hanged in black-and-white newsreels, with limbs knotted around themselves and head shapes turned to roars, flayed like lambs, or as pink as the dead young of mice.

And all the deformity and distortion he glimpsed, he knew himself capable of recreating. Depictions of the potential inside himself hung all about this reddish corridor, like gleaming cadavers in a butcher's cold room. Yellow fat, spiky bone, slick red: the meat and grease of human horror.

He too had glimpsed the first signs of this bestial rage, this annihilation of reason and decency, in the most prosaic of places. On a bus. On windy London streets. Browsing in the bright aisles of a supermarket. This terrible contamination made up of ugliness, cruelty and self-destruction, of compulsive narcissism, greed and hate, of bright flaring madness, had begun to emerge and crowd about him in the city. He observed it in others now they were stripped of the inscrutable facade of skin. He'd learned to see through, and down, to where the Devil lived. Hell was a living place inside every membrane of flesh that temporarily passed itself off as human.

Seth slumped to his knees. Tears stung his eyes, a merciful briny respite from what was nailed to the walls in front of him, roaring and contorted.

Genius.

He wept before the genius. Wept with gratitude at what he had been shown. A master class to guide his own pathetic scratchings and daubing. He needed to start again. The moment he got home. Cover the haemorrhages of paint with soiled bandages before making new scars on the walls and ceiling of his room. And then he would come back in here, night after night, to fill himself with this terror and learn how to re-create what was truly walking in this city. His squalid room would become a temple to a new renaissance. He'd work until he fell. Capture this impact, this dissolution of identity and the sickening jolt that came when standing before it.

On his hands and knees he crept to the nearest door. Opened it. Saw illumined, in the vague reddish light from the hall, walls filled with further wonders under cover. He wanted to be sick, to ejaculate and piss himself at the same time. It was too much. He had to take this filthy medicine carefully, in staged amounts, or he would lose the last bit of his mind he needed to create his own vision in oil.

In the next room, the one that terrified him in the dream, he peeked through the door and saw long, beautiful mirrors on each wall between shielded paintings. And he knew the visions under wraps in there could stop his heart or paralyse him with a stroke were he to look for too long. So he clambered to his feet and turned about, desperate to get out of the place where the paintings screamed at him. It was a din. A cacophony. They all wanted him to look and lose himself inside them. But before he could crawl away from the mirrored room he saw something move. From the corner of his eye.

Three times, moving too quickly for legs, it came at the surface of one of the mirrors, from deep inside the reflection of its counterpart on the opposite wall. And then vanished when he turned to stare. Too quick for his eyes to follow. Gone. Either back inside the reflection or vanishing from the fragment of his exhausted mind that could see such things.

There was no one in the room. Nothing so tall and thin. With a covered face. So tightly bound and red. He must have seen himself. Merging with the red walls. The murder walls all about him.

Seth broke from the apartment. He wiped at his eyes and pulled the wet shirt from the small of his back. Closed the front door and locked it. Went for the stairs. But paused before he descended, unable to move as he heard the inner doors of apartment sixteen closing, one by one.

Dawn was beginning to raise the solid darkness from the city outside, to thin and crispen the dense cold of the night air, but even the merest glimmer of daylight hurt the back of his eyes. Legs heavy with exhaustion, he pushed himself up the stairs inside the Green Man.

Ordinarily after a night shift, he would return to his room and slump into his unmade bed. Brace himself against the damp sheets and then fall into a coma. But not today. He had work to do.

Despite the painful swelling and bruising that still raged

from the beating, he was engorged with inspiration. It had been years since he'd felt this way, utterly preoccupied by ideas and images. And now he was compelled to dash them out before they evaporated from his mind.

After he'd left apartment sixteen, he'd sat behind the porter's desk and immediately filled two sketch pads with drawings. Just letting his bruised hands scratch the pencils blunt. A kind of automatic drawing had taken him over, filling page after page with suggestions and fragments of what he had seen up there.

And now he had work to do on his own walls. There was no time to waste. The desire to create could leave him again. For years even, if he didn't throw his entire being into his art right now. His very will and what dexterity his damaged muscles and tendons and sinews retained had to make their mark up there. On the walls.

The wall beside the bed and above the discoloured radiator he had left running and smeared with hasty impressions of the abominations he had seen about London. But he couldn't abandon the *line*. The perfection of the *line*. The artist in apartment sixteen had kept it intact beneath the chaos of colour and the violence of his brushwork. Seth could tell.

So the feeble beginnings on his own meagre walls would need to be covered with something black and smooth and flecked to suggest the greatest distances imaginable. Then he could begin again, and return to the impromptu canvas over and over until he was satisfied he had captured something of the spirit of those masterpieces in number sixteen. He needed to emulate the shock, the incapacity, and the complete involvement he experienced before them. He must acquire the style. But the subjects in here would be his own.

He needed space. The table and chairs and wardrobe had hampered his movements all through the night after the beating, when he'd hobbled about trying to splash and swipe an impression of those weasel faces onto the faded wallpaper.

The bed would stay. Now and again he would have to grab naps in the coming weeks. A few hours here and there. No more. He didn't want to waste time when his whole frame prickled with this static, when every finger and toe buzzed with an idea, an image he could not allow to die or fade from his memory.

And to think he had once been ashamed of these thoughts, these grotesque impressions of the world. How he had longed to be like others, considering his sensitivity a curse, a spoiler of any real chance of happiness. It was no curse. He was blessed. As the artist of those paintings had been. Given an epiphany when the alternative was routine and senseless comfort. Imbued with divine insight when ordinary eyes were glazed with illusion and a nonchalant acknowledgement of the surface of things. This was his one chance to inject meaning into his existence. To attain a purpose. To re-create an impression of whatever he was beginning to see in this city. Things he had learned to see, or been taught to see by god knows what.

He didn't want to think about why and how this impossible connection had been made. Couldn't allow himself to question its source, intention or meaning. It was just there and had brought him back from the dead. These nights alone had woken him up. Slapped him awake and made him realize that nothing mattered beside the vision; the insight into whatever was opening up in his dreams and eyes. Art. He would exist solely to create, no matter how great the sacrifice or loss.

The very thought of going back into that red place, of unveiling those things of horror and magic, chilled his skin. But filled him with a glee that made his soul shiver.

NINETEEN

Immediately, the phone at the other end of the line was picked up. 'Hello.'

'Er. Hello. Is that Harold?'

'Speaking.' It was a well-spoken and elderly voice, but Apryl instantly found herself disarmed by the hint of a confrontational attitude existing in one word alone.

'Mmm. I was calling about the meeting on Friday night.'

'The Friends of Felix Hessen, yes. Are you a Friend?' He said it quickly and with an authority and self-importance she thought ridiculous.

'Er . . . I'm not sure, but I'd like to find out.' She giggled, but the voice at the other end remained silent.

'Sorry, the meeting, I'd like to come.'

The silence continued.

'Sorry, are you still there?'

After another few seconds of silence, the voice replied, 'Yes.'

'It said . . . I mean, the website said to call for details.'

Silence.

Her resolve faltered. And not only because of the forbidding silence. It was on account of what she now knew about Hessen. Who would want to be a friend of that? 'Is it the wrong time to call? I apologize if it's too late.' She thought of hanging up.

'No. No. Not too late,' the voice said.

'Then can I come?'

'You know his work?'

'Yes, I just read the Miles Butler book—'

'Pah! There are better sources. My own work is published online and soon in hardback. I suggest you start there. It's definitive.'

'I will try.'

'Advance copies are on sale at all of the meetings. But as they are held at a private address and our interpretations are quite vigorous, not to mention the unwarranted infamy that hounds some of our visiting scholars, we do vet attendees. Who are you?'

'Mmm. No one really. Just visiting and I saw the website and bought the book.'

Silence again. Though it seemed loaded with disapproval. The guy was freaking her out. 'And, my great-aunt knew him,' she added softly, wincing with discomfort.

'What did you say?' he asked quickly, almost before she had finished speaking.

'My great-aunt, she knew him. They lived in the same building.'

'Which address?'

'Barrington House in Knightsbridge.'

'Yes, I know where it is,' he said, sternly. 'But why on earth did you not say so before?'

'I . . . don't know.'

'Is your great-aunt still alive?'

'No. She recently passed. But she mentioned him in her diaries. That's how I got interested.'

'Diaries?' The volume of his voice suddenly increased. 'You must bring them with you. I must' – he paused, as if to calm down – 'see them. Right away if possible. Where are you now?'

Immediately cautious, she lied, 'But I don't have them with me. They're at home. In the States.'

'No good to us there. Your fellow countrymen already have his sketches under lock and key. We must see the diaries.'

'I can copy them, or something, when I get back.'

'Have you got a pen?' he asked with impatience. She told him she had. 'Well take this down.' He recited an address in Camden and made her spell it back to him. 'Right, I'd suggest you get here early so I can brief you, and also to quiz you a little on your great-aunt. You're practically the guest of honour.'

'Oh, but I don't want to be. I don't really know anything about him—'

'Nonsense, you are related to someone who actually knew the great man. Someone who stood in the presence of genius. We'd be delighted to have you here. You must come. We can help with expenses.'

'No, that's fine. Thanks. I'll get there at sevenish.'

Harold then insisted on taking her number at the hotel, which she unwillingly gave, not being able to think fast enough to refuse. Then she rang off and sat back, feeling the perspiration dry on her brow. Her desire to go to the meeting had vanished. She began to suspect that anything connected to Hessen was weird and unpleasant. And she chided herself for mentioning Lillian's diaries. Why had she said that? To impress him? She felt she had been indiscreet in a way that would come back to haunt her.

The phone beside her bed rang. Nervously, she raised the receiver. It was Harold. 'Sorry, I pressed redial in error,' he said. 'See you tomorrow then.' He hung up while she was still thinking of something to say.

TWENTY

And he went up again and again to the blood-lit place where so many masterpieces were stored in secret. And he fed from their darkness. Drank in the sense of eternity on those walls and engorged himself on the horror of the things that came out of a moving nothingness, on what came up writhing. Different things and parts of different things every time he walked inside.

During the last three visits, Seth had concentrated his efforts on the paintings in the two end bedrooms. Spaces designed for sleep, but now converted into gallery space by an unknown presence; perhaps the one that flickered through the mirrors. And he had gone inside these rooms to learn. To stare like a child into a forgotten pond in an overgrown garden. Peering at the black surface to marvel at the slim white shapes moving through weed and water so cold an immersion of a single finger would take one's breath away. And maybe the finger too.

Once his duties had been taken care of, and after he'd lied to Mrs Roth following her continued complaints of noise from the empty flat beneath her – the bumping, the slamming of doors, the heavy dragging of things through the insulated darkness of number sixteen – only then, with the impediments removed, did he quietly retrieve the key from the safe in the head porter's office and enter the gallery.

Up he had gone, taking the stairs carefully, some time between three and four in the morning when the world slept, with his pager clipped to his belt in case a resident called the house phone, or arrived in the early hours from an airport and pushed the front doorbell. Excited by the trespass, afraid of what he might see but eager to be engaged, he had closed the door behind him and turned the lights on.

On his second visit, which seemed so long ago now, like a distant but still memorable nightmare, something was in there with him. Something he couldn't see. The presence, indistinct but powerful, that offered no threat to him physically. But something dangerous in a greater sense because it should not, by the laws of nature, be there. It manifested in the reddish light as a sense of motion and sound. Out of sight. Behind the closed doors of the mirrored room, where he heard occasional creaks caused by quick footfalls that moved back and forth rapidly, and then stopped abruptly by the threshold as he passed by.

He'd save the mirrored middle room until last. His instincts had told him to. He had caught a glimpse of movement in there on his first visit and was not ready to see it again. Not yet. So the correct sequence had to be followed. That room should be appreciated last of all. And perhaps when he did venture in, an introduction of sorts would be made.

His stomach still melted at the very thought of engaging with something so far beyond his comprehension, so far beyond all but his most recent experience. Or maybe that was just the old Seth trying to resurface; the vacillator, the dithering coward, the indecisive and contemptible weakling who had failed to follow his vocation, who had fallen at the first sign of criticism. Only now was he beginning to understand that the opinions of others did not matter. That they could not even begin to understand the places he must visit, and the visions he must record. There could be no half measures, no compromise. Not again. Not ever.

The hooded boy had suggested as much. Had told him that he was being helped and guided to see things as they were. He knew it, and was alarmed at how comfortable he felt with the steady insistent manipulation that surrounded him, slipped inside him, and pulled him up here. To study a master's work.

But had *they* arranged the beating? Thrown him under the clawed feet of jackals for that terrible kicking on cold, wet London paving because he'd entertained thoughts of escape in that bar? That hooded figure had something of the same brutalized innocence as his attackers, the same contempt for anything but itself. The idea that those vicious weasel faces in baseball caps were the hooded boy's emissaries made him feel as if he was out of his depth and the shore was too far away to reach. Or maybe, he tried to convince himself, they were just more evidence of what he must re-create in paint. Of what this city was truly filled with, resembling the things that shrieked and twisted on the walls of apartment sixteen. The final destination for us all. But if the beating was a warning then his will could not falter again. The will must triumph.

It was taking his body a long time to put itself back together. And parts of it weren't fixed yet. He walked with a limp and suffered shooting pains through his left hand. The cornea of his right eye was scratched and infected and bloodshot, and he still couldn't manage a deep breath.

Seth talked to himself as he uncovered the portraits in the

two end rooms for the fourth time, keeping his eyes shut as each was unveiled, before sitting on the bare floorboards, his sketch pad and pencils clutched in his white fingers. He muttered aloud to keep his mind together and aware of itself, because it was so easy to lose a sense of yourself before these things in rags that pulled themselves apart on the red walls. It was the only way to not cry out. To not allow cold panic to fill him up and force him to flee while scratching at the skin of his face, cutting it with his long nails.

He had to be strong. Courageous. If he was a true artist. Must learn to endure these sights and visions and learn how these truths could be depicted in his own studio at the Green Man. He knew it. Someone had been telling him all along. He just had to listen. They were inside him now. And they had opened the valves of his mind.

Later as he hung the key for apartment sixteen back on its hook in the safe, he heard the sound of a throat being cleared behind him. He slammed the safe shut and turned about quickly.

Stephen stood in the doorway of his office. 'Hello Seth.'

Seth nodded quickly, swallowed. His thoughts scrabbled and scratched about, but his mind was exhausted by what it had just tried to comprehend. His face was white and shaky and full of guilt, he knew it. He could not think of anything to say, an excuse, a reason for why he would be in the head porter's office, returning the key to a private apartment that porters were not permitted to enter without permission.

'Problem upstairs?' Stephen said, one eyebrow raised.

'Just Mrs Roth,' he blurted out, trying to think of the remainder of the lie but failing under the intense stare of his boss.

'Oh?'

'I . . . I didn't want to wake you. Was nothing really. But she keeps phoning down. You know how she is.'

'You're not wrong there. Anything I can assist with?'

God no. 'Nah. Peace of mind thing. That's all.' Stephen watched him closely. Seth tried to change the subject. 'You're up late.' He looked at his watch. 'Early, I mean.'

'Janet's having a rough time right now. I can't remember the last time I had a good night's rest. And you look as though you know what I'm talking about.' Stephen smiled, but the smile was not altogether pleasant. It looked sly. Seth's sense of guilt deepened and made him swallow, causing him to look even worse.

Stephen walked into the office and sat on the corner of his desk. 'Why don't you take yourself home, Seth. I'll cover for you.' He looked at his watch. 'You only have another two hours anyway.'

Seth frowned. Stephen should be interrogating him, balling him out, placing him under suspicion. 'I don't know . . . You sure?'

Stephen smiled. 'Sure. Take off. Looks to me like you've had a bad night. I know how demanding it can be. Before you came I had to cover the shift for a month before we could find a replacement – you. They never stuck around for long, Seth, your predecessors. Never had the stomach for it. Bloody art students. Not the right material for night guys. It's a hard slot to fill. Takes a good man to do it right.'

Seth held his breath while trying to work out what Stephen was leading to, if anything. He had no idea what this was about. 'I always wondered why you advertised in *Art and Artists.*'

'One of the oldest residents, it was his idea. Had a personal interest in artists.'

'Really. Who?'

Stephen waved a hand in the air. 'He's not around much any more. Doesn't matter. But I follow orders, Seth. As do you, I might add. I'm very pleased with how you've fitted in here at Barrington House. You're someone I can rely on. Takes a load off me, someone who does what's needed around here. Pulls his weight, so to speak.'

'Er . . . thanks.'

Stephen's smile widened. 'You know something, Seth, I might be looking for a replacement for myself in the not too distant future. Someone who can step up. Take responsibility for the building and all of its needs. And my successor would get the flat, rent free. Better salary too. I just need to put in a good word with the management. Might you be interested in that? A promotion? It's a great opportunity. And I'd like to leave this place in good hands.'

Seth rubbed at the stubble around his mouth, looked everywhere but at Stephen. He'd thought he was going to get the sack, but he was being offered the head porter's job. 'I don't know what to say. I mean, thanks.'

'Think about it. It has its moments. Its demands. But the worst offenders are getting on a bit. They won't be here for ever, will they? That's worth keeping in mind.'

'I guess so.'

'And life would be a lot simpler without them, that's for sure.' Stephen chuckled. 'Old Betty Roth wouldn't be missed, eh? She can't keep going for ever. I'd say she's had a good innings. Same as those Shafers.' He shook his head, smiling, then looked up sharply, straight-faced. 'But not a word to the others about what I've said. You can keep a secret, Seth. I've no doubt about that. You can be trusted.'

Seth nodded. 'Thanks.'

Stephen looked at the safe and then back at Seth. Touched his nose with his index finger and narrowed his eyes. 'Until then, keep up the good work.'

TWENTY-ONE

'Welcome, friend. Welcome.' The woman's body filled the doorway. Her garishly painted face was one big smile. Apryl tried to stop her astonishment freezing on her face. She'd barely recovered her bearings after the journey up to the twenty-eighth floor in a vandalized elevator that stank of urine and worse, before walking through a dim warren of yellowing cement corridors to find the front door of the flat Harold had included in his precise instructions.

'I'm Harriet, the host of our little gatherings, and the secretary of our illustrious society.' Harriet threw her great head back and shrieked, as if what she said was so funny a full laugh never had the time to slip out naturally and became a half-scream instead. 'But you can call me *Figure of a Woman in Crisis*. Many of the gentlemen do.' Again the shrieked laugh.

Now Apryl was doing her utmost not to stare at the woman's curious shape and ghastly apparel. A red velvet gown that swept about the floor had been draped over elephantine limbs and a thick torso. Great breasts festooned with strings of wooden beads stretched out the chest area. Thick but sloppily applied cosmetics lathered her doughy face, from which small watery eyes beamed with an intensity Apryl couldn't look into, so the path of her stare directed itself to the woman's large head. A turban of green and turquoise scarves was wrapped about Harriet's skull and loosely fixed at the front by a silver brooch. Like oily cobwebs, long strands of white-grey hair slipped out from beneath the headdress. Instantly, Apryl thought her mad.

'And you are Apryl. Our second special guest this evening.' The woman's podgy hands clamped on the outside of each of Apryl's arms to pull her further into the hot perfumed air of the flat. As Harriet moved aside, a cluttered and crowded living room revealed itself.

Incense sticks fixed in wooden bases burned around the large front room. They were placed with gothic candlesticks on sloping piles of books and on cabinets filled with tarot decks, oils, Indian jewellery, crystals, small ornate chests and carved statuettes.

'Come. Come. Wine?' the woman said. 'Harold Rackam-Atterton is here. Who I believe you have spoken to. We're all so excited by your visit. So thrilled.' Her tiny grey eyes widened with a fresh rush of excitement.

Apryl couldn't stop herself looking down at where the woman's jewelled hands held onto her arms. The fingernails were long, but uneven in length and yellow towards the tips. As if aware of their scrutiny, the hands disappeared.

'Please. Wine would be lovely,' Apryl said, nervously, and was steered between three men with long, thinning grey hair. Their clothes smelled of damp and old sweat.

Before a little table the huge woman slopped cheap Merlot into a wine glass. 'I'll just seize Harold and bring him hither.' Somewhere inside that high enthusiastic voice Apryl sensed a tremble of hysteria.

A curious blend of discordant jazz music mixed with

Gregorian chant and clanging industrial machinery was playing on a paint-spattered tape recorder, mounted on a wooden stool beside the entrance to the kitchen. About which two balding young men with intense faces whispered to each other. They both wore woollen trench coats and knee-length cavalry boots, like some new freakish subculture she was unaware of and doubted would catch on.

But for an apartment in a tower block the place was surprisingly big inside; it must have been designed for a family. Apryl even noticed a staircase leading up to another level. Between the worn and sagging furniture, dark bookcases, dried plants in amphoras and old photographs cluttering the walls, she spied some of the original decor. Very British; very seventies. In places a watery yellow paint appeared between the bric-a-brac and mismatching wooden picture frames. It was stained with rashes of black-spore fungus. She could smell its powdery wet rot amid the incense.

At least fifteen people had crammed into the living room and occupied most of the floor space. All of the guests appeared to have made some effort to dress, or half-dress, in vintage costume. Two of the men behind the sofa wore top hats, and Apryl glimpsed watch chains against their waistcoats. Others had adopted cravats for the evening. But despite their attempts at vintage styling, the gathering appeared universally dishevelled. Suit jackets were stained. Trouser legs too short. Waistlines heaved up too high. Dresses were creased beyond redemption. Everyone was overweight or unhealthily thin. And oh God, the teeth. Stained grey, or yellow from neglect, crooked, sloping or snaggled in their sunken or lipless mouths. British teeth. She wondered how they all managed to acquire such appalling mouths. She was not in the habit of dismissing people on account of their appearance, but she'd never seen such an extraordinarily ugly group of people assembled in one room.

Their dressing might have been sloppy and their grooming careless due to their eccentricity, because eccentric they certainly were, but she suspected another motive: they were displaying a wilful opposition to anything aesthetically pleasing. They had expanded or withered with no thought to the tastes of the world around them. It was as if they had made themselves deliberately grotesque. They could all be the living embodiment of a Felix Hessen drawing in ink and gouache.

Three of the five women present were seated together on a couch. They were middle-aged and all wearing veils over faces painted in an operatic style. Their thin bodies were draped in long, funereal dresses that suggested the First World War. Elbow-length lace gloves concealed their arms, but were fingerless from the first knuckle, revealing long nails, unpainted. The fourth woman was elderly and wore a floppy green hat with a sagging brim that concealed most of her small head. She sat like a little girl sunken into an armchair made for adults, and had struck an absurd aristocratic pose with her head. As soon as Apryl met the elderly creature's eye a sharp, surreal peal of laughter erupted from its thin mouth. For no reason that Apryl could determine. The woman then raised her chin and resumed a grim, imperious expression in silence.

Harriet was back, pushing through rumpled jackets and straggly heads, and bullying aside a bundle of thin legs. Behind her bobbed a fat, elderly man who Apryl presumed was Harold. Thick glasses in brown plastic frames magnified his eyes to four times their normal size, set in a large head, pink and hairless save for a circle of wispy white hair that fell about the shoulders of his stained dinner jacket.

'Ahhhh,' Harold sighed, opening his small mouth to reveal sparsely furnished gums. But the breath that rolled from it made her feel faint and sick. It was silvery and rusted with bacteria. The few teeth that remained in his mouth were the colour of wet peanuts. 'A bloodline that has brushed against the greatest mind in the canon of art history graces one of our gatherings. You are as rare as documents bearing his signature, my dear. But we must steer your fledgling scholarship on a more reliable path. I'd like to show you a small work of my own later. Fifteen years in the making. What I would call a critical appreciation of Hessen's artistic vision in the style of a dream narrative, in order to suggest what the missing oils must have resembled.'

'We're publishing it through the society,' Harriet said, with so much enthusiasm her whole body shook. 'The cover illustration is by one of our own members. I can take an advance order tonight. We're selling in royal hardback at ninety pounds. Signed.'

Apryl didn't know what to say, but nodded and held a smile on her face until it ached. But she didn't need to reply as Harold was keen to begin the introductions. Nor did she have to think of anything to say to the characters who shook her hand; as she was escorted about the room the members were only too pleased to do all of the talking. Elsewhere in their lives she sensed a lack of opportunity to converse.

'Yes, the American lady,' said an elderly man with a thin face and wild white hair brushed across his conical skull. 'Harold mentioned you. Have you been to the British

Library? It has some nice prints of the *Contortions*. Have you seen *Figure of a Woman Clutching her Face*? And *Childbirth: Figure of a Dead Woman*? They have good prints of those too.'

Apryl told him she hadn't.

'You simply must go to the Black Dog and the Guardsmen's Rest for a drink,' another man with a severe lisp said. 'Hessen used to go there. With Bryant, the poet. Of course the names have changed, but the ceilings above the bars are still original.' He blinked his eyes rapidly.

'I can take you,' said a portly man in a frock coat. He was drunk and stared at her legs.

'Calm yourself, Roger. Calm yourself,' Harold said, not without a hint of irritation, before guiding Apryl away to where the four ladies sat. Placing his plump fingertips on each of Apryl's shoulders, he whispered conspiratorially in her ear, 'You may find Alice a trifle strange at first. But, as I'm sure you'll agree, that is rarely a bad thing. She is in her nineties. And is someone you really must meet. We treasure her at our gatherings. You see, she is the only one of us who ever met Hessen.'

Apryl started, shaken out of her awkwardness in an instant. 'Met him?'

Harold smiled with satisfaction. His big watery eyes swam behind the magnifying lenses of his spectacles. 'Knew him, to be precise, in the late thirties. While the great man was emerging from his *Scenes After Death* phase, as far as we can ascertain. But her memory ... Well ... Not what it was.'

Apryl remembered reading in Miles's book about what difficult years the late thirties were for Hessen. He'd visited Germany in 1937, expecting to be embraced as a hero of the

Third Reich, due to the admiration of fascist ideals that he had expressed in *Vortex*. But by that time Hitler had grown tired of the obscure mystics and cults that were part of the early inspiration for National Socialism. Not only did lower-level Nazi officials reject Hessen's drawings and art theory, due to the growing abstraction and surrealism he dealt with, but they also refused his application to join the Waffen SS. So characteristic of a man accustomed to making more enemies than friends, Hessen had misjudged the value of his vision.

He returned home incandescent with rage and inconsolable at the thought of what he deemed a betrayal, only then to be imprisoned for his political affiliations shortly after Britain declared war, and kept behind bars until 1945.

'And we also suspect she knew him after he came out of prison too, for a brief while.' Harold grinned, and winked, so clearly aware of the importance of his final comment.

Hessen lacked any of the pedigree and connections of Mosley, or the achievements of Ezra Pound, to enjoy a relaxation of the infamy that surrounded him after the war. Miles Butler assumed this was the reason he'd hidden himself away in Knightsbridge. And even Mosley had distanced himself from Hessen by then, considering him 'decadent and unsound of mind'. Only an occultist and explorer, Eliot Coldwell, had championed his art in the fifties because of its connection with an 'unseen world'. And not until the late seventies was minor critical scrutiny turned again to his surviving work. Now it was only the Friends of Felix Hessen, their garish website, and their speculative limited-edition publications that kept his name alive. Apryl found it all miserable and depressing. Hessen's legacy, his enthusiasts, his art. Had it not been for his connection to her great-aunt, she wouldn't have given any of it a moment of her time, and she now wished she'd never come to this ridiculous gathering. What a place to end up on a Friday night in London.

Apryl perched herself on the arm of the chair into which Alice's thin body had sunk. Harold stayed close. Three fingers still maintained contact with her shoulder as if ready to spirit her away in a hurry.

She offered a smile to the three veiled women. Chalky faces glared at her through black netting. They muttered a greeting, but waited eagerly to listen to her talk with Alice.

'Hello, Alice, I'm Apryl,' she said, leaning down towards the hunched figure to see beneath the brim of the green hat. 'I hear you and Felix Hessen were friends?'

An old face embossed with rheumy yellow eyes rose to look at her. Then smiled. A clawed hand came to rest on her knee, below the hem of her skirt. 'Yes, dear. A long time ago.' The dry pads of her fingers moved in little circles on the fabric of her stocking.

'I'm sure you get asked about him all the time. My great-aunt knew him too.'

The frail hand moved from her knee to wave about in the air. 'I've told you before, it all changed after the accident. It was never the same again. Of course, once there were the puppets and everything else like that. He showed us at the, the, the . . .'

'Mews studio. Chelsea,' Harold prompted.

'Where are you, dear?'

Harold leant down. 'Here Alice. Right next to you.'

'Who is the lady with the pretty legs, darling? Doesn't she have pretty legs.'

Harold chuckled. 'I think so too.' The fingers strengthened their hold on Apryl's shoulder. She lacked the strength to swallow.

'This is Apryl. A friend of ours, Alice. A friend. Tell her about Felix.'

Alice sighed. 'Such a beautiful face. To lose it like that. We all thought him so handsome. And he painted the most wonderful puppets. Not for children, dear. No. Puppets in boxes. Stuck inside things, you know. But their faces you never forgot. I still see them.'

'It can be hard to follow, especially the dates,' Harold whispered, his mephitic breath hot against the left side of her face. 'But sometimes what she says is extraordinary. I have no doubt at all that she knew Hessen. She was his model. One of the few he used.'

Apryl coughed and writhed inside her own skin under the onslaught of Harold's breath. She tried to pull away but could get no further than the brim of Alice's hat.

'And the dancing,' Alice said, suddenly, her eyes widening. 'Oh, the dancing and chanting. You know. The most wonderful dancing. At his flat. Backwards dancing. Under the pictures, you know. Oh, the times we had.' Alice leaned towards Apryl's ear. 'But it all stopped when they took him away. They were so cruel to him. It was terrible, dear.'

Squinting against the smell of Harold's breath that was virtually being panted across her face, Apryl leant down closer to Alice. 'His flat? Where did you dance? At Barrington House? Was that when you saw the puppets?'

But Alice was oblivious. 'No, no, no. All rubbish, he used to say. All rubbish. It's not the figures, it's the background that counts. The stuff behind it you can't see. Very clever man. Of course he was right. He tried to help us to see it too. I used to take my clothes off for him, dear. But clever men have bad tempers. And they were all against him in the end, dear. He showed them so much, but they never appreciated him. They were afraid of him. But you just had to trust Felix. He was an artist. One must accommodate such. They'd all seen the pictures. No one had seen anything like it before. And the walls, dear. It's a part of it all, you know. All joined, you see. The background.'

What with Harold's continued exhalations behind her neck, Alice's disconnected thoughts, the effect of the Merlot she drank too quickly on account of her nerves, and the hot air saturated with the smell of incense and neglect, Apryl began to feel faint. She had to stand up. 'Harold, please. I'd like to get up. Please. May I? Thank you, Alice,' Apryl said, feeling an even greater need than ever to get away from Harold and the confused lady, whose recollections were next to useless.

Harriet's round face appeared behind Harold. 'The talk is about to start. Quick.'

Apryl stood at the rear of the crowd in the living room, not far from the front door, as Harold introduced a wizened creature in a shabby brown suit: Doctor Otto Herndl from Heidelberg. The doctor was the author of a small-press anthology of essays called *Gathered on the Right*, and the editor of some occult journal she missed the name of when the elderly man in front of her was racked by a coughing fit.

Otto Herndl began by saying something about the early philosophical influences on the precocious teenage Hessen. 'Particularly Professor Zollner, who asserted the existence of a fourth dimension, and used the paranormal phenomena of the time as proof.'

While he struggled to translate his thoughts into English, Apryl was distracted by the man's oddball appearance. The broken zipper of his trousers. A tatty briefcase resting against one scuffed shoe. His hair was razored up the back and sides of his head to a grey copse on top, then combed into a severe side parting. And he managed to convey the impression of being unsteady on his feet and about to topple over, without ever doing so. His brown, excitable eyes moved frantically behind his thick round glasses and his hands hovered out in front of him, as if strings had been attached to his wrists and were lazily controlled from above. It appeared he hadn't shaved for days.

When he began to talk about 'Max Ferdinand Sebaldt von Werth's five volumes of *Genesis*, a white supremacist treatise on eroticism, Bacchanalia, sexology and libido', she lost the thread of his argument and her thoughts wandered back and forth, in and out of the lecture, and settled on comparing his ideas about Hessen with what she'd learned from reading Miles's book.

She'd read how the young Hessen had been obsessed by Wotanism, the pagan cults and the millenarian sects of nine-teenth-century Austria and Germany – racist mystical ideas that influenced Germany's ideas of nationality between the wars. Hessen seemed to have approached it with the same passion modern kids follow rock or rap music. But Miles had been baf-fled as to how it had informed Hessen's studies of cadavers, his grotesque primitivist sketches of animal-human hybrids, and his ghastly puppet triptych of the 1930s. That interest, surely, must have come from his schooling in medicine.

But Herndl insisted that Hessen's sketches represented 'a middle-class reaction to the industrialization of Europe'. They showed, he claimed, how he was predicting both the bovine passivity in urban man and the loss of control and will 'zat ve see around us today'.

That contradicted what Miles had written. According to him, Hessen eventually mocked his own youthful interests in remote and rare folk movements, and acknowledged that they marked a young outsider's flight from mainstream culture. As did his dabbling with orientalism, hypnotism, and fascism. They were all part of his detachment and alienation from the status quo, a terrible force that he saw as the antithesis of original creativity. And as Miles had pointed out, Hessen's drawings reflected nothing of Nazi neo-classicism, or Aryan folk art. There was nothing idealistic or mythical in his art. It drew deeply from a complicated but brilliant imagination. Or whatever it was he saw in the shadows, or looking out from the murky windows of abandoned basements.

Miles Butler believed Hessen's disappointment with the Nazis and their nationalist occultism, after travelling to Berlin, was colossal. He'd pursued one subculture too far and hated the reality up close. Hessen never understood anti-Semitism, and *Vortex* championed Hebrew mysticism.

His failure in Germany and then his imprisonment signalled his final withdrawal from society, its ideas and purposes. But despite the inconvenience of prison, Miles suspected that everything he'd experimented with until 1938 was mere preparation for the Vortex. It was the source not only of his inspiration, but of nightmares, melancholia and despair too: 'the society of tragedy', Hessen called it in volume 4 of *Vortex*, which was entitled 'A World Behind This World'.

For her to be able to contradict Otto Herndl in this way, Apryl realized with horror, meant she'd remembered far too much about the man who'd cast such a spell over her great-aunt. The painter was fast turning into an unhealthy compulsion. She could even vividly recall what Hessen had written about the Vortex, because it seemed uncomfortably relevant to what Lillian had recorded.

> *I just want to dip my face into it. Now and again. And to paint what I see down there. But sometimes it shows itself to me: coming through the walls, or inside a laughing mouth, behind a vacant stare, or gathering itself in a wretched place. Either I am getting closer to it, or it is drawing nearer to me. Sometimes I can feel its breath on my neck. And my sleep is filled with it. Though my conscious mind banishes it, as if it has an in-built resistance to such things. But it is always there. Waiting. When I look over my shoulder, or walk past a mirror quickly and absently, I see it. Or when I slip into a torpor, it will creep into the room like a strange dark animal looking for food.*

After an hour and fifteen minutes of the lecture Apryl sat on the dirty floor, behind a sofa. While Herndl barked out the names of summoning rituals Hessen had purchased from Crowley and had performed 'with abzolute success', her head spun. Fatigued by the heat, the nervous excitement, and the thin, dirty air of the city, when she heard the smattering of applause and a final cessation in the bewildering broken-

English monologue of the speaker, she rose to her feet to leave. But Harold was upon her before she could find her coat.

'Leaving so soon? No, you can't – we haven't had our little chat about your great-aunt yet. And if you go now you'll miss the best part – the interpretations. Or, as we like to call them, the 'study of dreamers in a room'. You see, the Friends share their connection to Hessen's vision through a recounting of their dreams experienced under the influence of his art. We all try and find the missing paintings via trance. People resort to all sorts of means to get within the presence of the Vortex.'

'Really? Amazing.' Apryl barely had the energy to speak. 'I must get on. I have plans for dinner.'

Harold wasn't listening. 'You'll see why it's so important.'

At the front of the room, as soon as Harold called for order, a forest of tatty arms shot into the air to begin the procedure. The music was turned off. The chatter died. A shabby-looking man wearing an overcoat, and with a white chinless face and bulging eyes, was the first to take the floor. 'I returned to the same place twice. Lit up, but not with natural light.'

There was a murmur of acknowledgement. Or was it unrest?

'And in the gases, that were yellow, I saw the clothed face again. A tall figure briefly walked forward, at me, with its face covered in red. Then it stopped and seemed to be suddenly some distance away from me. It repeated the movement several times. Then I woke up and thought I was having a heart attack.'

Before he could continue, Harold pointed to one of the young men wearing cavalry boots and a trench coat.

'I was in my front room fasting and had deprived myself of any visual stimulation but the *Puppet Triptych IV* for two days and two nights. And when I slept, I glimpsed figures about a fire. Stick figures. Some of them fell in.'

There was a great impatience in the room. They weren't exactly dismissive of each other's dreams or hallucinations or visions or whatever they were, but each clearly felt his or her own to be more significant.

'. . . I saw hateful faces. Black and red with rage.'

'. . . they looked like clowns in dirty pyjamas.'

'. . . two women and one man, dressed in an Edwardian fashion. But they had no flesh on their bones. I couldn't wake up or run from the two women, who were unfurling the nets from the front of their bonnets.'

'. . . crouching on all fours, in the corner of a basement. The walls were wet, made from brick.'

Thirsty, Apryl gulped at a second glass of wine. It was a mistake. She hadn't eaten and felt light-headed. They were all jabbering out disjointed fragments of nightmares that had punched them from sleep and into the dreary alienation of their lives. What was the point of it all? Of them? The close stale air and the woollen heat and the crazy surrealist ranting of the guests made her move once again for the door.

'. . . teeth like an ape. Eyes completely red. But no legs. Just dragging itself about in the sawdust.'

'. . . The whole city was blackened by fire. Ash and dust in piles. But freezing cold. No sign of life—' The gentleman wearing a cloth cap that shadowed a purple face was suddenly interrupted by Alice.

'And they're all about my bed!' she wailed. 'They come

out of the walls, you see! No use in talking to them. They're not there for that.'

'I object to this!' the figure in the cloth cap roared. 'Must she always interrupt?'

Other voices murmured their assent. Harold appealed for calm. 'Now, now, if you please. There is time—'

But Alice was not to be stopped. 'Swirling up, all around, with backwards noises. Up in the corners of the rooms. I saw them once before the war and they never leave you.'

Irritated, the crowd began to chatter.

Harold leant towards Alice, a tense smile on his face while his eyes flitted about looking for the dissenters in the crowd. 'Alice, my dear, we agreed you should talk last. The others must be allowed to have their say too.'

The man who had stared at Apryl's legs and offered to take her to the Hessen pubs elbowed his way towards her. His fat face was shiny with sweat and it grinned lecherously. 'I wouldn't bother with this lot again,' he said. 'You should come and see us. The Scholars of Felix Hessen. Not so dreamy. This is a circus.' His fat fingers rustled inside a leather satchel that hung from one shoulder. He produced a flyer and pushed it at her. 'On the hush hush, we're breaking away. This lot won't get anywhere. Harriet's too wishy-washy and Harold puts far too much faith in Alice. She's as mad as a snake.' He laughed, unpleasantly.

On the other side of the room Alice had begun to sing 'Roll out the barrel' in a childlike voice. Others had begun to shout over her. Through the chaos Apryl caught sight of the little figure of Otto Herndl. His grin was wide but his eyes were full of confusion. He seemed even more unsteady on his feet, as if someone had finally severed the strings.

'I really don't think so,' Apryl told the leader of the splinter group. She struggled into her coat.

'Can I see you again?' he said.

'I, I shan't be in London for much longer. I'm very busy.' But in the din she wasn't sure he had heard her. She turned and pushed her way to the door.

Outside, the cold air rushed in to stifle her. It seemed unnaturally dark by the tower blocks and on the main road the traffic was relentless and moving too fast. She headed towards the lit-up area, to the centre of Camden Town. She wanted to get into a normal environment with normal people, and began walking away from the unlit buildings and ugly cafes, the empty fast-food restaurants and decrepit sunken pubs.

The meeting had depressed her. She'd expected the Friends to be eccentric after reading bits of their obscure website, but this fancy-dress party with its internal politics, splinter groups, and ludicrous claims of mystical dream connections struck her as adolescent. It was all fantasy. A gaggle of misfits attaching themselves to an artist who they imagined was a representation of their own alienation. They did nothing for Hessen's reputation, while masquerading as guardians of his legacy.

Apryl huddled deeper into her scarf and pulled the collar of her coat up, but it was as if a residue of the meeting's surreal dysfunction still clung to her. And pulled things in.

A junkie with a dirty whitish blanket across his shoulders ran across the road at her, narrowly avoiding two cars that sounded their horns. The violence of the sudden sharp sounds startled her. She held her breath, and then felt her skin ice with fear at the approach of the beggar. His thin, ashen face was scarred with purple lumps. A scrawny woman wearing a white baseball cap waited for him on the opposite side of the road, holding a can of beer.

'Can you spare us firty pee for a cuppa tea? Just to keep warm, like.'

She hadn't anything smaller than a ten-pound note. Apryl shook her head without looking at the beggar and increased her pace. He didn't follow, but she heard a long sigh of disappointment and frustration before he said, 'Oh fucking hell.' It wasn't directed at her, but at the cold, relentless misery of his life. At the dirty streets, the grey ugly council housing, the bent iron railings and the dying black grass, only lit up in part by the thin orange light of the street lamps that shrunk in the dense absorbing shadows all around the edges of anything solid.

The people here didn't need to dream of such terrible things. They lived among them.

TWENTY-TWO

Seth entered his room at the Green Man. In the dark, in the sudden stench of turpentine, he shrugged off his overcoat and let it fall to the sheets he had laid over the floor. He was almost hallucinating from sleep deprivation; felt like he could just lie down on the greasy dust sheets in his clothes and pass out. He'd been pushing himself too hard. Needed to sleep all day before the next shift. The strain of having just spent another two hours in apartment sixteen made him clutch both sides of his skull as if to still the carousel of wretchedness screaming through his mind. He thought of the blood-mired surgeons who amputated limbs for hours after battles. Reaching behind, he felt for the light fitting, then flicked the switch on. And fell against the door.

He stared at the wall over the radiator and at the section above the fireplace. At yesterday's work, at the things he'd painted before leaving for Barrington House. They punched him to immobility and left him breathless. They'd been waiting for him to come home.

He knew in an instant that these were the sorts of things the criminally insane produced in prison, where he might very well end his days. They looked like the nightmares that make you wake up with a gasp and then leave you nervous all day.

Animal teeth filled the stretched mouths. Pupils red with

pain and rage were directed right at him, the creator. And what were these things that walked on their hind legs but looked like apes with doggish faces? Hyena snouts and jackal laughter, piggish eyes and cattle-bone limbs: this was the work of a broken mind.

His genius. His attempts to mimic the work in apartment sixteen. Distorting the individual into fragments. Shattering the sense of being whole in an ordered universe. But all he had done was mortify and then shatter himself. In a cold and damning moment of clarity, he wondered if perhaps these were not images of any hidden truth, but only the suggestions of how a deeply disturbed mind sees itself.

He experienced a sudden hot desire to mutilate himself with a knife before erasing his face against a wall.

Falling to his knees, his eyes and teeth and fists clenched hard, he bit down on the hysteria that tried to burn its way up his throat. 'Jesus, God. Jesus, God. Jesus, God. What am I?' he muttered and then began to sob. He'd never seen so many tears. His soul was sick and melting away through his eyes.

The murk and dross inside his reddish thoughts were briefly rinsed away by the scalding salt of his grief, allowing him to think as he had once done so long ago. To know himself again for a moment. Something resembling free will, some final shred of his former self, seemed to have been washed clean. A tiny bright place within him grew in proportion to the dull mackerel light silvering the thin curtains.

But then he turned and saw the little girl with the tear-streaked face sitting up by his pillows, watching the door. Always watching the door.

He walked across to the curtains, his breath sobbing in

and out of him. A small part of him still clung on to a denial that such things could exist, and on to a belief that his exhaustion was just inserting part of his sickened and subconscious mind into his waking eyes. He would open the curtains and the window and take a deep breath and then, when he turned around, that tear-stained face would no longer be looking at the door.

But when he drew the curtain, his eyes were immediately pulled down to the scruffy yard at the back of the Green Man. Beneath whatever the adjacent apartment block had been built over, it seemed that a small assembly of former tenants were looking up at him from out of hollow sockets. Behind the railings and inside the little concrete moat outside the basement flats, he saw fragments of things whitish and indistinct reaching up to claw at the cold metal bars. The angle of their heads and the movement of the papery mouths suggested to him that they had suddenly seen a curtain twitch above them, and were now eager to engage the help of whoever was looking down upon their wretched state.

He let the curtains drop and stumbled back to the bed with his eyes clenched shut. Slapped off the lights. Then curled up at the foot of the mattress and whimpered.

'Me dad's coming soon. He told me to wait,' the girl said.

TWENTY-THREE

Behind the large desk Piotr moved heavily to his feet and wiped at his forehead. 'Hello Miss Apryl. How can I help you today? Maybe the umbrella it is you need?'

It was raining again and she'd been caught in a down-pour walking to Knightsbridge from Bayswater. Her mood had slipped further into the black when she'd seen Piotr grinning behind the desk. She'd been hoping for Stephen. 'Sorry, I'm dripping on the carpet.' Slowly, she warmed up after the chill from the wind and the heavy burst of rain outside, leaving her slightly dizzy in the heat of the lobby.

All about her brass door handles sparkled. Glass shone on the doors and picture frames. And the thick clean carpets beneath the heels of her boots made her feel self-conscious about tramping dirt inside. This part of the building was immaculate – dust free and show-home lit – but still unable to conceal the fragrance of age that seeped down from else-where. The reception area was nothing but a front. Behind this little capsule of bright light and warmth she could already sense the sepia gloom of its stairwells and rotten apartments, waiting up there to frighten her. How soon her impression of the place had changed. Staying in the hotel room and taking a few days out to explore the city had given her a distance, put her back in touch with herself, and now just the merest whiff of Barrington House made her remember the fear and confusion of her nights here.

But not long now and she would be free of the place. The cleaners would be in this week and then the estate agents. After that she'd never have to come back here again. Ever.

'Got caught in quite a storm out there,' she laughed and patted at her hair; the rain had flattened it. 'I never know what the weather's doing in this city. The sky was blue when I left Bayswater.'

She kept up her smile, but the affability of the fat porter failed to put her at ease. It always felt like he was making a pass. He came around the desk and stood too close, one hand reaching out to take her elbow. 'Please. Sit down. You must rest, no?' His shirt seemed too tight again, as if the collar was squeezing his round head up and out of his body, and then strangling him.

She took a step to the side and placed one hand on top of the desk to regain her personal space. 'I'm fine. Just a bit damp.' She put her bag on the counter, patted her leather coat down and then removed her black gloves. She couldn't avoid Piotr today; she needed him.

He maintained a constant and irritating banter. 'You know, it is nice to be in the warm and dry, no? And I am always happy to let the beautiful ladies come inside from the weather, yes?' He finished with a loud, excitable laugh.

It was becoming difficult to maintain the smile. But what she intended to do was invasive. She had shown up in the rain to interrogate the staff, and potentially a long-term resident, for information about apartment sixteen. She knew from Stephen that these exclusive apartment buildings in west London were often havens where the wealthy and famous expected the strictest privacy and security. Porters were forbidden to give out any pertinent information about the residents or the building. Stephen told her kidnap was now an ever-present danger for the children of the wealthy.

'So what can I do to help you, Miss Apryl? Today I am the happy man because of the pay day see? So anything at all I am happy to do for you.'

'Well, I have a strange request.'

Piotr slapped one hand over his heart. 'At last the day is a here. When the beautiful lady comes into the Barrington House and say she have a request for me, no?'

Don't push it, fat boy. 'I don't know whether you know, but this building has some history. You see, a painter lived here. A man called Felix Hessen.' Without revealing the fact that he lived in number sixteen, Apryl watched Piotr's face for traces of recognition, but it remained blank and slightly distracted as if he was merely thinking of the next thing to say to her. Before he could interrupt, she told him of her research into her great-aunt's life and of her desire to speak with a long-term resident, someone who had lived in the building since just after the Second World War.

'Ahh.' He raised one finger in the air. 'I think there are two peoples that live here after the war, no? Mrs Roth and the Shafers. Very, very old now, yes? But their nurses tell Piotr that they live here oh so long ago.'

'That's amazing. My great-aunt said she was friends with Mrs Roth, and Mr and Mrs Shafer. How do you spell those names?'

He moved back behind the desk and opened a leather-bound ledger on the desktop.

One of his plump fingers moved down a list of names and

telephone numbers stored beneath the laminated pages of the desk ledger.

Quickly, she leant over the desk. Her eyes became frantic, flicking up and down the names and searching for apartment and telephone numbers. She looked at the place in the ledger where Piotr's index finger had paused: *Mrs Roth*, followed by three phone numbers. One was next to what had been misspelled as *Dawter*, another was next to *Nerse*, and the third read *Landline*. This was an 0207 number and she quickly committed it to memory while fishing for her cell phone.

While Piotr talked quickly about them meeting for 'the coffee, no? To speak about the history and the aunt Lillian, yes?' she smiled and nodded, half-listening but trying to screen out the sound of his voice while she quickly added Mrs Roth's number to the address book of her phone. When she caught Piotr studying her, she raised the phone to her ear, as if to listen to a message. 'Sorry, I have to listen to this. A voicemail.' She rolled her eyes as if irritated. After a suitable pause she snapped the lid of the phone shut, shaking her head. 'Not what I thought.' Then looked into Piotr's eyes and smiled.

He went into a diatribe about 'the mobile', while her eyes scoured the page of the open ledger again to find the Shafers. There it was: number twelve, with one phone number given, which she also rehearsed and then surreptitiously inputted into her cell phone by holding it below the top of the desk.

'It is not so good at this time to speak to Mrs Roth and the Shafers.' Piotr beamed and held out his arms. Then closed his eyes. 'Ahh, but I will surely tell them that you asked about the aunt Lillian, no? In the mornings they don't like to be disturbed. Maybe if we meet and you tell me the interesting story about the aunt Lillian, then I can say to them: hey, I know this really nice lady who comes to our lovely building and is the relative of Lillian. Then I think they might say the yes, no?'

'No.' She couldn't keep the edge out of her voice. But then softened it to say, 'I don't have time. I'm very busy with sorting out the apartment and seeing ... friends in the evening. I can catch up with these people another time.'

Maybe the Shafers and Mrs Roth would be annoyed when she called. They'd already refused to see her once. It was all such a long shot. But it was a shot she had to take if she was to validate anything in Lillian's journals. Miles had said as much in the bar in Notting Hill the night before. After reading a few of Lillian's journals he was suddenly very keen for her to find out whether anyone had seen Hessen's paintings in Barrington House before he disappeared. For an art historian, this kind of information would be a coup.

Apryl was shepherded by Piotr up to the door that connected the lobby to the east wing. Close to her, his breath was unpleasantly warm on her face and neck, and the broken-English banter was relentless, insistent, until she practically fell into the sombre elevator to escape the bulbous shape beaming through the glass of the doors as they slid shut. He mimed the holding up of a phone, while showing her all of his little square teeth.

She half-turned and pretended not to see his hand signals. But then saw something else from the corner of her eye. She glimpsed it in the mirror at the back of the carriage. Something moving quickly behind her shoulder. Tall and thin and whitish, it rapidly vanished from her line of sight.

Sucking in her breath, she lurched around to see the gleaming but empty carriage. Nothing there but her. 'Jesus,' she said, breathing out. Then looked at the panel, as the elevator made what felt like a deliberately slow ascent. Six, seven ... come on ... eight ... nine. And why wasn't the door opening now? It hadn't ever taken this long before, had it?

With a swish the doors finally opened and she rushed out of the carriage, looking back over her shoulder, at herself in the elevator's mirror, at her frightened pale face. A face with an expression she'd only ever seen before in the mirrors of Barrington House.

'Who is this? What do you want?' The tone of voice was as unsettling as the smashing of crockery on a tiled floor.

Apryl cleared her throat, but the thin voice that slipped out was not one she cared to recognize as her own. 'I'm ... Er, my name is—'

'Will you speak up! I can't hear you.' Mrs Roth's voice rose beyond annoyance. Elderly, sharpened by age, too brittle for warmth, it instantly made her want to hang up.

'Mrs Roth.' She raised her voice, but couldn't banish the tremor from her words. 'I hope you don't mind me disturbing you, but—'

'Of course I do. Who are you?' In the background she could hear the music from a television show.

'My name is Apryl Beckford, and I'm—'

'What are you saying?' the old woman shouted, adding, 'I don't know who it is' to someone who must have been in the room with her. 'No! Don't touch it. Leave it! Leave it!' she shouted at the other occupant.

'The television. Perhaps you should turn the television down,' Apryl prompted.

'Don't be ridiculous. I'm watching it now. There's nothing wrong with it. Stephen fixed it for me. I'm not interested in anything you have to sell.' The phone hit the cradle with a sound like a stone hitting a windshield.

Apryl winced and listened to the dialling tone for a few seconds, too stunned to move.

Three hours later, sitting on the bed in Lillian's bedroom, she called again. This time there was no sound of a television booming in the background. Instead, the woman sounded as if she'd just been roused from sleep.

'Yes?'

'Oh, I hope I didn't wake you.'

'You did.' The words uncurled like something dark and mean, and in her mind Apryl saw small cruel eyes narrowing. 'I don't sleep at night. I'm not well. How can I sleep?'

'I'm very sorry to hear about that, Mrs Roth. I hope you get well soon.'

'What do you want?' The question was more of a bark than a sentence.

'I'm ...' Her mind went blank. 'Well, I'm calling because—'

'What are you saying? You're making no sense.'

Then shut your mouth, you evil bitch, and I'll make some sense. 'I'm very interested in Barrington House, Mrs Roth. The history. You see—'

'What's it got to do with me? I don't want to buy anything from you.'

Apryl imagined the phone crashing down again and braced herself. 'I'm not selling anything. I'm the niece of Lillian

Archer, Mrs Roth. I'm just trying to find out about her. I never knew her. And I believe you've lived here for a long time. I would really like to talk with you because I'm sure you have some very interesting stories. Especially about the artist—'

'Artist. What do you mean, artist?'

'Erm. A man called Felix Hessen. He lived—'

'I know where he lived. What are you trying to do? Frighten me? I'm not well. I'm old. And it's a cruel thing to call me and remind me of him. How dare you?'

'I'm sorry. I didn't mean to upset you, ma'am. Only, I'm visiting here from America to sort out my great-aunt's—'

'I'm not interested in America!'

Apryl closed her eyes and shook her head. What was wrong with these people? Apart from Miles, every tenuous connection to Hessen led her to the unstable, the dysfunctional and the senile. It was wearing her out. It was impossible to communicate with them. They didn't listen. She was just there to function as an audience for their craziness. She took a deep breath. 'You don't have to be interested in America. Please, just listen to me. It's quite simple really. I'm not trying to sell anything. Nor am I trying to frighten you.' Irritation gave a force to her words.

'You don't have to shout, dear. It's not very nice.'

Apryl bit her bottom lip. 'I just want to talk to someone who knew my great-aunt, and the artist Felix Hessen. She wrote about him a lot. Nothing more. Just a conversation.'

And then an extraordinary thing happened that filled Apryl with remorse at having raised her voice to this confused and elderly lady she'd woken from a nap. Mrs Roth's voice quivered with emotion and then thickened with a sob.

'He was an awful man. And I can't sleep because of him. He's doing it again.'

'Mrs Roth, please don't cry. I'm sorry I upset you. I just want to speak to someone who was here when Lillian was alive.'

The crotchety voice disintegrated into a few frail words interspersed with sniffs. 'I can still hear him. I've told them downstairs.'

Apryl struggled to comprehend what she was being told. 'Mrs Roth, I'm sorry you're upset. You sound so sad. My aunt was too. Because of him.'

'Well I am, dear. And you would be too. You believe me, don't you?'

'Yes, I do. Of course I do. And talking to someone might help. I think you need a new friend, Mrs Roth.'

Somewhere in the apartment, the metronome of a clock's hand struck a steely echo that travelled like sad tidings throughout the empty rooms. But she couldn't see the clock or seem to be able to get any closer to the far-off sound. And it was still hard to believe homes like this existed in Barrington House: peeling and faded with neglect from floor to ceiling, room after room.

As the small Filipino nurse, Imee, scurried ahead of her, Apryl found herself in a daze, dawdling down the long hallway of Mrs Roth's apartment, the soles of her boots landing hard against the worn carpet. It might have been blue once, but was now threadbare and grey.

To the side of the hatstand and telephone table, a small and aged kitchen presented itself, cramped with an old enamel cooker and refrigerator. It looked like it hadn't been used in years.

Apryl glanced into the living room. With her quick eyes she caught glimpses of elegant disorder. A silver drinks trolley sat idle, loaded with crystal decanters, an ice bucket, tongs, and half-empty bottles of spirits. Ageing heavy furniture retreated sorrowfully into the corners. The air was shadowed by leaden drapes, drawn by heavy gold braid. And all this beneath a magnificent chandelier, hanging like a gigantic ice crystal over a mahogany table.

The thin light caught these once glamorous but now dust-filmed objects. They seemed frozen in a forlorn disappointment at the absence of whoever it was who once peopled the space. It made her melancholy. In the noisy maelstrom that existed outside, of angry traffic and marching strangers, of ugly, tragic council estates, of wind-blown garbage, beggars, and the intense energy that both drained and invigorated you at the same time, how could such stillness exist? Shabby with neglect but undisturbed and ominous in its silence, it was another quiet relic from an era of elegant ladies in long dresses and gentlemen in dinner jackets.

And there was nothing on any of the walls. No pictures, no mirrors – not so much as a single watercolour. Nothing.

An open door beside the bathroom revealed a smaller bedroom with an unmade bed. The nurse's room, beside the Queen's chamber. Outside which they came to stand. The nurse paused before the closed door and lowered her solemn eyes, too tired to even attempt an encouraging smile. Behind the antique door the sound of a television boomed. Imee knocked so loudly it made Apryl jump.

When a voice, fierce with age, cried out from the other side of the door, she entered the master bedroom.

Apryl suspected the wizened figure had been deliberately positioned and prepared for her arrival. Small as a child, with mottled arms as thin as sticks resting upon the covers, the big hands incongruous below the lumpy wrists, Mrs Roth sat propped up in bed. She was clad in a nightgown of blue silk edged with white lace, an outfit that did nothing but add to the horror of the aged body inside it. The carefully arranged but grotesquely old-fashioned hairstyle had the unmistakable sheen of hair that had been recently attended to. It was as high and perfectly conical as a bishop's hat, but transparent. And the lipless beak of a mouth above the heavily grooved chin, protruding like the muzzle of a small dog, had been painted bright pink. Small eyes full of mistrust watched Apryl enter.

'Sit there,' the voice commanded while the hard eyes glanced at the two chairs at the end of the bed, arranged on either side of the television.

Smiling weakly, Apryl unlooped her bag from her shoulder and made a move for the nearest chair. 'Hello, Mrs Roth. It's so good of you to see me. I—'

'Not there!' the figure barked. 'The other one.'

'I'm sorry. I was just saying—'

'Never mind all that. Take your coat off, dear. What kind of woman wears her coat indoors?'

On either side of the enormous bed in which the tiny figure was huddled at the very centre, surrounded by large white pillows, two small dressers were cluttered with photographs. The black-and-white faces all looked towards the foot of the bed, where Apryl now sat, uncomfortable on a hard chair with wings that obscured the room on either side of her head, tunnelling her vision forward to the little creature among the pillows.

An audience had truly been granted. But what kind of audience? Mrs Roth's manner was hardly conducive to any kind of reasonable conversation – but that was the point. The clever old bird maintained complete control of both the discourse and the visitor by immediately unsettling and belittling them with her unpleasantness. And who was anyone to object, either as a guest or as a disempowered member of staff on her payroll, like the porters downstairs? Even the garrulous and feckless Piotr shuddered at the mention of Mrs Roth. And poor little Imee's face reflected the same fear and aversion. The nurse didn't enter the room – some rule probably forbade her doing so. Instead, she waited at the door.

But as Miles had reminded Apryl, Mrs Roth was one of a small and shrinking group of people still alive who could attest to the existence of Hessen's mythical paintings. She was now here on Miles's behalf too. More importantly, Mrs Roth had known Lillian. And the last tangible traces of her great-aunt's life were evaporating.

At least Mrs Roth was more lucid than Alice from the Friends of Felix Hessen, and beneath her inhospitable carapace there was a vulnerability about the old woman.

'I don't want to talk about him,' Mrs Roth said, as if reading her mind.

'Mmm?' Apryl asked.

'You know who I am talking about. Don't play games with me. I'm not stupid. But you are a bloody fool if you think I am.'

Then why did you agree to see me? She couldn't risk an argument. Mrs Roth was not someone to trifle with, but to weather until the woman's mood changed. And she knew from experience that the rude and unpleasant were not insensitive to flattery; the very insecurity that created a menacing facade could be turned into an Achilles' heel.

Apryl smiled her sweetest and most guileless smile. 'Not for a minute would I suggest such a thing, Mrs Roth. Would a fool live in such a grand apartment? I've never had the pleasure to see such a place.'

'Don't be ridiculous. It's terrible.' But no sooner had her attempt to win Mrs Roth been rebuffed than the old woman's mood changed swiftly to something more agreeable. Her cheeks flushed and her eyes flared with self-importance. 'You should have seen it when my husband was alive. We had such wonderful parties, dear. You've never seen anything like them. Full of lovely people. The kind of people you would never meet. You have no idea how charming the men were. You've never met such gentlemen. And the beauty of the ladies. You girls are nothing compared to how we used to be. I mean, look at you, dear. You should do something with your hair. It's awful.'

Apryl tried to maintain her smile. 'Yes, I should. Maybe you could recommend somebody. As soon as I came in, I noticed the lovely colour of your hair. It's so shiny.' Apryl looked at the carefully domed wisps and smiled as sincerely as she could.

Mrs Roth blushed. 'Would you like some tea?'

'That would be nice.'

The old lady picked up a small brass bell from her bedclothes and began to ring it furiously. 'Oh where is she?' she cried out at exactly the same moment she began to ring the bell.

In seconds the door opened and Imee shuffled in, her eyes lowered to her white gym shoes. 'We want tea, Imee. Tea! My visitor has been in the rain and you have forgotten to make tea again.'

'I am sorry, Mrs Roth,' the woman said.

'How many times must you be told. And cake. Bring in the cakes. I want the yellow one and the pink one.'

Mrs Roth glared at Imee until she'd left the room, then said, 'Look over here. Here, dear. These are my daughter's grandchildren. They are so beautiful. I took Clara to Claridge's for lunch yesterday. And when the head waiter asked her what she wanted she said, 'Fish and chips.' What a darling she is. You've never seen such a beautiful child. Look. Here. I said look here.' Irritated because Apryl hadn't moved quickly enough to satisfy her most recent and impulsive demand, she began pointing in the general direction of the cabinet on her right side.

When Imee returned with the tea and cakes on a small silver trolley, Apryl looked at the floor. Squirming in her seat and powerless to act, she listened to Mrs Roth humiliate the nurse, going so far as to call her a 'bloody fool' for not positioning the tea things in the manner she had been told to 'a hundred times'. Imee responded by saying, 'I am nurse, Mrs Roth, not waitress,' before scurrying from the room on the brink of tears.

'Cake, dear. Have a slice of cake, dear. I like the pink one. My daughter bought it for me.'

It was so cheap and dry, Apryl struggled to swallow a mouthful of it.

'You look like Lilly,' Mrs Roth said, dabbing crumbs from the side of her mouth with one swollen knuckle.

'I do?'

She nodded. 'When she was young. Very pretty woman. Such a shame she went mad.'

And then, quite suddenly, Mrs Roth asked Apryl to turn the television on so she could watch some quiz show, during which she was forbidden to speak. But by the first commercial break, Mrs Roth had fallen asleep while the television boomed within the room.

Watching the sleeping figure, who made infrequent whistling sounds through her nose, Apryl sat still for a few minutes. Then she called out, 'Umm, Mrs Roth. Mrs Roth,' three times, but to no effect. The woman could not be woken. Perhaps she was dead. But when Apryl became desperate for the toilet and stood up, Mrs Roth's eyes opened. Milky orbs drifted around her eye sockets, then locked on to Apryl. 'Where are you going? Sit down at once.'

'I was going to use the bathroom.'

'Oh.'

'You were asleep.'

'What?'

'You fell asleep. Maybe this is the wrong time.'

'What? Nonsense! I did no such thing. Don't make things up.'

'No. Well, I was mistaken then. I'll just be a moment.'

The bell was hoisted aloft and Mrs Roth began furiously ringing it again. Apryl and Imee passed in the doorway and exchanged tired, nervous but ultimately knowing glances. A look familiar to those beleaguered by the petty and the powerful.

When she returned from the bathroom, she tried to formulate a tactful way of bringing the conversation back to Felix Hessen, but Mrs Roth pre-empted her. It seemed she was now ready to speak of him without a prompt. It was as if until now she had been testing her guest's fitness for disclosure. Playing a game, unwilling to give her what she wanted until she'd tormented her first. And mercifully, the television was silenced.

'So you want to know about Felix. That's why you're here. I'm not fooled by you, dear. But it'll do you no good. You won't understand. No one does.'

'Try me. Please.'

'He drove Lilly mad. You know that much, don't you?'

Apryl nodded. 'Yes. Yes, I do. But I want to know how.'

Mrs Roth looked at her hands in silence. When Apryl began to wonder if the woman would ever speak again, she said, 'I don't like to think of him. I never wanted to remember him.' Her voice was tired. Every vestige of her brittle, difficult, impossible character was now absent from her words. But she was unable to meet Apryl's eye as she spoke. 'When he was finally gone we all hoped that was the end of it. But we were naive to have thought so. Men like that don't follow the same rules as the rest of us. Lilly knew that. She'd have told you the same. No one would believe us. But we knew.'

Apryl leant forward in her seat.

'When he first came here ... I don't remember when ... but after the war, when Arthur and I came back from Scotland, he was here.' She paused to paw at the bedclothes with her knotted fingers. 'He was the most handsome man I had ever seen. We all thought so. But he never smiled. Not once. And he never spoke to a soul. We thought it odd. It had never been a building for recluses. Quite the opposite. It was nothing like it is now. This was once a wonderful place where your neighbours were your friends. We all entertained each other. Only decent people here, dear. Not like today. It's full of rubbish now. People with no manners. You should hear the noise they make. We have no idea who is living next to us any more. People move in and out all the time. It's intolerable.'

Mrs Roth began to sniff. From under the sleeve of her nightdress she removed a white tissue and began to dab at her eyes. A long heavy tear that appeared incongruous on her face rolled down her cheek and splattered against her wrist.

Instinctively, Apryl went to her and sat on the side of the bed. Mrs Roth immediately offered Apryl her free hand. It was crooked with arthritis and very cold. Apryl warmed the fingers between her palms. The simple act made Mrs Roth cry harder, in the same way a child's grief intensifies within the safety of a parent's arms.

'One would often come across him in a stairwell. He never used the lift. He would be standing alone and looking at the pictures. He would take them from the wall and study them. But he would turn on you if you disturbed him. I hated it. No one liked to look into his eyes, dear. He was a lunatic. Quite mad. No one in their right mind had eyes like that. No one was comfortable with him here. Many of us were Jewish and knew he'd been one of those Hitler people. What are they called?'

'Fascists.'

'Don't interrupt me, dear. Nothing upsets me more than a woman with no manners.'

'Sorry.'

'But that was how it was for years. I never once had a single conversation with him. Nothing. No one did. The porters didn't like him either. They were frightened of him. We all were, dear. He lived in the flat underneath us. Down there.' She pointed at the floor. 'And he was always making such a noise at night. Moving things. Waking us up. This bumping. And shouting. You could hear him talking in a loud voice. As if he was in another room of our home. And right up against his ceiling we heard the other voices. Under our feet. But we never saw any visitors coming or going. No one knows how he got them up here. We asked the porters and they swore no one had called on the gentleman in number sixteen. But he had company. It wasn't a radio. Radios never sounded like that, dear.

'Sometimes it seemed like his flat was full of people. As if he was having a party, but not a very nice one. His other neighbours said the same thing. We all heard it in the west wing. And it got worse. Before his accident. The noises and voices. People were leaving because of them.

'And then one night – I'll never forget it – we heard such a dreadful commotion. Screaming. It was awful. This screaming from below us. Like someone was in agony, dear. Like they were being tortured. We were so shaken. We couldn't move. Arthur and I just sat together in bed and listened. Until the screaming stopped.

'And then Arthur went down there. He called your uncle Reggie, and Tom Shafer, and they went down with him. They were all in their dressing gowns. Reggie came because he had been trying to get Hessen evicted from here. The head porter was called too, and the police. And when they opened it up, they found him in the living room . . .'

Mrs Roth covered as much of her face as possible with the handkerchief and sobbed. When she spoke again her voice was broken. 'I went down with Lilly to help. He'd had a terrible accident . . . His face was all gone . . . Down to the bone.

'They took him away. We thought he would die. No one could have survived those injuries. And no one knew what had happened to him. He must . . . he must have done it to himself.

'But he came back. Months later. With his whole head in bandages. And there was a nurse, who he dismissed a few days later. Some of us even sent flowers and cards to the wretched man. We knew he was in there, but he wouldn't come to the door. Like before, he just wanted to be left alone. So we left him alone. At least until it began again. And the next time it was worse than before.

'He was evil. I told you that. And now I have them again. The nightmares. They killed Reginald and Arthur. It was the dreams, dear. No one would believe me now, but we knew then. He killed them both.'

Apryl couldn't remain silent any longer. 'How, Mrs Roth? I thought he was just a painter.'

'No. No. No,' she shook her head, the rims of her eyes now inflamed. 'I told you. He was all wrong. Evil. I never knew anyone could be so bad, dear. He should never have come here. I don't remember why he did. But he ruined the building. Killed it.'

'How, Mrs Roth? My great-aunt wrote the same things. What did he do?'

'The shadows have come back to the stairs. We could never get rid of them then, and they're back here now. They changed the lights but it never made any difference. People stopped coming here. People left. But some of us refused to let him ruin our home. It was such a wonderful place until he came here.'

'Did you see . . . his paintings?'

Mrs Roth nodded. 'Horrible things. You've no idea. He didn't know what beauty was. He made us all dream of them. We thought the Colonel was going gaga. He used to live here, the Colonel. And Mrs Melbourne. They saw them first. At night, dear.

'People took pills and went to doctors. Real doctors. Not like you have now, dear. They don't know anything now. They're bloody fools. But even our doctors could do nothing for anyone who had the dreams. Reginald had them next. And Lilly. Then me. I was only young.' She began to weep again and to squeeze at Apryl's hands.

'What were they? I don't understand. What were the dreams?'

'I can't say. I don't know how to. But he made us see things. You think I'm mad, don't you?'

'No, I don't.'

'Yes you do. You think I'm a silly old woman. I'm not.'

'No. No.' Apryl rubbed Mrs Roth's back, to which she responded with a surge of sobs.

She began to sniff and talk at the same time, in a tearful voice. 'The voices came out of that flat and onto the stairs and into our rooms. Arthur and I used to sit together and hear them. There was never anyone there, but we could always hear them around us. Anywhere near his flat, you could hear the things he brought with him. They came out of there.' Again, she pointed a twisted hand at the floor.

'Oh, it was terrible.' Mrs Roth began to speak in bursts between her sobs. Apryl moved her head closer as it was becoming difficult to make out exactly what she was saying. 'And Mrs Melbourne jumped from the roof. I saw her down there in the garden. She hit the wall. She wasn't the last to do it either.' The last sentence she spoke softly and with a genuine remorse that shook her words, but she wouldn't or couldn't look at Apryl as she spoke.

'Oh, Mrs Roth. I'm so sorry. They were your friends. It must have been terrible.'

'You have no idea. It was his fault. He did it.'

'With his paintings?'

Mrs Roth drew a deep breath and swallowed a sob. She nodded, once. 'They confronted him. Reginald and Tom and Arthur. They went to see him, dear. They were so angry, you can't imagine. We were all going mad with it. So the men went to his flat because he wouldn't receive our telephone calls and wouldn't answer letters from the management. The men took keys from the head porter and let themselves inside.

'And . . . and he looked terrible. They said his head was all wrapped up in something. Over his face he wore this mask. It was red. Cloth. And through it they could see the terrible shape of his face, dear. It was so tight on his face. No one knew what to say. But Reginald tried to be calm. Asked him what it was he thought he was doing to our home.

'He laughed at them. He just laughed. They were very reasonable. They were all good men. But he just laughed. His face in this . . . this red thing. They could only see his eyes.

'And then the men saw them again. On the walls. What he'd been doing in there for so long. They were worse than before. All the terrible things from our dreams. The paintings . . .'

'What were they like? Please tell me. Please.'

'And then Reginald lost his temper. They . . .'

'They?'

Mrs Roth sat up in her bed and released Apryl's hand. The sobbing and sniffing stopped abruptly, and her face froze back into a grim facade. 'I'm tired.'

'But . . . I mean, you were telling me . . . about the paintings?'

'I don't want to talk about it. It's not important.'

'But you were so upset. I want to understand.'

'It's none of your business. I want Imee. Imee. Where's my bell? It's time for me to eat. You shouldn't visit at mealtimes. It's rude.' The bell was ringing next to Apryl's ear, the action deliberate, she felt.

She moved back to the chair to collect her things. Then turned to speak as Imee came through the door – but Apryl found herself too bewildered by Mrs Roth's story to move her lips. And it was clear the woman was terrified and had told her far more than she ever intended to.

Apryl moved quickly from the bedside, only looking behind once she reached the safety of the doorway to see Imee beside the bed, bent by the force of the shrieked reprimands issuing from amongst the pillows. *A cushion over that old face would not be unreasonable.* Apryl felt shocked at the presence of such a thought that did not feel like one of her own.

She would let herself out. *What kind of woman lets herself out, dear?* Relief to be away from the dreadful woman pushed her down the aged hallway, and excitement at the revelations she would recount to Miles made her nimbler in her high-heeled boots. Until she opened the front door and passed through onto the landing.

With a breath-stealing suddenness, there was a quick flurry of whitish motion on her left side. Cringing, she sucked in air so fast she issued a tiny shriek. Then looked past the gloved hand she had raised to fend the thing off. In her peripheral vision she'd seen a flapping shape speeding towards her, with a smear of red above what could only have been bony shoulders.

And as she peered through her gloved fingers at the large polished mirror on the wall opposite the elevator, there was a brief billow of something white within the gilt frame. Which made her turn about swiftly to see the origin of the reflection on her right side.

Terrified she had flinched at a reflection and not the actual assailant, she staggered back two steps and braced herself for the impact.

But there was no one on the landing with her. She scoured the stairwells and elevator door for what had come rushing at her, but nothing moved, with the exception of the rapid ascent and descent of her own chest that struggled to take a breath.

TWENTY-FOUR

'What are you doing?'

The sharp voice pierced him from behind. Seth didn't even need to turn to identify who had caught him unlocking the door of apartment sixteen. It was a voice he'd heard on the house phone most nights for the last six months. But when he did turn to face Mrs Roth and saw her dressed in a pale blue housecoat and red slippers, the childlike vulnerability had gone, along with the frailty and confusion she exhibited last time they met, outside this very door. Now her hair was perfect; the bulb of thin silver covering the mottled skull hadn't even touched the pillow. She'd sat up all night waiting for the sounds to begin.

Panicked at being caught trespassing – he could be sacked for entering this flat, and would be blamed for the noises coming out of it – Seth tried to speak. But failed, muted by his own fear. Mrs Roth would be sure to tell Stephen first thing at daybreak, if not before. She wasn't just angry; she was furious at the sight of him before that door with keys in hand. Her face was red, her bottom lip trembling with emotion, the small eyes sharpened by rage. She raised her arm, the elbow bent, the quilted sleeve of her housecoat slipping down an emaciated forearm, stained with blue veins and continents of liverish discolorations.

'I asked you a question. What are you doing?' Her voice rose as she spoke until she was shouting. It could carry. He wanted to shut her up, but was powerless to act, to placate her. She was too clever. Too aware of the weakness of others, of his lowly status, and of her instant advantage as a resident. Too eager to expose and torment.

Seth swallowed. 'I heard something. I thought someone had broken in.'

'Liar. You are a liar. It's you. You! You make the noises in there. I knew it! You do it to frighten me because you know I am upstairs. You are a terrible man to frighten an old woman. I want Stephen now. Call Stephen. Now!'

He felt sick. Couldn't dislodge that huge lump of fear clogged behind his breastbone. It was like being a kid again. She always flustered him.

Bitch.

The very sight of her filled him with a rage of such intensity he imagined smashing her dried-up stick body against a wall. That idiotically big head, the threadbare hair, the pointy, vicious face above that child-puppet body of old sticks and loose flesh: why couldn't she die? Her own family despised her. She couldn't keep a nurse for more than a month. Reduced them to tears every day. No one could work for her. Or stand her. She had even driven the taciturn Stephen grey with her impossible demands.

Seth felt himself go white with loathing from head to toe. An antipathy that frightened him; the kind that would astonish him once it passed. Something he regularly experienced now, but never grew accustomed to; he'd never before been able to hate with such intensity, or to create from it with such integrity. And didn't she understand that he had no choice – that something far greater than him was calling him up here to study its genius?

At last he found his tongue, but managed to suppress the anger, quickly thinking of a tactic to sidestep this mess. 'I am responsible for the health and safety of the residents in this building at night. And I am sick of the noises in here.' He jabbed a finger at the door. 'And I can do nothing because of some stupid rule about the key. And you phone every night complaining to me about the noises in the empty flat beneath you. It's gone on for too long, Mrs Roth. And tonight, I decided to go inside. So phone Stephen if you want. I really don't care. Because I've had enough.'

At first she seemed startled that anyone would dare to take such a defiant tone with her. But the anger gradually softened from her face, only to be replaced with an expression of suspicion as she regarded him in silence, and thought on what he'd said. After a few seconds of deliberation, she raised the crooked hand again, showed him her big knuckles and fingers lumpy with arthritis. 'Don't you lie to me. You have been going in there. At night. And moving things. Making noises.'

Seth did his best to muster a stance of impotent frustration. It wasn't hard, he'd had plenty of practice. He shook his head, stared at the ceiling as if to beseech a higher power. This had to be good; even though most of the sting had gone from her voice. 'Mrs Roth, you believe what you want to believe. I am only doing my job. Would you rather I sat downstairs and ignored a break-in? So be it.' He locked the door and walked towards the stairs.

'Where are you going?' she asked, the bent finger jabbing the air again.

'I'm going back downstairs, Mrs Roth. Isn't that what you want?'

'Don't be a bloody idiot. Get it open. I want to see for myself. Go on, open it. Now.'

He tried to fight a smile. He could tell Stephen she forced him to open the flat because of the noises, and that he only entered the apartment to finally shut her up. He should have called first, but he didn't want to wake Stephen, knowing how tough he had it with Janet being so sick and everything. Maybe he and Stephen could keep it between themselves. Didn't they have an arrangement of sorts, anyway? So what was the point of making trouble?

But what would Mrs Roth think of the paintings? He imagined her pale with shock, moments before the impact of a stroke; envisaged some tiny black blood vessel inside that heavy brain, its hard wall cracking, springing a lethal leak.

And she would ruin everything if she survived the ordeal of looking at them, by shrieking her ignorant complaints at Stephen. Seth might be fired; no head porter job for him. At the very least, the locks would be changed and the door alarmed. Sealed off from him. His access would be over.

Why tonight? Why did she have to make her move tonight? He was desperate to see the last room. Terrified, but alert to the potential of its influence on his own work, back at the Green Man. On the walls. Wet on the walls. So vivid. Something to bring the London art world to its knees. Oh yes, he was having his doubts. Was sick with fear at what he was doing, what he was becoming, what he was seeing inside his very home . . . But an artist must be courageous, and what was flowing from his hands was too spectacular to deny.

'You bloody fool! I own the flat, it's my property. Get

it open. I'm telling you to open that door. Do as you are told.'

He started to fret again. To taste panic at the back of his mouth. He removed the keys from his pocket. Fumbled with them. But how was this possible? How did Mrs Roth own this place and the ghastly wonders inside it?

And then another voice spoke. From the stairwell, behind Mrs Roth. A voice he also knew well, its words coming from the cold, windy shadows of deserted council flats, from the rain-blurred streets of Hackney, and from the dim horrors inside the rooms of the Green Man. His hooded companion had returned. 'Go on, Seth. Open it up for the old lady. There's someone down there who wants to see her. An old friend, like. She'll be taken care of. She'll get what's coming.'

Inside the mouth of the stairwell and half-obscured by the wall, Seth glimpsed the lowered cowl of nylon hood. The face was lost in darkness and the melted hands were tucked away in the rustling oversized pockets.

She'll get what's coming.

What did he mean? Seth felt sick.

'Give them to me! Get out of my way!' Mrs Roth came across the landing, quick on those clawed feet for an old lady. Her face animated by fury at his indecision, one of her lumpy hands snatched for the bunch of keys.

He held them up, out of her reach. Stared down at her, keeping his voice even. 'Please. Would you just let me do my job?'

It was no use; she gave him no choice. He slid the front-door key inside the lock. He was not responsible.

'Hurry up. Hurry. Why are you just standing there?'

Seth unlocked the door and pushed it open. He stood

there and stared into the darkness in front of him. A cold draught wiped across his face and made his neck shiver.

Around his elbow he felt the clutch of her hand. Despite her anger and the way she had spoken to him, she still expected to be escorted in there. And protected.

He glanced down at her. Could see how agitated she had become. How frightened she was of the place. What did she know about it? She knew something. She'd lived in this building since the Second World War, and must have known the former resident of this apartment. They had been neighbours. And now she owned the flat.

Seth led her into the darkness, pausing inside the front door to reach for the lights. Into the hallway came the crimson glow.

'Don't they work? It's so dark. Have you got a torch?'

So her eyes weren't that good. No surprises there; she was nearly a hundred. Seth looked over his shoulder quickly. The hooded boy stood on the landing, watching.

'Leave the door open. I don't like it,' Mrs Roth muttered. 'Can you see anything?' The strength had gone from her voice. Now she was just a frightened old lady, squeezing his elbow. Asking for reassurance. How could he ever have been afraid of her?

And yes, Seth could see everything: the paintings covered by the dirty ivory sheets, hung upon red walls, and all lit by the dim rose light silting through patterned glass. Just as he'd left it. But Mrs Roth didn't appear to notice the paintings, which he thought odd. She was still complaining about the dark. Pressing herself against him, her head only rising to his bottom rib. A flicker of sympathy caught in his chest before he banished it, knowing this was no mark of friendship between them, or of respect. She despised him. She needed him now, that was all. In the morning she'd be reporting him to Stephen. Ruining everything between him and the treasures in this sacred place.

'Can you see anyone?' Her voice was shaky and imploring. Then she called out, 'Who's there?' into the darkness; the obtuse tone was back in place, but seemed to lose its power inside the hallway.

'Mrs Roth, who lived here?'

'A terrible man,' she said. The strength in her voice was slipping away again. She sounded confused and frightened. Misery and fear combined to sag around her mouth, to bow her head, as if she were being forced to remember something acutely painful. She seemed more stooped over than ever before. 'We don't want him coming back.'

He led her down to the middle of the hallway, aware of her breathing, that seemed laboured, as if she were enduring some strenuous exertion as opposed to merely wandering on slippered feet between these red walls. Walls she took no notice of. He heard her whimper.

'An artist lived here, didn't he, Mrs Roth?'

Mrs Roth said nothing as she looked at the closed doors.

'Someone you didn't like. Probably didn't understand. So tell me, Mrs Roth, who was he, this terrible man? And what did you do to him?'

'I don't want to think of him. Don't ask me again. I don't want to talk about him. I don't want to remember him. Not in here. I bought this place to get rid of him.' And then, her voice practically a whisper, 'After he'd already left.'

'What did he do, Mrs Roth?'

'Shut up!' she suddenly shrieked, then pointed at the door

to the mirrored room. 'In there. Do you hear it? I can hear him in there. He's laughing. It can't be. We got rid of him.' The sudden force of her fear made Seth jump. She was shaking. White with shock and looking so frail now, he was practically holding her up: a papier-mâché puppet with bones of bamboo.

'He can't come back. It can't be him. Someone is playing a trick on us. We got rid of him. We wouldn't allow him to be here. Open that door. Open that door and turn the lights on. I want to see. I don't believe it.'

Unsure of what to do and so aware of the power inside that room, he hesitated. Just standing near the door made him tense with an unpleasant anticipation. And Mrs Roth was witless with fear. Was trembling against him. What could she hear? She said she could hear *him* laughing. But Seth could not hear laughter ... Just the wind. Yes, the suggestion of a far-off wind. The sense of some tremendous cold distance approaching, as if a black sea were making its way towards them on some impossible tide. One that washed in from above them, and somehow below them at the same time.

'No. It's not safe. We have to go,' he whispered desperately at her.

'Open it! Open the door. I want to see. This isn't right. It's not right. He can't come back.' She was becoming hysterical. The perfect dome of silvery hair was falling apart. What pitiful remnants of blood still survived inside her veins appeared to have drained from the surface of her skin. She looked ready to collapse; her flesh had taken on a greyish tinge and he was seeing far too much of the whites of her eyes.

But he couldn't just stand here and let her scream. She might wake someone. Right now another resident might be banging on Stephen's door, or calling the front desk. Or worse, the police. He was losing control again. Control of this stupid panicking old bitch. Anger replaced his unease and fear. Anger could do that; it had its uses. 'All right. All right,' he said, his teeth clenched in a grimace. He reached out and seized the cold brass handle of the door. But when the moment came to give the handle one full turn, it was pulled from his hand. Opened from inside with a force that made them both cry out.

Seth sat behind his desk. Unmoving. Staring at the glass of the front doors and the blue-black of dawn behind. Shivers ran across his skin, beginning somewhere inside, but spreading out and over his entire form. In the ceiling the lights made tinkling sounds from their own heat. Somewhere outside, a powerful car accelerated into the distance.

He wanted to keep his mind clear but couldn't even follow the action on the television screen below the desktop. It was just a senseless mosaic of flickers and colours and distant voices. The pictures in his head were far more compelling. And they refused to stop or be still, but surged forward to reassemble the events that had occurred so quickly around him upstairs.

He remembered jumping back, instinctively, away from the dark, empty rectangle of space behind that middle door. At least that's what it had looked like. A room that failed to materialize when the door had been torn from his hands by an eagerness within.

And then he saw Mrs Roth fall. Slowly, sideways. Down to the marble tiles at his feet. She went down quietly. Never cried out for help. Or got her arms out to break her fall. Just hit the hard tiles with a smacking sound. And lay still, with her face turned towards the door. She looked dazed. Her lips moved but she made no sound.

Seth had looked into the room. Some of the dim reddish light from the hall fell through the doorway, to reveal the glint of a distant mirror and the suggestion of long, shadowy rectangles on the opposite wall. As if solid, tangible matter had suddenly recomposed itself inside that space that had previously appeared dark and empty. And just for the briefest moment, he was sure he saw something lope quickly across the face of the door. From right to left. Hunched over. Indistinct and moving with a rustle, just below the sound of the approaching wind.

'Quick, Seth. Quick. We got a deal, mate. I told you. So hurry it up. Put her in. Put her inside. There's not much time,' the hooded boy had said from behind him.

Mrs Roth had seen something too. Her eyes bulged from a face so ashen it looked like a plaster death mask. They seemed strained to bursting around the corneas and were fixed, unblinking, on the open doorway. A long dribble of spittle hung from the side of her mouth closest to the floor. She began to make a low moaning sound, like an animal. A frightened, wounded animal trying to breathe from injured lungs and growl at its attacker at the same time.

Seth felt disgusted by her. Repulsed at this display of incapacity. Wanted to get away from the broken figure on the floor.

She wouldn't listen to him. Not a word. It served her right. The stupid bitch shouldn't have been in here. He'd tried to tell her.

'Seth. Seth,' the boy said in an urgent, hissing voice. 'Do it. Do it. Put her inside. Get rid of her. You got to be quick. It don't stay open for long. And she's hurt bad. Yous'll get in trouble. They'll blame you. Do it. Do it now.'

And that compelled him to kneel down beside the old lady. To reach for her narrow, pointy shoulders. He acted on the instinctive assurance that once he put her inside this room, the problem would be solved. Once and for all. So he did it.

She moaned as he tried to move her, but she didn't move her eyes from the doorway. She felt so thin and hard under the nightgown. The housecoat flapped open. It was hard to get a grip.

'Quick, Seth. Quick like. Put her in and close the door. You got to. Do it now. Do the bitch.'

Desperate to put an end to this confusion, this fear, this terrible suspension of reason and decency, he slipped his hands under her warm armpits, hoisted her up in front of him and turned her to face the door. Limp, unmoving, and now strangely silent, she hung from his hands, her eyes still open, about to be offered to the room.

You should never move an old person who's had a fall. He remembered the first-aid training they'd had down in the staffroom. *They can go into shock.* She'd probably busted her hip. But they were past all that now. Way past it all.

'That's it. Get her in. Put the bitch inside,' the hooded boy said, his voice breathless with excitement and starting to break into a humourless, eager laugh. 'But don't look up, Seth. Just don't look up.'

Seth obeyed. Knowing this was going to lead to a swift end to the nuisance she had become, he walked forward. Not breaking his step, or looking left, right, or up above as he marched to the middle of the room. And then he laid her down.

It felt like walking through a dream in there. His own body was weightless. The air was strangely thick around him and so terribly cold it punched the breath from his lungs.

Nothing made sense, but it didn't need to, as he immediately obeyed the rules of this space and did what he had to. Did what was asked of him. Did what was necessary in a room in which the ceiling – he was quite sure of this without even looking up – had vanished and become a terrific circling of air and half-formed voices. Rushing downward from somewhere miles away towards where he stood, a cold and fathomless turbulence above his head was rotating backwards at a frightening speed and getting closer. Spiralling down. He'd heard this sound before and hoped it had been a distant radio. But he knew for certain now that it was no such thing. It was the infinity he had seen depicted in the oil paintings that hung upon these red walls. And it existed with a force and energy that made him feel more insignificant than he had ever felt before any wonder of nature.

As quickly as he could, Seth turned and scurried back towards the door and the hall outside. He lurched through the doorway, his legs shaking, knowing that he was only back in the hallway because he had been allowed to leave the room. And then he wasted no time in closing the door behind him. He kept his eyes down, so that when the door moved on its arc to become flush with the doorway, he never saw, clearly, what it was that suddenly rushed across the room and covered Mrs Roth up.

Her scream was short. Started deep. Went high, warbled, then ceased abruptly. This was followed by a loud snap, then a series of dry cracklings that put in his mind the image of fresh celery being broken between strong hands. And of dry kindling being snapped to fit into a small fireplace.

And the noise of the wind, that inexplicable circling, the static crackle swooping, and inside it the sense of figures being swept away, their voices whipping through the air, suddenly built up to a crescendo he was sure every resident in Barrington House could hear while sitting bolt upright in their beds. A climax of such force that he waited, cringing, for the sound of the windows to blow out.

It never came. And before the noise suddenly stopped he heard what sounded like an assembly of hooves against a wooden floor, scraping in their haste to get to the place he'd left Mrs Roth.

The silence that followed was almost harder to endure than the preceding series of noises that had sapped all feeling from his arms and legs. Because it wasn't a tranquil silence. Instead, it was loaded with anticipation. And when the silence lengthened Seth wondered if whatever grisly business had been conducted on the other side of the door had finally been concluded.

The hooded boy had moved down the hallway from the place where he had directed the proceedings. He stood beside Seth, who winced at the sudden gust of spent gunpowder and singed cardboard.

'You's done all right, Seth.' The boy giggled and the hood of the parka trembled from the activity inside that Seth was glad he could not see. 'Bitch had it comin', mate. Bitch. Old bitch. He's gonna be pleased wiv us, mate. He's wanted that old bitch for ages, like. Now you get inside there and clean up, mate. You's ain't finished yet.'

He had to go back inside there. And clean up. A terrible shudder racked his body and he bit his bottom lip to prevent the mighty sobs that wanted to shake him from head to foot.

'Come on Seth. You's got to be fast else yous'll get caught, mate.'

Pressed against the door of the mirrored room, Seth listened intently. Strained to hear through that heavy wood to search out any sign of occupation or activity. If he'd heard anything he was sure he would have fled and not stopped running until he'd cleared the building. But he heard nothing. It was only the gradual recession of his shock and fear that made him think again of Mrs Roth. An aged woman lying on the floor of a flat he should never have set foot inside. A woman badly injured now, or worse. He opened the door.

And saw her lying on the floor, hunched up, in much the same position he had left her, on her side, facing the mirror. The mirror in which he could see her face, contorted into a mask of such extreme fright he could almost hear the scream all over again. And above the reflection of Mrs Roth's unmoving clump of nightgown and stick limbs he saw a flurry of movement.

Way down inside the mirror, inside the silvery rectangular tunnel of reflections created by its position opposite another identical mirror on the facing wall, something moved in quick flits like the images from a film struggling through a projector. But whatever it was he thought he had seen vanished before he had taken more than two steps into the room. Even after all he had endured and heard and seen in this place, he was still sickened with fright at the suggestion of something long and pale, with a reddish smear for a head, moving away inside the reflective distance of the mirror. And it was dragging a pale blue lump by the ankle, away from this room and deep into whatever existed down there.

Seth then turned and briefly looked about him, at all eight of the undraped paintings; one on either side of the mirrors positioned in the centre of each wall. And inside him everything seemed to stop moving, as if shut down by the sheer force of the images.

Each painting depicted the same face, but in different states of disintegration amid a terrible upward blast of air, moving so fast it must have seared the flesh from the bone with the efficiency of an acetylene torch. It was as if the entire demolition of the head above the seated body had occurred instantly. The eight portraits showed, in sequence, the head of the figure being pulled apart, torn and then sucked upward, while the body was still fastened to a chair. He recognized the bits of face in the piecemeal head. It was Mrs Roth.

Seth closed his eyes and shook himself. Rubbed at his face.

Don't look up.

He knelt beside the cold body of Mrs Roth. He prodded and whispered to her, but elicited no response from the stiff shape, bunched inside the blue housecoat. Her eyes were still open, but he preferred not to look into them, either in the reflection of the mirror or on the actual face, that had been stretched by terror into the rictus of a scream that barely had time to leave the lipless mouth.

Wasting no more time, he scooped up the bundle of bone

and its lolling head and moved quickly with it through the flat, out the door, up one flight of stairs, through the open door of flat eighteen, and then down the hallway to the master bedroom. And positioned the body at the foot of the bed, as if it had fallen heavily, head first against the floor, after losing its balance. Not even little Imee was roused by the sounds he made. Perhaps that tormented drudge only responded to the sound of a bell.

Seth then stood back and surveyed his work. Satisfied with the position of the shrunken, broken thing, with one foot tangled in its bedclothes, he turned on his heel and moved quickly out of the flat. He pulled the front door closed behind him and then went back downstairs to apartment sixteen to cover both his tracks and the paintings in the mirrored room, deciding he would keep his eyes closed when so near the shrieking horror of that face, depicted in paint still wet.

TWENTY-FIVE

'They killed him, Miles. They murdered him.'

Miles paused in the process of removing his jacket. 'Who? What are you talking about?'

Apryl was breathless, wasn't making any sense – she knew it – but couldn't stop herself the moment Miles entered her room at the hotel. 'My great-uncle, Reginald, Mrs Roth's husband and Tom Shafer. The men who lived there. In Barrington House. They killed him. They went to confront him. About the dreams. The shadows. They thought he was haunting them. Like my great-aunt, in the journals. It all changed after he moved in. Then he had some kind of accident. And it all got worse after that. Don't you see it all makes sense?'

'No, I don't. What the hell are you talking about?'

'The residents killed him. They saw the paintings. In his apartment. They must have destroyed them. Burned them. And killed him too. He didn't disappear. They killed him.'

'Sweetheart. Please. Sweetheart, sit down. Here. Please. Slow down. I don't understand. It doesn't make any sense. You're talking like a crazy thing.'

But Apryl continued to pace back and forth. 'She didn't mean to tell me, but she wanted to. Part of her wanted to confess. She's very old, Miles. But she's not senile. Oh, no.

She's as sharp as a cut-throat razor. She knows exactly what she's doing. My God, she's a control freak. But she can't control her conscience. No. It's why she's such a miserable bitch. She's got a guilty conscience. And she wants to confess to someone. Anyone. I caught her at a vulnerable moment. Whenever she wakes, she's vulnerable. Her judgement is impaired – you know how it can be – and she just needs to get it off her chest.

'She's so spoilt she's still like a child,' she went on. 'But she doesn't have long left now. She knows it. And it's all been building up inside her. She did something terrible. A long time ago. Lillian too. They all did, and kept it quiet. And now her mind is playing up and she's convinced that Felix Hessen has come back to the building. For revenge, or something, I don't know. She claims she has heard him in his apartment again. Moving about underneath her. Like he used to do. She lives right on top of his old place. And the stairs are full of shadows again. Like they used to be. Shadows he brought with him years before. She can hear the voices again and is seeing things and everything. Like Lillian. It's contagious. It's so creepy up there. I mean, Jesus, I . . . thought I saw something. Again. But it's like . . . it's her conscience. It's just so fucking gothic, but it explains everything. What happened to Hessen. To the paintings.'

'Are you out of your mind?'

'Listen. Listen to me.' Apryl sat beside him and held his forearm tight with both of her hands.

'But—'

'Just listen. Please. Do me a favour, Miles. Just listen to me.'

*

When Apryl finished a less frantic account of her meeting with Mrs Roth and what she'd gleaned from her, Miles leaned back on the bed and rested on his elbows. He looked at her, his face inscrutable.

'You see?' she said, her eyes and hands still flitting with excitement.

'Jesus, what a terrible story.'

'Yes. It's the story of Hessen's missing years, and of the proof he painted.'

'Maybe. And it's just a maybe.'

'Oh Miles!'

'Hang on, sweetheart. Just cool your boots. I'd like to speak to this Mrs Roth myself before I make up my mind.'

'She won't see you. I'm sure of it. Or me again. I just know it.'

Miles raised his eyebrows. 'But what do you make of it? All that business about the shadows. And the sound of raised voices in his apartment. It's pretty damned eerie if you ask me. It's exactly the same thing Lillian wrote.'

Apryl smiled; she was so excited she wanted to scream. 'Isn't it! Have you read all the journals? Tell me you have.'

A frown creased his forehead. 'I have. Finished the last legible one this afternoon at work. In fact, I've read some of them twice. But darling, Mrs Roth is probably crazy. Like that Alice character you told me about at the Friends, who claims she knew him. And like your great-aunt . . .'

'Lillian was nothing like Alice.' Then Apryl paused and clapped her hands to her cheeks. 'Oh, God. Alice. Alice said the same thing. About an accident. She said Hessen had an accident. She *must* have known him. They both must have known him after the war. I think he self-mutilated.'

'Oh, hang on, girl.'

'Why not? You're the expert aren't you? Didn't Van Gogh cut his own ear off? Hessen was all alone in there, tormented by his vision. Working furiously. His mind disintegrating. A mind that was never truly like anyone else's to begin with. You said so. It all adds up. Talking to himself. Shouting. Doing those rituals that got him thrown out of places. God, he must have lost the plot in there and . . . mutilated his own face. His own beautiful face.'

'Apryl. Let's not get carried away. Please. Let's just bring it down a notch. You've no proof. Just a couple of half-crazy old women telling you stories. I mean you were telling me a few moments ago how the residents of Barrington House carried out an Agatha Christie murder mystery. Mrs Roth in the dining room with a candlestick.'

'If you're going to laugh at me, Miles, then I want you to leave.'

'Hey.'

'I mean it. I followed the clues my great-aunt left me. And it led to this. The man was murdered in his own home. Who knows why? Who knows what he really did to them? She said there were a lot of Jewish people in that building and they would have known he was a fascist. Mrs Roth is Jewish too. I mean, her name? There's all kinds of motives.'

'Well, yes, that's one, and it's pretty flimsy. Oswald and Diana Mosley had Jewish friends before and after the war. They didn't rub them out. Different rules applied up top. Far more forgiving of each other's faux pas, darling. But—' Apryl turned to him with an expression suggesting a complete absence of patience with his doubt. '—if you truly believe he was murdered, then it is a matter for the police.'

She nodded. 'But I need to know more. Find out more.'

'How?'

'I need to go back and talk to the Shafers. Get it all confirmed. They're still alive. I'll even stop them in the street if I have to. I still don't know how Reginald died. I didn't get the chance to ask. But I know, I just know, it's connected to this.' She turned and looked at Miles. 'I want the whole story. For Lillian's sake.'

TWENTY-SIX

Bruised by worry and lack of sleep and from having seen things he had no defence against, Seth didn't recognize his own frightened eyes staring back at him from the dirty mirror he kept on the mantel in his room. He looked away. Inside his mind a crowd jostled in fear.

He struggled to breathe. His heart beat too fast and cold sweat leaked from his pores. He couldn't sit still and paced up and down his room instead, looking from the walls to the windows. He thought he might be sick.

What had he done?

Shivering by the glowing radiator, he rolled and lit another cigarette; the sixth in as many minutes. Smoked half of it then stubbed it out in the saucer already overcrowded with a hundred other butts on a thick bed of ash. The sight made him feel worse.

He couldn't remember the last time he'd eaten. He'd been living off mugs of tea and cigarettes for days. Too much tobacco, caffeine and stale air. Nor could he recall the last time he'd opened a window.

The watery grey light of the late-afternoon sun, soon to die into dusk, turned the orange fabric of the curtains whitish in the places they were most worn.

The grubby half-light revealed red-black colours smeared

across two walls. The sight of it made his guts convulse. How had it come to this, to fall so far? Had he lost his mind? Or was this a new mind that painted such fragments of faces and body parts over his walls before killing an old woman?

Dear God, did he?

He wasn't sure what he'd done. In his memory the events of the previous night had a jerky, insubstantial quality. If he could only slow his head down for a moment, maybe then he could remember what he had done, and what he had seen in that flat, on the walls. See if any of it was possible. But his hands still seemed to bear the weight of her bony body. And he couldn't suppress the image of Mrs Roth lying on the floor, her face stricken but staring. Or of the quick shadow racing across the floor of the mirrored room and covering her up. The room he'd carried her into like a priest taking a sacrifice into the heart of a temple. And then he recalled her body on the floor of her own bedroom, where he'd planted it, at the foot of the bed, unmoving and broken. Where they would find it today. Her nurse would be there already. Any moment someone could call, maybe Stephen, maybe the police.

In the mirror – what did he see in that mirror? Something scrabbling like a thin white bird with a broken wing, with something red stretched over a face that didn't look right. And dragging her away, deep into the reflection.

He couldn't trust his memories. Couldn't even distinguish what was real and what was a nightmare. No. It was not possible. He'd been hallucinating for weeks. First the dreams and then the visions of that boy. His sick mind had made it all up. This is what happened when you spent too much time alone. Sleep deprived, not eating properly, depressed and anxious, a consciousness turns on itself. He'd left the path so long ago and now he couldn't get back on it. It was too late for all that.

Seth sat down again. Closed his eyes. Clenched his teeth and bit down against the sudden re-emergence in his mind of Mrs Roth's sharp dead face, and against the morbid hints of that other head framed on the walls of the mirrored room. The one coming apart, being stripped down to the bone. In paint that was still wet.

He had to leave London. Get out of this vandalized and smeared room. Get away from apartment sixteen and what it made him do. Break out of this blockade of misery, aggression and indifference the city was perpetually shrouded within.

He'd completed a shift pattern and now had a few days off work. If questioned, he could say he'd only gone home to visit his mother. Then his desertion of the city might not be seen as an admission of guilt, were he suspected of causing Mrs Roth's death.

Clinging on to this logic, he rose to his feet. Unsteady on tired legs, his vision almost pixelating from lack of sleep, he fumbled through the pile of clothes in one corner and retrieved a rucksack. Stuffed some dirty clothes inside it. Then snatched up his overcoat, keys and wallet, before leaving and locking his room – a room that was a testament to delusion, to mania, to futility. A place he would never set foot inside again.

The traffic never stopped on New North Road. He waited by the kerb, blinking in the dim light that still managed to make his eyes burn. Cold winds buffeted him from three directions. Dusty, fume-drenched air swirled up around his face.

Eventually the lights changed. He moved on, further up the Essex Road, into Islington. Angel tube station his target. And then King's Cross and away. As he moved he shivered and sweated at the same time. Feared a re-emergence of the fever. He just didn't feel right. Staggering about to avoid the loitering pedestrians, he felt like he was either stuck in one place or moving backwards.

The sky was so low. Disconsolate and grey, it appeared to be no more than a few yards above the top storeys of the tallest buildings. Sodden with muck, it silted a brownish murk down to the ugly red bricks and stained concrete of the buildings, so that it was hard to see much further than a few hundred feet ahead.

And the people here, how they looked like the final dregs of a diseased race. Shambling under the grotesque loads of their fat bodies. Huffing irritably, elbowing and shouldering each other as they walked the cramped pavements. He tried not to stare at these faces about him. What had the city done to them? They made him feel sick.

Everyone was being worn down in increments here. Some, like him, had just fallen further than the others. And it didn't help to dwell too long on those who were most damaged, in case you hastened your own descent to their musty forgotten corners: the stale bedsits, the damp rooms and labyrinthine concrete estates where trees didn't grow and where the air constantly shouted with the belligerent voice of the fast angry traffic.

Away from this. Oh God, to just be removed from this place that didn't work. A city regenerating its timeless contamination through the misery of the occupants. That was how it found nourishment. By dousing hope and disturbing minds. By instigating crisis and breakdown. With the shock of poverty and the tyranny of wealth. With the eternal frustration of being late; the suffocation of mania and the binding of neurosis; the perpetual cycle of despair and euphoria; the murderous anger at the trespasser who sits too close; the dead stares of faces at bus windows; the mute absorption and quiet humiliation of the underground; delinquency and drink; a thousand different tongues snapping in selfish insistence. City of the damned. So ugly, so frenetic. And all beneath the white sun in the forever greyness of sky. Where the damned are swallowed and forget who they are. He loathed it.

His horror spurred him on. Made him walk faster even though he was out of breath and uncomfortably sweaty under his bag. In the dull windows of the shops and cafes he caught glimpses of himself: shabby and hunched over like a beggar with its old sack. And when he saw his face it looked sickeningly white. Bleached by fear, sharpened by anxiety, lengthened by misery, but the eyes were full of the bewilderment of a man tormented by an absence of sleep. 'Jesus Christ,' he whispered, amongst the other mumblings in which he rehearsed the directions of his journey, over and over again: 'Northern City Line to King's Cross. Buy a ticket to Birmingham. Get on the first train . . .'

Near the glassy face of a building society he rested before the final surge to Angel tube station. He was close to the crossroads and the air was all wrong. It felt like a hand on his chest was holding him back while his legs went numb with pins and needles. At this place a stream of visions poured into his head, appearing and vanishing quicker than heart-beats. They were everywhere, the damned.

The two tramps on a bench told him to fuck off. They were using drink to hold back their own visions.

This was a place only the mad could see. But the insane are so filled up with it they can only stand and stare, or wander and mutter like forgotten prophets and dethroned kings.

'You cunt of a whore,' he said to the pavement that tripped him up. 'You cunting shite of Christ the devil,' he said, before spitting at the speeding cars. 'Stinking bile and shit of shit of shit . . .' he said at the tube station when he found it closed due to industrial action.

He prayed for the strength to destroy the city with a hammer.

He'd have to continue on foot. Stumble down the Pen-tonville Road to King's Cross Station. Rage drove him. He ground his teeth to sand. He would not be defied. Not by the uneven pavement, the lights that never changed, the sud-den roadworks that forced a lengthy diversion, or the yel-lowy faces that looked up, beseeching, with their horrible parchment mouths moving in the darkened windows of base-ment flats. Something like a crab, with legs as thin, scuttled behind a dusty privet hedge. He closed his eyes against it.

It seemed to take hours, with frequent stops becoming necessary to wipe the sweat from his eyes and readjust the backpack that was close to giving him a spinal injury. His vision was beginning to dissolve at the edges into white flashes. Sound was slowing down, and elongating.

At King's Cross most of the road was open around the front of the station and surrounded by orange plastic mesh.

No one was working in the strata of tarmac, soil and clay piping. The signs had been knocked down. People were walking across them. The sound of their heels against the dented tin ricocheted inside his skull. The roof of his brain was a bruise now, pushing darkness into his eyes.

Two police cars were parked outside the main entrance to the station, but he couldn't see the officers. Six feral dogs on rope leads were fighting, blocking the main entrance. One of the owners had a beard that reached his waist. It was grey and tangled into dreadlocks. The other was a skinny punk with acne-covered cheeks and stripy leggings, trying to sell the *Big Issue*. They tugged at the ropes fastened to their dogs and swore at each other. People with jobs walked past the commotion eating sandwiches from Pret A Manger and talking on mobile phones. Inside the station someone was screaming, 'Get your stinkin' hands of me. Get them off me you stinkin' ape,' and then three police officers burst out of the station dragging a black woman out. She had no shoes. All of the officers had lost their hats.

The black woman looked derelict, homeless, insane from huffing crack. In one hand she still clutched the stub of a half-chewed baguette. Two little Chinese women followed the struggle. They wore the red and white uniforms of catering staff. Their expressions were identical – silent indifference.

If he'd had a gun, Seth believed this would be the time to start shooting. To clear his path of dogs and degenerates. But the red flare of anger only made him feel weaker. Close to a faint.

Once inside King's Cross Station, and once he'd managed to keep his eyes focused on the departures board, he realized he was in the wrong place. Trains didn't run from King's

Cross to Birmingham New Street. It was Euston he needed. Fucking Euston.

Hands on his knees, head bowed, he tried to contain both his anger at himself and his delirium from lack of sleep. It had been so long since he'd left London for even a day. A year since he'd travelled to Birmingham. He'd forgotten how to get out. But he would get out. He'd walk all day if necessary, until he collapsed, to find a way to leave this hell.

Back out on the Euston Road, he plodded west. Euston Station wasn't far. The signs said so. Above him the sky was turning white. Or rather, he could see a bright shimmer through the gaseous sheet of grey. His face was hot and now his vision swam. Streets, buildings, lamps, cars, stunted trees, road signs and pedestrians all rotated and blurred about him. If he lay down he would pass out.

Slowly, slowly, he made his way up the long white glaring tunnel of the road to the station. A sudden flood of hope pushed him across the grass to the main doors of Euston.

But inside the station he felt even worse. The effect was immediate. He began to panic. Within the glare of white lights and chatter of sound, the push and sweep of the crowds, the buffeting of bags and screech of cases on wheels, he felt an overriding desire to run back outside.

An echoing announcement he couldn't fully understand was listing delays and cancellations. He couldn't see Birmingham on the departures board. Woozy and screwing up his eyes against the vertical judder in his eyesight, he soon found it too painful to look up at all.

He went in search of help, which was in short supply. Non-existent in fact. He decided he would ask at the ticket office, then saw the enormous queues that turned in serpentine coils and decided he'd better head for the toilets. But in the middle of making his way through the crowd on the main concourse he suddenly paused. Standing before the red-yellow smear of the Burger King facade was the figure of a hooded child. His hands were pressed deep into the nylon pockets of the snorkel coat and the face was lost in darkness, but he turned in Seth's direction.

A man behind Seth knocked him off balance, then wheeled round in a whirl of overcoat and tie not in order to apologise but to grimace. Seth looked back to where he'd seen the hooded figure, but it had gone.

Breathing hard from the shock at the sighting, he told himself it was a hallucination. But then he caught a flash of schoolish trousers and scuffed chunky-heeled shoes flitting past a concession that sold sunglasses and watches.

Impossible; the boy couldn't move so quickly. There were other kids in here. it must have been one of them. He was being paranoid; was paranoid and sick. He pushed his way through a cluster of French travellers and headed for the ticket office.

But maybe the boy was here to prevent him from leaving. There had been nothing but obstacles in his path since he left the Green Man. It was like the whole city was conspiring to keep him stuck within certain boundaries.

In the queue, he kept his eyes down and closed so he wouldn't see something in a hood watching him. Trying to focus his vision, he took deep breaths of the warmish air to hold the panic back; the panic boiling at the back of his throat and threatening to come up as a high-pitched scream. It made him want to tear at his clothes and run madly through the crowd.

Instinctively he believed that if he moved back eastward, back towards the Green Man, he would feel better again. Something was letting him know he was not allowed to leave the city. Something he had willingly gone into partnership with the night he opened the door to apartment sixteen.

Finally he stood before the glass screen, behind which sat a fat man in a red waistcoat. Seth rediscovered his voice and asked for a ticket to Birmingham.

The man looked exasperated. 'Have you not heard the announcements or seen the signs? No services to Birmingham today.'

'What?'

'No services from Euston.'

'So how do you get to Birmingham?'

'Marylebone. Chiltern Railways. Or the coach station at Victoria.'

But just the names of those distant places, so far off in the cluttered and crowded city, doused the last flicker of his spirits. He wanted to punch the wall until his hand was jelly and bone fragment loose inside purple skin.

'Can you move aside for the next customer,' the man in the red waistcoat said.

Seth drifted away from the counter. He knew the Tube and the buses wouldn't take him anywhere he wanted to go, and he didn't have the strength to walk any further. All of his energy was gone apart from the reserve set aside to feed his panic. Even if he managed to reach another station the swift sickness would swamp him again.

He had to sleep. To go home and lie down. Maybe he could try later, after some sleep. He could think of nothing else now, and refused to even acknowledge the hooded boy who waited for him outside the ticket office, and who then fell into step beside him as he left the station.

The following day he tried to walk south, but could go no further than the Strand, where he vomited in a pub toilet.

The north presented an impossible maze. He was disoriented by brick walls, pointy black roofs, iron railings, bitter air and the half-seen whitish things that called out to him from building sites and moved quicker than rats down there in the uprooted foundations. His effort to escape was turned back to the centre, where he discovered himself to be in the evening, somewhere between Camden and Euston, wasted by hunger and exhaustion.

On the third day, in the east, he nearly suffocated between a row of grey terraced houses with front gardens full of rubbish. He shook and wept, watched by Pakistani children in strange clothes. And then he turned for home: the only direction that offered any relief from the nausea, the hot-cold sweats, the gasping for breath, and the constant calls from the bone-things in windows with their yellowy faces and wide-open maws.

The next evening, he went back to work.

TWENTY-SEVEN

Outside the Shafers' apartment the smells of Barrington House clouded: wood polish, carpet shampoo, brass cleaner, and dust. And something else. A hint of sulphur. Of something recently burnt, like gunpowder.

Descending and ascending on either side of the elevator, the stairwells were lit by the electric lights, but the very air was gloom. Half-lit like a photograph taken in poor light. It made Apryl uneasy, but strangely apathetic too. Unless she kept moving and focused on specific tasks, she could imagine herself just lying or sitting in silence and waiting, alone, in here. But waiting for what?

At the thought of knocking on the Shafers' door, her stomach went hollow with nerves. They were old and difficult and didn't want to be disturbed. Stephen and Piotr had said as much. Their rejection of her request to meet them was down to their connection to Hessen and what they had done to him. With her great-uncle Reggie leading the way. Only under emotional stress had Mrs Roth confided in her. Maybe she had even expected her own end was near. The thought made Apryl deeply uncomfortable, as she must have been one of the last people to see Betty Roth alive. Stephen confirmed as much that morning when she arrived.

But the elderly resident had confided enough, and Lillian

herself had hinted at the same ghastly series of events occurring half a century ago. But in her fear of interrupting Mrs Roth's scant and haphazard disclosure, she had failed to ask about Reginald's death. Not even Lillian had been able to share those details, because the final truth of what happened back then was too unpalatable for Mrs Roth and her great-aunt to recount. And so she was left with suggestions of Hessen's evocations of unnatural powers and terrifying sounds, of hideous paintings and a plague of nightmares that even direct confrontation with the man had failed to erase. Things she too had glimpsed and was terrified of encountering again in these dim halls and wretched rooms, where the shadows were all wrong and where every mirror she looked into suggested a presence. She looked about, anxious when her eyes moved over the mirror on the landing.

But there had been a conflict and it had ended badly for Hessen. Of that she was certain. A murder they had kept secret all these years. A secret that drove them apart and into isolation and madness. But it was a story she would have retold now. She would know how Reginald died, and how Hessen had been murdered, and she would know this afternoon.

She raised her hand.

Her index finger met the cold brass of the door buzzer.

She pressed the button softly, too softly. It made no sound. She depressed it more firmly and held it down within the decorative brass surround.

What did you do here?

There was a pause and then the buzzer vibrated against the tip of her finger. At the same time, behind the heavy wood of the front door she heard a faint chime.

And across the greyish glass of the window in the stairwell, the weak sun must have moved its face further behind the ever-present cloud, because she felt the air cool and darken about her.

She stepped back and waited. And waited. Because no one came. She leant forward and pressed the bell button again. And again.

And then she heard footsteps rapidly descending from the floor above, down the communal stairwell, and felt the guilty urge to run away like a kid. The waiting was draining her confidence, her purpose. A shadow reared up the wall and she turned to greet the figure coming down in such haste. It must be a child, to move with such alacrity and speed. But could a child cast such a shadow?

To her right voices eventually came forward from deep inside the apartment. They gathered around the sound of the chime. A woman's voice, sharp and anxious. Though Apryl could not make out the words. And then much closer. Close enough to be directly on the other side of the door, an elderly man's voice came to life. 'Well I'm trying to find out.' It was raised in annoyance and directed back down the hallway towards the distant cries of the woman.

Apryl looked back at the staircase. The shadow grew larger but thinner and dissipated up near the ceiling. The footsteps on the stairs stopped. No one came around the bend in the staircase. 'Hello?' she said, her voice weak. 'Who's there?'

'Who is it?' For an old man, the voice on the other side of the Shafers' front door was surprisingly strong, his American accent still detectable, though tempered by decades spent in London. His voice was directed at her, so she guessed he was peering through the little spyhole in the door. She could hear the rasp of his breath from the exertion of moving.

She looked away from the stairwell, suddenly eager to get inside the apartment with the elderly couple. 'Hi, my name is Apryl. I just wanted—'

'Who? I can't hear you?'

She sighed with exasperation. 'Apryl Beckford, sir! Can I come in, please?'

'I can't hear you.' And then he shouted behind himself again, at the woman. 'I said I can't hear them. So how do I know? Would you just quit it! I said I'd take care of it. Don't bother. Don't bother getting up. I said I don't need you.'

'I just wanted to . . .' Apryl began to say. No use, he wasn't listening and couldn't hear her even if he was.

Old fingers scraped and fumbled at the latch as if it were the first time they had performed the operation. Tom Shafer's breathing grew louder and more strained, as if he were lifting something heavy.

When a gap appeared between the edge of the door and the frame, the man was so tiny she had to look down to see his face, which nudged forward. Severely lined baggy skin, dotted with bright white stubble, hung about a wet mouth, from which the lips had withdrawn. A rivulet of clear drool shone in a deep ravine at the corner of his mouth. Thick glasses magnified his watery eyes. They were so dark as to appear black in the moist discoloured whites. A blue mesh baseball cap was perched untidily on the little figure's head.

'Yes?' Like that of a cigar smoker, his rough voice seemed to emerge from somewhere behind his breastbone and was liquescent but incongruously deep and bone dry at the same time.

'Hello sir. You don't know me.' She spoke loudly, but not at a volume that would carry to the woman back inside the apartment who she assumed was Mrs Shafer. 'I'm the great-niece of Lillian from apartment thirty-nine and I really need to speak with you, sir. Please, just for a few minutes.' The door was partially open, but she instinctively felt it could close very quickly. She cast a final nervous look over her shoulder at the staircase, suffering the feeling that whatever had thrown such a shadow and moved so swiftly was now waiting just out of sight, and listening.

Occasionally blinking, Tom Shafer looked at her in silence. His expression crumpled into an anxious suspicion that she felt was a near-permanent feature. Slowly, he shuffled his body about to look behind him, down the hall, as if making sure his wife was not visible. Then turned back to face her. 'You look just like your aunt. But I can't see you. I'm sorry. We told Stephen. He should have made that clear.' He began to close the door.

Apryl stepped forward, surprising herself. 'Please, sir. I have to know what happened to my great-aunt and uncle. They were your friends. Your neighbours.'

He breathed out noisily. 'That was all a long time ago. We don't remember anything.'

'I know about Felix Hessen.'

At the mention of that name, he looked up, his wet eyes startled into an animation they'd previously lacked.

'I just need to know if what my great-aunt wrote is true. That's all. Some closure on her life. Please sir, it's just for me and my mother. We won't tell a soul.'

Tom Shafer squinted at her. His heavy glasses moved up his small nose. 'Young lady, your great-aunt was as crazy as a snake. And you're starting to remind me of her. She used to come up here with just the same attitude. We don't want to be bothered by any of that.'

That? What did he mean? She smarted at his flippant remark about Lillian. 'She had her problems. I know that. But you know why too. Mrs Roth told me. She told me what happened. Before she died.'

The door reopened, wider than before. 'Betty wouldn't say a word. She was many things, but she was no gossip.' Despite his wizened body and little head in the ludicrously oversized hat, she was again surprised by the power of his deep voice. It suddenly made her feel foolish and guilty, like a kid caught misbehaving and bothering adults.

She cleared her throat. 'Mrs Roth didn't tell me every-thing. But she was very frightened before she died. And she needed to confide in someone. In me. She felt she was in danger. That something in the past was having repercussions right now. She told me about the paintings, sir. And about Hessen's accident. What he did here. How he changed things for all of you. My great-aunt wrote of it too, in her diaries. Between them they've told me a lot of things. Including what happened after Hessen came back here and started tor-menting you all over again.'

Tom Shafer didn't speak for a while, but the tension of the space between them was filled with his raspy breath. He suddenly looked ill and terribly frail as if he could easily fall and not get up again.

'I just want a few minutes of your time. That's all. I have to know.'

'I can't. I'm sorry. My wife . . .'

This aged and fragile man suddenly made her think of

Lillian, alone and afraid and abandoned, but never relenting in her struggle to escape the ghosts in her memories that had become the terrors of her every day. She'd never given up. Not like Mrs Roth and the Shafers, imprisoned here until death with their nurses and pettiness and powerlessness. Apryl wiped at the tear that tickled her cheek.

Without looking at her, as if he was too ashamed to meet her eye, Tom Shafer opened his front door and then hobbled away into the darkened hallway. He paused after a few unsteady steps and turned his head to the side. 'You coming in or what?'

Dabbing at her nose, Apryl walked behind him. But now she was inside she wasn't even sure she wanted to hear what he had to say.

'Keep your voice down,' he whispered. 'If you disturb my wife you'll have to leave.'

She nodded, but wondered whether he'd said this out of protectiveness for his wife or out of fear of her.

She followed him between the bare and stained walls of the hallway and into a large living room. It appeared the couple only used the one little corner of this space, the part with the television and the two worn armchairs huddled together about a little table on wheels, covered with small Evian bottles, tissues, sweets, a half-eaten bunch of purple grapes and scattered packets of medication. The rest of the room was empty save for an ancient sideboard and a dinner table piled high with cardboard boxes, faded towels and wrinkled bed linen. It was another poorly lit and miserable little pocket of Barrington House. With all their money they lived like bums in one corner of a penthouse. The carpeted floor was covered with crumbs and bits of paper. There were no pictures on the walls. No mirrors. Only the outlines of frames that once hung there, the paper bleached around the dark rectangles and squares.

The *Financial Times* was spread over one of the two chairs. 'Take a seat. I can't offer you a drink. It'd take me an hour to get to the kitchen and back. And we don't have that much time.'

'Please, don't apologize. I'm sorry to disturb you. I really am. I know I came here uninvited. I don't want anything but a few words. An explanation. It's just—' She swallowed the tightness in her throat. '—I've found out so many things since I've been here. Things I now wish I didn't know. But I can't go home without knowing the rest of my great-aunt Lillian's story.'

After falling into the chair and panting to get his breath back, Tom Shafer peered up at her. His aged face was calm now, his stare unfaltering, resigned, with no time for social discomfort despite the squalor of his surroundings. 'You really do look like Lilly,' he said, and finally smiled. 'She was a very beautiful lady.'

Apryl's face suddenly suffused with warmth at what he'd just said. Not because he thought her attractive, but because he'd confirmed the connection between her and Lillian. 'Thank you. She really was, wasn't she? I've seen the pictures of her and Reginald.'

Tom Shafer kept on smiling. 'Sometimes it hurt just to look at them. They were something else.' He looked away, at nothing in particular. Just out there into the scruffy room he occupied every day. 'But things change. Enjoy what you have when it's there. Don't go looking for trouble.' It sounded like a warning. He looked back at her. 'I hear you're going to sell that place of Lilly's. Well I'm going to ask you to do it, right away, and to get out. Don't waste any more of your life here than you have to.'

'What makes you say that?'

'I thought you knew.'

She avoided his eyes and looked instead at her hands clasped in her lap. 'I know some things. But not everything. I can't put all the pieces together.'

'And you think I can?'

'But you were there. Back then.'

He shook his head. 'But who can say what happened? I'm not sure I can. Betty sure couldn't. Nor Lilly. And the others aren't with us any more. It was not something in the normal course of a person's experience. Not something we were prepared for, or could deal with. It should never have happened. We just got caught up in it because we were too proud and too damn stupid to get out when we had a chance.'

'But caught up in what?'

He let out a long sigh. 'I don't suppose it makes a god-damn bit of difference who knows now. I can't believe Betty told you anything. I really can't. But who would believe a damn one of us old fools? And I have no idea what the hell Lilly was writing. She wasn't herself. Not for a long time. It all beats the hell out of me, but something happened for sure. By God, we've paid our dues for it. We all have.'

Apryl looked down at her lap again, feeling herself fill up with a familiar frustration and despair. 'But you can tell me how Reginald died. Lillian couldn't bear to write it down.'

Tom Shafer looked up at her. 'You ever heard the expression that two people can love each other too much? Well that was Lilly and Reggie. We never thought she'd survive Reggie's passing, and I guess we were right in some ways about that.'

'But how did he die?'

His stare hardened. 'He killed himself. Jumped from the living-room window of their apartment.' He spoke without a pause, blink or stutter.

'Where the roses were,' Apryl said. 'Where she put the roses. It was a memorial.' She looked deep into Tom Shafer's eyes. 'Because of Hessen. Because of the way he tormented them and drove them crazy. But how did he do it?'

Tom Shafer shook his head. 'I don't know.'

'You must. My great-uncle was a war hero who flew missions over Europe. I have his medals. He survived and came back here to the love of his life. And then killed himself over a dispute with a neighbour? And in the process broke his wife's heart so badly she went crazy from it. I can't accept that no one knows the reason why he would do that. You were close to him once.'

Tom Shafer shook his head. 'Now you are getting ready to understand why we don't speak of it and never have done. Beside your aunt, who never let it go. Maybe she had more cause than the rest of us. But how can I explain it? You can't understand unless you were there. Reggie wasn't the only person to take his life. Mrs Melbourne did too. She was the first. Went right off the roof and hit the damn fence. They had to cut her from the railings. And then there was Arthur. Betty's husband.'

'No.'

He nodded. 'Oh they covered it up with some damn bullshit about heart failure, but he took an overdose.'

'But why did none of you leave? Why can't you leave? Lillian died trying. I don't get it.'

Tom Shafer's voice rose in anger. 'Don't you think we damn well tried? But we can't! And that's all there is to it. Can't go further than a damn block in any direction and we don't know why.'

'The paintings. The Hessen paintings. It's about the paintings. My great-aunt said it was all connected.'

Tom Shafer's little body seemed to shrink further into the large chair. Now he looked like he was just bone and skin inside a plaid shirt and sweatpants. His gnarled hands trembled on the armrests. He closed his eyes and soon his entire body was shivering. Apryl felt an urge to go to him, like she had done with Betty Roth, and to hold him. To go to this tired and broken-down old man and to comfort him as no one had comforted Lillian. 'I don't want to remember them if I can help it,' he murmured.

'Lillian dreamed of whatever was inside those paintings. Then she started to see it. Around her.'

'We all did. Somehow it never stayed inside those damn paintings.'

'It's why Reginald took his own life. And the others.'

Tom Shafer nodded. 'Maybe they were the lucky ones who had the guts to get out of this. But we suffered too you know. We never had any children because of it. She miscarried every time.'

'I'm sorry.'

A silence thickened around them in that dusty little corner of nowhere. Tom Shafer broke it and spoke as if to himself. 'My wife still thinks she can protect us in here. She doesn't know any better. I can't afford for her to be upset. Not in here. So you'll have to go soon.'

'You burned them.'

Tom Shafer never said a word or even nodded.

'And killed Hessen. Together. I know you did. You and Arthur Roth and Reggie. I don't want to make trouble with this. I just need to know why Lillian couldn't come home to us. It's what she wanted. She said so in her journals. But something was done here that drove her husband to kill himself. The same thing that kept her here until she died. I want to know how Felix Hessen could make all this happen after his death. Can you tell me?'

Tom Shafer shook his head in despair. 'You have no idea what he was. I don't know what Betty told you, but he brought things here. We didn't know what. Or how he did it. I still don't. None of us ever did. Lilly had some crazy ideas, but we weren't buying it. But whatever it was, it was more than us. All of us together or individually. We soon found that out. And it was the end of Reggie and some other good people too. Including your aunt and now Betty. I'm pretty damn sure. That woman had a strong heart. I don't believe it failed. Me and my wife are all that's left.' He stopped talking and swallowed. Perspiration had begun to make his forehead shiny and he began to look grey in the thin light as if he was seriously ill.

'Are you OK, sir?' She reached for his arm.

'Don't believe a damn thing they're saying downstairs' he said, his voice a whisper. 'Something's not right down there. Just get yourself out of here, girl. Like we should have done.'

Tom Shafer then shook his head and sighed as if reluctantly accepting bad news. It was the weariest sound she'd ever heard come out of a person's mouth. 'The whole damn building used to shake. It came out of his apartment. About a year after he moved in here. Make no mistake, he was a crazy bastard before all this started. Never left the building. Not once, I'm sure of it. You'd bump in to him on a staircase, or down where the staff used to live, making his weird signs in the air like he was drawing. Messing around with the pictures on the walls. Talking to himself, and not in English or any goddamn language I ever heard. The porters used to catch him all the time. They kept an eye on him. They never liked him.

'And at night he was doing things in his apartment that could dim the lights on the other side of the building. Used to fill the air in Betty's apartment with something you couldn't see, but could tell was there all the same. And if you listened real hard you could hear voices. Not like you and I are speaking, but a hundred voices. All going round and round down there with him.

'We all heard it for the first time in Betty's place. We were having dinner and we heard it coming up out of the apartment below. In Hessen's place. And once you heard it you never stopped hearing it.

'Whatever he had in that damn place came out. It came out of there and got into everything else. Came through the building. Got behind the walls and inside mirrors and pictures. You saw things in them that weren't there before. Even if you were the only damn human being in a room you suddenly knew you weren't alone when you looked into a mirror. Sometimes it was one of them *things*, sometimes more than one. But you saw them. Moving. And then they came into our dreams. They got inside our sleep.

'I don't know how he did it. I made a hundred million on Wall Street. I'm good with what I can see and explain. But not with this. We had no defence against it. Neither did he.'

'What makes you say that?'

'He lost his own goddamn face down there. He lost his whole face and his whole goddamn mind in whatever he had moving around down there. Something he couldn't control once he got it started.'

Apryl swallowed. 'What happened to his face?'

Tom Shafer kept his eyes lowered. He thought for a while and then swallowed. 'Arthur called Reggie and Reggie called me. Betty and Arthur had heard screams. Hessen screaming. So we went down with the head porter and let ourselves in. And found him in the living room. All on his own with all the rugs pulled back to the wall. But you could see how messed up his face was. Like frostbite, Reggie said. Black and burnt-looking, with the flesh gone down to the bone and eyes. But there was no fire. No chemicals. No blood. And he sure as shit hadn't been to the North Pole, though we may have wished it on him. We had no idea what caused those injuries.

'An ambulance took him away. And we thought that was the end of it. But he survived and when he came back, he just started it up all over again. All them noises, circling. Like a whirlpool. All down in his place.' Tom Shafer broke his train of thought and looked at her. 'How did Betty die?'

'In her sleep, Stephen said.'

He shook his head. 'That's a damn lie.'

'Betty said he's come back. Do you think he could really come back?' Apryl prompted him, terrified he'd stop talking, like Betty Roth had done.

'Back? He never damn left. He's kept us here and he's

been waiting for something to start it all over again. He's still here for us. Which makes me as crazy as Lilly for just saying such a thing. He's been biding his time. Until now, he couldn't do much else beside scare the shit out of us if we went near a picture or mirror. Or make us sick as a dog if we tried to leave the neighbourhood. But things have changed again. Now it's different. Like he's got some help.'

Apryl struggled to control her voice. 'And Reginald . . . You all killed Hessen.'

Tom Shafer shook his head. His voice was barely audible. 'It wasn't a case of killing a man. Reggie just put him in there with it. We did nothing to stop it. And that crazy bastard never came back out again.'

'Put him in with what?'

'I don't know. None of us did. But it sounded the same as whatever was in them paintings on his walls, or filling that room that must have been the size of a football field.'

'I don't understand . . .'

Tom Shafer swallowed, noisily. 'Second time we went down there, we took the keys from the head porter's safe ourselves. Reggie took a pistol too. We let ourselves in and Hessen was waiting for us in the hall. So damn thin he looked like he could barely stand on his own two feet. Just wearing his dressing gown with this mask over his face. Made from something red that went over his head like a hood and tucked into his collar. But you could still see through it. See that fool's messed-up face.

'Reggie demanded to know what he was doing. What he had in that room, making all that noise. The living room. And Hessen just laughed at us. Like we were nothing. Like we were pointless. That's how he made you feel.

'And Reggie lost his temper. Got him by the collar and mixed it up with him. Knocked him down over a chair that busted right from under him. We tried to hold your uncle back while all the time trying not to look into those pictures on the walls. But your uncle was a strong man and he just shrugged us off and dragged Hessen by an arm across the hall floor. Right up to that room he dragged him, and opened the door.'

Tom Shafer stopped talking and began shaking. He reached for a bottle of water, which Apryl quickly uncapped for him.

'Well, Hessen really started struggling then. And carrying on like he did the time he lost his face. Screaming like a lunatic. But Reggie tossed him into that dark space. With all the cold coming out of it. And those noises. All them voices speaking at once and crying out for help. A room where you couldn't see much beside the bit of the damn floor with all them markings on it. Voodoo shit or something, right behind the door. But it was a place you knew went on forever. And Reggie threw Hessen in there. Like he was a doll. Just picked him up and threw him through the damn door.

'And we all held that door shut on him.

'We heard him carrying on for a while. Screaming and banging and begging for us to open the door. And then just bumping against it, like he had no strength left. Until he stopped that too. Until it all stopped.

'It was like he faded away, with all them other voices in the wind and cold. Don't ask me what it was. None of us had a goddamn clue. But we all felt about twenty years older the day after.'

Apryl gulped. Her voice was only a whisper when she spoke. 'Hessen was dead?'

Tom Shafer shrugged. 'When we opened the door, the room was empty. Not a soul in there. Just them four mirrors and the candles that were still burning in the middle of all the marks on the floor. I swear to God almighty that's what we all saw. But he wasn't there. He'd vanished. Hadn't gone out the window either. They were all locked, and anyway, no one would walk away from a fall from the eighth floor.'

'The paintings . . . You . . .'

'Every damn one of them. Took them down from the walls in the hallway and in all the bedrooms. Burned them to ash. Bust them out of the frames and burnt that crap he'd done and all the strange markings under them. Put them all in the furnace they used to have here to burn coal.'

From the hallway outside the lounge door, a shrill voice suddenly destroyed their whispered sharing. 'Is there someone in here? I can hear ya'll talking through that damn wall! It's driving me crazy.' The voice was breaking down into tears and hysteria.

Tom Shafer suddenly broke out of the miserable trance he'd fallen into while recounting the story. His face was now stricken with panic. The door handle turned. He struggled to his feet. Apryl stood up quickly too and turned to face the doorway, her own discomfort turning to fear. In this place it was contagious. The door opened.

A huge bulk of a body filled the gap between the lounge and the hallway outside. The moon of Mrs Shafer's face was terribly old, but the skin had a curious sheen to it, as if she were wearing a thin plastic membrane over her features. It must have been some kind of face cream. Coils of black hair were piled under a blue headscarf that was sloppily pinned in place. It was squashed flat on one side where she must have been lying against a pillow. The small black eyes were ferocious.

Mrs Shafer clasped each side of the doorway as if to support herself from the shock of seeing this stranger in her home. Immediately her lips began to tremble, whether from rage or grief it was hard to say. 'What is going on in here?'

Tom Shafer raised two thin arms that wavered out in front of his little doll body. 'Now don't go getting all upset.'

'I ... I ... I ...' She stared at her husband in astonishment, as if the greatest betrayal of their entire time together had suddenly been revealed. 'She's got to go! I'm telling you. I want her out of here! I don't believe my eyes! I mean, what were you thinking? God damn you for bringing trash into my home!'

She was insane. Apryl understood this in a heartbeat. 'Ma'am, I'm sorry. I never meant to disturb your rest.'

Without even looking at her, without breaking her stare from her husband, as if the sight of Apryl was intolerable, she began to speak in a deeper and more controlled voice that was somehow worse than the shrieking, 'We don't want you here. You're not welcome. I told Stephen and you pushed your way inside here. You took advantage of this dear old man.'

'Now dear. All she—'

'I'm not talking to you!' she suddenly shrieked at the tiny figure in the crooked baseball cap, her face flushing a dark crimson. 'I surely don't want to be speaking to you for a long time!'

'It's not his fault. I meant no harm.'

'Leave here now! I won't have such, such, such *things* in my home. How dare you! How dare you! I'm calling Stephen.'

'You won't call a damn soul!' Tom Shafer suddenly roared at his wife.

Apryl fled for the door. 'Then excuse me and I'll leave,' she said to Mrs Shafer, who still wouldn't look at her for even a moment.

'I'm sorry,' Tom Shafer said to Apryl in the hallway, as he hobbled after her. 'She's not herself. Not today. It's all very hard for her.'

'Can I call you?'

'No you cannot call! Or come up here again!' Mrs Shafer shrieked. She would follow them, stop, then follow some more and clasp her hands over her mouth. As her little husband shuffled in front of her, Apryl half expected to see Mrs Shafer reach out and seize her diminutive mate, before dragging him into the great belly that pressed through the stained front of her floral housecoat.

Tom Shafer reached out and touched Apryl's elbow by the front door. She turned about and looked into his frightened eyes.

'I can't believe this is all still going on!' Mrs Shafer had recovered her voice. 'I wonder how long it has been going on!' And now she had begun to cry, while crowding behind them, her great body hovering protectively and threateningly behind her tiny husband.

'For the love of Christ,' Tom Shafer whispered to himself. Then turned and shouted, 'Would you shut your damn fool mouth!'

It made Apryl shake and want to be out of this terrible place without delay, but the old man's crooked fingers dug into her arm. He was breathing so hard now she thought he could die at any moment. His lips were moving. She leant down towards his wet mouth.

'Don't trust them,' he said. 'None of them downstairs. They're helping him.' And with that he released her arm and turned back towards his weeping wife.

TWENTY-EIGHT

'Heart attack. A big one.' The news about Mrs Roth was delivered quickly by Stephen. The head porter had been waiting for Seth to come in for the evening shift. Piotr stood beside Stephen, beaming. The nurse, Imee, had found Mrs Roth at the usual time, six o'clock, when she'd taken her breakfast in that morning.

But to his barely concealed amazement, Seth wasn't asked about the events of that night. Whether she had called down at all. Nothing. Neither of his colleagues seemed upset either. At least she wouldn't be troubling them again, that seemed to be the tone: relief. Stephen was even whistling, which Seth only remembered him ever doing after receiving a big tip. He clapped Seth on the shoulder too, which he had never done before, and then passed through the fire door to enter the staircase that would take him down to his flat.

A ninety-two-year-old woman's sudden death in the night as a result of heart failure, while alone in her room, was hardly likely to arouse suspicion or instigate a forensic investigation. Wasn't that exactly what he'd been telling himself, as if he had been rehearsing a mantra, as he'd stumbled towards all four points of the compass looking for a way out of London over the last few days? And tonight he had to assume, with a relief that made him shake, that he'd got away with it.

A respite short-lived. His fear of the police swiftly turned into a terror of what occupied apartment sixteen, of what it was capable of, and of what it might want from him next. Because there was no saying no. It changed him. The same as when he was painting – he could forget who he was. He became its tool, its assassin. He understood that now. The hooded boy, that stinking bastard in the parka, had said as much. They'd make him a great artist, liberate him from living death, if he did things for them. Like murder. Fucking murder.

When Piotr went home, Seth waited out the hours under the hum of the lights in reception. And it was not an easy wait. What was left of his conscience kept him company as gravity increased its pressure in the building. In anticipation. It was palpable. Sleeping or awake, things happened here. On terms that were not his own.

At certain times he would be required to act. Always. Here. To be complicit in a vengeful business he seemed to have brought back to life. Business long unfinished at Barrington House. And he could do little but guess at its origins, while having no control over its ghastly outcome. But people had to die here. Old people. Maybe lots of them. Old bitches who had harmed the thing that was once a man in apartment sixteen.

Impossible. Just preposterous. But happening, right now.

He fidgeted in the leather chair, or paced up and down the hall.

By eleven he'd smoked 12.5 grams of hand-rolling tobacco: Drum Yellow. Too wired to yawn, he stared at the screens of the security monitors, the greenish view never changing. He drew nothing. His desire to re-create the world in red and ochre and black upon his walls was absent. He now knew such insight demanded a terrible price. His new talent was only there by virtue of a collaboration with something in this building. A presence that wouldn't let him leave the city.

Jesus Christ.

Why had he waited until he had no control over anything? His dreams, his actions, and now his movements were not his own. And to have been pulled back here tonight. To have been summoned and not given any choice in the matter accounted for this brief renewal in his health. The stomach cramps and nausea and dizzy spells had gone. Completely.

Had they ever existed? Yes, and he feared their return. Would do anything not to feel like that again. Seth slid his face into his hands and shut his eyes. Shut his eyes at the impossibility of it all. Of what had been done.

The hours passed him like indifferent pedestrians. Six thirty became midnight. But where was the watchdog? The hooded one, able to enter his dreams at will and shepherd him around the streets of London and the floors of Barrington House for its own purposes. Maybe the boy was here right now spying on him. Able to read his thoughts and be aware of his every intention.

Or maybe Seth was schizophrenic and hallucinating. No one else could see the figure of the boy. And Mrs Roth had been unable to see anything in the dark flat, which to his eyes was a place lit red. And he was seeing the city in a way all others were blind to. Maybe this was how it was for those who killed because of the voices in their heads, or obeyed commands uttered by visions of the dead or heard messages from televisions and radios. So maybe it was time. That time to surrender. To turn himself in to the authorities. How was that done? They would have to come to him. He could get sick if he tried to go to them. Break down before he even reached whatever doctor or constable was required to remove him from life. And could any of it even be explained?

A terrible shudder racked his body. A lump closed his throat down. He clawed at his cheeks and tried not to cry. 'Jesus. Jesus. Jesus Christ,' he said. There was no barrier between sleep and waking. No division between what was real and what was not real. All of it was the same thing. Coming together. Out of him and into him.

'Come on Seth. They's got summat to show you.' The hooded child's voice woke him at two and his sinuses filled with the scent of firework sulphur, cold winter streets, cheap clothing and the seared flesh that stuck to it.

The boy's coat swished as he turned and walked away from the reception desk. How long had he been standing there watching him? The thing in the hood moved to the lift doors and paused to wait for Seth, hands in the pockets of its snorkel coat. 'Don't mess about, Seth. Get the keys.'

'Go on, Seth. Look. She's in there now. Where she belongs. Down there with the rest of them.'

He couldn't stop the shaking in his arms, or in his hands that tried to cover his eyes, or in his legs that seemed ready to give way and reduce him to his knees.

Up there hanging on the wall at the very end of the hall was Mrs Roth. Depicted in bright oil paint. Recognition carried an impact that stopped the ticking of his watch, the pulse and pull of blood in his veins, the flit and reprise of thought. But by no means was it a literal portrayal of the former resident of flat eighteen. More of an impression of her. Incorporating suggestions of her distress at the very end. Distress both at her dispatch and at her sudden realization of her fate thereafter, because there was no end to awareness.

The skin of the face was twisted about the skull. Skewed somehow as if wrenched by invisible hands. The watery eyes had been rearranged. They were on different parts of her head now, but they were hers for sure. Bright with surprise and wide with something else. Thin bones, stripped of flesh, clawed for purchase where there was none in the black torrent of upward. Through which she seemed to both travel and hang. A frail configuration of sticks taken away. Away with it all. With no delay.

'No,' Seth mumbled.

Here he was again, between the red walls, to view a painting that was absent the last time he'd knelt before some contortion inside a gilt frame. This one was new. And worse than all the images combined of Mrs Roth that he'd seen on the night of her death. Because this one told him where she was now. Where he'd put her. And his sense of incapacitation was stronger than ever, if it was possible, as he lost himself before those bones in the rags of a nightdress, propelled through the dark.

'There's more, Seth. Come on,' the boy said, and stood outside the mirrored room. 'Gotta see it through, Seth.'

Seth turned away from the painting. Forced himself to remember where all his limbs were, so he could move, directed by the boy, to the mirrored room. He felt ready to scream, but never for a moment did he even consider resisting the will of the hooded boy. An unpleasant desire to see even more, until he was again taken to the boundary of himself, to endure the psychic strain of these creations, pressed him into that mirrored room.

Where a new exhibition had been organized for his eyes. The fragmentation of face series was gone. In its place he was treated to five blank canvases, reflecting an impossible sense of depth no two-dimensional medium should have been able to create, preceded by a triptych that began next to the door he had entered.

The three new paintings were in frames, but still gleamed wetly as if recently finished. He could smell the oil paint from where he knelt. It was a series of paintings in which, as he sat still and unblinking, he glimpsed something resembling a narrative. The first two pictures were separated from the third by a mirror positioned directly across from its counterpart on the opposing wall, creating an infinite silver corridor that retreated to a distant pinpoint.

In the first picture, out of the smudge of background came the suggestion of a staircase in Barrington House. He recognized it immediately from the hundreds of times he had walked those passages on patrol. Only here the walls were coloured like dried blood. Orange orbs glowed to light the darker places using some technique and mix of colour he couldn't help but think masterly, despite the sight of the three figures in the foreground. Monstrous things that made him recoil.

Three men in evening dress, with peeled heads and thick sullen lips that parted with an imbecile vacancy, moved up the stairs on legs that never fully formed or separated from the grey swoops at the bottom of the frame. And it was as if all three figures grew from the same source and were in possession of only one arm. There was an oversized and raw hand at the end of the arm, clutching a metal object that had been designed for hammering or shooting.

Which is precisely what they seemed to be doing to the swathe of bloodied robes and naked limbs inside the next frame. It could have been a fourth figure, and the three grotesque idiot figures, their faces now animated with a hideous mirth, were destroying it. No face was visible within the wet linen that surrounded the victim, only two thin legs that shot out from the coils of the slaughter in progress.

In the third and final picture only the fourth figure – the victim – remained in view. It was inside some kind of transparent membrane that possessed a bluish tinge to its see-through walls. But the victim now resembled meat still wet on the bone, and it lay upon a gore-sodden platform of some kind. What looked like a head, with no face, hung over the side, flattened and misshapen, with the solitary eye closed. A long shadow crept away from it like running blood and filled the entire lower portion of the picture. And beside the crude plinth it lay upon was a red rag that could have been a mask or some sort of deflated hood, with a partial face still embossed upon the front of it.

And then something moved. Quickly and backwards, in the mirror before him.

A figure. The indistinct face reddish, as before, but hunched over and vanishing the same moment he caught sight of it. Leaving only a reflection of himself, seated and bewildered, in the silvery corridor of mirrors.

'Others are gonna get done in later for what they did to our friend, Seth. And you got to help out wiv 'em,' the hooded boy said, faceless inside the tatty fur trim that circled the hood.

'No,' Seth said, unable to stop the shaking that began again as he crawled towards the door. 'No more. No more. I don't want to do any more.'

The boy crossed the room quickly and blocked the door. Seth winced as his mouth filled with the smell of scorched flesh and charred cloth. 'You bring them Shafers down here. Call 'em up and get 'em down here quick,' the boy said. 'You owes us. We got a deal, like.'

Behind him and up above him at the same time, he then heard a sound that washed his face of colour. A distant wind. Moving anti-clockwise, beyond the ceiling of the mirrored room, with the faint suggestion that within the turbulence, many voices were crying out in the blindness and unreason of terror.

'And be quick about it, like. It can't stay open for long, uvverwise too many fings get out, like. And we want them old Shafer cunts chucked in before it closes.'

'A fire? What do you mean?' Mrs Shafer's waxy face confronted him from the open doorway. Then she looked away, down the stained hallway of her flat, in the direction of the distant bedroom, where her husband was still in bed, and cried out, 'I don't know what he's saying, dear . . . Something about a fire?'

'Who is it?' Mr Shafer called out in that southern accent of his.

'It's . . .' Mrs Shafer couldn't remember his name. 'The porter!'

'Hold on, would you? Let me get ... my glasses.' Mr Shafer sounded preoccupied and breathless. He must have been trying to get out of bed.

In all the excitement his wife's bottom lip quivered and her eyes were watery from interrupted sleep. 'Are you sure?' she said to Seth. In her tone a prelude to hysteria was making itself known.

Seth nodded. 'Afraid so, ma'am. We have to evacuate. Now.' He had to get them out of their apartment and into number sixteen quickly, before anyone heard or saw what he was doing. The floor above was occupied, and if Mrs Shafer raised her voice any higher, he wouldn't be surprised to hear a door unlatch up there.

'But ... I'll have to get dressed. I mean, look at me.' She was in her nightdress; a baggy red garment beneath a scruffy tartan housecoat that looked like it had been made for a man. Whatever was on her head – a wig under a scarf, or possibly real hair dyed black – had begun to drape about her ears. They were multi-millionaires – Stephen had once mentioned a fortune of over one hundred million – and they dressed like vagrants. They disgusted him.

'There's no time, ma'am,' he said, raising his voice to a command. 'Go and get your husband. Now.'

Immediately she shambled back inside the apartment and Seth wished he'd been as firm with her before, during all of those evenings when she'd tormented him with her pettiness. But she wouldn't be able to inflict herself upon him for much longer, not if she walked between those mirrors. The very thought of them, and of what flickered through their silver-white depths, and of what was spinning above it all, made him so weak he leant against the door frame to wipe the sweat from his forehead. His skin was cold. He felt sick.

Mrs Shafer reappeared further down the hallway, holding her husband by one elbow and leading him out of their bedroom. A black walking stick in his other hand, Mr Shafer looked up, blinking. 'Where is he? Who is it, dear?'

'He's there!' she scolded the old man. 'Right before your eyes. We have to get out because of a fire and you're asking me these questions now? I mean, for God's sake.'

As usual Mr Shafer fell silent, knowing better than to argue. He just sighed with the fall of every foot, his face tense from the exertion.

'We'll take the lift.' Seth struggled to find his voice. The enormity of what he was doing took his breath away: waking elderly residents in the early hours with a story about a fire, in order to lead them to a grisly execution in *there*.

He held the door of the lift open and watched them shuffle inside. Seth crammed himself in too, ignoring Mrs Shafer's murmurs of annoyance.

He stopped the lift on the eighth floor, but they didn't seem to notice they'd gone up instead of down. 'Here we are,' Seth said. 'That's it,' he added, helping Mrs Shafer out onto the landing by holding her arm.

He then steered them toward the unlocked door of apartment sixteen; left shut but on the latch. 'We're going to evacuate through this apartment. Downstairs is blocked,' he said, praying they wouldn't question his instructions that were patently ridiculous: there were no external fire escapes and they were on the eighth floor, between flats sixteen and seventeen. It was no place to make an evacuation.

'Well I guess we better do what the young man says,' Mrs

Shafer said to her husband, leaning down and shouting into his face.

'Well, yeah, but where's the fire marshal?' he asked her. 'This man isn't qualified. I'd like a word with the fire marshal. I mean, do you smell smoke? I thought I did back there,' he said to his wife, but allowed himself to be led.

Only when he came to cross the threshold of the flat and enter the red hall did Mr Shafer stop. 'Let go, dear. Let go. I said let go a me. This ain't right. Where are we? This says sixteen, right there on the door. It's that apartment, dear. He's taking us into *that* apartment.'

No mistaking the emphasis. Seth's neck stiffened.

Bewildered, Mrs Shafer stopped tugging on her husband's thin but wilful arm and looked about herself until she also saw the number on the door. 'What? I don't understand? In here. We can't go in here.' Her voice was rising again.

'What is the meaning of this?' Mr Shafer demanded, his voice growing in strength and volume. A voice of business, one that must have come in useful when he was amassing all of those millions.

'Look. There is . . . I'm trying to help,' Seth said uselessly as they talked over him.

Mr Shafer was pushing his way back out now, around the bulk of his wife. His head was lowered with a determination to escape. 'Call Stephen now. I want to speak to whoever is in charge. This is ridiculous.'

Seth tried to regain control of his voice. 'You have to. You must. In there.'

'I'm not going anywhere until I've seen the fire marshal. Stand aside.' The old man prodded Seth in the stomach with his cane.

He shouldn't have done that. Belittled him with the stick. Shouldn't have touched him. Seth couldn't breathe. Inside he felt himself go black. And too hot for reason to act as a coolant.

Mrs Shafer was still looking at the brass number on the door, then down inside the unlit hallway, then back towards her husband with her mouth open and her eyes all wild, when Seth kicked the stick out of her husband's hand.

It hit the wall.

Mrs Schafer screamed.

Seizing the old banker by the collar of his nightgown, and then fisting another handful of thermal cloth near the small of his back, Seth lifted the figure from the ground and walked quickly through the front door. Mr Shafer's feet never touched the ground.

'Outta my way,' Seth said to Mrs Shafer, his teeth clenched. And she stood aside, which surprised him. Just stood aside and let him pass, like he was carrying an unruly child to a family car on a trip the child had spoiled with a tantrum.

Mr Shafer never made a sound. Not a word. Nothing. Just hung from Seth's hands and let himself be carried down the hallway. It was only when they stood outside the partially open door of the mirrored room, where the sound of the wind inside embraced them and the unnaturally cold air gusted out to burn their faces, that Mr Shafer spoke. He said, 'Oh dear God. No. Not in there.'

Seth kicked the door open.

The lights might have been off, but it was clear the air of that room was occupied. Alive and electric with wind and animate with something else on the floor he couldn't see, but could hear as a swish of eager movement around the edges. Just audible under the spinning.

As if he were simply throwing a log into a furnace, he hurled Mr Shafer into the room. Head first, into the darkness. And the old man didn't make a sound as he hit the floor, as if something was there to catch him when he came down in the dark. But Seth didn't have time to stop and think about what he was doing and what had become of his victim – best not to think of that – he just returned his attention to Mrs Shafer, who stood mute in the entrance to the hallway and stared at him.

He grabbed hold of her and marched her through the flat. 'That's it. That's it. Come on. Here we go,' he said to himself, to drown out the part of his mind that was screaming at him to stop.

She didn't make a fuss either. Just whimpered. Dazed with shock, she even walked right into the room after her husband, requiring not so much as a shove. And it was noisy in there now. In the dark it sounded as if the ceiling had opened to let in a thousand voices all crying out at the same time, but not to each other. It was as if they couldn't see each other, but were crowded together in some terrible dark confusion.

Seth closed the door on it all. Then fell to his knees and held the handle with hands white as bone, forcing it up so nothing could get out. And he tried to shut his ears to the new sounds defining themselves from out of the wind, and the cries so thick inside that room.

When he heard the bumping up against the door, as if someone had lost their balance and fallen heavily against the other side, he desperately wanted to take his hands from the brass door handle and block his ears, but knew he couldn't afford to leave the door unsecured. This instinct for self-preservation was reinforced when out of the circling swept-away voices came a snarling in the foreground, like a dog worrying something between its teeth, up near the door where he had heard the bumping. And when someone tried to twist the handle down on the other side to get out, Seth was sure he heard the scrabbling of clawed feet on a wooden floor.

The wind and the voices were gone, the red lights were switched on, the paintings were all covered with dust sheets, and Mr Shafer was dead. Seth could see that straight away; the eyes turned around and gone all white, the mouth wide open, the hands frozen into claws and the legs wide apart. You didn't strike a pose like that when you were still breathing.

But his wife was moving. She was hunched over before the mirror on the wall opposite the door. On her knees. Tottering ever so slightly, from side to side, and looking into the mirror for something she had lost in there. Her lips were moving too, but no sound was coming out of her mouth.

Seth locked her inside apartment sixteen in case *they* came back for her, and then carried the frozen bundle of sticks that was her husband's body up the stairs to their flat. He then placed the thing that had once been Mr Shafer back inside the bed and covered it with the sheets, up to the chin, all the time taking care not to look at the face. And then went back down to collect Mrs Shafer, or whatever was left of her.

She was still kneeling, but now silently rocking back and forth. Her mind must have gone out like a blown fuse. And she offered no resistance as he coaxed her to her feet and slowly walked her out of the flat and into the lift.

'She's finished, Seth,' the hooded boy said, reappearing when Seth guided Mrs Shafer out of the flat. 'She won't say nuffin'. Her head's all bust inside. It was the 'usband he wanted most. Don't forget his stick. Take it up wiv his missus. He won't need it where he's gone. You's done well, mate. Our friend's gonna be pleased.'

'I don't want to do any more. It's finished. You tell him that.'

'Nah ah. Yous don't tell us nuffin'. We tells you what to do, like. And I fink you might be ready for a little treat for being so helpful and all. Summat nice might be comin' along soon. 'Stead of all these old uns.'

Seth scowled at the reeking thing in the tatty hood, who trailed him as he led Mrs Shafer inside her apartment. He decided to put her back on her knees beside the bed. The Shafers only had an occasional visiting nurse, but they always came down in the early evening to walk to the local shop on Motcomb Street. Piotr would soon notice they'd not been around for a while. He'd check on them soon enough.

TWENTY-NINE

'Apryl, please. Just take it easy. For your own sake. You're starting to worry me. I mean, really worry me.' Miles leant over his desk, his fingers wound tightly together, trying to look into Apryl's wild and excitable eyes and to still them because they were flicking about and blinking as fast as the thoughts and ideas were streaming into her head.

'I'm starting to worry myself. Jesus.' She stood up again from the chair on the other side of Miles's desk. Could not keep still, and walked across his office to the door. Then stopped, and clasped both hands on either side of her cheeks. 'I have to, Miles. I have to do something. I can't walk away from this. People are dying. Lillian tried to help them, but they wouldn't listen.'

'Have you any idea, any idea at all how preposterous this all is? I mean, you are suggesting that Hessen is still in that building in some . . . some . . . I don't know, altered state and murdering those who wronged him back in the forties, one by one. Listen to yourself, woman. It's nuts.'

Apryl was deep in thought and did nothing but shrug Miles off. She removed her hands from her cheeks and slapped them against her tight-skirted hips. 'I need to go in there at night. That's when it all happens. When people are in danger. And someone is helping him. That's what Mr

Shafer said. Before he was killed. Murdered. I'm sure of it now. Mrs Roth, then him. And I'm responsible.' She turned to Miles, her eyes moistening with tears. 'Don't you see? I made them talk to me and now they're dead.'

Miles sunk his head into his hands and slowly drew his long fingers down his face. 'I cannot believe I am hearing any of this come out of your lovely mouth. You know, a gay friend of mine claims that all women are latently mad, and by degrees the lunacy gradually surfaces. Right now, you are a testament to his insight.'

Apryl sat down and sniffed, then dabbed her eyes with a tissue. 'I'm not going to cry . . .' By the time she was attempting to pronounce the last word a big bubble popped in her throat and she was crying. 'Fucking eyeliner's going to go everywhere,' she said, sniffing again.

Miles came around the desk to her. 'Hey. Hey. Go easy on yourself. You are putting yourself under a lot of strain. Just sell that bloody flat and put all of this behind you. Come on.'

She moved away from his embrace and shook her head. 'I can't. I just keep thinking of Lillian. All those years, Miles. On her own. That terrible . . . thing, frightening her. Night after night. That poor old lady. Who lost the love of her life. And then suffered for so long without him. And . . . I know what it's like. Hessen, I mean . . . I saw him too.'

'What?'

'You're not someone I can tell things like that to.'

'Hey. Now that's not fair.'

'You're not. But I did. It . . . he was in the mirror I brought up from the basement. And in the painting of Lillian and Reggie. And in other places. Whenever I'm in that building,

Hessen is watching me. Trying to scare me away, I think. Because I'm getting closer to him. He follows me about, like he did the others, who just hid and waited for the end. Lillian never did. That brave, brave woman tried to escape every day for fifty years. Every day, Miles. After he killed her husband. Drove him out that fucking window.' Out of the corner of her eye, she caught the look of disbelief and pity on Miles's face. 'You've never seen him, Miles. And be glad you never have.' She said this with such force she surprised herself, and Miles leant back, away from her.

'Before I even met Betty Roth and Tom Shafer, I'd already seen the same thing. In mirrors, paintings. Hessen. The residents didn't suggest it to me. I saw it independently. Because when I arrived he'd become more active again. Because someone is helping him. That's what Tom Shafer said. Shafer was as sane as you and me. He said someone in that building is helping Hessen now. To kill, Miles. To kill those terrified old people. Hessen's been able to keep Lillian and the others all stuck there, and has tormented them with his population of the Vortex, or whatever the fuck he brought into that building, but he hasn't been able to kill them. Not until now. Because now someone in that building, maybe someone who works there, is doing his bidding. Maybe all of them. Piotr, Jorge, Stephen. This morning, when Stephen told me about the Shafers, I pressed him about the coincidence of three elderly residents dying like this. Three people who knew Hessen. Tried to talk to him about what Betty Roth and Tom Shafer had insinuated about Hessen still being in the building. And he looked really uncomfortable. Cagey, you know? He's avoided me ever since. And there's another guy too I haven't met. Who only works the night shifts. Or who knows? Maybe it's a resident behind all this. They could all be in on it.'

'Then go to the police.'

'Don't be fucking ridiculous.'

'Because that is how your story will sound. Because it *is* fucking ridiculous. It's wild and unsubstantiated. You can't just go around accusing people of murder.'

Apryl turned to him, her face tight and fierce. Miles raised one hand, palm outward, in an appeal for silence. 'Now hang on. Let me finish. Mrs Roth and this Shafer chap were in their nineties. Their nineties, Apryl. That is a fact. People in their nineties can keel over at any moment. That is also a fact. Your great-aunt had been ill for a long time, and she was in her eighties. There was no evidence of foul play in any one of these deaths. That is a fact. Heart failure, strokes, all natural causes. I've no doubt at all that they knew Hessen. Or that his antisocial behaviour and his paintings, which they destroyed I might add, affected them profoundly. They never forgot him or his work. And I'm also beginning to believe they may have killed him and burned the evidence. But as they got older, their minds ... well, their memories became less effective. And now the trauma of the original crime and its lingering influence have warped into this ... this ghost story.'

Apryl sat quietly and stared at the floor. 'But why didn't they ever leave Barrington House? Explain that.'

Miles shrugged. 'I really don't know. The rich often huddle together in a castle-keep mentality. Look at all of these gated communities springing up. Safety in numbers.'

'That's bullshit. None of them have gone more than a block from the building in fifty years. Fifty years, Miles.'

For a moment Miles looked at his lap in silence, his eyes half shut, his lips pursed. Then he said, 'OK, OK. Let's look at this from another perspective then. From within your current point of view. And I am only speaking hypothetically here. By no way is this an endorsement of your theory—'

Apryl waved a hand in the air with frustration. 'Yes. Yes. Just tell me.'

'Well let's just say, for argument's sake, that Hessen did summon something into Barrington House. Something demoniac. From one of those rituals he learned from Crowley. And that the Vortex exists somewhere in that building. If this is truly the case, then what in hell are you going to be able to do about it?'

She had no idea. None at all. But she was going back to Barrington House. To stake it out. To harass Stephen, the rest of the staff, whoever she could suspect of an involvement. And she was going to get proof ... somehow. She'd even break into apartment sixteen if she had to, to find out what the hell was still inside that place. There had to be something, inside there, allowing Hessen's presence to remain. Something that her great-uncle and his friends overlooked so long ago. Betty had been hearing Hessen at night in there, right up until she died. She said it had become worse all over again. The noises, the voices. It was all coming out of there, that apartment. Where it began, so long ago.

Something was going down inside that place. Something very wrong that she had found impossible to accept, no matter how hard she thought about it. Until now. Until Betty and Tom died. That was no coincidence. So soon after Lillian. People were dying who had known things about Felix

Hessen. Who had made him and his art disappear. And maybe there were others, still inside that dreadful building. Trapped. People in grave danger. Imprisoned and stalked and tormented like Lillian and her circle from way back, until the time was right to take revenge, if that's what it was; something coming back from the dead to settle a score. And she couldn't just leave them in such a situation. That crazy bastard had killed her great-aunt and uncle, her own flesh and blood. And maybe even now, after death, they were still trapped inside the building, like Hessen. Didn't Lillian suggest as much? She couldn't leave her there, in limbo, for ever. Inside those terrible places with those hideous things he painted.

But as she walked away from Miles's office at the Tate, with the wind gusting and darkness coming down over every building and turning the stone a darker grey, she felt herself suddenly seize up inside, in a paralysis of fear, at the very thought of setting foot inside Barrington House again, at night. *Could I*, she asked herself, as she steadied her body against a bus stop with one hand, *could I get trapped inside there too?*

THIRTY

And the next night Seth waited for the call, all the time unable to stop shivering in the warm reception area. Anticipating the moment the solemn hooded figure would appear before his desk, to instruct him on who was next. Who he was to escort not merely to their death, but to something infinitely worse that came after.

But would the boy come for him first? Or would it be the police, wishing to speak to the porter on duty when two of the most senior residents had died within a week of each other?

It had been just over two hours since Stephen left him alone. The head porter had been waiting for Seth to come in, and had told him there was 'some more terrible, terrible news'. Mr Shafer had died in the night and his wife had suffered some kind of breakdown. 'Looked like a stroke to me. Poor thing must have lost the plot when she realized her husband was dead. They were very close, you know. They had their moments. We all know that. But they were inseparable.'

And Stephen had nearly called him at the Green Man this time, to ask how he'd missed finding Mrs Shafer while he was on patrol in the night. Mrs Benedetti from flat five had discovered Mrs Shafer on the first-floor landing the following morning just before six, looking as if she had been slowly making her way down to the ground floor all through the night. She was found, still dressed in her nightgown, on her hands and knees, catatonic with shock and cowering in front of the mirror on that landing, as if she was looking at something above her. But then Stephen had assumed by the state of Mrs Shafer that her husband must have died after Seth's last patrol at two and that she'd lost the presence of mind to raise the alarm.

'Terrified. Absolutely witless,' Mrs Benedetti had told the front desk before Piotr went up to investigate. An ambulance was then called and Stephen ventured up to the Shafers' apartment to find the front door open. Inside the main bedroom he found Mr Shafer, still tucked up where Seth had left him. 'His face, Seth. Must have been very bad at the end for him. Perhaps that's what set her off.'

'Must have been,' Seth had muttered, his entire body so tense he expected his mind to snap like a corroded rubber band stretched too far.

'And you know what they say, Seth. Death comes in threes. Makes you wonder who's next, eh?' Stephen had said, trying to add levity to a conversation that made Seth so deeply uncomfortable he'd forgotten to breathe. 'Or was Lillian the first? Which would make Shafer number three. Who knows? Still, let's keep our chins up, eh?' he added, with a smile that seemed to be battling with his casual solemnity.

Had he got away with it? Too early to tell. But he would be caught soon enough. Surely. Because he sensed his work here was unfinished; and knew that another death during his shift would certainly put him under suspicion. There had been no sign that he would be released from the tasks set him by the presence upstairs. From his involvement in it all, to procure revenge, because that was what this was: a murderous vengeance, and there was no refusing a call when it came. He wondered who was left; who else had wronged that enduring genius in apartment sixteen. He just had to sit here and await guidance.

But what would become of him when his grisly work was finally done? He wondered this with a tightening of the gut, followed by a wave of anxiety so acute it made his heart hammer and his head feel dizzy.

Despite his fearful anticipation of the malevolent presence that required so much of him, his hands seemed to automatically resume their work with charcoal and paper. As if they had a story to tell, and needed to record the further progression of this nightmare there was no waking from, his scratching and smudging and rubbing on a sketch pad were soon audible in reception.

Unaware of the passing of the early evening, and only mildly conscious of the pain in his bladder that demanded he urinate, Seth withdrew inside himself to where the world had been reshaped. For once he wasn't disturbed by the men from Claridge's delivering Mrs Roth's supper, or by the calls from Glock for cabs, or by the shuffling nuisance of Mrs Shafer. He was permitted to fill the hours and the pages with what only he and the presence in apartment sixteen could see of the world.

It wasn't the hooded boy who finally interrupted his frantic work just after the security clock clicked nine; it was the appearance of an attractive young woman standing in front of the reception desk of Barrington House.

*

She was pretty. Verging on beautiful. Unchanged. Unlike the creatures with the lumpy grey complexions hidden by make-up whom he saw on his journey to and from the building, or glimpsed on his rare forages for food in Hackney. This one was slender and well-groomed, and walked with grace. Like something off the silver screen; a vision from the past.

He'd never met her before, but had seen her captured on the security monitors coming in through the back door of the east block. An American girl. The niece or something of crazy old Lillian who snuffed it in a black cab. The girl Piotr lusted after, always rolling his eyes whenever he mentioned her. And Seth could see why.

So chic in a black leather jacket and that tight pencil skirt and high heels, her hair styled like a film star from the forties, with her big dark eyes flicking up to the camera as she came in through the rear doors, either alone or with that guy with the half-smile, like he knew something about you he kept to himself for fear of embarrassing you.

But tonight she came through the main entrance of the west wing alone and into reception to speak to *him*. Immediately, his eyes dropped to the flash of the new leather of her boots, and to the smoky gauze of dark nylon clinging to her shapely knees. Then his stare roamed up across her tight curves to her pale throat and pretty turned-up nose. She smelled so good.

His body warmed with desire. A feeling so alien and incongruous its sudden re-emergence made him dizzy. Glock's escorts used to make him feel the same way when their painted and scented loveliness had been summoned to service the rotund body of the director. He'd forgotten a woman's body could offer any pleasure.

Seth stood up, both to receive her as he had been taught to greet all residents and visitors, and also to continue his admiration of her figure before it was concealed against the front of his desk.

Under that smile she was nervous. 'Hello,' she said, with a beautiful painted mouth and perfect white teeth. He felt his idea of himself immediately shrink and hunch into something unkempt and unwashed. His uniform was a creased disgrace. His shirt unclean, the collar brown and rubbery against his skin. He could not recall the last time he had bathed or shaved. Or cared about such things.

'Good evening, miss. How can I help?'

THIRTY-ONE

It had been a while since anyone had called her 'miss' here. Apryl's smile changed into something not so tight.

Despite the intense stare and the look of harried surprise on his pale face, this one was younger and less sure of himself than the others. She hadn't seen him before, but she made him nervous; he kept clearing his throat and was unable to hold her stare for long. She'd seen this look many times before, in the faces of men infatuated with her.

'I'm sorry to bother you so late. I'm not staying here any more, but I've been coming back in the day to show real-estate people an apartment. And when I was leaving the building this morning I saw an ambulance out front. So I just wanted to check in and make sure it was nothing serious. What happened to Mrs Roth made me a bit jumpy.' She would have continued to keep up the charade, but the sudden clench of anxiety on the porter's face stalled her. 'Was it serious?'

The porter cleared his throat. 'Yes. Someone died.'

Someone else, she wanted to say. 'I am sorry. Who ... was it sudden?'

He cleared his throat. 'He was quite old. Mr Shafer hadn't been well for a long time.'

'Oh, my God. The ambulance? Was that him? I mean how

. . . When did it happen? I was only just there with him . . .'

'Would you like to sit down, miss?' He motioned for her to sit in one of the cane chairs arranged before the garden windows. 'Can I get you something?'

'No. Thank you. I'm just . . . a bit shaken. After what happened . . . to Mrs Roth. But what about his wife? Mrs Shafer? Is she all right?'

'Not really. No. She's taken it very badly and is in hospital.'

Apryl shook her head. 'I'm so sorry. Look at me here, being so selfish. It must be hard for you. I know how close you guys get to the residents. Stephen said you become part of the family. And to lose two of your people so quickly. I am sorry.'

When she said that the expression in his quick eyes changed again and she thought she detected embarrassment, even guilt, as he still failed to look her in the eye. Painfully shy too, and possibly disappointed in life. To be young and working night shifts in a building like this, it had to be tough.

Slowly, she crossed her legs, and didn't hurry to correct her hemline, which slithered along her sleek thigh. 'Please, why don't you sit down? Tell me what happened. Maybe it will help to talk about it. And I haven't even introduced myself properly. I'm Apryl. Lillian's great-niece. Lillian Archer . . . who also passed away recently.'

He cleared his throat. His eyes flicked from her face to her legs, back to her face, to the floor. 'Seth.' He sat in the chair opposite her. Perched on the end and rearranged his hands and feet several times. 'I believe it was very quick. For Mr Shafer. Heart attack they say. I wasn't here when they found him. I work night shifts. But I was told this evening when I came in. You see, miss—'

'Apryl, please. You can call me Apryl.'

'Apryl. Many of the residents here are quite elderly. It's a terrible loss, of course, but it happens quite often. I mean, it's not unusual.'

She nodded. 'So I hear. But isn't it so strange that three people should die in such a short time? I mean, they all knew each other, from way back. Did you know that?'

He looked up from his shoes quickly, but said nothing.

Apryl nodded. 'My great-aunt wrote all about it. And Mrs Roth told me a few things too. And Mr Shafer. Right before they died. You know, they all thought they were in danger here.'

Seth's face was very pale now and one of his hands started to twitch. He tucked it under his thigh. 'Were you . . .' He paused and cleared his throat. 'Were you and Mrs Roth close?'

'She was helping me with some research about my great-aunt. And this building. They both lived here for a long time.' Apryl paused, noticing how alert Seth had become.

'Research?' he said quickly, then swallowed and leant forward as if afraid he might fail to hear everything she said.

'Yes. Because so few people seem to be aware that an artist lived at Barrington House.'

'Mmm,' he said, and his face was so drained and twitchy it was becoming uncomfortable to look at.

'After the Second World War. They all knew him. Mrs Roth, my great-aunt, the Shafers. He disappeared, you know. Did you know that?' Apryl watched Seth's face closely so no flicker of recognition could escape her scrutiny.

'No,' he blurted out. Then gathered himself to control his voice. 'What was his name? The painter? I studied fine art.'

Odd how he assumed the artist was male and a painter. His body and his quick anxious eyes were betraying him. He knew something. He spent all night here; could hear and see and come across all kinds of things. She shivered at the thought of what might be roaming these corridors at night. What could come out of that empty but still active place. A place Mrs Roth had bought in order to keep it silent; as though she had purchased the scene of a crime. Stephen had told her she'd bought it and kept it empty for fifty years. Piotr and Jorge had just blinked with incomprehension or mystification when she'd pressed them earlier about Betty Roth and the Shafers. But Stephen had stiffened. And now Seth was twitching.

'Felix Hessen.' She watched Seth's face closely.

He looked into the middle distance and his eyes narrowed as if struggling to recall the name. 'It sounds familiar. But not a painter I recognize.'

'Only his sketches survived. And he fell out of favour with the establishment because of his politics. He was a fascist. Was into all kinds of weird things. Like the occult. Used to draw corpses and stuff. Really freaky. Then he came to live here and disappeared. Just vanished from out of this building. Did you not know?'

Seth stood up quickly. He looked like he was going to throw up. He rubbed at his mouth and closed his eyes, then rushed across to his desk. Snatched up a pen and paper. 'Felix Hessen, you say.' His voice was a whisper. 'Sounds German.'

'Austrian-Swiss.'

'This is incredible,' he said to himself, and scratched down the name on a notepad.

His teeth were terribly stained. Brownish. She had no idea what this young man had been through, but the aspect of neglect and melancholy and tension about him suggested he carried a serious burden, like depression. Yeah, maybe there was a touch of the bipolar about him. She recognized the manic signs from what she'd seen in her own mother and in her roommate, Tony, back home.

'So why here?' She couldn't resist the question.

Seth had become preoccupied again, and was staring down the hall as if she was no longer there. 'Sorry, what?'

'Why do you work here?'

He suddenly flushed. 'I . . . Well . . . Well I'm an artist too.'

Apryl sat stunned for several seconds. 'Then why would a painter hang out here all night? I thought you guys needed natural light and stuff to work by.'

He looked embarrassed. It was another question that seemed to cause him discomfort. 'Well, I only draw here. Nothing really. Just sketches. Now and again. Ideas. And I thought this would be the ideal job. You know, some peace and quiet. The solitude of night. That's why they wanted an artist – thought it would suit one.'

'They?'

'The building. The management. The ad I saw said the job was ideal for an art student. But then . . . but then it never quite worked out that way. And yet . . .' He seemed distracted again, anxious and uncomfortable.

Behind the desk on his leather chair, she saw a large white pad and a pencil box. She stood up and moved towards the desk. 'Is that some of your work?' When she entered she must have disturbed him. He had been drawing, though she still couldn't see what. Not clearly from this angle. Leaning forward, she screwed up her eyes and angled her head to one side to get a better look.

Detecting her interest in his sketches, he snatched up the pad and concealed the drawings against his chest, leaving her with only the memory of what she had glimpsed. Of what had momentarily stunned her.

Seth was breathing fast now and beginning to perspire. She could see his forehead glistening.

'Please. Let me see. I want to see that. Did you do it?' She couldn't help herself. Couldn't restrain her interest, her desperation even, in seeing that sketch.

She reached out for the pad. 'Go on, please. Let me see.'

He lowered the pad from where he clutched it to his chest. 'I'm sorry. But ... Well, my work is not very pleasant ... I mean, it's not finished ... No good. I'd be glad to show you when I'm done.'

And then he looked to his left and swallowed hard, like he'd suddenly seen something unpleasant, even threatening. She followed the direction of his stare, but saw only a wall and an indoor plant with long waxy fronds drooping to the immaculate carpet.

'Go on, Seth. Show the pretty lady. You's pictures are good, mate. I told you, didn't I?'

The terrible reek of damp ashes, spent incendiary chemicals and melted fabric had preceded the arrival of the watching child a fraction of a second before he appeared. But the advance warning did nothing to ease the shock of his appearance. Seth stared at the hooded thing with a stronger aversion than ever before. Of late its presence was an omen for imminent death. He shook his head.

'You's shouldn't be shy, mate. Go on, show the tart. She'll love 'em. I told yous he was bringing you summat sweet, like. And she's been sticking her beak everywhere, mate. Looking for 'em. So go on, give the slit a fright.' The kid giggled and the hood shook in a way Seth found loathsome. 'Her aunty-bitch was just the same. And she saw more than she bargained for.'

Seth swallowed again, cleared his throat and shook his head, now aware of Apryl watching him intently.

'Go on, Seth.' The boy's voice dropped to something low and mean and uncompromising. 'Fuckin' do as you is told, mate.'

Apryl softened her face into a smile and looked straight into his eyes. 'Seth. What I just saw was . . . good. Please, let me see.'

He looked away from the plant that he seemed to have been having some kind of unhinged communication with, and peered down at what he had drawn. Winced, hesitated, then passed the pad to Apryl. As soon as her painted nails touched the paper, he shoved his hands deep inside his pockets and looked at his shoes, like a bashful and diffident child.

Apryl stood back from the desk and stared into the smear of shading, lines, smudges and scratches, elements that together formed a hunched, faceless and yet tormented parody of an old man, or something composed of sticks and made to look vaguely more human than animal, imprisoned inside some sort of transparent cube or rectangle. Quickly, she flipped over the page.

Seth said something in objection, but she didn't hear him clearly because she was so engrossed as she stared at a bird-like effigy, clutched in the hands of something implausibly thin. And to the next page she turned, and the next and the next, unaware and uncaring about how fast her heart beat, how quickly her chest rose and fell as if in shock as she observed these dreadful suggestions of torment and incapacitation and despair, as she saw how haunted the eyes and slack the mouths of these things in the porter's pictures were, and realized how they filled her head and rendered her unable to think or feel anything besides what they demanded of her. When she reached the final sketch she forced herself to look up, to regain her presence of mind. The similarity between the styles was indisputable. They could actually be forgeries of Hessen's work. 'I don't understand why you would say you were unfamiliar with Hessen.'

He looked hurt at the tone of accusation in her voice.

'Because these look just like Hessen's sketches. You must have seen his work.'

His eyes flicked from left to right as if searching for a place where he could hide. He had lied. Maybe he'd learned from Mrs Roth or one of the other residents about Hessen, then researched him and begun to replicate the style so convincingly, it was as if . . . as if Hessen himself had drawn them, or at least tutored his hand.

'Seth, I'm sorry. But I'm at something of a loss here. These could have been drawn by Felix Hessen. I'm no expert on art. But these are so like his pictures. Pictures I've spent a lot of time looking at. The ones that survived.'

'I . . . I don't know the name. Maybe I saw something once . . .'

He was frightened. Really scared of what she was saying. If she wasn't careful she'd lose him. 'Please understand, Seth, why I'm saying this. I find an artist working in this building as a security guard who has produced what look like original Hessen drawings. But you claim you know nothing of him. I don't know what to say. I mean, how could you not know?'

Seth started to speak. Then stopped. He tried again, but held back.

'What is it? Tell me. You were going to say something.'

He shook his head. 'I have seen something.' He glanced at her then looked away. 'But I didn't know it was this Hessen who painted it. I mean, I don't always check. You know. When I see something I like.'

He was lying again. Jabbering to cover himself and unable to look her in the eye.

'Where, Seth? Where did you see it? Did you see it here?'

When she said that his fringe shrank back from his forehead. He swallowed but was unable to speak and was showing too much of his eyes. It was the only answer she required.

Her thoughts became frantic. Some of Hessen's work had survived inside Barrington House. Tom Shafer said they destroyed it all: he and Arthur Roth and her great-uncle Reginald took 'that crap' down from the walls and burned it in a basement furnace. And maybe the artist along with it. But not everything went up in smoke.

The story Shafer concocted about Hessen disappearing had frightened her, but her sense of reason had still clamoured that it couldn't possibly have been true, as if Hessen were some kind of illusionist with a mangled face who could vanish from inside a locked room full of mirrors and ritualistic markings. She had kept telling herself it was bullshit. All day. That his crazy wife had locked the truth down inside him a long time ago. Same with Mrs Roth. Who also tried to confess to something too improbable and terrible to actually say out loud. Something like *murder* – a murder they were all complicit in.

But as soon as she was inside Barrington House she believed it. She knew, instinctively, that no one – not Lillian nor Betty Roth nor Tom Shafer – had been lying. Stephen had though. And so was Seth now. She could tell. They were both lying to her, covering something up. She could barely breathe.

Only cranks like the Friends of Felix Hessen would ever believe such a thing. But here was Seth, right here in Barrington House, nervous, stuttering, anxious Seth, right underneath the place where so much had been done and now refused to be forgotten. 'They're still here, aren't they? His paintings.'

His hands were shaking and one foot tapped quickly against the floor.

Apryl tried to calm him with a smile. He was freaking out. Though he appeared frightened and vulnerable and not at all threatening, she wondered if he was dangerous. And maybe unstable enough to confess what he knew.

'I'd like to see more. More of your work. Like this. I mean it. And the work that inspired it. What you saw. In here. I won't tell a soul. We can keep this between us. And then I'll share something with you. You see, I know about Felix Hessen. About . . . what he left behind. A legacy. Here. At Barrington House. That no one else knows.'

Seth didn't speak. It was as if he couldn't. He just kept swallowing.

She placed the sketch pad upon the desk. 'We need to talk, Seth. Not here ...' She looked about herself nervously. 'Tomorrow. Can we do that?'

'I don't know.'

Reaching out, she touched his hand. 'I'm not trying to get you in a bind here, Seth. We'll have a nice dinner. And just talk. It seems like fate. For us to meet like this. When I came here tonight I never expected this. But it's a connection.'

He began to wet his lips. He wanted to speak but couldn't regain his voice.

'Let me give you my number,' she said. She took the pad from behind the desk and wrote the number of her cell phone down on the top sheet.

THIRTY-TWO

Sitting alone in a window seat of the theatre bar, which was empty at this early hour of the afternoon after the lunchtime crowd had thinned and before the workers rushed in to anaesthetize the day, Seth shifted about in his chair and anxiously scanned Upper Street for her approach.

After a long bath, his first in weeks, and dressing in the cleanest clothes he could find, Seth had briefly looked about the walls in his room. And was satisfied Apryl would be astounded. Particularly when he told her it was just part of a much greater project.

He tidied the floor space too, so that she would be able to walk about and see his work from different angles. Three walls were covered now. And neither the grainy daylight nor the electric light from the unshaded bulb could relieve the darkness in them, or how it crept across the floor and the stained ceiling. Even the corners and right angles where the walls met were lost unless you looked hard to see the joins.

But out of the sheen of flat lightlessness came the figures. Out of a depth that would mystify an audience. How had he created it, she would ask. How was it possible to suggest such a distance? And to convey the sense of the terrible cold that gripped you while staring into it? He had no idea.

Using the small stepladder from the kitchen, he'd

increased the height of the piece to improve the sense of the characters being suspended in nothingness. Though he wasn't sure, either, how he'd then created the effect of movement in his subjects. Because there *was* motion in the whole piece. The endless cold darkness upon which their torments were repeated to infinity now seemed to seethe as if with strange currents.

Sometimes when his work caught him unawares, he was tempted to believe they were no longer walls at all, but a long space opening to another place, one so vast and deep you would never find the end. And the images of the figures all drawn at various angles, who were rising to the surface as if attracted by the light in his room, still gave him a start whenever he came in. Even if he was merely returning from the toilet and had been away for a few minutes, he would find himself staring in mute shock at what he had done, at what was up there now.

It was impossible to become familiar with them, with all of those things holding themselves, or being held against their will, his lines capturing the tension and resistance in the suggestions of the limbs, or the perfect nuance of an eye open in terror, or the curl of a lip after a despairing scream.

All covered over, redone and then perfected until the best angle and posture had been achieved for each of them. Until the teeth chattered idiotically, and the mouths stretched to issue cries you thought you could hear, and the eyes were red with a pain that made your nerve endings spark.

Because of Apryl, his efforts had redoubled that morning. His hands had been more careful in the way they had swept and cut and reworked the dark red and black swathes from which the twisted figures were born wet and howling. It was as if he had something to prove now, as if an exhibition was being prepared for a sympathetic audience. If his sketches affected her, she would be in awe of his painting.

She was not in danger. Couldn't be. That hooded kid and their friend in apartment sixteen couldn't have anything against her. She'd only been in the building five minutes. And there was no need to dwell on Roth and the Shafers. She couldn't possibly have known them well. And anyway, if she had, she would have applauded their demise. Old scores needed to be settled. And in return maybe he was being rewarded now. *They* could make anything happen. Like a beautiful girl walking into your life when your mind was in pieces; someone who admired your work and wanted to know you. Someone who could put all of those pieces back together again and make you whole. That hooded freak had suggested as much, had told him that they were bringing a 'treat' to him, 'summat sweet'.

Dare he suggest such a thing to himself? That she was an offering for all he had given to that place of mirrors? Apryl had woken something vital in him that had long been moribund. And despite his dishevelled and haggard appearance, she'd seen something behind it. Intuited something inside him that appealed to her; she had even spoken of fate at their meeting after seeing his sketches. *A connection.* And now she wanted to see more of his work. To eat and drink with him too. Spend time in his company. This most rare of women might even accompany him home, to gaze upon his walls. These walls would be the test. His art would show her what he was all about. And she would tell him more about his master and why he had come back to visit those who had wronged him so long ago. Was that not what she had been suggesting?

Perhaps the killing was done now, and his work would continue to flourish. Maybe even within the security of a head porter's position with sexy Apryl as a companion. *They* could do anything. Bring you to your knees in shuddering horror, or cast you into the freezing nothingness like driftwood, or show you wonders that left you gaping in awe. This was going to work out; he was being rewarded, he told himself over and over again until he believed it, at least for short periods of time. But it had to work out to his advantage, it simply had to, because he had no control over any of it.

He couldn't lose his nerve when she arrived. He had to keep himself together. Be cool.

And here she was. Walking slowly and checking the names of the buildings as she searched for the place where he'd told her to meet him. A pleasing shudder passed through his body. She was beautiful. Here for him, an artist. God, he was an artist. Finally, an artist.

As she teetered into the bar, he stood up to greet her. The sweet and heady scent she wore stunned him; perfume's potential for mystery only truly realized when wafting from the pale throat of a beautiful woman. The sound of her high heels clacking so enticingly against the wooden floor turned the barman's head.

She had dressed for Seth. Dressed to please him. In a simple but elegant black dress under a long overcoat made from fine and expensive-looking wool. The neck of the dress was cut to partially reveal the heavy white softness of her breasts. Her make-up was full but carefully applied to her exquisite features. Shimmering from black to blue, her hair was elegantly arranged on top of her head. And what he could see of her legs glimmered in barely visible stockings, before tapering into black high heels.

'Hi, Seth. Good to see you again,' she said, and leant forward to kiss him on either cheek. Briefly, he indulged himself with the scent of her lipstick and with the aroma of her skin as she came close. All of his opening lines vanished. But his eyes flattered her. He shook his head, managed a smile, and said, 'Wow.'

THIRTY-THREE

To which Apryl laughed. And felt her efforts confirmed. She was a little overdressed, but had come prepared for this afternoon with Seth to become an evening with Seth. It could take that long to win his confidence, his trust. Her drinking would be measured. Tonight was going to be about Seth. What he had to say. And she was not accustomed to having her attempts to impress men rebuffed.

Nerves skittered about her stomach and she would rely on them being calmed by the first glass of wine, which Seth promptly went to buy at the bar. It had been hard to settle since she met Seth. She had tried to distract herself with meeting the estate agents and by conducting some aimless shopping during the day, followed by a meeting with Miles, where he struggled again to accept her gush of conspiracy theories about the vanishing of Felix Hessen, right from his own living room, followed by the incineration of his work. And as for her assertion of his lingering influence at Barrington House, and her intention to interrogate Seth, Miles had become both pale with concern for her and terribly disappointed in her ability to believe such things.

But Seth had been, she was certain, in the presence of Felix Hessen's work inside Barrington House. Tom Shafer must have been wrong: some of the paintings had survived and were still in existence, somewhere in that building. Maybe in number sixteen itself. Seth had discovered them. And she intended to find out how. It was preposterous: Miles was wrong and the Friends of Felix Hessen were right.

There was no mistaking the signature Hessen thematics and style in Seth's drawings, but they also contained an anticipation of what Hessen might have achieved as a painter. Seth was a capable artist. A man able to emulate the vision in what he must have seen in Hessen's actual work – oil paintings that took the horror of Hessen's surviving sketches one long step further. Miles would believe her when he saw Seth's work and confirmed the comparison.

And if she was careful, she might even be able to show Miles the unthinkable: a surviving original. Something the strange, lonely night porter had discovered in that wretched building. Or been shown by Hessen's presence. But something that had guided his own hand as an artist and, perhaps, even his role as an accomplice in the murder of the most senior residents. She found it hard to associate the lanky, introverted figure with violence. But someone was helping the residue of Hessen in that building. Someone was in collusion with the indistinct but palpable evil that had haunted the building for fifty years. Right now, with Stephen avoiding her, Seth was the number one suspect. He was involved somehow; he gave himself away last night. But how and why he was involved, she had no idea, and needed a lot more to go on than hearsay and guesswork. In that respect, Miles was right.

Seth returned from the bar holding a large glass of white wine. She forced herself to hold back from deluging him with questions, reminding herself to work him carefully for the information required. Like she had done with Betty Roth and the Shafers. It took coaxing. They had nothing to gain from telling her anything and much to lose when they did. Or so it seemed. She let Seth start the conversation.

'So tell me, please, about this Felix Hessen,' he said, in between nervous sips of his pint.

'Well, I'm no expert, and from what I have seen of your work I suspect you could tell me a lot more than I can tell you. About his style anyway.'

Seth looked down at his hands on the table as they fumbled with a cigarette paper. She'd made him nervous again and she quickly changed tack. 'You can borrow this book. I know the author, Miles. It's the only book in print about Hessen's work.' She withdrew Miles's book from her bag and passed it across the table. 'I know Miles would be impressed by your drawings too. He works at the Tate.'

Seth blushed and nodded quickly. He seized the book and held it in his lap. 'You said some really kind things. I don't get much encouragement these days.' He laughed nervously. 'But things are changing. I'm working on something quite ambitious. At home. In my room. More of a studio really.' His eyes were suddenly alive with an intensity she found startling. 'Maybe I could show this Miles guy before I move it to canvas.'

Slowly, she crossed her legs and moved them out from under the table so he could see them. And she asked him more about himself, his background, where he studied, his family, to which he became immediately awkward and evasive. Or possibly none of these things held any interest for him. He seemed uninterested in anything but his most recent work, of which he talked enthusiastically, but gave little away.

Or, she even suspected, was unable to articulate what it was he was producing.

After she returned to the table with the third round of drinks, having switched to Coke for her second, he seemed more loquacious. 'I've stopped trying to analyse everything that comes out, Apryl. It gets me nowhere. But I feel like I'm in touch with something right at the bottom of myself. And it has some relevance with what's out there. And maybe what comes after all this. You know, life. But it is only relevant in images. There isn't language for it. I can't explain it.'

She carefully studied his quick eyes and perpetual smoking and fidgeting, but didn't suspect him of trying to cultivate a mystique by being evasive about his work. It was something else. She had a hunch that Seth was deeply anxious, if not even afraid, of what he was doing, despite his compulsion to do it.

He spoke at length about London, about the people, and had nothing good to say about either. 'It's a terrible place, Apryl. Everything here is difficult. It's falling to pieces. It changes people. Anyone who stays here. The energy is all wrong. It doesn't work. I've been trying to work it out ever since I arrived.' He tapped the cover of Miles's book on Hessen. 'I think he was on to the same thing.'

At times it was hard to follow the thread and meaning of what Seth said. His head was a storm of ideas and thoughts all struggling to find their way out at the same time. It was like he was trying to make sense of his own manic temperament by speaking out loud to her. She found him exhausting, and after his third pint had been drained, she suggested they go and eat, wary that he might otherwise become irreparably drunk and a hindrance to what she needed to learn.

Over dinner she would find the right moment to ask about Barrington House and apartment sixteen. He was becoming garrulous and wanted to impress her, desperately. It was nearing the right time to seek from him a disclosure about what he'd seen, what he knew, and what he'd done.

It must have been a long time since he'd been in the company of a woman. She caught him staring at her with an intensity that made her uncomfortable. It was no longer only a question of seducing herself into his confidence, but also one of regulating the consequences. But in the small Indian restaurant he led her to, Seth's mood changed. After they'd ordered, it was as if something caught his eye outside the window. She turned her head to follow his gaze, but saw nothing out of the ordinary except for the usual diverse mix of humanity and fashion that filled every sidewalk in a city that seemed unable to stay still.

'What is it? Someone you know?' she asked.

THIRTY-FOUR

There he was, standing in the side street directly across from where they sat.

The silhouette emerged from the dusty shadows and orange light emitted from the interior of a bar; hands in pockets, the oval mouth of the hood turned in their direction, watching. Briefly it disappeared behind the shambling passage of a number nineteen bus and then reappeared. 'Barrington House,' he heard Apryl say, as if it were some cue for the hooded figure to appear and molest their privacy.

And now she was looking too. Out into the darkness that quickly fell and absorbed detail, merging brick with concrete with car with road, swallowing walking legs and fading colour into the vagueness of London dusk. But no matter how keen her pretty eyes were, he already knew she would be unable to see that sentinel. Watching and waiting, the figure was there for him and him alone.

'What is it? Someone you know?'

Seth shook his head, his face draining further beyond its normal pallor. 'No. I thought it was.' He turned his attention back to her, but failed to concentrate on what she was saying as his eyes darted, continually, back to whatever it was on the street that had so abruptly stolen his attention from her.

'Tell me about Felix Hessen,' he said, suddenly serious and failing to acknowledge the arrival of two plates on the table, one sizzling, the other steaming. 'Please.'

He ignored his food and listened intently while she concluded a brief history of Hessen by telling him that his vision had remained unfinished because none of the apocryphal oils had survived. But she never gave him the full story. She often checked herself. There were certain details she omitted to tell him. Particularly from the unofficial history she had pieced together. She didn't tell him of what Mrs Roth or Tom Shafer or Lillian had said about the changes in the building, or of what they had all dreamed of after Hessen's arrival: the things they saw in mirrors and paintings and on the stairs, and heard behind his front door. All of this she didn't mention, preferring to portray Hessen as a misunderstood eccentric and recluse, thinking it would appeal to Seth's sense of himself.

He began to ask tight, direct questions. Probing her about Hessen's study of the occult, about theories of his disappearance, what was known about his ideas, his obsession with death, the titles of journals and books that mentioned his peculiar life, why he studied anatomy, and what she thought he was trying to achieve. And during her attempts to satisfy his insatiable need for information, she mentioned the Vortex.

Seth's face stiffened with shock, or fear, she wasn't sure which. His eyes became wild and his voice shook as he pressed her, over and over again, for details of this Vortex, for clarification of Hessen's desire to stare into it. Did she have other books? Could he read her great-aunt's journals? It was important, he said, and he even stretched one hand across the table to hold her wrist tightly. 'I have to know,

Apryl,' he said, looking into the street, his bottom lip moving as he muttered something to himself. 'Please, it's very important to me. To my work. Can you help me?'

'Why, Seth? Why is it so important?' she said, smiling and trying to put him at ease.

'I can't really say why. Not yet. But maybe soon.'

'I really want to help you, Seth. And do whatever I can. I'm so intrigued by your work. Miles will be too. I think he will want to help you once he sees how talented you are. And he'll be better at explaining Hessen than me. I'm no academic.'

'You do all right.' Seth looked down at his plate. Pushed some basmati rice about with his fork. Closed his eyes for a few seconds, then excused himself and went to the toilet. Where he remained for ten minutes.

When he came back one of his hands was shaking. She pretended not to notice, but asked him why he wasn't eating. At which he sniggered nervously and said he preferred to smoke. Then looked back outside again, to that spot across the street that so fascinated him.

Apryl was losing him. He looked so utterly miserable. His fidgeting had become manic and he was trying to catch his breath as if in the clench of an acute anxiety attack. At any moment she suspected he might make an excuse and leave.

She reached across to him and held his hand. 'Something's wrong, Seth. Don't be embarrassed. I can see you've been under a lot of strain. Would you feel better if we went back to your place? Maybe you could show me your work. If you feel uncomfortable here.'

'I'm sorry,' he said. 'I . . . It's just . . . I . . .' But he couldn't finish.

'Let me get the bill. We'll go somewhere more comfortable.'

Outside on the street, Seth walked too fast for Apryl to keep up in high heels, and she asked him to slow down.

'I'm sorry. Really sorry, Apryl,' he said three times.

'It's OK. It really is,' she said. It was freezing. A dry dusty wind whipped them from behind.

'Sometimes . . . It's just . . . I get . . . It's hard to describe.'

'Then don't try. Let's just get you home.'

'It's good of you. Really is. I feel so embarrassed.'

'Don't be silly. Shall I get something? Maybe some wine?'

'I have some, I think. In the fridge. There's not much in my room. Just a fridge and a bed. It's more a place to work. But it's pretty shocking. I mean, it's a bit of a mess.'

'You don't have to apologize, Seth. You should see some of my old apartments back home.'

'Yeah?' But he was distracted again and jumpy. Watching anyone who passed them, and peering across the street into darkened shop doorways or up narrow side streets.

From Upper Street to where he lived in Hackney, the atmosphere changed. She felt it as much as noticed it. There were fewer people on the streets and the shops were run down. They passed betting stores and unappealing pubs, a plethora of fast-food places with home-made advertisements in the windows. Large rectangular cages of social housing surrounded by iron fences loomed up and over the pockets of cramped Victorian buildings.

'I hope I'm not being too forward. I don't want to intrude.'

'No. Not at all,' he said, distracted, then looked over his shoulder. 'I'd really like to know what you think. There's no one I want to show more than you, Apryl. I think you'll understand. I really do.'

'Why?'

'Everything you've said about Hessen's vision. I think I've been chasing the same thing.'

THIRTY-FIVE

Up the dark and cluttered stairwells she climbed, all the time wishing she hadn't insisted on seeing his painting. But not from a fear of him – she thought him harmless. Intense and emotional and sensitive, but not aggressive. But there was another side to his character she had only just begun to understand. Seth's self-absorption and rapidly changing moods, the endless tangents that sprang from his hurried and excitable monologues she could deal with, but that haunted look, and at the root of it something akin to real terror, unsettled her far more here than in the restaurant. Because she could see it better in him now. As if he was drawing her closer to something she should be afraid of too.

But when she thought of him living above this scruffy pub, in a warren of peeling walls, smelly carpets and dark passageways, with its grubby windows overlooking cluttered yards and vandalized garages, she even felt sympathy for Seth and his dismal life. Working nights at Barrington House in the glaring white light of that reception area, and sleeping in one of these rooms during the day, only to wake late in this depressing neighbourhood filled with the damaged and the dangerous and the marginalized, while trying to complete some abstract and tortuous vision – it was enough to send anyone crazy. But then she put a stop to her natural empathy intruding upon her purpose: she was here to discover the extent of his involvement with that terrible thing, that murderous force, that still haunted Barrington House.

Up she went behind him in a building that stank of male sweat, of fried food and damp clothes dried on radiators, all making her wince as she climbed too many staircases and turned tight corners, while all about her corridors vanished into darkness, or stopped before reddish doors.

When finally he turned from the stairs and led her across a landing cluttered with old wardrobes, tables and broken chairs, and then down a narrow passageway to his door, she was exhausted. And as Seth opened his door, she looked down with irritation at her leg to inspect where she had scraped it against some splintered object in the dark. The fine material of her stocking had run down to the heel of her shoe in three places.

'It's in a terrible mess. Please understand, it's just a work space. I don't usually live like this.'

'Sure. Let me in. I don't like it out here,' she said, a hint of annoyance hardening her voice as she peered over her shoulder into the dark passageway they had just squeezed through. The place should be condemned. How could anyone live here?

I don't usually live like this.

Who could? Without losing their mind.

He'd painted the fucking walls.

Covered three-quarters of the entire room with a mural most psychiatrists would attribute to the work of the insane.

The figures hanging in that darkness with no end shut all of her senses down, apart from that of sight. It was childlike in its simplicity. Primitivism loud and raw. Eschewing literal portraiture to immerse the onlooker in a shock of distortion and psychic panic.

She had to sit down. On the bed, where she gaped at the walls. At the twisted things, grinning or shrieking before the infinite and the lightless.

'It's just a place for ideas. Studies of figures. The preliminary sketches are behind you. I did most of them at night. And I've got lots more in that case and in those folders. I'm just trying to find the colours on the walls. A combination of textures in the background too that really . . . really arrests.'

It certainly did that. If Hessen had ever painted, his work would have looked like this. She took her eyes from the wall and looked at the floor, covered in sheets saturated with paint and grease stains. In one corner of the room was a mess of tangled clothing. Apart from the old yellowing fridge and the sweaty bed there was nothing. Not a thing was permitted to distract her gaze from the walls and what cried out upon them, disfigured, crucified, flayed and nailed in place.

The tormented and tortured never asked for a dialogue, or suggested much of a narrative; they just existed to create seizure in whoever looked at them. They hit her with a fist of horror, but also with a cold shock of recognition. As if the bleakest and most painful experience in the viewer – the disabling moments of doubt and despair, the choking of self-loathing and hate, the binding of grief and the tether of fear – had all been personified in these figures. They were the same morbid flashes of the half-formed in agony, enduring a violence of disintegration, that Hessen had begun to sketch in his work dated 1938. But Seth had taken the ideas another step forward, using Hessen's studies as a platform, so all that they promised could be achieved on the bigger canvas and in the richness of oils.

'You have seen his paintings, Seth. Somewhere. You must have. Tell me, Seth. Please. It's why you work in that building. You knew.'

He shook his head and stepped away from the window, where he had been standing witnessing her paralysis before his walls. 'No. I never knew about him. Not in my entire life. I studied Brueghel and Bosch and Dix and Grosz. They all appealed to me. Maybe that's what made me right for this. To continue the work. And London is the perfect medium to get it out. The divide is thinner here. Nothing leaves.'

'What do you mean?' she asked, half understanding but not wanting to process the truth.

'Something happened to me. In my dreams. At work. Here. And bits of the dreams came into my head when I woke up. Then the world was different from how it was before. I thought I was mad. I started seeing things, Apryl. After the noises in apartment sixteen. Like it was trying to get my attention. So I went in. And I saw the paintings. And understood what I'd been seeing. What I'd been shown in my dreams, by a master.'

He stopped talking. The look on her face silenced him. When he'd mentioned the paintings in apartment sixteen, Apryl felt the skin shrink under her hair.

'Paintings? Hessen's paintings are still inside the flat?' She stood up. 'Tell me, Seth. Tell me the truth. There are paintings still inside that flat?'

He turned his face away and grimaced as if someone had just entered the room, then said, 'Fuck off.'

'What?'

'Sorry. Not you.'

'Seth?'

He shook his head. His mouth moved, as if he was about to speak to the door, then he turned his face away, drew his hands over his white quivery features and sighed. 'It's . . . it's not safe.'

'Safe? I don't understand. What do you mean?'

He slumped on the bed and held his head in his hands. 'I can't say. You wouldn't believe me. I should never have gone in there. It's not allowed. You can't tell anyone. I just needed to make sure no one had broken in. Because of the sounds. And the phone call. But then I saw them. The paintings. My God, those paintings.'

After he finished speaking, he looked again at the red door of his room, as if someone had suddenly knocked, or called from the other side.

'You watch your mouf, cunt, when you's talkin' to me. And you's gonna show her them pictures, Seth. Our mate says so. He wants to meet the little tart. Shovin' her fucking snout in, like. Just like her old aunty-bitch. Well there's plenty to see if you go to the right places. Ain't there? You's knows that better than anyone, mate. So you bring her up them stairs. You know where.

'She's the last one, Seth. You's almost done, mate. And you's'll get what's comin'. He's gonna fix things for you. Yous'll do alright out of this, mate. You's comin' to live there with us. Do some paintin's and stuff and live downstairs. Close like. We's always gonna be together, like. So you's do as you is fuckin' told, like, and bring that tart up them stairs.'

*

'What paintings? Hessen's paintings?'

Seth heaved out a great sigh. Then swallowed. He took his eyes from the door and looked at her, with pity, she thought. 'You have to understand. Nothing has ever given me so many ideas before. No other artist has ever spoken to me in the same way. He's taught me to do everything all over again. Taught me how to find a voice, Apryl. But . . .'

Apryl felt dizzy. Disoriented from his crazy mixed-up talk and the sudden realization that Hessen's paintings actually existed. It was like reading Lillian's journals all over again. And to have it confirmed like this. By this nervous obsessive young man with eyes so bruised by lack of sleep he was beginning to look like he had a terminal illness.

'I need a drink.' Apryl gulped at the cheap and acidic white wine Seth kept in his fridge. At least it was cold. Then she sat on the bed again to put herself back together. 'Seth, I want to know what is still inside apartment sixteen.'

He winced and slopped wine into a dirty coffee mug, then lit another cigarette.

'I want to know what happened, Seth. To my great-aunt. To the others. You know he killed them, Seth. That he's still in the building. You know that, don't you?'

His body seemed to deflate as it sat on the edge of the bed. He hung his head down between his knees, his bony spine arching upward, every joint visible through his thin shirt. She crossed her legs so quickly they hissed. 'Did you help him?'

Seth raised his head. 'I was tricked.'

'How? How did you do it?'

He looked at her, his face pale, his eyes wild, feral. 'I just let it back in. I didn't know . . .' He swallowed, looked up at the door, his wide eyes watering. 'Then it was too late.'

She put her hand on his forearm. He looked down at it and sobbed.

She spoke to herself as much as to Seth. 'No one would believe us anyway. About what we know. What only we know.' Then her eyes suddenly hardened to an intensity that clearly frightened him. 'But he has to be sent back, Seth. You know that. Whatever he is coming through has to be closed. He killed my family. And you helped him. So now you are going to help me. Or there will be trouble. More than you can handle. And Miles knows. My friend. He knows everything too, so nothing had better happen to me when I go into sixteen and shut that shit hole down. You get it?'

Outside the room, someone stumbled through the darkness and swore in a heavy Irish brogue. They both started on the bed. Apryl clapped a hand to her chest.

Seth swallowed. 'It's not that. I could get you in there easy. Easy. It's not that.'

'Then what?'

He looked at the door and whispered, as if terrified someone might hear him. 'It's not safe.'

April felt her skin ice and then shrink around her muscles. 'How?'

'The apartment. Changes things. Seeing it isn't safe. And . . . I don't think everyone can . . . is able . . . to see it . . . the paintings . . .' He said this with such conviction she shivered as if suddenly affected by a draught from under one of the old wooden window frames, painted white and peeling.

He pointed at the wall. 'This is nothing compared to what he has done. It's just a facsimile. But his painting is . . . it's

not right. It's just impossible. They change. They're alive.'
And then he had to look away as if unable to withstand the
sight of her fear. 'He's still in there. Hessen. In that flat. And
he's not alone.'

THIRTY-SIX

And at last the hour had been reached when he could walk down the final flight of stairs to his flat in the basement. So weary in mind, back and legs, like his whole being was bruised with fatigue, Stephen headed down. Back to his wife. He would usually go to her for thirty minutes during his lunch break at one, and then again at six thirty once the night man was in.

Stephen was the only company Janet had these days. The only real voice she ever heard, though he wasn't so talkative any more. The residents liked to do the talking and they liked him because he listened and never troubled their space or time with his own personality. Such a tactic had advantages. The less you said, the easier life was.

In the only part of the basement that was carpeted, he reached the front door of their staff flat. Around him he heard the clank and grind and shudder of the lift motor room, its harder sounds rising above the distant thrum of the boiler. Sounds that could be heard all of the time down here if you concentrated. When he took the job and they moved in, he and Janet doubted they would be able to tolerate the constant noise. But if he had learned anything as head porter of Barrington House, it was that you soon get used to all kinds of things, and you accept what cannot be changed.

As he slipped his key into the lock, he wondered if Janet was always aware of the labouring of the building's utilities, or the passing vehicles on the road one floor above their sub-terranean-level flat. These days, she never left the apartment unless he took her somewhere. Which was never much further than a mile in any direction.

Inside the flat, in the little hallway where it was too cramped to bend right over, he slipped his shoes off. The warmth and the smell of Janet's patient exhalations hit him immediately. The flat wasn't big enough for one person, let alone two. But Janet didn't move much, so they managed as best they could.

Reaching out, he felt for the light switch where the hall opened into the living room. The old curtains and cheap carpet made the flat look orange, the colour somehow shrinking the dimensions too. He didn't like spending too much time in here and tried to get off to sleep pretty quickly in the evenings. To put every day out of its misery.

He'd not been down at dinner time to turn the television on for Janet. Not today; there had been too much to do upstairs. So Janet had sat down here all day and into the early evening in the dark.

Silent and still, she was sitting in her chair in exactly the same position as this morning when he left her, dressed in the pink housecoat, with the tartan blanket over her lap and legs.

He could smell piss.

She must be thirsty too; the glass with the straw inside, on the little side table beside her arm, was empty.

But no shit. Yes, she'd been that morning before he'd gone upstairs for the day.

He would have liked to open a window to air the tiny room. Being so close to the boiler the heat became insufferable. But the window was right behind Janet's chair and he didn't want her caught in a draught.

In the kitchen that always made him think of the caravans they used to rent in Devon, he opened the fridge. All Formica surfaces in the kitchen and everything built in miniature like it had been made for a child's Wendy house. What a way to live.

The fridge began to hum and vibrate. There were three microwave dinners left. He'd have the Lancashire hotpot. Didn't feel like curry tonight after smelling Piotr's armpits all day. Once he'd finished, Janet could have the macaroni cheese, after he'd let her meal cool down properly. She couldn't tell him if it was too hot; he had to watch her eyes instead.

While the microwave purred and tinged and lit itself up, he went through to the lounge and turned the television on with the remote. Immediately, he lowered the sound. Slowly, he undid his silver tie. Then unbuttoned his cuffs and rolled his sleeves up his forearms. Janet watched him.

From the little cabinet built over the fireplace, he retrieved the single malt Mr Alfrezi gave him last Christmas. The last bottle, but the residents were very generous at Christmas. You look after them and they'll look after you, he told his staff. And would tell Seth the same thing when he handed the staff apartment over to him. Pass on the simple instructions and advice – that he had longed to do for ten years. The moment was almost upon him.

Stephen drank two big gulps from the mouth of the bottle. And winced as it burned down his gullet. Yes, it should be a good Christmas.

Last Christmas he made three grand in tips and received four bottles of champagne, two good reds and eight single malts. This year should be even better. His wife was very ill, they all knew that; and he had dealt with the sudden deaths of Mrs Roth and old Tom Shafer too, with 'considerable sensitivity' Mr Glock had said. Betty Roth's daughter had even held both of his hands and said as much with tears in her eyes. Apparently, her mother was very fond of him. Not that he'd noticed.

He went and sat down heavily with a big sigh, on the sofa next to Janet's chair. Then placed his feet on the little cushioned stool. He removed his glasses and rubbed at his eyes.

Janet looked at the floor in front of her chair. No real expression on her face. She didn't seem to react to much these days. Beside one thing: now *that* always got a rise out of her.

Stephen took another gulp from the neck of the bottle and sighed appreciatively. 'You know, dear, I'm very glad that I have never actually seen whatever it is that you saw up there. Inside that flat. I mean Seth is going in there tonight to do the kid's bidding. And it'll be that gorgeous little thing he takes up there with him. The one who inherited Lil's old place. You know, the niece? And then I'm out of here, my dear. Long gone. Vamoosh.'

Janet continued to stare at the floor. He was really getting fed up with her now. If he were honest, she'd never been good company. But what did he know back then when they got married? You never had as many choices and opportunities as the young people did today. With hindsight, he'd certainly have done things differently. But there was still time.

A little time left to get out there and enjoy himself a bit. Instead of living in these demoralizing shoeboxes at the beck and call of rich tossers like Glock and Betty Roth.

He nodded in her direction, raising his eyebrows to emphasize his point. 'And we both know only too well what can happen if you go messing around with things in there, don't we dear? I've said it before and I'll say it again, what's dead should stay dead. Bring it back and there'll only be trouble. But you wouldn't listen, would you. Eh?'

From the kitchen the microwave pinged its little bell. Stephen rose from his seat and went through. As he peeled the steaming wet lid off the hotpot, he spoke distractedly over his shoulder. 'You had to go up there with old Lill, messing around in that place looking for our son. If you'd not gone up there to find him, none of this would have happened. So I reckon this is all your fault. I mean it. Had you not brought our proud son back from wherever he was causing havoc, old Roth and the Shafers would still be breaking everyone's balls at Barrington House. And we wouldn't have been stuck here until they died. Did you know that? Eh? Well you do now, dear.'

He turned away from the counter with his meal on a tray. 'Hard to believe that such a vicious little sod was ever our flesh and blood.' He shook his head. 'Jesus, I still can't believe he's had Seth do those old Shafers as well as Betty. Though I don't know why I am surprised. All those years ago when I was serving my country in Ireland, you let that little shit run wild, until he ran into borstal. Eh? Loved trouble he did, and then got himself all burned up. Christ almighty. But he's far more dangerous dead.'

He emptied the slurry of vegetables and cubes of stewing

beef onto a Pyrex plate and retrieved a fork from the side of the tray.

Blowing on the surface and then forking it quickly into his mouth, he spoke around mouthfuls. 'I'd have to guess that Seth has pretty much done his job. As have I. Though I take pride in the fact that I did my share a little more thoroughly than he has. He's always leaving doors open. Never thought it through. Too jumpy for the job. But I cleaned up thoroughly after him. Got it sorted. Like I have always done in this bloody place. Making sure the symbols stayed behind the pictures, in all the right places, like our kid showed me, no matter how many times the directors messed around with the decor. I had a right job with the stairs in the west block when they bought all those new prints. I had to work fast outside the flats the kid had an interest in too, to keep things as they were and to keep certain people here until they died. Which Seth is making happen with an efficiency I honestly did not believe he was capable of when I hired him. So I'd like to think our lad, and those *others* he knocks about with now, are satisfied with my work. Though the little shit is coy, dear. Very coy. Takes after his mum, he does.'

He sat back and smacked his lips. Moved a tongue over his gums. 'But I'll guess Seth has been shown things up there in much the same way as you were. The night you spent up there.' He pointed his fork for emphasis. 'For Seth, being a painter, it was exactly what he wanted to see. You know, for inspiration. Painters need this. That's pretty much what the kid said last time I saw him. And Seth's got more stomach for it. In there, with those things. Fancy that. Not like the rest of us. Or you, for that matter. Now look at you, eh? That's what comes from meddling. Makes you wonder though, doesn't it, what's in store for that girl, Apryl, dear. I never asked the kid about what he's got Seth to agree to up there, but I can't help thinking it'll be something she isn't expecting.'

He finished the last of his hotpot in silent concentration. He was hungry and chased every pea to the edge of his plate. 'Mmm. I'm going to give you macaroni cheese, dear. You used to like it, but I think it tastes and looks and smells like shit.'

Back in the kitchen he tossed the hotpot carton into the bin and then settled his plate into the blue washing-up bowl inside the sink.

When Janet's meal was ready, he knelt on the floor before her chair and scooped a forkful from the side of her plate where it was cooler, and blew on it too to make sure. 'There, that should be just right.'

Without meeting his eyes, Janet accepted the fork into her mouth, chewed a little and then swallowed.

'The girl though,' he said. 'It's still upsetting. It's why I need a drink. And I'll see that bottle off tonight, you mark my words. So I'll thank you in advance for keeping a low profile this evening.'

As she looked at her husband, Janet's eyes widened.

'She's very pretty, Janet. I've told you before. Lovely-looking girl, with good manners too. Even though she has all of those tattoos, she's every bit as courteous as Lillian. She reminds me of old Lil. She really does.' He shook his head with a sigh and fed Janet another three heaped forks. His knees were hurting and he wanted to get this over with.

'It was bad enough seeing Betty's face and old Tom Shafer, but I really don't want to see what they'll do to a young and pretty thing like Apryl. The girl is an unfortunate accident, I reckon. She's just been in the wrong place at the wrong time. Poking her nose in. Like you did. Fatal. Fucking fatal, dear. And like you, after that first time in there, dear, I doubt she'll ever be the same again. No one is once they've been up there with *them*. You know, up close. She'll be lucky not to have a stroke as well. I hope it's her heart that goes. I really do. So she doesn't end up like you.'

He dropped the fork onto the plate. 'That's enough. We don't want you losing your figure again. You can't exercise and this shit is full of fat.' With a groan, he slowly rose to his feet, using the arm of Janet's chair as support. 'I'll get a cloth, it's all over your ruddy chin.'

When he came back with the damp cloth he used for wiping down the kitchen surfaces, Janet was crying. He dabbed at her chin.

'Now if you're going to make a fuss, I'll put you in the bedroom again, and close the bloody door. I've had a very trying day. Let's just get through the next few weeks and stay out of each other's way. Then it'll be all over and done with. I expect Mrs Roth's daughter will sell both flats. And you know as well as I do that properties don't hang around in this building. So after that I can finish up here. I don't think I can risk waiting any longer than a month at most. Because when someone moves into sixteen, then what? Eh? I could get stuck. Mixed up in it all again. Thanks to you. It's already a little risky. Two deaths, Mrs Shafer all crazy, and the girl soon to get hurt. So I'll do the handover to old Seth as quick as I can, and then I'm off, me dear. Like they promised. They'll let me out then. I haven't been able to walk further than Bond Street in a fucking decade.'

He sucked his teeth for a moment and looked up at the

ceiling. 'And it could also work in my favour too. It'll look good, if you think about it. And I do. I think it through, dear. Not like you bleeding hearts. You see, the strain of recent events and all these years enduring the incapacitation of my wife, then getting widowed. Who could blame me for handing my notice in? Just packing in and heading for the sun? I think I'll be all right.'

Janet began to make a moaning sound. A hard keening that came from deep within her chest. Her eyes flitted around as if she were looking for a way out.

Stephen took no notice. He'd talk to himself if she wasn't going to hear him out. Set it all down inside his own head. Talking out loud helped. They all did a lot of that here. 'They've no problem with me. I've done my bit and can go now. Our kid will show me how to remove whatever the fuck it is that keeps me inside a square mile I now know every single inch of. Seth's turn now. They wanted a painter and I gave them one. Though he has a different agreement with them, I'd say. I stood me ground and wouldn't kill those old bastards. Though God knows I've thought about it often enough, just to get out of here. But Seth stepped up. Right off. Christ, he's cold.

'So I'll give it another fortnight and I'll take you back up too. For the last time. One more trip will be sufficient. I'll give you plenty of notice, though. That's only fair. But I don't know the exact date yet. I'll have to play it by ear for a while, so do be patient. Then you and the kid can spend all the time you want together.'

Janet tried to move forward in her chair. Her eyes bulged from the effort, and without even looking at her, Stephen

410

gently put his hand between her breasts and pushed her back. She gasped and sat still again.

'After that, your guess is as good as mine. It's only a theory, mind, because different rules apply up there, but Seth won't ever be going far from this place. Life sentence for old Seth. He'll live in this flat till he croaks. Nor will you, dear. Your body might, when it's over, when they've had their way up there. But you won't. You'll go where our kid and old Roth and Shafer went. So maybe you can all be chums again. In that other place with the rest of them. And I don't want to be around when you are. Spending so much time together in here has been bad enough, so I don't want to keep seeing you in mirrors or popping up in the pictures on the stairwells. No good for the nerves, dear. I think you of all people will appreciate that.'

Stephen took a seat beside her and took another swig from the neck of the bottle. Janet began a constant rhythmic sobbing sound.

'There's no point in making a fuss. This had nothing to do with us until you made it our business.'

He stood up again and approached her chair. Janet flinched. He took the brakes off the grey rubber wheels and moved her away from the wall and pointed her feet in the direction of the bedroom door. 'I don't know what gets into you women, I really don't. Got to poke your beaks where they're not wanted. And then you start fussing and moaning when it all goes tits-up.'

He wheeled her chair into the tiny bedroom and parked her in the corner beside the bed. 'I want some time to myself now. I've been on my feet all day. I'll change you in the morning. I don't have the patience now.'

The head porter closed the door and left his wife in the dark. As he resumed his seat on the couch, he guessed, and it was just a guess, that the residents would be very generous at Christmas when he announced his retirement as head porter of Barrington House.

THIRTY-SEVEN

When Apryl arrived at one in the morning, Barrington House was enshrouded by a wet darkness. The lights in most of the apartments were out. Only in the communal areas did the discoloured electric bulbs illumine the hazy stairwells and dismal landings. But there was nothing comforting about this light, nothing warm, and nothing about the dim glow to make a person want to take shelter in there, even if it was wet outside.

At the end of the reception area Seth watched Apryl peer through the main doors, at the place he occupied once the sun was dead. Around her silhouette the night was a blur of depth and reflection, like a combination of inner and outer worlds. Two separate places joined on the thin layer of glass.

She was wrapped in a long, dark coat and her hair was concealed by a headscarf. He could almost smell her. That sweet sweet smell. Even on the other side of the door, before she let herself in with the pass code, he anticipated the taste of her.

Behind Apryl's svelte shape, he caught the shudder and then the rattling whoosh of a black cab passing away. Had she come by taxi? He'd told her not to. Not to allow anyone to see her enter this building tonight. Or to tell anyone where she was going. They had a deal. Who knew how things could go up there? Just the thought made him sick with fear.

He looked up at the ceiling. Bits of whatever was in there must have escaped from the mirrored room back when the residents and Barrington House were younger – before the building was aged by what came through, by what it now held within its feeble bricks.

He had come to think *it* began when life began and that this building was nothing but a keyhole through which a few draughts had snuck. But he could only guess at the invisible byways by which its influence had then spread. Hessen used it to find allies and to destroy enemies. From amongst those close to his presence, and that of the terrible collective that used madness and nightmare to make itself known in the places it could only be brought into by men like Hessen. And not sent back.

Hessen had waited fifty years for someone to finish his business. He was greater than Seth, and Seth could not defy his will. His tutor had waited too long for this opportunity. Had even hobbled Mrs Roth and the Shafers to keep them close, all this time, while he waited. Never forgetting. Unforgiving. Pure in purpose as an artist must be.

Seth clambered out from behind his desk and walked over to greet Apryl. 'You came in a cab. I told you not to. I told you to be discreet.'

'I didn't. I only took a cab to Sloane Street, and then walked from there. Like you said.' She reached out and touched his arm. 'It's OK. You can trust me, Seth. I want you to trust me.'

Looking into her pretty eyes and then letting his stare linger on her red lips, glossy with a scarlet that contrasted so arrestingly with the white skin of her face, he would believe her. Cabs always passed by this place, looking for fares in the richest part of town. That's all it was. But God he was jumpy.

'You have the keys?' she asked.

He fished them out of his pocket. Made them jingle on the silver hoop in front of her face. 'Remember, if anyone sees you, if the head porter sees you, you don't mention number sixteen. He won't be around, but just in case. OK?'

'Sure. Right.' She was nervous but her eyes were excited. He liked that. Stupidly, he wanted to kiss her before she went in there. But the thought of where she was going made him swallow to try and force the panic back down his throat.

'Let me get the pager. Then we'll go up by the stairs. The lift makes too much noise. Sometimes it gets stuck. I don't want to leave anything to chance.'

'Seth. What you're doing – it has to stop. You know that. And we are going to stop it. Together. You understand that, don't you? What you brought in can be sent back. Somehow.'

It did something to his stomach, the way she looked at him. Right into the middle of him. He shivered in a nice way. Felt a bit dizzy too. She was the kind of woman he could just look at. For ever.

But she really did not have a clue.

THIRTY-EIGHT

She followed him up the stairs, behind his narrow shoulders in the blue blazer and his long thin legs in the creased flannel trousers. He walked quickly and whenever he turned to take the next set of stairs, she noticed how pale his face was. And how quickly his lips moved as he muttered to himself.

Breathing harder than she liked, or thought she ought to, she went up seemingly endless stairs thickly carpeted in green. Twice on the verge of losing her balance in the high-heeled boots she had worn, she skipped after him, trying to control her fear. The idea of going inside that apartment made her nauseous with the wrong kind of excitement. She had not been an accessory to Hessen's end, or to the destruction of his art, but she could not stop wondering what his presence would do to defend itself against a threat or an intrusion.

At least Miles was outside the building awaiting her signal. She'd given him the pass code to the front door and directions on how to find the flat once he was inside. If she felt threatened she would summon him immediately. He'd tried to stop her coming here tonight, but this arrangement was his compromise.

And then Seth stopped walking. Turned to her quickly. His face a shock of nerves, his hands clenched. 'Here we are,' he whispered, his voice weakened either by the climb or by the prospect of trespassing.

She looked over Seth's shoulder at the door marked with the number 16, fixed in brass on the teak. This is where Hessen had lived and worked. Where he had tried to seal himself off from scrutiny and interference within the city he drew his inspiration from. The place in which he suffered and where he nearly revised the direction of modern art. But a place where he also achieved the most extraordinary contact with an unseen world. And where his own face was mutilated before he was put away by her flesh and blood, who had led her here in a strange, meandering confession in a series of handwritten journals. But this was now a place that needed to be sealed by more than a locked front door. Whatever still allowed Hessen access needed to be removed and destroyed, and more thoroughly than the last attempt in 1949. Exactly how this was going to be achieved she wasn't at all sure. But searching the apartment, she swore to herself, was at least a start.

'You ready?' Seth whispered.

She nodded.

'Let me go in first. You wait here. Until I call you.'

'Sure,' she thought she said, but her voice was so faint now it probably sank through the warm air and vanished around her knees.

Carefully, Seth unlocked the door.

The moment the front door closed behind Seth, Apryl flipped open her cell phone and hissed into it. 'It's me. Yes, yes, I'm fine. I'm outside the flat now. He's gone inside. I'm going to leave the phone on and hold it in my hand so you can hear everything … OK, I will … It'll be fine.'

THIRTY-NINE

Leaving the catch on, Seth pulled the door shut behind him.

The lights were on in the hallway. Stretching away like a red funnel the passage looked fleshy, with clots of shadow pooling on the floor in the spaces between the lamps. And the place was silent. Every painting was covered in muslin as it had been the last time he visited here, accompanied. Pushing the recollection away he walked down the blood-lit hall to the mirrored room, with his skin acutely aware of how the air swelled about him, as if some restless energy rolled and thickened about these rooms, even when he was not here.

And things seemed to be quiet tonight in the mirrored room. From the other side of the door he heard no one cry out from the ceiling in a far-off rushing of air. There was no bumping or crawling or dragging of something out of sight. Nothing. Just the still, cold air in which the greatest art man had ever known hung behind its coverings.

He paused a moment. Slowed down the spinning in his head. Steeled himself against what he might see, against what might be shared with him tonight, and against thoughts of what would become of Apryl, sweet Apryl. In there, in that room. She was *the last one*. The boy had said so. He'd learn to live with himself later. If that Miles guy raised the alarm, then so what? What could he or anyone prove? He'd say she forced him to show her that apartment because she was obsessed with some conspiracy about a dead painter. He just had to hold his nerve and keep that door shut until *they* took what they wanted. But would she still be breathing afterwards, like old Mrs Shafer? She'd have to be. What the fuck could he do with a dead girl? Where was the boy? He had to speak to the boy before he put Apryl inside.

He swallowed and opened the door, looked into the cold, unlit room. Nothing but the bare wooden floor, the covered picture frames and the empty mirrors. His body shuddered with relief. Maybe, just maybe nothing was going to happen tonight. You never knew, he told himself, when you had dealings with such things.

Reaching inside the door, he felt the bump of the light switch and flicked it down to flood the space with faint reddish light. Some unseen curator had concealed the paintings again, but left the four large mirrors that faced each other uncovered, their silvery corridors reflecting each other and tunnelling away to the furthest reaches of light and sight. Carefully, he walked into the middle of the room, watching the mirrors for movement. For the one who wanted to meet Apryl.

But saw only himself.

Seth then steeled himself against the very idea of what would shriek and twist and unravel between the borders of the gilt frames before his eyes tonight. It had been prepared. Was he to unveil them? Would that kick things off then, and get it all going round and round?

Time to collect his guest.

But as he turned to face the door, a sudden dart of

movement pulled his eyes to the mirror on his right, above the empty fireplace. When he turned to look all he saw in the glass was a reflection of his own shabby visage again – shoulders hunched, face tense and pale.

It was nothing. Just his imagination.

But then again, at the periphery of his vision, to his left, he detected a quick but distant movement inside another mirror. He turned quickly to look into the glass. And saw nothing again save his own dark eyes reflected back at him.

It struck him that the mirrors were connected at the side of each reflection. As if all four faced each other to offer some means of passage for whatever flitted within them. Before serving as an exit for whatever was taken back inside.

Anticipating a circular movement, he looked quickly to the next mirror, at the head of the rectangular room. And saw a pale shape flap across the bottom of the silvery square, halfway down the tunnel of reflection, but closer to the surface of the glass than before. With a smear of red this time, a momentary blossom of scarlet near the floor of the mirror, as if a coloured face atop a stooped body was turned inward, towards the room where he now stood alone.

He was too afraid to turn and see how close it came to the skin of glass in the next mirror, the one behind him. The skin on his neck goosed from an unwelcome static.

He moved his eyes down and to the right, but couldn't bear to turn his head completely. Instead, he stared at the wooden floor at his feet. And listened.

The lights hummed. There was no other sound. Or maybe there was. In the distance. Maybe it was the far-off traffic from the world beyond the curtains, windows and walls. Or the swish of an approaching storm, draping its hem across the roofs and through the stony ravines of street and lane as it came towards Barrington House.

No. It wasn't moving forward, it was moving down and from a great distance that lessened by the second.

A moment of dizzying panic filled every molecule within his body, before he suddenly broke from a stunned paralysis and made for the door. But the hooded boy stood before him, in the open doorway of the room. Hands in pockets, face drawn back into the volume of dark hood, he said, 'They's coming for the tart, Seth. They want to show her the next bit. He didn't get the aunty-bitch, but he'll have the tart, mate. You can be sure of that, like.'

The enormity of what the delinquent was suggesting stopped his breath. Seth shook his head. His nervous smile made him feel idiotic. 'No. I don't want to.' He took another step towards the boy.

The hood shook. 'Nah-ah. You's gonna get her in here fast like. It don't stay open for long. I told you before. You's got to be quick, like. Get the tart in here and shut that fuckin' door behind you. You know how it's done, mate. You's gettin' good at it. So don't go gettin' all soft in the 'ead, like. She's just using you, mate. Finks you is a cunt, like. She's tryin' to fuck it up for us. So she's gonna disappear. Summat special tonight, Seth. She's goin' right off the edge. Down there wiv him, our mate.'

'But what do I do with the body? I can't just put her in a bed and walk away. There's a guy. He knows she's here.'

The boy closed the door of the mirrored room with them both inside it. Looked up. 'Won't be no body, mate. I told ya, like. Gonna be nuffin left of that tart once he's had his way. She's going off the edge, like he did. All them years ago. Won't be fuck all left, innit.'

'But—'

'He's comin'! It's all going off, mate.' The voice was tight with childish glee. The little arms left the pockets and a row of fingertips all melted together were displayed.

Above them, the light flickered. Then suddenly dimmed. It was like a cloud moving over the sun. Shadow tinted the room, then darkened the very air before his eyes. And there was a voice from beyond the room, but too far away to be a part of this place. A voice that called his name: 'Seth? Seth? You're freaking me out now. Where are you?'

It was Apryl. 'Apryl, no!' he cried out. 'Don't come in. Stop!'

'You's shut your gob!' The boy shouted at him, then raised stubby arms as if to start a fight with him.

Then the temperature suddenly collapsed to a cold he could feel like frosted pins inside his bones. What was left of the room – the walls and floor and skirting board, the hooded boy, the very substance of the solid and visible – melted into darkness so quickly he could no longer see the wood beneath his feet.

Instinct begged him to flee. To rush quickly for the direction of the door and to leave the building, with Apryl in tow. But he knew he had no choice. He had been so limited in this city ever since he'd arrived, and choice was no longer an asset he could command. Had it ever been?

And this meeting was inevitable anyway. Whatever presence had been inhabiting his dreams and watching him from afar, and opening his eyes to the world, would eventually present itself. He'd always suspected as much.

He took two faltering steps towards where his memory told him the door was, every muscle in his body shaking from the icy temperature and from the sudden sweep of cries that came down from above, circling, helpless, and torn about by the cold turbulence.

From behind him something issued a sigh. It filled the cold room with a rasp that seemed to have escaped from lungs greater than anything that could possibly be housed inside a man's chest. The sound continued in one long exhalation, dispersing like a frosted gas to the four corners of the room, rolling across the floor to swallow the last traces of definition before him.

There was no sign of his hooded companion. No trace of him now. Or of warmth, or of any evidence that the world existed or had ever done.

And down came the rest of them. From above, in a multitude of distant cries and screams. Moving so fast towards him, he wanted to be sick with terror on the floor he couldn't see.

He took several stumbling steps on legs he could barely feel, and was sure his heart would stop and his blood would freeze, then shatter, if anything touched him in here, in the darkness.

Behind him, so close now, and competing with the maelstrom from above that he dared not look into for fear of seeing its descent, he heard the sound of footsteps upon a hard floor.

The tone of the continuous sigh that gushed and filled this blind place rose in a note of expectation. Or excitement. Within the shroud of his fear, he didn't know. Couldn't possibly think clearly. Didn't know much at all any more – which way he was facing, if his feet were still on the floor, whether his body was tilting back, down and down and down to the place where a floor should have been. Or why in a place of no north or south, no ground or sky, he could still see so far ahead of himself. Or maybe it was an inch from the end of his nose. But he could just make out something red that moved as he blinked and tried to focus. And it only became clear for splinters of seconds in which he glimpsed what appeared to be a red cloth bound about a small head. With sharp features pressing hard against the taut scarlet fabric. And out of what could have been an open mouth came the sigh.

Seth covered his eyes when the cold burnt the flesh of his face.

FORTY

Seth had been gone for over five minutes. And she had stood, nervously, outside the front door of apartment sixteen, fingering a cigarette lighter inside the womb of a deep coat pocket, while listening for any sign of him inside the apartment.

Once she thought she heard him approach the door on swift feet, almost as if he was running back to the front door. But the door hadn't opened. And the feet had sounded tiny, like a child's.

When she called out, 'Seth? Seth?' the footsteps stopped and her memory of them became vague, making her believe they had occurred somewhere else in the building, in another apartment, on another hard floor. Maybe they had.

And then she thought she heard a door close deep inside the flat. Far off, far behind masonry and wood. But again, the sound might have been generated from another place somewhere inside the building. It was hard to tell.

But she couldn't stand outside for much longer. And what was he doing in there anyway? She wondered if Miles was right. That it was a setup, an ambush. This couldn't go on any longer. She took her hands out of her pockets.

'Hello. It's me.'

'*Apryl. You all right?*'

'Yes.'

'What's going on?'

'Beats me.'

'Are you inside?'

'No, I'm still waiting outside. He's been in there ages. I don't know what he's doing. He told me to wait here. Do I wait all night?'

'I don't like this. I'm coming in.'

'No. Don't. You'll ruin everything. I promised him.'

'It could be a trap.'

'No. I told you . . . I think he's harmless,' she said to calm Miles, but wasn't sure she believed it any more.

'You think he's harmless! Jesus, Apryl.'

'I just don't know what's taking him so long. So I'm going in. The door's on the latch. I just wanted to tell you I'm leaving the line open. You know, just in case.'

'Apryl, don't go inside. I don't want you to. This is all wrong. You're trespassing. I don't like the sound of this at all.'

'It'll be fine. Trust me. Just listen out. To be on the safe side. I won't stay long. I just want to see what's in there. I'll see you in a few minutes.'

'I'm getting fed up with this. It's so damn foolish. Don't you feel absurd?'

Apryl pushed the front door open.

The hinge squeaked and then whined as the heavy door swung inwards. To reveal an unlit hallway. From the light of the landing she could just make out its shadowy far end in a derelict penthouse apartment. 'Seth,' she whispered into the gloom. 'Seth. Seth.'

Taking a step inside, she looked for a light switch. And found an ancient ceramic device that looked like her grandmother's butter dish turned upside down. She flicked the switch down but it clunked, emptily, and there was no response from the elaborate glass lights attached to the walls.

Guided only by the light from the landing, she moved further down the deserted hallway, her feet creaking the floorboards. The place smelled of dust and stale air.

'Seth', she said again, louder this time. 'Seth. Where are you?'

Passing another two light switches, she flicked them up and down. They were useless. Dead.

She was running out of light from the landing. The darkness in the apartment swallowed the yellowish glow before it could spread fully from the mouth of the front door. Then it suddenly went even darker, right around her.

Looking over her shoulder, she saw that the front door had silently swung half shut, its weight pulling it back to the frame. She retreated, anxious with every step that her heels didn't make too loud a sound on the floorboards, and propped the door open by wedging her compact underneath. Then returned to the middle of the hallway.

This time she took more notice of the doors she was passing. The smaller ones painted white she assumed had cupboards behind them; the others must open to rooms like they did in Lillian's apartment. 'Seth,' she said. A note of command mixed with irritation sharpened the word to cut the silence.

Taking out her lighter, she sparked it into life and raised it to see better.

The walls were skinned with an ugly paper. It was browned with age and had a rough texture against her fingertips. Every other thing had been taken down from the walls as in the other apartments she had seen. Like they were not to be trusted. There was no sign of the paintings Seth promised to show her, or any sign of him either.

'Seth? Seth? You're freaking me out now. Where are you?'

A few steps further and she ran out of all but the thinnest electric light and the pale flicker from her disposable lighter. Its bright but short flare scattered into the cold, heavy atmosphere, showing little beyond a small radius. But it managed to reveal a closed door on the left-hand side of the passageway. In her great-aunt's flat this would have been the living room. And inside it, she heard a distant voice. 'Seth? Is that you?'

As if from a great distance he cried out, 'Apryl, no! Don't come in. Stop!'

A draught seeped out of the gap between the door and the floor and cooled across her hands. The flame of her lighter flickered blue, then flattened itself against the metal cuff before going out. Impossibly, it was as if he had been calling from a great distance. She stayed still, her body tense, the nerves down her spine prickling. She listened.

Someone else was speaking again inside the room. Yes, she could hear a voice. No, voices. Was that a television? A radio? Moving closer to the door, she pressed her ear to the wood. The sound seemed distant, like she was passing Yankee Stadium during a home game. It must have been coming from beyond the building.

Her mind suddenly filled with what Mrs Roth and Mr Shafer had told her about the noises they heard inside this apartment. She pressed the phone to her ear and stood away from the door. 'Miles?'

'Yes, I'm here. What is it?'

'I don't know. There are no lights in here. I can't see much. But I can hear something. Or is it outside? Can you hear anything down there?'

'Like what?'

'Like a crowd.'

'What do you mean?'

'Is it windy out there?'

'What?'

'Windy? Is there wind outside?'

'No. It's bloody cold and wet, but there's no wind for once. What are you talking about?'

'I can hear something.' And she could. Either it was getting louder by the second or her hearing was improving. It was like a storm. Or like something really loud and far away but not tuned in properly. From beneath the door the cold air increased its force and made her take another step away.

'Apryl? Apryl?' She heard Miles's little voice chirping from the phone.

'Seth? What are you doing?' she said at the door and repositioned the lighter before her face. It sparked but wouldn't ignite in the draught.

'Down here,' a voice called from inside that room, from right behind the door. At least that's what it sounded like. Was that Seth?

'What?' Quickly, desperately, her fingers scraped at the metal wheel of the lighter. She raised her phone. 'I think I can hear someone. In this room.'

'Apryl, you're worrying me. What the hell is going on?'

Apryl held the lighter up. It sparked, then died. Then lit up again on the next attempt. She took a hesitant step right to the threshold of the room, the flame held up near her face. Choked by the thump of her own heart, she squinted over the lighter and decided to take a peek into the room to see what Seth was doing. It must be him in there. With someone else. Or he was talking to himself? She touched the door handle.

And the door swung open.

It had been pulled open from the other side. She sucked her breath back inside her mouth. The little flame of the lighter was extinguished, instantly, by the sudden darkness and cold that rushed out of that room. That came roaring out like a tremendous pressure forcing itself from a confined but volatile space. Yes, it was all alive in there. The air was alive and full of so many screams she lost her balance before the force of it all.

The thin light from the landing was doused and all definition from everything in her line of vision – the dirty wallpaper, the vague suggestion of a ceiling, the cornice – vanished. All gone. Eclipsed by something so dense and black only her sense of temperature remained.

As Seth came out of there, fleeing right out of forever, her hair plastered itself against her skull and her eyelids trembled in the sudden punch of an arctic wind. And with him came a slipstream of howls so wretched and frantic she was forced to add her own long scream. But at the very least, hers came from a living mouth.

FORTY-ONE

Seth collapsed in the hallway, on the other side of the door, panting, sobbing. Then looked up and saw the hooded boy a few feet to his left, agitated, the hooded head whipping from Seth to the traumatized figure of Apryl. She leant against the wall a few feet to his right, one boot turned at an awkward angle and no longer supporting her weight. Further down the hallway, the front door gaped.

'Seth! Seth!' the delinquent voice shrieked from out of the trembling hood. 'Get that fuckin' tart in there. Bang her in there. Do it now or you'll be sorry. He'll take you down there wiv 'em instead. You or her, like. Fuckin' do what I says!'

Apryl stared at Seth in shock, unable to speak.

'He wants to meet you,' he said, his voice sounding pathetic and wheedling to his own ears. 'In there.'

Apryl shook her head, then turned to run.

'Seth!' the boy screeched, and rushed after her. 'Get her inside. In there I can help you wiv the bitch. Just fuckin' get her in and we'll do the rest. Come on!'

As Seth got to his feet and began the pursuit, he realized he was crying.

'Apryl. Apryl.' He seized the collar of her coat and yanked backwards. In one long motion she came back at him, her feet airborne. Before clashing hard against the floorboards.

Her face screwed up to cry. She was hurt, had banged her tailbone against the floor. Immediately, he wanted to apologize.

'That's it. That's it. You got her,' the boy shrieked from between the pointy toes of her boots that kicked out and scraped for purchase on the marble tiles.

'Seth. No,' she said, in between the moans and sobs she made from the pain that prevented her from struggling, that shut her down.

Walking backwards with long strides, clutching her collar, he slid her along the floor after him. Slapping her hands against the hard smooth surface she tried to slow her inevitable passage towards that door, which rattled from the force of the storm that hammered it from the inside, as if eager with excitement. The collar of her coat passed up the back of her head as she tried to wriggle out of the jacket. He twisted the collar tight in his fists and pulled her shoulders towards each other so the movement of her arms was lessened. He heard his own breath, loud about his ears. 'I'm sorry. I'm sorry,' he sobbed at her.

As the hooded boy followed them down the hallway, its short arms swished in the air. 'In. In. In. In.' Its voice had begun to squeal.

'Oh, God no. Please, Seth,' she wept at him, her pretty face all red and smeared with eyeliner as she turned her head to the side to watch the door she was being hauled closer to. The terrible icy air belched around the frame, giving her a taste of the black infinite void that waited to claim her

Seth quickly reached one hand behind his back and seized the door handle. Apryl's struggles became frantic when his grip loosened on her collar, and she almost got to her feet.

But he kicked one of her legs and she went down and onto her side, whimpering, with her leather jacket all twisted around her face and neck. It had become an effective sling and he could just yank her through there with it.

The hooded boy skipped and panted with eagerness beside their struggles, like a weasel at the sight of a small hole with a rabbit inside. Its legs started a stamping motion and a strange little whinny came out of the dark hood as it readied itself to follow her into the darkness, to finish up.

The door swung itself open wide and a colossal blast of freezing turbulence swept over them, like a wave across the deck of some floundering ship. Just beyond the door a tremendous number of voices gathered, emitted from mouths Seth did not want to see. They screamed from above, and howled from below; they screeched from the sides and hurtled upwards towards the door, as if another chance at life were presenting itself in this unexpected pinpoint of light.

With all his strength, Seth took a step backwards into the darkness and wind. And then took another, and pulled the screaming girl in there with him.

FORTY-TWO

'Apryl! Apryl! Fuck it!' Miles tore the phone from his ear and began to run towards the front entrance of Barrington House. Up the steps he went, taking all three in one long stride, landing on the polished marble before the wide glass doors. Skittering sideways on leather-soled shoes, he was unable to breathe for the fear and shock and panic that scream had brought into him: the terror in her voice, lost inside a battering wind that made the signal crackle, break and then end. He reached for the keypad and punched at the stainless steel buttons. One. Nine. Four. Nine.

Inside the heavy brass clasp that held the two glass doors together he heard a loud *thunk* as the lock mechanism disengaged. And through the doors he banged, then hurled himself down the long carpeted hallway. Only as he neared the wide circle of the reception desk and the silent conservatory with its chairs and coffee table and magazines and dried rushes in vases did he manage to breathe again. To suck a great draught of warm air into lungs unused to vigorous exercise.

Through the fire doors, she'd said. These fire doors. To the staircase and elevator. He could hear her street-smart voice with its *apartments* and *elevators* and movie dialogue words, all swirling inside his thoughts that he couldn't slow down.

He launched himself up the stairs. Then stopped. And stood uselessly with all of his limbs shaking and his reason trying to douse enough of the fire of panic to tell him that the flat was eight floors up and he was almost broken from just running through the reception area. There was the lift. Take that. It was on the ground floor. Yes, he could see inside the carriage: the mirror at the back and the wooden panels and yellowish light filling the space.

By the time he got inside the lift his hands were shaking. His index finger depressed the wrong button, the button for the fifth floor. Then hit number nine. Five stayed lit. So did nine. 'Fucking hell!' he shouted at himself, then steadied the finger and pressed eight, the floor with the numbers 16 and 17 stencilled next to the button.

What was he doing, that crazy bastard Seth? Attacking her? Or worse?

How long did this thing take? It seemed like a full minute dragged by while the lift carriage clunked and wheezed before it even began to ascend, up there, towards Apryl.

What would he do? Only now that he'd stopped running and stabbing his fingers at the buttons and was forced to stand still and wait did he have time to consider what would be required of him. He wondered if he could even fight if it came to it. He simply wasn't sure. The last time had been at school, decades ago.

'Oh Jesus,' he said, at the preposterousness of the whole night. What had Apryl been thinking? As the lift stopped, uselessly, at the fifth floor, his trepidation turned into anger at her. The crazy stories, the wild speculations about murder, and now this, going undercover with an unhinged security guard as if she were some amateur sleuth. He swore at himself for allowing himself to become involved. He'd never really stopped to consider that she could be just as batshit crazy as her aunt.

The lift finally reached the eighth floor. But now he was this close he didn't want to get out. Peering through the little latticed observation window in the door of the lift, he checked the landing outside. No one there, but the front door of an apartment was open. Must be sixteen.

'Fuck it.' Trying to be as careful as possible, he opened the outer door and peered to the side to make sure no one was waiting out of sight. 'Apryl!' he hiss-whispered. 'Apryl.' Then waited, halfway out of the lift, for a response.

Nothing.

He moved out of the lift and walked forward to peer into sixteen, at an unlit shabby and empty hallway.

Standing in the doorway, he called her name twice more. Screwing up his eyes, he peered at the far end of the passageway, but it was too dark to see anything clearly. He'd have to go inside.

Which he did, slowly, hardly able to believe that he was actually doing this: trespassing inside a private flat in a private building. And he'd taken no more than two steps inside when he tensed into a squat and said 'Jesus!' out loud.

He could hear it too now. The crowd. The storm. The voices. What she had been asking him about. And it was sweeping and circling beyond the middle door on the left side of the hallway. The one through which Apryl's great-uncle had hurled Hessen.

Outside the room, he doubted whether he'd have the strength to even touch the door handle. But then he heard her. In the distance, in there, over there. Crying. In all of that roaring and excited screaming as if a tribe of apes had gathered in thrashing trees above a leopard, he heard her. In tiny broken snippets. Wailing and calling out for mercy, as if she were being murdered.

'Christ!' Miles threw himself at the door.

And fell into nothingness. Into absence.

A place where only the freezing temperature and the din of thousands of screaming voices registered. But he fell against a solid floor that he could not see, with his hands clamped about his ears. And when he twisted his body about to look for the screaming girl, he felt his feet and lower legs vanish over an edge, in which an even colder and faster wind belched upwards, as if it was striking the side of a great sheer mountain face and had nowhere else to go but upward, into forever.

Scrabbling backwards, he managed to crawl away from the lip of whatever he had fallen onto, when a collection of things like fingers, as thin as pencils and as hard as bones, snatched at his ankle as if it were an unexpected handhold presenting itself in some terrible climb up through oblivion.

He scrambled to his knees, his arms held out to prevent being blown into the precipice he sensed was gaping all around him in the pitch black violence. His shirt ballooned outwards and his tie slapped his face like a dog's tail. 'Apryl!'

He saw her, thrashing from side to side, her fingers raking upwards at the two stooped figures busy about her. Her booted feet kicked out and she threw her hips in a desperate struggle. He could see the silver tips of her heels flashing in what little light struggled to get through the open doorway he had fallen through.

On his hands and knees he crawled closer to the struggle.

And saw a child. In a coat. Impossibly, a child in a hooded coat was whipping its little arm in and out, in and out against her face, that thrashed from side to side to evade the blows. It then started to kick at her body in order to move her. To shuffle her towards ... Miles thought of what his own leg had just been hanging over. The other man, barely able to stand in the typhoon, snatched at her arms, trying to gain a purchase.

On his feet, Miles took two steps, steps that were more like the staggers of a drunkard, towards them. He had to wrap his arms about his ribs in a desperate attempt to stay the terrible racking shivers that threatened to topple his freezing body over the edge. But then pulled up short at the sight of what flashed in and out of the lightless void around the struggling figures.

He saw faces without flesh, and raw meat on bones twisting horribly in and out of the thinnest light, and hind legs kicking out at the other blind grasping things. And before this moving tapestry of disfigurement and whipping bone-things with jaws too far separated from skulls, a reddish face with long, brownish arms extended from impossibly small shoulders seemed to be rushing forward at the struggling trio. And then flashing backward as if pulled on some invisible harness, away from the light, before repeating the motion, in which it came closer each time to Apryl and the wind-blasted silhouettes that would not be coming back if they went over the side.

The hooded child looked up at Miles at the last possible moment, when Miles's foot connected with the middle of its torso. Helped by the wind, it surged backward like a kite in an updraught, and was immediately swallowed up by moving, sinewy limbs too thin to be of much use apart from clawing at the darkness. But against the sole of his shoe the hooded thing had been palpable, as heavy and solid as an actual child. And practically sucked off the ledge upon which they all clung.

In his dimming senses and great upheaving struggle to breathe, Miles knew that the man in the white shirt, with frost bearding his face and eyebrows, was Seth. And with the last of his strength in this terrible exposure, the deranged nightwatchman tried with all of his might to haul Apryl over the edge, and into the abyss, by the one arm he had managed to seize by the elbow.

She flopped onto her belly and her head and shoulders disappeared over the edge and into a cluster of writhing white things with snatching hands. The swooping thing with the reddish head was almost upon them again.

Miles fired himself off his front foot and hit Seth in the centre of the chest with his shoulder.

Before he landed, half on and half off the invisible platform, the only thing supporting them in the maelstrom, Miles heard Seth issue a high-pitched scream. And at the edge of his upturned eyes as Miles fell, he was sure he saw the thin reddish thing embrace Seth's flailing shape in a horrible motion that reminded him of a crab using its pincers to stuff matter into its jaws.

And then Miles's head was plunged for an instant into what felt like bracken and sharp sticks, and then thrust against cold dead meat the next. Until he hauled himself backwards, away from the edge and onto the ledge.

Only to see Apryl from the waist down. The rest of her was lost as if decapitated, and hung over the edge of the platform. She was being clawed into the void by whatever was thrashing in a place that was mercifully only partially lit. On his knees, screaming for several seconds before he realized he was screaming, he snatched at her ankles. Seized one, then another, with numb fingers, and hauled her backwards. And onto the solid surface he still could not see. Where Apryl rocked from side to side, clutching her face, blind and concussed by the terrible cold.

With the last of his strength, shouting until his vocal cords threatened to snap, he maintained his grip on each booted ankle. And on his backside, he shuffled like he was rowing a skiff, and pulled her after him. Back towards the open door and the light.

She moved. On the floor, beside him, where she was all huddled against the wall across from the door he had slammed behind them as they came out of there on their backs, frozen and gibbering. On the other side, in what disguised itself as a room, the last murmurs of the wind and the highest screams of the damned finally hushed away into silence.

Then came another movement and a sound from Apryl. A whimper. Miles rolled to where she lay crumpled inside her own coat and the shadows. 'Apryl. Apryl. Apryl,' he muttered, as much to himself as to her, to add something real and familiar to this sinister place. 'It's me. I'm here, sweetheart.' He reached out to touch what he thought was an arm, but she pulled herself quickly against the wall, withdrawing every limb inside the coat, keeping her face covered, while making those little crying noises.

'It hurts.' Her voice came out of the sobs.

'Apryl, it's me. Miles. It's all right sweetheart. I'm here.'

But she didn't respond and just shivered underneath her coat against the wall.

Looking about himself in the darkness he made sure all of the doors were closed. From somewhere inside himself a red spark of anger lit up and spread. He got to his knees. 'The police are on their way,' he called into the echoing apartment. 'Do you hear?'

Apryl began to cry softly now and rock back and forth as if she were in great pain. As his sight adjusted just enough to see more of her down there on the floor, Miles could tell she was holding her arms tightly to her body with her head dipped down. She was really hurt. He had to get her out. Right now.

She came away from the floor without resistance. Up and onto her feet as if she were used to being led. But she didn't unwrap her arms from about her chest, and she kept her body bent over and her face angled towards the floor until they were outside the apartment and on the landing in the yellow light before the lift doors. Where he coaxed her and said, 'Show me, Apryl. Show me where it hurts.' Only then did she reveal her injuries.

He saw the black flesh about her wrists and all over her hands, as if they had been injured as they reached out to fend something off. Those beautiful white hands were black with something that shone dully like hard leather, or frostbite. And not all of the fingers were there any more.

Her frail arms wavered in front of her as she raised her face at last, showing him the beautiful parts that were pale and tear-stained, and the place where the hair was missing from one side of her head.

He clutched her to his chest and swallowed. Clamped his

eyelids shut on that final sight of the thing that had followed them right up to the threshold of that space. Something on all fours, snatching at her within the doorway. Until she kicked at it. Stabbed her boot heels into it with what was left of her mind and strength. Stamped it away like a bundle of sticks. And he knew that what had vanished, still clutching as it was propelled back into the seething absence, had been all that was left of Felix Hessen. And Miles had been close enough to the painter to be seeing him again, and perhaps every night for the rest of his life, as Hessen reached for the girl with arms so long and thin they must have been bone.

FORTY-THREE

Stephen paced the cramped living room, the hems of his uniform trousers whisking past Janet's inert toes where they protruded from beneath the tartan blanket draped over her lap.

'And now there's no sign of Seth at all. I'd guess they took all of him. Amazing, isn't it? That things like that can actually happen. I mean, I checked the tapes this morning before I erased them and did a switch. He never left the building. You can see him going out of reception to the lift on camera three, with that girl, Apryl, and then nothing. He never came back down. Imagine that, dear. He never came back down.

'But he's not in flat sixteen either. I checked every inch of it. Empty. What must have come in folded itself all away again. Took what it wanted and then just melted away without a trace. The police want to see Seth. But they'll have a bloody job finding him.' Stephen laughed, but there was no humour in the sound that came out of him.

He sat down on the sofa, the material worn shiny by the anxious occupation of his buttocks over the last ten years. 'The girl left here in an ambulance. And she wasn't a pretty sight.' He took a swig from the whisky bottle in his large hand and winced through the after-burn in his throat, before pointing the sloshing bottle at his silent, motionless wife, who merely watched him with her quick eyes. 'Now I'd guess that things didn't go to plan, dear. I knew the moment her boyfriend, or whoever that chap was, got me up in the middle of the night. No, dear. I'd hazard a guess things didn't go to plan up there last night.'

And then he was just about to ask his mute wife if she could smell that ... that terrible stench of something both burned and rotten. But stopped himself when he saw the little figure appear just beyond the radius of the standing lamp's glow, in the tiny hallway before the front door.

It stood still, and made no sign that it would fully enter the living room, for which they were both grateful. Considering the miasma that preceded its appearance, the head porter expected the uncovered head to still be steaming.

Stephen stood up and swallowed. Janet started a frantic keening sound from behind her sternum. She began to rock back and forth in her wheelchair parked by the window, using what few muscles in her abdomen still functioned after the last of the three strokes she had suffered in succession, shutting down ninety per cent of her nervous system the night she'd ventured into apartment sixteen and encountered her dead son for the first time.

'Jesus.' Stephen took a step back from the grinning apparition. 'Jesus Christ.'

'You wish,' the blackened head said.

There was no hood encasing its face any more. It looked like the hood had been completely torn away from the coat. As had one sleeve, along with the arm that had been inside it. From within the socket, something dark glistened. The rest of the parka was blackened and smeared with long, ugly stains, as if wet hands had wiped their palms down the outside of the garment while seeking purchase. But the worst part, the feature that made Stephen whimper out loud and drop the bottle of whisky, was the head from which the voice issued.

The whites of its eyes and the gleaming little teeth in its pained grin made the tar-black ruin of the surrounding flesh all the worse for the contrast. 'I's come with some news, like.'

'We don't want any. Not any more. Nothing from you.' Stephen swallowed and wanted desperately to remove his stare from the tottering mess in the doorway. 'It's over. Finished, you hear? I've done what was asked of me.'

'Nah-ah. Fings have changed, like.'

'Not for me. We had a deal.'

'Is all fucked up, innit. Unless you can get that tart back here, and put her in that room with them fings, you's going nowhere. But I don't fink she'll be wanting to see that place again. Do you?'

Stephen shook his head slowly, as the full impact of his dead son's words sank in.

'You's gonna be all right, like. No one knows you have anyfing to do wiv it. But someone's got to keep all them markin's on the walls, like. And under the floorboards. Else, who is gonna do it for us?'

'No. No more. You have Seth. We had a deal.'

The crispy dark skull grinned. 'Seth's outta the picture now. All's we got is you.'

Stephen dropped to his knees, his hands clenched together in entreaty. 'Tell him. Tell that thing . . . No more.'

'Go and tell him yourself. In the darkness. Where I just been, like.' The child looked at where its arm had once been, and then down its stained coat, and chuckled. 'You's going nowhere, Dad. You's gonna stay here and look after Mum. Happy families, like.'

EPILOGUE

'Jesus. Jesus fuckin' Christ,' Archie said, looking up at the walls. 'I just never get used to it.'

Beside him, Quin didn't speak. Just blinked a couple of times as if staring into the glare of the sun.

'What ya think it is?' Archie asked, his hands on his hips, standing at the foot of the unmade bed in the abandoned room.

Quin didn't or couldn't answer. It had been four weeks since rent had been paid on the room, and about as long since anyone could remember seeing Seth leaving or entering the building, or using the kitchen. And they had told the police as much when they came looking for him.

He should have taken more of an interest in Seth, but hadn't wanted to pry. Everyone had their reasons for living at the Green Man. Reasons that were their own. There was never much choice involved in residency here. And Seth had always been a good tenant. Paid up on time and never bothered a soul. So he didn't mind him falling behind on the rent for a while. But four weeks was taking the piss, and he didn't want the Old Bill looking round the pub again either.

There had been no one in the room when Archie let the police in a month back, or at any other time since whenever he had tried to raise a response or peered inside the room from around the door. People had done it before; lived here, sometimes even for years, and then vanished without a word. The cellar was full of stuff left behind by previous tenants. There were no records kept at the Green Man or questions asked. That was the beauty of the place. You could take time out here. As long as you paid your seventy quid every week and didn't bother anyone, then no one was going to be your keeper.

But now he came to think of it, hadn't Seth said something about being a painter? Once, a long time ago. Maybe. He couldn't remember. But he'd definitely been painting something up here. On the walls, and even the ceiling.

'What should I do wi' his stuff? Archie said, and pointed at the jumble of clothes in one corner, and at the dried-out paints, the stiff brushes, the mess of sketches strewn across the spattered dust sheets, the white saucer piled high with gnarled cigarette butts, and the rucksack beside the fridge. 'Quin?'

'What?'

'I said, what should I do wi' it?'

Quin broke his stare from the reddish colours on the chimney breast. It was like looking at an autopsy. 'Put it in the cellar. In case he comes back to fetch it.'

Archie nodded, then looked at the wall across from the door. 'Poor bastard was twisted. Don't think we're gonna be seeing him agin.'

Quin looked at the side of Archie's face, wanting him either to elaborate or to exchange a look of mutual understanding. But then he wasn't really sure what he wanted. Not at all sure of what was on these walls, or in his own mind as he looked at them. The pictures made him feel uncomfortable and unwell at the same time, like he was suddenly worried sick about something. And yet, he wasn't entirely sure what he was actually looking at.

Archie shook his head. 'What is that, a face or summat? Maybe a dog. Looks like it's got teeth in it.'

He was talking now to ease the shock that had accompanied their turning on of the lights and opening of the thin curtains. They should have been angry at the way these walls had been defaced, or full of mirth at the preposterousness of what Seth had done. Even full of admiration at the skill involved in the way he'd got these things up there to hit you so hard when you looked at them. Took your breath away they did. But Quin couldn't feel much now beside a deep discomfort he had no words for, and a desire to shut his eyes tight. He didn't want to see any more. 'Leave the dust sheets where they are and get this covered up today. You'll have to use two coats of the white emulsion left over from the kitchen.'

'It'll take a roller.'

'I don't fuckin' care what it takes, just get rid of it. I want this place let by Friday. Kenny's cousin has left his missus and is looking for a place. He can have it.'

Archie nodded, still staring at the walls. Quin left the room.

'Christ,' Archie said to himself, and shook his head one final time before removing his glasses. He'd paint the room without his specs on. At least then he wouldn't have to see too closely the things that climbed these walls and crawled across the ceiling. But even when they'd been covered over, he wondered if he'd ever forget them.

extracts reading groups
competitions books new
discounts extracts extracts
competitions extracts discounts
books new extracts events
events books reading groups
new extracts new
new books titles reading groups
interviews
events extracts extracts
discounts events books
new books events events
events new interviews new books extracts
discounts extracts discounts
www.panmacmillan.com
extracts events reading groups
competitions books extracts new